A Very French Wedding

Maeve Haran is an Oxford law graduate, former television producer and mother of three grown-up children. Her first novel, *Having It All*, which explored the dilemmas of balancing a career and motherhood, caused a sensation and took her all around the world. Maeve has written sixteen further contemporary novels and two historical novels, plus a work of nonfiction celebrating life's small pleasures.

She lives in North London and a much-loved cottage near the sea in Sussex.

Maeve Haran

A Very French Wedding

PAN BOOKS

First published 2021 by Pan Books
an imprint of Pan Macmillan
The Smithson, 6 Briset Street, London EC1M 5NR
EU representative: Macmillan Publishers Ireland Limited,
Mallard Lodge, Lansdowne Village, Dublin 4
Associated companies throughout the world
www.panmacmillan.com

ISBN 978-1-5290-3518-6

1 3 5 7 9 8 6 4 2

A CIP catalogue record for this book is available from the British Library.

Typeset by Palimpsest Book Production Ltd, Falkirk, Stirlingshire
Printed and bound by CPI Group (UK) Ltd, Croydon, CR0 4YY

Visit **www.panmacmillan.com** to read more about all our books
and to buy them. You will also find features, author interviews and
news of any author events, and you can sign up for e-newsletters
so that you're always first to hear about our new releases.

*For my fabulous friend Carol Danti who helped me research
the region and her lovely daughter, Lucie Spence, who suggested
we escape to the delightful Château Carbonneau*

One

_____

'Oh shit,' wailed Stephanie to her husband. 'That was Meredith, and she wants to come and stay with us. For two whole weeks!'

David looked at his wife curiously. 'Meredith Harding, your old school friend? Isn't that good? Because one, we're running a B&B, and two, I thought she was a great friend of yours.'

'She is. One of my oldest. But David, they call Meredith the Queen of the East! She's used to staying in five-star hotels, or even seven-star hotels, if there are any. We're much too humble for her. I mean – the thought of all the guests dining together at one table. She'd have a fit!'

'Then you'll have to explain that the idea of the *chambre d'hôte* is all about people getting to know each other,' David replied calmly. 'Anyway, what makes her so grand? You're making her sound like Cleopatra and Madame Mao rolled into one.'

'She works in some incomprehensible high-powered job in finance. She's always moving from Hong Kong to Singapore to Shanghai making vast amounts of money, so I hardly ever get to see her. That's why it's so great that she's coming here.'

'And what brings her?' David asked, intrigued by the prospect of meeting this dazzling-sounding person.

1

'I don't know. I expect she'll tell us when she gets here.'

'And when's that?'

'The day after tomorrow.'

Steph and David had opened their B&B in France ten years earlier. Since it was only March and the season hadn't really started yet, they had plenty of room.

'Do you want me to get something special from the butcher?' asked David. 'I imagine you'll want to kill the fatted calf?'

'Absolutely. I'll get down my recipe book. Did you pick up the croissants?'

'Of course I picked up the croissants,' he replied patiently. 'As we have discovered, fresh croissants are part of the fantasy of staying in France and people get pissed off if you try and palm them off with French bread, no matter how delicious.'

It was this same fantasy that had lured Steph and David here themselves. No other country seemed to have quite the same alluring effect on the British mind as France. That and their love of this particular landscape in the south-west, with its clear, shining rivers – so clear that people actually swam in them, unlike their British equivalents – and its rich sprinkling of châteaux for their guests to explore on day trips; not to mention its lush farmland, deep gorges and gentle rows of vines. They had been here on countless holidays and utterly lost their hearts to the place, so when they'd decided to finally take the plunge and buy somewhere to turn into a B&B, it had to be round here.

They had found a handsome *maison de maître*, a solid stone house, more practical than a crumbling château but with oodles of charm. In order to do it up they had enlisted the help of Steve, a local builder beloved of his fellow expats because he seemed to be able to do his work efficiently without speaking any French. He managed this simply by pointing, gesticulating and having a way about him that the suppliers seemed to regard as engagingly *rosbif* (eating roast beef being – obviously – the most defining of British characteristics).

Over three years – trying not to get discouraged by rising damp or sudden holes in the walls or floorboards so riddled with damp rot that David had almost fallen through – they had prepared six bedrooms, each with the essential en suite bathroom no tourist could live without, put in a swimming pool, and got ready to open just as their money was about to run out.

The life suited them both. Steph loved to cook and David was the most sociable of beings, happy to host the large shared table that was the big feature of the *chambre d'hôte* – where all the guests got to meet each other. The only drawback was the grinding tiredness that sometimes enveloped them both as a result of the constant shopping, cooking and bedmaking.

Steph finished laying the table and putting out the pretty pots of home-made jams (another must at a *chambre d'hôte*), the fruit salad and the cold meats.

'*Madame, s'il vous plaît,*' called a voice from the staircase.

'Oh my God,' Steph muttered, 'it's that Belgian family again.' A large family called LeBrun had recently arrived, trying to pack extra children into their bedroom and constantly demanding assistance of one sort or another. 'What do they want now?'

'I'll go and see,' soothed David.

'Ideas for what to do today,' he announced when he got back ten minutes later. 'Perfectly reasonable, really. That's what we're here for, after all.'

'What did you tell them?' Steph murmured. 'To get lost in the caves, I hope!'

'Now, Stephie.' David smiled at her. 'I suggested a day-long boat trip on one of those barge things with the sails. That should get them out from under your feet.'

'Let's hope they fall overboard and drown!'

David looked at her in consternation. This wasn't like her.

'And why on earth you let them bring that bloody dog . . . !' The list of his sins was growing.

He was about to answer crossly that it had actually been Steph who agreed to the dog, when he noticed the deep lines of tiredness under her eyes. 'Hey,' he said, his voice softening, 'come out here on the terrace and look at the view.'

'Really, David,' she answered irritably. 'I've got too much to do.'

He watched her anxiously. She was like this more and more at the moment. He never knew when he was going to get his head snapped off. Eventually, Steph realized she was being a cow and followed him, wiping her hands on the jokey apron he'd given her, proclaiming 'I Kiss Better Than I Cook'.

Beyond their terrace the land slipped away, gentle, green and fertile, right down to the river. 'Nice, huh?' David ventured.

Steph smiled, looking suddenly pretty and years younger. 'Very nice. Beautiful.'

'It's the reason we came, remember?'

'I know, I'm sorry. It's just that I get so tired and then I start to get grumpy. Sorry.' To think she'd imagined running a B&B together would be good for their marriage! She tried to concentrate on Meredith and how silly she was being. It would actually be great fun to see her old friend after all this time. The realization made her feel instantly better.

'Why don't you put your money where your mouth is?' David suddenly grinned.

'What on earth are you talking about?' she replied.

He pulled her against him and pointed to the slogan on her pinny.

'That was just a silly joke.' Steph eased herself out of his embrace.

'So I'm beginning to learn,' he observed, in a tone of weary irritation she hadn't heard from him before.

'Good morning, Miss Harding,' the flight attendant prompted gently, offering her a glass of wake-up orange juice.

Meredith sat up and stretched. She had slept well on the business class bed, as she always did. Years of flying across continents had accustomed her to dealing with jet lag and making sure she slept as long as possible. She wasn't like the real pros, though, who got on, donned their masks and ear plugs and lay straight out on their beds till they arrived at the destination. Meredith liked to enjoy dinner served on a tray with its own white linen cloth, with proper knives and forks and glassware. She also particularly enjoyed the glass of champagne you were offered as soon as you took your seat, while the rest of the passengers were still queuing up to board. She always made a point of having dinner and watching a film before settling down; and as for all that wellness nonsense about no alcohol – there was too much of that sort of telling you what to do in modern life. She'd actually bought a bottle of water the other day that had instructed her to 'Do the right thing today.'

She sat back, enjoying her fresh fruit and thinking about her visit. Her colleagues had been stunned when she'd announced she was suddenly taking two weeks off. Meredith was famed for putting work first in her life. She had plenty of other pleasures, of course. She loved spa weekends and opera and she had a sprinkling of good friends she spent time with, even though moving between cities as she did could mean it was tricky to maintain friendships. She knew she was admired and also a little feared, but she didn't think much more about it.

So she had been taken aback recently when a young woman she was mentoring blurted out that Meredith was her role model in everything but her personal life. Realizing what she'd said, the girl had instantly tried to cover up her tactlessness, but it was too late. The damage was done. My personal life is perfectly fine, thank you very much! she'd told herself. Somehow, though, the comment had really stayed with her.

And then her father had died so suddenly. He and Meredith had always been very close; it had been he who told her she could do anything with her life, so often that she began to really believe it. Her mother, on the other hand, had been both difficult and distant, and seemed to find having a child faintly irritating. She clearly resented the closeness of father and daughter. Obviously Meredith was sorry when she died, but with nothing like the dreadful void that had opened up when her beloved father had a heart attack while Meredith was on the other side of the world. It had been sudden and unexpected, but everyone had said it was a merciful release, as he was beginning to decline in other ways. Even so, losing him had rocked Meredith's well-ordered world. She had come home for the funeral, said her own personal goodbyes and gone back to work even more feverishly.

Yet something had changed. She found herself thinking all the time about the years when she and her father had been happiest together. He had always loved camping and his favourite place to do it had been south-west France, where people took camping really seriously. When Meredith was a child, he had found a campsite where the tents were fixed and even quite luxurious – with their own camping loos! It was right on the banks of the Savarin River and her father would take three whole days to drive the family there, being honked at by angry French motorists and overtaken on the inside on motorways, but staying at the speed he blithely thought appropriate. Then they would arrive and move in, having brought their special put-u-up beds and pillows, and Meredith would dash off and see if any of the usual children had arrived since it was the kind of place people came back to every year, often at the same time. To an only child, it was bliss, and it meant that Meredith learned to get on with lots of different nationalities – a skill that would become very useful in her adult life.

But the best moment of all was when she and her dad would walk along the banks of the river into the nearest village to buy the bread in the mornings. If they dawdled enough, this could mean a whole hour together, just the two of them. Dad would talk about all the possibilities ahead for his clever daughter, and how her dreams must never be limited by the realities of life, as his had been. He was saving, he told her, so that by the sixth form when the important exams loomed, she could go to a really good school where the teachers would do nothing but encourage her, unlike the local school she was at now.

Sometimes Meredith would notice a beautiful butterfly and ask him about it, and he would always know. His knowledge of nature was encyclopaedic. The sun would be beating down on her back and she would run ahead, laughing. And when they got to the village he would buy her a delicious, flaky *pain au chocolat*, fresh from the baker's oven, and whisper not to tell her mother about it. Her mother was forever carping that he spoiled Meredith too much anyway.

On the way back he would tell her about the region, its history, the wars that had shaped it, what made the landscape so special. They would cross the river on a small narrow bridge that swayed when it was windy, like something from *Indiana Jones*, and halfway home they would always stop at the same spot, where they had a perfect view of the château on the other side. It was the most beautiful building Meredith had ever seen, built of golden stone, with four turrets that looked to a child's eyes like giant pepperpots. It even had its own moat, as every proper castle should. She could just imagine Rapunzel letting down her hair from one of the towers, or one of the Disney princesses waiting for her prince to come and rescue her.

'Now there's a real château!' her father had said. 'None of your nineteenth-century rubbish. Think of all the history that's taken place there. Tell you what, one day I'll buy it for you and we can run away and live there. I'm sure your mother would be all for it,' he added with a grin.

And they had both laughed and gone back across the rickety bridge to the campsite, where Meredith grabbed her things before dashing off to find her friends for a swim in the wide, shallow river.

And now, all these years later, a very strange thing had happened. A couple of months ago Meredith, flying to Berlin for a meeting with some banks, had opened an in-flight magazine. There, in an article about France, she had come across a photograph of their very own château.

At first she dismissed it as a silly coincidence; but when she idly browsed places to stay near the château and Steph's B&B came up, she decided that was it. She was going to drop everything and go there. It would mean she could say goodbye to her father properly and catch up with Steph at the same time.

And here she was.

She handed her tray back to the attendant with a smile and

headed for the toilet before the masked sleepers woke up and took it over, working their way through all the goodies in their freebie Calvin Klein bags and forgetting the existence of anyone who might be stuck outside, desperate for the loo.

One glance in the mirror told her she didn't look too bad. Her shoulder-length grey-blonde Helen Mirren hair needed a comb, but her skin was clear and healthy. All those facials had paid off. She touched up her natural lipstick and dusted her face with Dior powder. The beauty writers might claim shiny skin was fashionable, but in Meredith's view, ladies of her age looked better flatteringly matte.

She patted her well-cut beige trousers and surveyed her silk top. She always travelled in silk – both light and warm – usually with a cosy pashmina to wrap herself in if it got cold. Her long cashmere cardigan was perfect too, both smart and comfortable.

'Right then,' she told herself with a smile. 'They might all think you've lost your marbles at work, but what the hell. The adventure begins!'

And, for the first time in months, she felt a happy anticipation about what the next two weeks would hold.

Once she'd cleared immigration at Charles de Gaulle she would find the driver of the comfortable Mercedes she'd ordered and go straight to sleep in the back. It was a crazy extravagance, of course, when she could perfectly well get a high-speed train; but hell, she could afford it.

With a bit of luck and not too many traffic jams, she would be at Steph's by early evening.

'Where do you want to put Meredith?' David asked.

'In the Oriental Room,' Steph replied at once. 'She's coming from Shanghai, so that should be appropriate.'

During their renovations Steph had found a gorgeously exotic length of fabric at her favourite *brocante*, the French version of an antique shop, which also sold superior junk. She had taken out her old sewing machine and run up floor-length curtains and a canopy to go above the bed. There had even been just enough left over to cover a stool, which she had put in front of a French dressing table she'd picked up and repainted. With a few oriental prints and a Japanese fan fixed to the wall, the effect might not be authentic, but it was good all the same – both inviting and exotic.

It was in the same *brocante* that she had found most of the treasures that gave the rooms their themes: the Flower Room, where a marvellous set of flower prints was ranged across the walls, and the Chandelier Room, named after a fabulous gilded chandelier she'd discovered that somehow took you straight back to the lost elegance of the eighteenth century.

Steph had always fancied sleeping in the Oriental Room herself, or at least having a bath in the en suite bathroom, which had a wonderful old tub with feet. One afternoon, after Meredith was gone, maybe she'd sneak up there with a glass of champagne . . .

She sighed. Not very likely.

Their young helper, Marcelline, who came in two days a week because that was all they could afford, would make up the bed and ensure everything was ready for Meredith's arrival. Steph returned her focus to the plan for tonight's dinner. It looked like a full house – twelve people – which was good news, as it meant she'd make a bit of profit if she budgeted cleverly enough. Before she left home she'd bought a little book called *Running a B&B in France*, and it had become her bible. By doing dinner, the book asserted, you could double the income from every room. Most people who stayed in places like theirs didn't want to go out to eat because they'd often be doing a lot of driving anyway. And of course, there was the drink/drive risk, which the French gaily ignored, as they did any troublesome bureaucratic imposition. So most guests liked to eat in.

The standard fare at a *chambre d'hôte* was a four-course meal – usually soup, an entrée and a pudding plus a selection of cheeses and a glass of wine – all for a *prix fixe*. Nowadays, of course, there had to be a vegetarian option. Fortunately, Steph had taken a brief professional cooking course just before they'd moved to France. Before then, she'd been rather an extravagant cook who wasted a hideous amount of food. Now she was the queen of portion control and detailed planning.

It had been a challenge at first but she had soon realized preparation in advance was the key; and thank God for her freezer! Messing about with anything last-minute was a potential disaster. Thankfully, most guests didn't seem to expect haute cuisine.

Tonight, in honour of Meredith, they were having something more special than usual: iced courgette soup and then a traditional *coq au vin*, but with Steph's special *dauphinois au gratin* potatoes, which always went down a treat. They would finish with *tarte tatin*, another sure-fire winner. And then, of course, cheese. It was the cheese you had to watch or it could make the cost of the meal rocket, so she always stuck strictly to three very good local ones.

As she peeled the potatoes, it struck Steph that you learned some funny things running a B&B. Beds, for example. She'd discovered that the British and French liked double beds but the Americans, Germans, Scandinavians and especially Japanese preferred twin beds. Funny, because after all, the British were famous for not being interested in sex!

The other thing she'd learned was that most people didn't bother to unpack, so vast wall-covering wardrobes were a waste of space – which was a pity, since they were very cheap nowadays. In fact, she'd bought a couple and repainted them, and hadn't been able to resist a delightful, vast *armoire* with pastoral scenes of shepherds painted on the panels.

It always made her laugh, too, that the French for chest of drawers was *commode*. She certainly hoped her guests wouldn't emulate the use of a commode in her chests of drawers! They'd had one guest who'd thrown up after much too wine at dinner, leaving the mess for Steph and David to deal with; and another had dropped black eyeliner on the pale carpet and hidden the resulting stain under a stool.

She looked at her watch. Five o'clock. Meredith would be here any minute.

She thought about when they'd first met and decided not to compute how many years ago it was. Far too many, anyway.

Meredith had only arrived at Meads House in the sixth form. She was a spiky girl: tall and slender with extremely straight fair hair, which Steph had suspected her of ironing (quite common at the time even if it sounded barmy now, not to mention downright dangerous). She was not well off and had only come, Steph later discovered, because her father had insisted on it, borrowing against his pension to pay the school fees. He believed in education above all, and Meads' teachers had a towering reputation locally. If anyone could get his daughter into university, they could, he was convinced.

Meredith had obviously felt way out of her depth surrounded by posh Pony Club girls, some of whom had known each other forever. For a while she had kept herself to herself and stayed silent, burying her head in her studies. She had always been the last to leave the library.

And then she'd discovered Steph – and they'd just seemed to click. As her father had told her, you only needed to make one friend and then everything would change. Later on, Joanna had joined their little group and they'd suddenly become quite a force: three pupils who were actually interested in their work and loved to argue about *Jane Eyre* and Lizzie Bennet from *Pride and Prejudice,* and whether Mr Darcy was A Good Thing.

Meredith was convinced it was he who had almost single-handedly – maybe with a bit of help from *Jane Eyre*'s Mr Rochester – provided the stereotype for most subsequent romantic heroes. 'And why any sane woman would want to live with a dark and handsome but proud and moody man, God alone knows! Even if he did get a bit nicer in the end! Just the profile for a stalker, if you ask me. Once phones came along Mr Darcy'd be checking up on poor Lizzie all the time and asking her where she'd been!'

It had been fascinating how much Meredith had minded. She was a natural feminist before the name was in common use. I wonder if she still is? Steph thought to herself. It was such a long time since she'd seen her properly, just the two of them. The only sad thing was, they wouldn't get much privacy tonight; though Steph could probably get David to take over the guests at some point, so that she and Meredith could have a bit of time to themselves.

There was a sudden commotion downstairs and she realized Meredith must have arrived. She ran to the window and looked out, feeling nervous again. A sleek black Mercedes, the kind Russian oligarchs seemed to favour, was parked outside on the gravel drive. Steph shuddered at how much it must cost to be driven all the way from Paris to Bratenac. But Meredith's life was one of limos and swish hotels.

She ran down the stairs to find Meredith, surrounded by a

mountain of smart luggage, saying goodbye to the driver while David struggled with the biggest case.

'Meredith!' she shouted joyfully and, forgetting all her reservations, skipped down the front steps.

'Stephanie!' replied the sleek and elegant figure, dressed in various shades of taupe. She looked as if she could walk straight into the Ritz despite having just flown halfway round the world.

They hugged each other enthusiastically. 'Get you!' Steph teased. 'Fancy taking a limo all the way from Paris!'

'I know,' grinned Meredith, clearly guilt-free. 'Outrageous, isn't it – but I do work very hard. Anyway, forget me and my extravagant ways. I'm so excited,' she added. 'Two whole weeks together!'

'I know,' grinned Steph. 'Pity Joanna isn't here too! Maybe we'll give her a call on FaceTime or whatever it's called while you're here. She caught me on the loo the other day! Come on, let's go upstairs to your room. Dinner's all prepared. You'll laugh, but I have a minute-by-minute schedule of what to do when.'

'Very professional. I applaud you. I wish the people who worked for me were so thorough.'

'Meredith, what is it you do exactly? I know it's all to do with money, and very high-powered . . .'

Meredith laughed. 'I work in M&A – that's mergers and acquisitions – which means I spend my time advising businesses whether to take over their rivals. We also buy a few companies. It can be quite exciting, despite the boring name. Scary, even, at times.'

'And you aren't ever tempted to take things easy?' Steph didn't add 'at our age' as it would probably infuriate Meredith. She didn't like the subject of ageing and had clearly decided it was a choice, not an inevitability.

Meredith grinned. 'Can't think what I'd do with myself. I'm not exactly the garden centre and National Trust type. Besides, you look pretty busy yourself.'

'True.' Steph opened the door to Meredith's room.

'It's beautiful!' Meredith pronounced. 'Did you come up with the idea?' She walked round, admiring the curtains and the canopy. She even noticed the stool. 'And the bathroom's wonderful!'

Stephanie visibly relaxed. She'd been so worried Meredith would be demanding and hard to please, but she seemed ready to be happy with everything.

'I'll bring you up a glass of champagne before dinner and you can have it in the bath. I've been fantasizing about doing that myself!'

'We should do it together!' grinned Meredith. 'Imagine if we'd done that at school!'

'Scandal! That was just the sort of thing they were terrified of, yet they didn't seem to mind you having pashes on older girls.'

'You had one on Karen Ricci,' Meredith reminded her. 'Mind you, she was Italian and gorgeous.'

'Actually, it was because she was captain of the netball team and I was so crap at it. She seemed like a goddess.'

'Hmm . . .' Meredith laughed. 'And there were those lovely long netball-playing limbs.'

Steph surveyed her friend. 'You don't look too bad yourself,' she observed.

'Regular spa treatments, facials, manicures and pedicures. Pampering. That's the answer.'

Steph repressed a sigh. She couldn't remember the last time she'd been pampered. 'I'd better leave you now and get back to dinner, but we can bunk off later and take up where we left off.' She looked at her watch. Six already – she'd better get a move on. 'I'll send David with the champagne.' They hugged again. 'It really is great to see you. I always wanted women friends here but never found the time!'

Meredith nodded. To be honest, she didn't have any real girlfriends at all in Hong Kong, Singapore or Shanghai. 'I'll start unpacking. I was never any good at travelling light. Why have two pairs of shoes when you could have six?'

'Especially when you have a limo driver to carry them!' teased Steph. She waved and went back downstairs to her schedule.

Five minutes later there was a knock on the door and David appeared with Meredith's champagne. He smiled with genuine good humour. Steph had done well with her choice of husband. He seemed an unusual blend of niceness without dullness. And he still had his hair. Meredith pushed aside all thoughts of her own different life choices: marriage hadn't been for her, and that was that.

She took the proffered glass of champagne, returning his smile. She was always being offered glasses of the stuff back in the East – where, along with whisky, it was currently seen as an important status symbol – but this one was going to be extra special, in that beautiful bathtub, with two weeks of real friendship ahead.

Downstairs, Steph was going into autopilot. Marcelline had laid the big table where they would all have dinner together. They did have lots of little tables people could sit at, but most guests seemed to prefer it this way; they said it was convivial and fun, like a house party. Dinner was at seven thirty, but people often drifted down much earlier and were sent with a drink (which they paid for) into the lounge.

16

David was busy advising the noisy LeBruns on some more outings. It was good to get guests out from under your feet during the day. They didn't actually make them go out, like Blackpool boarding houses were famous for doing, but there was plenty to see in the area and very few stayed around.

Meredith came down at seven twenty-five, looking glamorous in pale grey silk. All the other guests turned to look at her and she smiled graciously.

'Goodness,' she couldn't help commenting, 'is this where we all sit?'

'Come on, Meredith,' David replied cheerily, 'meet Mr and Mrs LeBrun. They're from Belgium.' This could have been a conversation stopper, but Meredith, veteran of many a gathering of foreign businessmen and women, plunged in with aplomb.

The food was delicious and every mouthful seemed to disappear, as if the guests were hungry lions rather than upmarket tourists. Better than people not appreciating it, Meredith supposed.

By the time Marcelline cleared the last plates, it was almost ten o'clock.

'Right, everyone,' David announced. 'Coffee and liqueurs in the lounge. And of course, fresh mint tea,' he added in the tempting tones of a carpet seller in Marrakech. 'Chamomile tisane and all manner of interesting potions. You can make it yourself from our array of exotic teabags.'

Steph led Meredith into the sparkling kitchen with its large catering oven and vast fridge-freezer. 'What would you like? *Un petit cognac*, as the French always call it no matter how huge the measure? More wine?' She smiled, looking suddenly less careworn. 'I know, we could finish the champagne in your room. Your sofa's more comfortable than it looks.'

Meredith laughed, recalling the spindly-legged, gilded Louis XIV-style love seat that looked as if it would be more at home in Versailles. 'I'll take your word for it.'

David came in to get some glasses. 'You go off with Meredith,' he smiled. 'I'll look after the guests.'

Steph's response took Meredith by surprise. 'David,' she replied sharply. 'You did remember to put out the coffee cups, didn't you?'

'For God's sake, Steph,' was his weary reply. 'Yes. I always remember to put out the coffee cups. And the sugar.'

'And the warmed milk as well?'

'Yes.' Again the weary tone, this time with a thin veneer of irritation. 'Of course I did. Just the way you like it. I'm not a complete idiot, you know.'

'Sorry.' Steph rubbed one eye. 'Just a bit tired, that's all.'

As they climbed up to her bedroom, it struck Meredith that all was not well here. Steph and David had chosen this life, following a dream of living in France; apparently running a B&B was the number one dream of all Brits moving to France. But it was a demanding business, and by the looks of things, it was overwhelming them.

'Come on, sit down, you're exhausted,' Meredith insisted.

'It's been a bit of a heavy week. Those LeBruns are very demanding, always wanting something new. And they do have five children. To be honest, it's the one downside of running somewhere like this.' She took Meredith's hand and squeezed it. 'You don't know how great it is to be able to admit that. It's so lovely here, and David is really patient. I just feel so guilty that I'm always so bad-tempered these days! Anyway, forget about me. Tomorrow we'll ring Jo and be three Meads girls together! Maybe we can persuade her to hop over while you're here. You could always share a bed . . .'

She chuckled at Meredith's shocked expression. 'I don't mean it, you idiot!'

Meredith clinked her champagne glass against Steph's. 'Long live good old Meads. I wonder what it's like now? They've probably got en suite bathrooms!'

'And underfloor heating,' laughed Steph. 'Do you remember how bloody freezing it was?'

'Do I?! I used to get dressed in bed!'

They giggled away, bonded by the memory of that tougher era, until Steph found herself yawning unstoppably, suddenly overcome by tiredness. She tried to suppress it, but Meredith couldn't help noticing. 'Come on – drink up and get yourself off to bed.'

'But you're only here for a little while,' Steph sighed.

'There's plenty of time. Do you get any time off tomorrow morning? I'd like to walk along the river and find the château, if that's OK with you.'

'St Savarin? It's about a mile away. Yes, that'd be lovely.' She hugged Meredith one last time. 'Eleven o'clock? Then I could get the dinner sorted first.'

'Perfect. Sleep well.'

'I will. See you in the morning.'

When she'd gone, Meredith opened her French windows and stood on the balcony for a moment. All didn't seem to be well in the Adams household. It was just as well she was a solutions woman – they clearly needed some solutions here.

Two

Guillaume, the barman of the Café de la Paix, stood behind the bar twirling his moustache in the small mirror he kept for this very purpose.

In his view the moustache was a work of art, far more interesting than Salvador Dalí's famous version. It had taken him three whole years to perfect it. Dark brown in colour, it unfurled in perfect symmetry over his top lip, ending in a dramatic curl at either end like the strong man in a Victorian circus.

Guillaume and the moustache had just finished an hour's lively French lesson with the expat members of the Bratenac Ladies' Luncheon Club. He made a little money from these sessions, but did it more for the *entente cordiale* and the belief that if all these *Anglais* were going to come and live in his country, the least they could do was to learn the language. It also helped that the English ladies liked a drink and spent enough to keep the owner, who happened to be Guillaume's partner, very happy.

Among the club members present was Jackie Brown, well over seventy but still bursting with energy under her mahogany permatan. Jackie considered herself the doyenne of Bratenac's expats. She had left Essex and settled here long before a lot of the other arrivals and, unlike many of them, spoke good French, albeit with a truly terrible accent.

In her view, Jackie was the opposite of retired, and that was the way she liked it. Like most expats looking for ways to make ends meet in their French paradise, she had a variety of jobs, from managing empty properties to doing the change-overs for Airbnb rentals, making sure villa swimming pools hadn't gone green and unusable, and organizing her toyboy husband of sixty-two, Steve, who happened to be Bratenac's most popular builder. Perhaps toyboy was an exaggeration, looking at Steve. He was big and muscular, but had a large paunch and an arse that hung over his trousers when he bent down, in a classic case of builder's bum. Jackie was forever nagging him about this unsightly appendage. After all, she didn't want him popping his clogs before her, even though he was thirteen years younger, did she?

The other regulars in Jackie's *coterie* were Janine, who did dog walking and dogsitting, often moving into people's houses for the whole time they'd gone back to the UK; Mandy, who made money catering for the expat parties; Shirley, who was a happy housewife; and Suzi, who saw herself as the group's *femme fatale*, since she had a weakness for other people's husbands. Jackie knew that this came from insecurity and a fear of ageing; but even so, having lost her own first husband to another woman, she knew Suzi definitely needed watching. Fortunately, Steve wouldn't have noticed if Suzi had posed naked across a plate of chips – or rather, he'd have noticed the chips. He'd lost interest in sex long ago, which was a pity because Jackie certainly hadn't.

'Hey girls,' she suggested, 'how about an early lunch

tomorrow in that new pop-up restaurant down by the river?' Shirley declined because, being a happy housewife, she liked cooking for her husband, but the others looked keen. 'It's been taken over by a famous chef. From Paris,' Jackie added ominously.

'Why does he want to open a restaurant in a portacabin in Bratenac, then?' asked Mandy, who resented all new culinary competition. 'Anyway, who wants to eat beetroot prepared five ways? You can't understand half of what you're ordering with these trendy new menus.'

'Well, let's go and see for ourselves,' soothed Jackie.

They arranged to meet at twelve for a pre-lunch glass to inspect the new venue.

Just as they were leaving, that nice man married to Stephanie Adams came in and quietly went up to the bar, avoiding the lustful glance cast at him by Suzi. It was becoming a bit of a habit with him to slip in here for a drink, Jackie noticed.

'Suzi!' hissed Jackie, catching her in the act of undoing her top button. 'Behave. And do that button right back up. Stephanie Adams is a nice woman and Steve helped with their building work and said her husband was a really good bloke.'

'You mean he gave Steve a beer on the job, I bet,' retorted Suzi, tossing her luxuriant black curls.

Jackie ignored her, although it was probably true. Steve had also commented that David Adams had as much grasp of DIY as a gorilla, possibly less. According to Steve, most of the Brits who bought châteaux round here fancied themselves as artists with the Black & Decker. The usual story was that the wife was convinced she was Kelly Hoppen – probably someone at home had once complimented her on her cushions – and the husband thought he could do all the refurb work himself. On the basis of such illusions many wrecks were purchased, Steve said – and often they completely took over the buyers' lives, destroying their marriages and eating up their entire life savings. He'd seen it time and time again. Still, it was all good business for Steve.

'Hello, Mr Adams,' Jackie greeted him cheerfully. He looked startled and slightly guilty. Clearly his wife had no idea he came in here so often. 'Jackie Brown,' she enlightened him, 'Steve the builder's wife. I'm sure we've bumped into each other before.'

'Oh, hello Mrs Brown. How are you?'

'Very well, thanks, Mr Adams. How's business?'

'Not bad, thank you. Full house at the moment.'

'That's good. Give my regards to your wife.' He picked up the drinks list from the bar.

'Guillaume!' Jackie bellowed. '*L'addition, s'il vous plaît!*'

'*J'arrive! J'arrive!*' Guillaume appeared with the bill with all the speed and elegance of a figure skater.

Jackie twirled his moustache, smiling. 'Worth every second of the three years it took you to grow. It's wasted on all of us. It ought to be in a moustache museum.'

Joanna Walker checked her bank statement, as she did every day now since The Discovery.

When her husband Mark had left her for upwardly mobile PR exec Amanda, she'd assumed their finances were in order, since he'd always seemed very financially savvy. According to Mark, Jo was 'an arty-farty type with her nose constantly in a book', and he would therefore take over all things financial. And she'd let him.

Ladies, a lesson. Never leave all the money matters to your husband, no matter how much you think you can trust him.

It was no longer the 1950s, when women didn't understand money and men were possessed of godlike wisdom, as Jo had found to her cost. Mark had emptied their joint account and borrowed against anything he could. She'd thought of trying to sue but instead had worked flat out as an events organizer. Now, three years later, she was solvent and their house was safe.

And now Mark and Amanda were getting married.

And although Jo thought she'd got over the worst of the heartbreak from the divorce, the news of their engagement was still ripping her apart. Despite all her mindfulness and effing CBT her mind kept going back to this wedding and comparing it to their own happy day, which had seemed so full of love and hope and promise. Huh.

The mornings were the worst, somehow. When you woke, your mind was raw and undefended. Instead of feeling angry, she started to ask herself if it had partly been her fault. Had she let him down somehow? The truth was, when your husband dumped you for someone else, you couldn't avoid feeling a failure.

But she mustn't let herself go down that road. Trying to revive some healthy cynicism, Joanna thought of messaging Amanda that she'd better keep her money in her own account – but the irony would probably be lost on her. She didn't seem the brightest of sparks.

Instead, Jo longed to get away.

The trouble was, she was busy with a big exhibition and it would be letting down her daughter Sophie, who ran the business with her, if she just disappeared. Besides which, the wedding might affect Sophie too, though all she had said so far was 'I hope she dresses like a teenager at a school disco like she usually does. She'll look bloody ridiculous!'

Jo would just have to go to the cinema with her lovely neighbour, Liz, who had seen her through some of the worst times. Women were so much more reliable than men. Pity she wasn't gay, Jo thought, it would be so much easier. But then gay women no doubt made stupid choices and fell in love with the wrong people just like straight women. Bloody love, she mused, for about the millionth time. We'd be better off without it.

She got out her phone and browsed all the local cinemas. The choice seemed to be between an action adventure or a serious and important film about the plight of the planet. Poor old planet, it was even worse off than she was. She must save more plastic bags. Ah well, she'd go over to Liz's instead. It would have to be a bottle of fizz and *Mamma Mia* on Netflix.

She looked outside. It seemed to be rain, rain, rain this spring. Even her daffs were drooping. 'You look how I feel,' she told them. 'Careful,' she added sternly, 'talking to yourself is the first sign of madness. If you don't watch it, you'll end up a batty old bird!'

She stared out again at the sheets of non-stop drizzle. Looking on the bright side, if the weather stayed like this, at least it might ruin Mark and Amanda's wedding!

'Are you ready, Meredith?' Steph called up to her friend. 'Everything's sorted for dinner so we can have all the time in the world!'

Meredith skipped down the stairs, beaming. 'Will these shoes be OK?' She pointed at her expensive Tod's loafers.

'As long as you don't fall in the river in them, fine.'

It was a lovely spring day, with a clear blue sky and the promise of a warm sunny walk along the riverbank. Meredith realized she was actually quite excited.

They walked down a path by the side of Steph's house that

meandered from a small vineyard right down to the Savarin River. 'I wonder if the campsite is still here,' Meredith mused.

'What was it called?' asked Steph.

'God knows! I haven't been there since I was twelve.'

'I *think* it might be still here,' Steph suggested. 'The French are nuts on camping. Some of them come the moment the school holidays begin and stay six whole weeks! That's why the motorways are all madness at the end of August, for the famous *rentrée*, when they all go home on the same day. It's an amazing sight as long as you don't get caught up in it – like migrating wildebeest! The queues into Paris go back twenty miles.'

They walked along, arm in arm, admiring the lush green landscape. 'Look at that!' Meredith said suddenly. 'That pond over there on the other side of the field. There's a little boy standing in the middle of it and the water is making perfect circles all around him. It's like something from a Chinese vase!'

They continued their walk for about half a mile without meeting anyone until they came to a narrow bridge. It was no longer the rickety structure of her childhood but a sensible, solid-looking affair. They crossed the river and stopped to look back from the far side.

'Oh my God,' Meredith breathed. 'There it is! Rapunzel's château!'

Steph was about to point out that she didn't think Rapunzel lived in a château, but decided to let her friend enjoy the precious memory.

They both stared at the fairy-tale castle built of grey-gold stone with its four russet-tiled towers, surrounded by its own moat. 'It's exactly how I remembered it,' Meredith announced with a catch in her voice. 'My dad and I used to stop at this very spot every day on our way to get the bread. It was the best moment of the day and Dad used to laugh and say one day he'd buy it for me.' She shook her head at the touching absurdity of her dad, in his menial job, being able to buy a château.

'We could probably look round it,' Steph suggested. 'It's quite a well-known wedding venue now. The great selling point is that the old duke and duchess will come down and mingle if you want them to, and the duke will even give the bride away if there's no father around. He's an old sweetie, actually. People come from all over the world to get married here. They have a very grand lady called Héloise who organizes everything, but she must be about eighty now.'

Meredith was hardly listening, still wrapped in her memories. Steph let her have her moment.

After five minutes Meredith turned back to her friend. 'I'm so glad I came,' she announced with a kind of suppressed passion Steph hadn't sensed in her before. 'I'd lost him, you see. Missing his death, and then coming back for a funeral that could have been for anyone, not my amazing dad. But here I seem to be getting him back. I thought I was mad to race across the world all because of a photo in a flight mag, but I was right. It's really going to be worth it.'

'Meredith.' Steph put her arms round her friend. 'I'm so glad. Do you want to stay here a bit longer?'

'No, let's wander on. I can always come back. We have two whole weeks!' She looked at her watch. 'I wouldn't mind a bite to eat.'

'Fine,' agreed Steph, realizing her friend might like to come back alone. 'Why don't we try the new place everyone's talking about? It's right on the riverbank about half a mile on.'

'Sounds great.'

They wandered on happily, arm in arm, watching the wide, green depths of the river with willows dipping their branches into the water's edge, creating secret hidden places.

After about fifteen minutes they spotted some tables and chairs ranged along a decking platform that hung right over the river. Most of the tables were for two people, but three had been pushed together and were occupied by a noisy group who seemed to be accompanied by a large number of dogs, much to the disapproval of the other customers.

'Oh my God,' Steph giggled. 'It's the Bratenac Ladies' Luncheon Club!'

'And what on earth is that?'

'They're all expats who hang around in the Café de la Paix. The permatanned one is Jackie Brown, married to our local builder.'

Jackie was at that moment speaking in French to a young man who was waiting at their table. Her accent was terrible, for which she compensated by declaiming at full volume. '*Qu'est-ce que vous allez faire maintenant, Jean-Christophe?*' she enquired. And then, for the benefit of the others: 'I'm asking what he's going to do now he's finished interning with his dad in the restaurant.'

Jean-Christophe, a young man of about twenty-two possessed of the dark, broodingly handsome looks of a Gitanes ad, was smiling down at her.

'Amazing how she always knows what's going on,' Steph whispered to Meredith as they took their seats. 'Be warned. Never tell her anything unless you want the entire region to find out.'

'I will be looking for a job, madame,' Jean-Christophe replied with a smile that could have melted every female heart within a half-mile radius. 'Perhaps three days a week, so I can still help here when needed.' He tucked a strand of luxuriantly curling black hair behind his ear.

The gesture suddenly reminded Meredith of her favourite rock star, a famous bad boy of the early seventies. Good heavens, she told herself firmly, I hope I'm not becoming a jaguar – or is it a cougar? Why on earth the cougar should be burdened with representing predatory older women was beyond her. But then, she didn't imagine newts got pissed, yet they were lumbered with that label whether they liked it or not.

Along with the rest of the restaurant she couldn't help hearing Jackie's question to the young man. It seemed he was a chef who needed a part-time job. How interesting. Meredith, with her highly evolved business brain, stored the information away.

Before they'd even given their order, Jackie was grilling him again.

'Does it need to be near here?' she enquired in hundred-decibel tones.

'Yes, madame, in Bratenac if I can find one.'

'You don't miss the bright lights of Gay Paree?'

'I grew up there, madame. But you can tire even of Paris. Now you could say I am a country boy.'

He smiled with the half-modest, half-flirtatious air of a young Belmondo; then, noticing the two newcomers, he turned towards them. 'Can I get you a menu, *mesdames*, or are you just here for a drink?'

'A drink first, and then something to eat.' Meredith returned his smile.

Five minutes later they were settled in the sunshine, Meredith with a *gin-tonique* and Steph with a glass of local white wine, so cold that it made the glass look frosted. Steph knew the experts argued that you should drink white chilled rather than cold like this, but it was the way she loved to drink it.

They both studied the menu.

'It's much less up itself than we were expecting,' Jackie informed them loudly, twisting round in her seat with surprising agility for someone who resembled a barrel wrapped in Lycra. 'The chef has moved here from Paris and has quite a reputation, so we were expecting some incomprehensible nonsense covered in dots of balsamic vinegar.'

'Thanks, Jackie.' Steph went back to the menu.

Meredith was looking around her and had become so entranced with the landscape that she didn't even hear. The river danced in the golden light of spring; it seemed to sparkle and shimmer like a mirror reflecting the sunshine. Further in the distance, the russet brick of an ancient bridge looked almost like a mirage in the midday heat.

'I can't believe the air.' She threw back her head and closed her eyes. 'So clear you can almost drink it. In Eastern cities, sitting out like this, we'd all be choking with the smog and pollution!'

'Did you manage to find a parking space?' Jackie enquired. 'We'd forgotten it's market day and had to leave the cars miles away.'

'We walked, as a matter of fact,' Steph replied. 'My friend used to come here as a child and wanted to see if the château was still the same.'

'And it is,' laughed Meredith, mellowed by the beauty of her surroundings into a rare personal disclosure. 'Exactly the same. My father used to say he'd buy it for me one day.'

'Your luck's in, then,' Jackie remarked with a flourish, waving her blackberry martini. 'The duke and duchess have put it up for sale. Hoping some mad Brit will buy it.' She sipped her drink, warming to her subject. 'You know Louie Worth, the ballerina, owns a wedding château nearby, and one of the Spice Girls another. Château weddings are big business round here.'

Meredith put down her drink. 'How bizarre. How much are they asking?'

Steph stared at her, eyes widening in surprise.

'Four hundred thousand euro, I think,' said Jackie. 'Though they'd probably take an offer,' she added confidentially, as if she were an intimate acquaintance of the duke and duchess.

'Good God,' Meredith laughed. 'My apartment in Hong Kong cost four times that – though of course, it does have a concierge and swimming pool.'

'Why don't you buy it, then?' challenged Jackie. 'I hear you're a businesswoman. If you've got money and a business brain, I gather it could be quite a good venture.'

Meredith smiled and stared out at the river. 'Not really my kind of thing. I'm more into banks and hedge funds.'

'God, how dull,' said Jackie, as Jean-Christophe arrived at her table with their food. 'Think of all the drama you get at weddings!'

Once they were served, he turned to Steph and Meredith. 'Are you ready to order, *mesdames*?'

'I think I'll have two starters, please,' Steph replied. 'The hot *foie gras* and then the asparagus. Are they local? Not flown in from Brazil?' She smiled, undercutting the pointedness of her question.

'*Bien sûr*, madame.' The young man looked shocked, as if Steph had just sworn in church. 'My father insists. Everything is local and seasonal.' He turned to Meredith. 'And you, madame?'

'I'm actually quite hungry after our walk. I'll have the *confit de canard* and some *sauté* potatoes. Oh, and a *salade verte. Merci bien.*'

She gave him one of her special smiles, the one she reserved for friends rather than clients.

'I didn't know you spoke French,' commented Steph.

'Menu French, you mean. We all do that.'

'No, you have the accent, and that little way of waving your hands as the French do.'

Meredith looked out at the river again. 'How much would it make my dad laugh if I bought that château?'

Steph stared at her, astonished. 'You're not serious? Could you afford it?'

'Easily. A year's bonus. And that'd be a bad year.'

'But your life's in the East.'

Meredith produced a sphinx-like smile. 'Indeed it is. Are you going to have another glass of wine with yours? I certainly am.'

Jean-Christophe appeared with the drinks menu.

'I'll have a glass of Sancerre,' Meredith said decisively, not even bothering to look at the list.

'*Non, madame, je suis desolé,*' a laughing voice insisted from somewhere behind them. 'Sancerre is from the Loire, and here you must drink the local wine.'

An older version of Jean-Christophe suddenly materialized. They even had the same hair, although the newcomer's was streaked with grey. Yet this version struck Meredith as shaggy and craggy, unshaven to the point of scruffiness, wearing an old and not very clean suede jacket over his chef's overalls.

He was holding a bottle of unlabelled white wine in one hand, and a tiny glass of golden liquid in the other. 'Montbazillac,' he announced, indicating the glass. 'Our famous dessert wine, and the perfect partner for the *foie gras*.' He set it down in front of Steph, and then poured Meredith a glass of the paler wine from the bottle.

Meredith, used to ordering – and paying – for exactly what she wanted, was about to protest that she'd have what she bloody well asked for, *merci*.

'Try a little, at least,' he insisted with a smile. 'It would be a crime to drink Sancerre. And think, you would become notorious – the tourist who ordered Sancerre in the middle of Savarin!'

Meredith took a sip, annoyed that he seemed to be mocking her. To her irritation it was absolutely delicious: flinty, as she liked her wines, and yet with overtones of fruit that never strayed into sweetness.

'The grapes are grown no more than a mile from here. Is there not a special pleasure in knowing that, when it accompanies your *confit d'oie*?'

'I know,' Steph interjected, suspecting that Meredith might say no simply because she didn't like being told what to do. 'You must be the famous Philippe!'

The man bowed, an ironic expression lighting up his warm brown eyes and producing engaging crinkles in the corners. 'Not so famous in the circles I suspect your friend moves in. Enjoy your meal.'

Meredith had been about to comment that his jacket didn't exactly look like suitable wear for a kitchen, but she could imagine his sardonic reply. No doubt she was more used to pristine overalls and the white chef's hat of five-star establishments, he would reply; and she would somehow end up looking foolish again.

Instead she waited till he had left. 'How is he famous?' she enquired huffily.

'He grew up here, then went off to Paris and ran his own restaurant – with three Michelin stars. He's just come back to Bratenac to start again and rediscover his roots.'

'I bet he lost one of his stars and knew the whole thing would go pear-shaped,' Meredith said cynically. 'So he's come home to keep the food local, seasonal and very, very simple, and give a positive spin to his failure at the same time.'

'Meredith! Don't be so mean. I think he's rather wonderful. Also, his father's ill, who used to be a big influence on him when he was growing up. Taught him to cook and everything.'

'He's got dementia, as a matter of fact,' interrupted Jackie from the next table. 'Wanders round the town making a spectacle of himself.'

'Is there anything that bloody woman doesn't know?' hissed Meredith under her breath. She added at normal volume: 'Poor man. I do sympathize. As a matter of fact, I'm pretty ill myself. I've just had a cancer diagnosis.'

Steph was so startled that she almost dropped her glass of Montbazillac.

Jackie leaned even closer until she was practically in Meredith's lap. 'Oh, poor you. Is it terminal?'

Meredith simply looked forlorn. 'Nothing the doctors can do. That's why I'm here, as a matter of fact.'

'You won't be buying the château, then,' concluded Jackie unceremoniously. 'You have my deepest sympathy.' She moved back, as if Meredith's affliction might be infectious.

'Meredith! Behave!' Steph tried not to completely dissolve in giggles. 'You really are the end!'

Rather to Meredith's disappointment, there was no sign of the annoying Philippe for the rest of lunch. Several times, Steph noticed her friend glance towards the kitchen and smiled secretly to herself. But not secretly enough for the all-seeing Meredith.

'What are you looking like that for? That's the kind of smile Jane Austen probably smiled as she sentenced Lizzie to fall in love with that moody Darcy bloke. Come on – let's walk back through the town. I used to like the market here. Will it still be open, though?'

'It's all day on Saturdays, though some of the really early stallholders may be closing up shop. Let's go and see.'

Meredith clicked her fingers and Jean-Christophe did a slight double-take before he came towards them.

'Meredith,' whispered Steph. 'That's considered rude in France. You call the waiters "monsieur" here. It's considered an honourable profession.'

Meredith looked impish. 'You can do what you like when you're as ill as I am!'

'I don't think we should let that silly rumour go any further,' Steph replied. 'Besides, it's really quite offensive. Plenty of people really are seriously ill!'

'Don't be so PC,' countered Meredith. 'Humour has to be a bit outrageous, or it wouldn't be funny. You're probably right, though,' she admitted. 'It's just that I can't bear the way she claims to know everything.' She picked up the bill. 'I'll get this, by the way.'

'Thanks,' Steph smiled. No point arguing with Meredith about money. 'Then I'm going to put Jackie right about this silly story.'

She headed for Jackie, who was in the middle of revealing some particularly juicy gossip about a Parisian couple who had bought a house in the village. 'She's incredibly stylish,' Jackie was saying confidentially, 'but wait till you meet the husband. Camp as Christmas!'

'Jackie.' Steph leaned in and spoke firmly. 'That stuff about my friend being ill. I'm afraid it was just a joke. Meredith's perfectly fine.'

'Is she indeed?' replied Jackie stiffly. She didn't like to be made a fool of. 'Then rather tasteless of her to say so, if you don't mind me pointing it out.'

'I'm sure she's very sorry.'

Meredith, who was striding towards them, looking expensively elegant, didn't appear in the slightest bit sorry.

'So,' Jackie mused as she watched the pair of them walk away, 'is she just being tasteless, or is she really ill?' She turned back to her coterie with eyebrows raised.

'You don't think,' Suzi posited, still smarting from the rebuke about undoing her top button yesterday, 'she was trying to make the point that you can be a little bit nosy, Jackie?'

Jackie looked as shocked as a nun at a hen do. 'Me? Nosy? What a completely ridiculous idea. Half the time I'm the last to know about things!'

Janine bit her lip, trying not to giggle, as Mandy kicked Suzi under the table on her bare fake-tanned leg. 'Time we left, I think.' Jackie rose with all the hauteur of Elizabeth I on a royal progress and marched out of the restaurant.

Behind them, Meredith and Steph were settling their bill with Jean-Christophe.

'You do not think, madame,' commented the slightly husky voice Steph recognized as Philippe's, 'that you should not make jokes about being struck down by serious illness?'

Meredith whipped round to find that he was, in fact, roaring with laughter. 'Congratulations. You have finally turned into a laughing-stock the biggest busybody in Bratenac. By tonight the story will be everywhere.' He bowed like an eighteenth-century chevalier and blew her a kiss.

'The cheek of the man!' Meredith exploded as she dragged Steph swiftly towards the river. 'I loathe his type. Men who are rude to you, then pretend it's all a joke! Absolutely bloody outrageous!'

*

Bratenac market's indoor area contained three butchers, two fishmongers, a bread shop and three different cheese shops, as well as some fruit and vegetable sellers. It always left Steph in exasperated amusement that you could queue for twenty minutes in the vegetable shop, but when you asked for lettuce the shopkeeper would shrug at the extraordinary ignorance of the foreigner and patiently explain '*Mais ça, c'est salade, madame!*' – and you would have to queue for another twenty minutes to purchase your lettuce and cucumber from the salad man next door. No wonder some people fell for the lures of the hypermarket.

Despite that, Steph loved French markets. The outdoor market area consisted of about a hundred stalls, selling everything from the enormous knickers beloved of the farmers' wives to a magnificent array of handbags imported by two Senegalese with megawatt smiles. There were also 'Persian' rugs made from suspicious-looking polypropylene, and a glorious selection of herbs tied with ribbon or displayed in baskets, perfuming the air with their fragrance as if preparing for the arrival of the Queen of Sheba. Another stall sold jars of olives and nuts, especially walnuts, one of the proudest products of the region, found in everything from savoury tarts to salads, puddings and stuffing. A couple of local winegrowers were offering samples of the sweet Monbazillac wine Steph had had with her *foie gras*, which Meredith gaily accepted.

'I only tried the local white, remember. Whether I liked it or not.'

Steph tried not to smile at how much this clearly still rankled.

Next was a clothes stall selling dresses in thick, slubby Italian linen. Steph stopped and fingered one of the dresses hanging up on display. 'It's really good quality, feel.'

Meredith raised a disdainful eyebrow.

'OK, OK, I know you only wear designer . . . but this one would really suit you.' She held up a knee-length dress in bright pale green, the colour of a new shoot, patterned with the outline of leaves in a darker shade. 'Go on, try it on!'

'What – there?' Meredith pointed to the half sheet slung across a tiny alcove set aside for clothes-trying.

'Don't be so pompous! Try it!'

'Madame, try,' encouraged the vendor. 'It could be made for you!'

'I'll be the judge of that.' Meredith reached for the dress and carried it off, still shaking her head at the ludicrousness of the situation.

When she emerged a moment later, Steph burst into smiles. 'It's really great! That colour is perfect for you.'

Meredith studied herself in the mirror. The cut was surprisingly stylish, just the right length, shaped at the waist and with short sleeves that covered any incipient bingo wings. Not that Meredith would ever have those.

'How much?' she enquired in a bored tone.

'Twenty-five euro, madame.'

'Twenty-five euro? God, I pay that much for parking when I'm at home. OK, at that price I suppose I'd better have it.'

'Come on, big spender,' Steph teased, 'let's go home and we can ring up Jo.'

'What a lovely idea!' laughed Meredith as they passed through the remaining stalls, who were now beginning to pack up, the best of their business accomplished.

They started off towards home, passing a pancake stall, the distinctive aroma filling their nostrils as the young woman spread the mix astonishingly thinly onto the hotplate. Seeing this always made Steph think of the LPs she'd played on the Dansette record player in her teenage bedroom.

Meredith stopped, breathed in the glorious scent and enquired, a saucy grin suddenly transforming her sophisticated manner, 'Have you had a crêpe lately?'

Steph came to a halt, her hand over her mouth, totally shocked at the lavatorial *double entendre*. Something was happening to Meredith. The high-flying businesswoman seemed to be shedding her cool and blasé demeanour and returning to the mischievous, irreverent Merry of their sixth-form days.

'I love you, Meredith Harding,' Steph stated and gave her a sisterly hug. 'Come on, let's get home and call Joanna as soon as we can, or the dreaded LeBruns will be invading the homestead.'

'Hi, honey, I'm home!' she called out as she opened the front door, sharing the private joke both she and David often called out as they got in. Silence. He must have gone out and left me to do it all, she thought irritably, somehow forgetting that she was the one who'd just been out for hours with her friend.

'Come on, let's call Jo while the house is quiet,' she said.

They sat in the empty sitting room and she dialled Jo's number. 'I hope she's not at work,' she remarked as the phone rang out and no one picked it up. Then on about the tenth ring, just as Steph was about to put down the phone, Jo's voice came on the line.

'Hello. Joanna Walker speaking.'

'Jo!' they both chorused gleefully. 'It's Steph! And Meredith!'

Jo sounded as if she almost had to sit down. 'Meredith! Are you in France, then?'

'Staying at Steph's. It's a long story. You'll have to come and we'll tell you.'

Steph grabbed the phone. 'Yes, Jo, please come. Meredith's here for two whole weeks! You've got to come. God knows when she'll be over again! We miss you! It's time we Meads Girls were together again!'

They heard Jo speaking to someone in the background, no doubt explaining who was generating so much excitement down the line. 'I'm with my lovely next-door neighbour, Liz,' Jo explained. 'She's been saving my life, as a matter of fact.'

'Oh, Jo.' Steph instantly guessed why. 'Are things pretty horrible, then?'

'Fairly crap, as a matter of fact,' Jo confessed, her voice sounding ragged at the edges despite every attempt to sound normal. No point beating about the bush with Steph and Meredith. They'd been almost as close as sisters before life got in the way. 'My horrible husband Mark is about to get married again.'

'Oh, Jo, the bastard!'

'Too true! I was tempted to call you, Steph, and offer myself as an extra pair of hands at your B&B. I know how busy you always are, and there's nothing like a bit of bedmaking and a lot of white wine to help you forget your troubles.'

'Oh, Jo, you don't need to do any bedmaking,' Steph re-assured. 'You'd be a treasured guest. Look, you have to come over while Meredith's here! It'd be amazing! All three of us together again!'

Hearing Steph's voice, the thought seemed more tempting than ever to Jo. And Meredith was there too! Meredith, who already thought men an inferior species and would waste no time in saying so. Jo could almost hear her funny, astringent tones now.

'The thing is,' she insisted finally, 'no matter how much I want to, I can't. You remember I'm in business with my daughter? We're right in the middle of this major exhibition, the biggest thing we've had for ages. Liz . . .' She stopped, her voice sounding suddenly sharp. 'Liz, what are you doing?'

'Calling Sophie,' was the matter-of-fact reply in the background. 'Hi Sophie, it's Liz here. The thing is, your mum's just had this great invitation to go and see her two old school friends in France and she doesn't think it's fair to you. Yes, that's what I thought, and I could help you out with any boring admin. Here, I'll hand you over.' She held her mobile out. 'It's Sophie. She says of course you should go.'

'Liz, you wretch. I'll kill you!' laughed Jo. 'Hi, darling. Yes, Steph invited me and Meredith's over there too.'

'That settles it, Mum. Of course you must go,' her daughter repeated. 'Look, Mum –' Sophie's voice was unusually serious – 'for perfectly understandable reasons you've been cocooning yourself away. But it's time you took a few risks. You mustn't let what Dad gets up to define you! Go to France with your friends. You need an adventure. I can cope fine with the exhibition.'

'But, darling,' Jo replied hesitantly, 'the exhibition's one thing . . . but what about the gruesome wedding?'

'I can just as easily run her over when you're away as when you're here!' Jo could hear her daughter's laughter, and felt a little reassured. 'I'm kidding! I'll be busy flogging paintings to art galleries and making our sponsors happy little bunnies. Sad, because it means I'll have to miss the nuptial celebrations, which quite frankly is probably much better for my head; and then when the show closes, maybe I'll pop out and join you!'

'Soph, you're wonderful!' Delight struggled with guilt, and delight won. 'OK, then. I'll go.'

She handed the phone back to Liz. 'Good on you, girl,' Liz congratulated Sophie. 'And I mean it about the boring admin. I used to be quite a whizz in my day.'

'I expect you heard all that!' Jo explained to her two school friends, but her words were lost in all the clapping and jumping up and down that seemed to be greeting her response.

'Jo, that's so bloody brilliant!' Steph managed to reply. 'Just let me know when you're arriving. David'll come and meet you.'

'What a luxury!' Being met at airports was one of those rare treats Jo missed from her marriage. Not that Mark had ever done it unless forced to. 'I'll look up flights,' Jo suggested, full of excitement. 'Does any day suit you especially?'

'Tuesdays are usually quiet for some mysterious reason.'

'Then I'll come on Tuesday. How absolutely lovely!'

'It will be. And the weather's gorgeous. This is always a lovely time of year here, before it gets summer-hot.'

'I'll let you know the details as soon as I've booked. Byeee!'

Steph was still smiling delightedly when David came back into the room, so she didn't notice his slightly guilty demeanour. But Meredith did, and wondered what he'd been up to. Maybe she'd better speak to that nice young chef soon about an idea she'd had.

'Jo's coming!' Steph blurted delightedly.

'Well, that should cheer you up,' smiled David. 'The Meads Girls are back in town.'

'And she even wants to help a bit.'

'Well, there you are. You boarding-school girls are brought up to help other people, I know. Except husbands,' he added with a grin.

'Come here, you.' And Steph gave him a kiss to silence any more complaints he could think up.

Jo could hardly control her excitement the next day as she booked her flight and started packing. What would she need? Some old jeans in case she really did do some cleaning. Her trusty white capri pants and some pretty blouses, plus two or three smart dresses. Sandals! She looked out of the window at the driving rain. How wonderful to need sandals! Finally her make-up, sponge bag and a hopeful swimsuit. Would she need suntan lotion? She delved into the bathroom cupboard in case, pushing aside a can of mosquito spray.

Jo picked it up and laughed. Last time she'd spent any length of time in France she'd been a student, grape-picking near Carcassonne during her long summer holiday. It had been the fashionable student thing to do then, even considered rather daring in Basingstoke, her home town. She sat down on the bed for a moment. Where had all the time gone between then and now? She'd been so hopeful and optimistic, full of excitement at having life ahead of her.

Her daughter was right. She had been hiding herself away. It was time she broke out of her cocoon and tried to be a butterfly!

She got up to go and join Liz and heard the faint sound of an insect batting against the window. Probably an early fly or bee. In fact, it was a large moth. As she watched it, it opened its wings and revealed shades of delicate celadon green, patterned with zig-zag lines like Venetian paper. Jo smiled as she let it out. Even moths were beautiful, she told herself, feeling suddenly light-hearted and hopeful for the first time in months as she went next door to join her friend.

A powerful whiff of patchouli assaulted her nostrils as Liz showed her in. The Sixties were still very much alive where her friend and neighbour was concerned. Jo hadn't even taken off her coat when Liz handed her what looked like a shoebox wrapped in stripy paper and adorned with a large green bow.

'What on earth's this?' Jo asked.

'A revenge gift!' replied Liz with a smile.

Jo began to unwrap the layers of tissue until she uncovered a bright purple rubber object, about six inches long, shaped like some kind of tree or cactus without the spikes, with what seemed to be a small animal climbing up the side. Perhaps it was a koala bear?

It was Liz's favourite hobby to go to every artist's open house in the area, and Jo assumed she'd bought this at one of them.

'Right.' Jo tried to sound enthusiastic. 'Does it go on the mantelpiece?'

'I sincerely hope not,' smirked Liz, reaching out and pressing a white button on the side of the trunk that had escaped Jo's notice. The object began to buzz loudly and jump about. 'It's a Happy Rabbit!'

'What on earth is a Happy Rabbit?' Jo enquired.

'A vibrator, you nitwit! You'll never have to think of Mark ever again once you discover one of these! Guaranteed!' Liz produced the beatific smile of a highly satisfied customer. 'Off home with you. I have to go out. I'll pick you up at six a.m. on Tuesday and drop you out to the airport. Have fun with the rabbit!'

Three

'Jo! Over here!' Steph shouted, jumping up and down and waving like a windmill to the astonishment of the other travellers at the tiny local airport.

Rather than sending David, Stephanie and Meredith hadn't been able to resist meeting their old friend themselves. As soon as she came through the barrier they both flung themselves at her and Jo, determined to keep her cool and not bleat on about how crap she was feeling, found herself dissolving into tears mixed with giggles of delight at being in the company of her oldest friends.

Meredith insisted on taking her pull-along bag and the two of them put their arms round her as they walked her to the small car park.

'Welcome to *la belle France!*' Steph smiled, gesturing around her.

'I can't tell you how delighted I am to be here,' Jo said, allowing herself to be led along. How wonderful to be looked after and not have to make any decisions for a while.

'We've planned a full programme for today,' Meredith announced briskly, rather as if she were announcing the agenda to a business meeting.

'Unless you want to have a little lie down,' Steph interjected, knowing everyone wasn't made of the same steel as Meredith and that Jo certainly wouldn't have enjoyed the luxury of business class. 'You must have got up very early.'

'I did, but my lovely neighbour Liz drove me to Luton Airport.'

'I like the sound of this Liz,' Steph grinned. 'You'll have to bring her with you next time.'

Jo toyed with telling them about the Happy Rabbit, but was still too embarrassed to describe its true function. Maybe after a few glasses of wine. Fortunately, she'd left it safely at home, terrified she might have had her bag opened by some diligent customs official. She could just imagine some uniformed jobsworth holding the object up and demanding, 'And what, pray, madam, is this for?' in front of a giggling hall of travellers. She found herself blushing at the mere thought.

'We're taking you back to Steph's to dump your bag, or unpack, whichever you prefer,' Meredith explained as they headed for the car park, 'and then we'll go on to a lovely lunch at the cafe in Bratenac – that's Steph's local town. And then this afternoon, there's a bit of a surprise.'

'Sounds blissful. Actually, I would quite like to unpack.' Jo always found she slept better in a strange room if her things were neatly hung up and her make-up bag stowed safely in the bathroom.

Steph had managed, by rejigging a couple of guests who hadn't arrived yet, to give Jo a lovely room on the top floor. The only drawback was that it was next to the ghastly LeBruns.

'Here's Jo, David,' she announced as they arrived back.

A harassed-looking David turned round. 'Hello, Jo – welcome to Fleur-de-Lis.'

'A bit flowery, I know,' Steph explained, 'but the fleur-de-lis is a royal symbol of France. The mason who built the house was probably getting a bit above his station when he named the place.' She pointed to where the name was beautifully carved into the huge chimney piece and then, noticing her husband's harassed demeanour, demanded: 'Have those bloody Belgians been driving you mad?'

'The little one's got diarrhoea.'

'And they say it's only the Brits who get the shits,' Steph grinned. 'The French think we're obsessed with our bowels,' she enlightened the others. 'They can talk. You should see inside a French bathroom cabinet. More drugs than the NHS. I hope it's not all over my new sheets,' she added unsympathetically.

'They've taken him to the doctor and left the other five here.'

'Oh God, poor you.' She looked at her watch. 'I'm afraid we've got to go. Lunch at the cafe at twelve thirty.'

'Couldn't we go a bit later and help David out . . . ?' suggested Jo.

'No,' replied Steph firmly. 'This is our special Girl Time. David will cope, won't you, dear? I'll just show you where your room is, Jo.'

She opened the door and four noisy children burst into the kitchen demanding orange juice and biscuits. Meredith and Jo exchanged glances as Steph ignored the chaos and led them upstairs. David clearly had a tough time of it. Jo didn't really know him, and hoped he was the type who didn't mind. Unlike her ex-husband, Mark. Stop! she told herself. France is a Mark-free zone. That was the whole point of coming.

She quickly unpacked and hung up her two dresses on a pretty padded coat hanger. How like Steph to get those important little details right.

It was only a short distance into Bratenac, and as Steph proposed that they should share a bottle of wine – if not two – it made sense to walk. Jo found herself instantly charmed by the allure of what the French reverently describe as *la France profonde*: deepest France, which meant totally rural areas like Savarin, where agriculture and winegrowing were still the main industries and time seemed almost to have stood still. They passed a red road sign featuring two fat geese and the legend *Route du Foie Gras*. Clearly the fashionable vegan vibe had not penetrated Bratenac and geese were still having their livers stuffed until the poor birds could eat no more and obligingly expired, or were despatched in the cause of gastronomic greed. On the other hand, the stuff tasted so bloody delicious. Oh dear; another modern dilemma to add to the list.

Once in Bratenac they passed a *pharmacie*, stuffed with enticing beauty and slimming products, the window adorned with a false leg wearing a lacy black pull-up stocking – perhaps it was a support stocking, such as might be found in our own dear Boots? Jo giggled. Only the French could come up with a seductive support stocking. She must go and have a look after lunch. Then there were creams and moisturizers – one of Jo's weaknesses when she could afford them, which wasn't often – promising an instant reduction of ten years.

Even though it was early, the Café de la Paix was crowded and almost every table filled, mostly with men in characteristic blue overalls or the uniform of the postal service or EDF, the major electricity provider, with one or two mud-splattered farm workers. Some were already enjoying a *petit blanc*, the small glass of white wine the French didn't consider a drink at all.

'It's because the *prix fixe* menu here is such amazing value,'

Steph explained. 'Eight euro for four courses, including cheese and a small *picher* of local wine.'

Jo looked round in wonder. Clearly the concept of the sandwich *al desko* had not hit Bratenac. 'I'm just so amazed they all drink at lunchtime!' she marvelled.

'They don't count a *picher*. David says no one in Parisian banks wants to be sent to the UK or the US. What did St Joan burn at the stake for if it wasn't to preserve the freedom to have a proper lunch?'

'Did she?' Jo asked naively. 'I thought it was all about religion.'

'I'm joking, you noodle,' Steph laughed.

'And why aren't there any women?'

At that precise moment the door opened and the Bratenac Ladies' Luncheon Club trooped in and ceremoniously sat down.

Guillaume instantly appeared with menus.

'My God,' Meredith whispered loudly, 'don't they ever go home?'

Jackie, still offended by Meredith's tasteless joke at her expense, studiously ignored them.

Guillaume turned his attention to the three friends. '*Votre plaisir, mesdames?*' he enquired with a raffish smile that made his moustache seem to curl even more at the ends.

'I'll have the duck *rillettes* followed by the wild boar and haricot soup and then decide in a while about the dessert,' Meredith said crisply.

'The walnut quiche and duck breast for me, *merci*,' smiled Steph, 'and I'll decide afterwards about the dessert as well.'

Jo looked bewildered. 'Are you having two starters, then, Meredith?' she enquired, assuming the soup was a starter as well as the paté.

Meredith laughed. 'The soup is actually a main course. They call it soup but it's a very hearty stew. It's delicious. Try it.'

'I think I will. I'm starving after getting up so early. I'll have the same as my friend.'

'Très bien. Et pour boire? Du vin blanc ou rouge?'

Jo knew she should pass on the wine, but it was all so deliciously different from the usual dash for a Tesco's Meal Deal.

'The white for me, please. And some tap water,' she added, trying to be virtuous.

'Red for me,' Meredith announced. 'I may even have to have another with the cheese.'

'Red for me too,' Steph smiled, trying not to feel guilty about abandoning David to the LeBruns and their diarrhoea.

'So what's the surprise this afternoon?'

'It wouldn't be a surprise if we told you,' hedged Meredith.

'My father always used to say the best surprises are the ones you know about,' Jo laughed.

'OK.' Meredith lowered her voice almost to a whisper. 'We're going to see round the Château de St Savarin.'

'How fabulous,' squeaked Jo, her voice getting louder in her excitement. 'You mean that wonderful fairy-tale castle we passed on the river?'

Meredith could almost sense Jackie Brown leaning forward, straining with every atom in her ample body to hear what they were saying.

'Yes,' agreed Meredith, determined not to feed Jackie's gossipmongering. 'Now tell us about what's happening with your horrible ex-husband.'

'He's marrying Amanda, a brainless floozy who calls herself a sales executive. Bet she couldn't sell beer to a thirsty Belgian.' Jo smiled impishly and raised her glass. 'Not that I'm bitter, you understand.'

Steph and Meredith raised their glasses in support. 'Here's to your exciting new life!'

'Absolutely,' Jo agreed. 'Once it bloody well starts!'

The meal, when it was brought out, was absolutely delicious. After their main course, an array of cheeses arrived. Jo chose a local goat's cheese rolled in herbs, peppercorns and the crushed walnuts that seemed to feature in so many local dishes round here.

'You'll have to come over for the walnut harvest,' Steph told her. 'Everyone in the entire place, from ninety-year-olds to tiny children, joins in shaking the walnut trees onto cloths on the ground, and the *père*, the parish priest, comes and blesses the crop afterwards.'

This sounded idyllic to Jo, who drove to work every day on the M25 with belching trucks and white van drivers opening their windows to give her the benefit of their accumulated wisdom.

As they finished their desserts of *îles flottantes*, islands of meringue floating in vanilla custard, followed by tiny coffees, Jo looked at her watch. 'We've been in here nearly two hours,' she marvelled, looking round at the still packed restaurant. 'Don't people have to get back to work?'

'They will soon,' Steph reassured. 'You have to remember, lunch is a religion here. To rush it is heretical.'

'Back to poor old St Joan. What time are we due there?'

Meredith started to get up. 'In half an hour. Plenty of time. I'll get this.'

Steph smiled at Jo and shrugged. Meredith seemed to be in such a different financial stratosphere that they might as well let her, and enjoy it.

They walked out past the other tables, finally beginning to empty, and politely saluted Jackie and her friends.

Jackie watched them, smiling smugly, and waited till they'd passed before commenting: 'Well, if that stuck-up bitch does buy the château, I hope she knows the old duke and duchess have bought a house right at the bottom of the driveway. Margot de Savarin will haunt that place like the Ghost of Christmas Past, only twice as interfering – heh heh! It'll all be highly entertaining. I almost hope she does buy it, silly cow.'

'But Jackie,' Shirley, always the gentlest member of the club, commented, 'don't you think you ought to warn her?'

'Not on your nelly!' announced Jackie. 'And you're not to breathe a word either, Shirley Harrison. On pain of being drummed out of our little lunch club! Understood?'

'Let's walk along the riverbank,' Meredith suggested. 'I want to get the full-on memory, if that's OK with you girls?'

The others nodded. It was a glorious day and walking would be a pleasure.

It only took ten minutes to arrive at the once-rickety bridge of Meredith's memory. Jo looked down into the green depths of the river, watching a fish rise, creating ripples for a second and then disappearing, while Meredith stood transfixed, her eyes on the château ahead.

'Isn't it the most amazing place?' she asked Jo.

'Hang on,' Jo replied. 'I think I can see Cinderella waving from the battlements. Or is it the Sleeping Beauty?'

Their appointment at the château was for three p.m. and to Jo's amazement they were to be shown round by the duke himself. Meredith clearly expected nothing less. His secretary met them at the entrance and informed them that his grace *le duc* would join them soon.

In fact, it was only a moment before the duke made a true Hollywood entrance, suddenly addressing them from the minstrel's gallery above their heads in the Great Hall.

'Bonjour, mesdames,' he greeted them, leaning out precipitously. 'If I were a troubadour like the famed Jospin de Bratenac, who lived here back in 1483, I would sing you a song praising your beauty. Sadly, it is the twenty-first century, so I will simply welcome you to our home!'

They found themselves looking up at a dapper and sprightly man, probably in his eighties though apparently still full of youthful vigour, wearing a jacket of English tweed with a dotted silk cravat and matching handkerchief.

'You have entered through the *donjon* – I think *keep* is the English word – which is from the twelfth century. You will have noticed the crenellations for firing weapons.'

'So that's what crenellations are for,' whispered Jo. 'You always hear about crenellated castles, but I never knew they had a purpose.'

'There are also loopholes for the archers,' continued the duke. 'It was a very warlike time.' He began to descend the staircase, still talking non-stop. 'By the eighteenth century the de Savarins had become more civilized.' He gestured around him at the painted ceilings, the elaborate plasterwork and vast chandeliers, each of which looked as if it would have been lit with a hundred candles, as well as the faded Aubusson carpets.

He had finally reached the bottom of the staircase. Jo realized that he was actually quite a small man. Perhaps that was why he liked to make his entrance from above.

'Come –' he favoured them with a smile as twinkly as any chandelier – 'the salon is more comfortable.'

He led them into a dazzlingly elegant room with walls painted in pale green decorated with gold, and vast gilded mirrors that wouldn't have looked out of place at Versailles. Spindly velvet sofas and marble-topped side tables with lion's-paw feet dotted the room.

Steph found her gaze fixing on a large painting of three fat cherubs, crowned in flowers, swimming face down in a turquoise sea, their chubby bottoms the focus of the picture.

The duke smiled. 'I have to apologize for the bad taste of that decoration. My wife is inordinately fond of cherubs. She purchased it at auction.' He shuddered visibly. 'It goes down well at weddings. But my wife will tell you about that later. Let us sit down and share a cup of English tea. The only thing, in my view, you British do better than the French.' He softened the comment with another of his twinkly smiles and went towards the huge chimney breast to ring a bell.

'What an old rogue,' commented Jo in a low voice. 'No man with that much charm can be genuine.'

Meredith laughed softly. 'That's new – Joanna the cynic! Since when have you been so distrusting of male magnetism?'

'Since I met my husband, I expect,' replied Jo, attempting an arch smile which somehow managed to look sad instead. She felt Steph's arm creep round her and felt suddenly better. 'Not that he had much, anyway. More of the "call a spade a spade" school, was Mark.'

'We'll just have to find you someone else, won't we, Meredith?' said Steph.

'Don't look at me,' Meredith laughed, then added in an undertone, 'I haven't been to bed with anyone for ten years! On the whole, I prefer a massage.'

'What a waste! Still, I hope your massages had happy endings,' interrupted the duke with a broad wink. 'Ladies, the tea has arrived.'

Meredith raised an eyebrow at her friends. Clearly, the duke had not caught up with Time's Up.

Behind them, a maid had laid out a silver tray on a table by the long window to the inner courtyard.

'Which was just as well,' Meredith told the others later. 'Or I might have had to slap the old lech. I can just see him as Maurice Chevalier singing "Thank Heavens for Leetle Girls" and meaning every word.'

Steph was delighted to see that Meredith was still militant.

They arranged themselves on uncomfortable gold chairs, hoping they weren't priceless antiques that might collapse under their weight.

'My wife will join us in a moment,' smiled the duke. 'How do you like your tea?'

'I bet he wants me to say "Strong, like my men,"' Meredith whispered to Steph. 'Milk with no sugar, thank you, your Grace,' she replied primly.

'We take ours with lemon,' he contributed unnecessarily, clearly feeling the situation needed rescuing.

A rustle of silks behind them made them turn. A vision stood waiting in the doorway to be admired before she went any further.

Margot, *duchesse de Savarin*, wore a beautifully cut ruby-red velvet dress with long sleeves and a Peter Pan collar and matching belt which were, if Meredith had any eye for these things, made from genuine leopardskin. A velvet pillbox hat adorned her suspiciously auburn curls. To complete the outfit she wore a slash of red lipstick, which Meredith instantly recognized as the colour worn by every woman who intended to make an impression, from Elizabeth Taylor and Joan Crawford to Rihanna and Alexandria Ocasio-Cortez.

Steph had seen the act before, but Jo had to stop herself looking on in open-mouthed amazement like the kind of medieval village idiot who would once have hung around the castle gates asking for alms.

'*Bonjour*, ladies.' Unlike her husband's charm-drenched

tones, Margot's voice was clipped and efficient. She crossed over to them and took a chair. 'I am sure you want to know all about the wedding business.'

'Do we?' whispered Jo, who had not been put in the picture about the precise reason they were here. For that matter, neither had Steph, but she intended to sit quietly and see what Meredith was up to.

'Is somebody getting married?'

'I'll explain later,' said Steph.

'We had thirty-one weddings here last year. Given the length of the season, that is between two and three a week,' announced the duchess.

'And are your customers mainly British?' asked Meredith. Steph had explained to her that getting married in France was all the rage amongst the younger generation.

'By no means.' The duchess shook her head. The small net veil that seemed to be part of the hat threatened to fall down across her face, and she swept it back with an imperious hand.

Jo found herself idly thinking that Leslie Caron would have to play her in the movie of her life, but perhaps she would be too soft; maybe pouting man-eater Jeanne Moreau?

'A large number of English, certainly, but also Dutch, Scandinavian, Chinese and even American. We have had a number of Americans who come here and hire the whole château so they can get married alone.' She began to pull herself up from her chair. 'If you have finished your tea, I will take you round.'

Despite her advanced age and the killer heels she was wearing, the duchess made a surprisingly swift job of their tour. They started back in the Great Hall, where, she explained, the wedding guests were greeted as they arrived. 'They usually have a drinks reception in the salon before moving to the dining room, with overflow into the orangery. We can accommodate one hundred and fifty guests between the two,' she explained proudly. 'If there are more, or if they wish to be outside, we use either the courtyard . . .' She pushed open the orangery door, revealing a large area within the four towers of the château. '. . . Or if they prefer a view, we certainly can provide that.' She led them briskly back through the salon to another set of huge French windows and threw them open with a dramatic gesture.

The view was indeed breathtaking. A vast terrace gave onto a low balustraded wall below which the ground fell away, rolling through serried ranks of vines right down to the banks of the Savarin, sparkling and dancing in the afternoon sun, and straight on to Meredith's bridge.

'It's my view in reverse!' breathed Meredith, so enchanted that she forgot her surroundings. She was momentarily lost in a vision of herself and her father standing on the bridge – it was so clear, it seemed more real than the scene around her.

Margot watched her, fascinated. What strange people these British were. This brisk, efficient woman, not unlike herself, Margot decided, looked almost as if she were experiencing a beatific vision – like Bernadette in Lourdes, or one of the visions St Joan claimed to have been given, which had taken her off to some other world more vivid than their own. Still, the canny Margot decided, it might be a vision that made her more open to purchasing.

'The vineyard also belongs to us,' Margot continued. 'We feature our own wine at the weddings. A tasting forms part of the weekend package. We find it's very popular. Why don't you go and take a little look outside while I look for our wedding organizer?'

Jo gazed out at the vineyard. Ever since the weeks she'd spent grape-picking she'd had a bit of a fantasy about moving to France and having a terrace shaded by her own vines. Some chance of that!

When they got back inside, Jo gently tugged Meredith's sleeve. 'This place is absolutely gorgeous,' she said quietly, 'and I can see what it means to you, but somehow this duchess seems to have got the wrong idea. She seems to think you're interested in buying it.'

Meredith turned to her two friends, beaming. 'Perhaps that's because I told them I was,' she replied.

'But you live in Shanghai!' blurted Joanna. 'Or was it Hong Kong? You're a high-flying businesswoman, not a wedding planner!'

'That's what I tell myself,' Meredith grinned, 'but somehow I don't seem to be listening.'

'But you don't know the first thing about it!'

'Not now, I don't,' agreed Meredith fatefully. 'But how hard can it be to plan a few weddings?'

Four

Steph and Jo both stared at their friend in astonishment.

Meredith started to giggle, something she'd hardly ever done since their schooldays. 'Your faces! I've never seen anyone's jaw actually drop like that before . . . Look, I know this is probably insane. But I've been feeling so different since I got here. I hadn't realized how much I was grieving for my father until I came to Bratenac; I had some kind of locked-in syndrome where I couldn't feel anything. I was frozen. And because of the nature of my work, I didn't even realize it. But this is a real place, full of real people. I know that sounds corny. And on top of that, it's the place my dad loved. I feel at home here. This may be the biggest mistake of my life, but *tant pis* as the French say – I'm going to have a go. Look, it may never happen. Buying a place like this will be a complicated business – but then I'm a pretty effective businesswoman!'

She shrugged in a convincingly Gallic way, to reinforce that very French sentiment of 'never mind'. Risks needed to be taken and if you failed, what the hell? And somehow, the way Meredith said it, you believed her.

'But that'd mean you'd be just down the road!' The thought suddenly dawned on Steph.

The duchess, who had disappeared into the bowels of the château, re-emerged with a tall, elegant woman in an unmistakably couture dress – Meredith guessed it was Givenchy – and heels as high as the duchess's own. It was hard to guess how old she was, though hadn't Steph said something about her being eighty? She had that timeless elegance only the French seemed able to achieve. Another French expression, *jolie laide*, came into Meredith's mind. Literally 'pretty-ugly', but in practice it meant striking rather than conventionally pretty or beautiful. The newcomer was certainly that.

'*Mesdames*, may I introduce you to Héloise d'Aubigny?' the duchess announced. 'Héloise organizes all our weddings here. She becomes a best friend and mentor to our brides during this wonderful but stressful process.'

Joanna glanced at Héloise, with her haute couture and her chilly expression, and found herself thinking, Poor brides!

'Perhaps, *mesdames*, you would like to hear about the arrangements we offer at the Château de St Savarin?'

Without waiting for an answer, Héloise launched into a rapid description of the entire process, from first enquiry to last drinks at the reception. It was an impressive performance. She didn't pause or stumble for a good fifteen minutes, but kept up the commentary like high-speed gunfire until she finally came to a halt with a brisk, 'Any questions?'

'I think she's done this before,' Jo murmured to Steph under her breath.

Héloise shot a look in Jo's direction, as if one more slip and it would be the guillotine for her, and proceeded to tell them more about the unique advantages of a château wedding.

'I am most impressed, madame,' soothed Meredith. 'Can

the wedding party stay inside the château? I'm told that's often part of the package these days.'

'*Hélas, non.* We thought of renovating the rear wing of the château with eight bedrooms plus en suite bathrooms and a kitchen for guest use; but the duke is unwell, and we thought it too much to take on.' She skipped swiftly past this small obstacle to another of the many facilities the château offered.

Jo found she'd stopped listening. Someone was knocking on the long French windows leading to the terrace and being completely ignored by Héloise, as if they didn't exist. Jo felt her irritation levels rise. Really, this woman was more *grande dame* than the duchess herself.

A man stood outside. He was wearing the characteristic blue workman's overalls of the region, yet there was something about him that told you instantly he was not just a horny-handed son of the soil. He had a way of holding his tall, loose-limbed frame that made Jo think of the Westerns she had seen, as if this man would be more at home in the saddle than on foot. His deeply tanned face suggested an outdoor life, and there was a certain relaxed confidence about him that contrasted sharply with Héloise's chilly grandeur. His engaging smile held the faintest hint of irony when he saw who was speaking, as if he'd had plenty of experience of Héloise before.

Jo decided to let him in. 'Ah,' he murmured in a low, deep voice that certainly wasn't French or British either, 'better not interrupt Her Majesty. The duchess requested some grapes from the hothouse.' He handed them over with what she could have sworn was a wink, except that it passed so quickly she might have imagined it. He saluted and slipped away, smiling to himself. After a few yards he glanced back, as if he were assessing Jo and liked what he saw.

Jo shook her head, deciding she was suffering from middle-aged delusions.

'Some grapes for the duchess,' she explained when she found Héloise's basilisk stare fixed on her. 'She asked for them, apparently.'

'Really! Why didn't the man take them round to the kitchen instead of interrupting our conversation?' she asked irritably.

'Who was he?' Despite the deliberately casual tone of her request, Jo found two pairs of quizzical eyes suddenly trained on her. 'Just asking,' she added lamely.

'That's Liam, our *vigneron*. He's from New Zealand. We don't compete with the great wine houses, but we do produce some wines that get starred in the *Guide Hachette*.'

Jo would have liked to ask what a *vigneron* did, but thought better of it. She would be teased enough for showing interest as it was.

'It remains for me to show you the de Savarins' apartment, where the new owner of the château will be living.' Without waiting for a response, Héloise started walking briskly towards the enormous staircase. 'The reason the duchess wishes to move is that the duc's back is not what it was,' she confided, lowering her voice. 'He does not like to admit it. We explored installing a lift, but it would be ruinously expensive.'

'Why not a stairlift?' suggested the ever-practical Joanna. 'They're quite reasonable these days.'

Héloise raised a haughty eyebrow. 'Can you see Louis, duc de Savarin in a stairlift?'

'I see what you mean,' Jo conceded. The Maurice Chevalier charmer they had met earlier wasn't exactly the type for mobility aids.

They climbed the enormous stone staircase, carpeted with a richly coloured runner that was going bald in parts but still made a dramatic impression. As they reached the top, the duke suddenly emerged.

'Hello, ladies! I hope you have enjoyed your tour. Welcome to our private residence. If anyone is to blame for the extravagant style, it is my wife; and also the sixteenth duke, who had an unfortunate taste for the rococo.' He flung the doors of the apartment wide, revealing a vast pale blue room with enormously high ceilings that were decorated in elaborate plasterwork and from which hung no fewer than three giant chandeliers. 'My wife's feeling is, why have one chandelier when you could have several?' He gave his most dazzling smile and bowed to let them all pass. 'By the way, has Héloise told you about our resident ghost?'

Meredith and Jo shook their heads while Steph found herself glancing round nervously.

'The White Lady of Savarin,' the duke continued with relish, ignoring Héloise's discouraging expression. 'The tenth duke, not the most tolerant of husbands, I'm afraid, found his wife in the arms of another man in 1598 and had her locked in the west tower until she died, getting food through a hatch in the ceiling. I can show you the hatch, if you like,' he offered gleefully. 'He had her lover executed and hanged from a branch of the tree outside her window where he was sure she could see him. Servants in the château claim to have seen a ghostly form in a long white dress, wandering around at night looking for her lost lover. They call her La Dame Blanche de Savarin.'

'Right,' replied Meredith briskly. 'I wouldn't put that on your publicity material. I'm not sure prospective brides would go for it.'

'Fortunately, times have changed,' agreed the duke, suddenly struck with the realization that this might not be the best sales pitch. He hoped his wife wouldn't discover he had told them. 'It's probably just a myth anyway,' he added lamely.

'You haven't seen her yourself, then?' asked Jo with a touch of humour.

'It would take more than a ghost to wake me up in the night.' He winked. 'Unless she was trying to get into bed with me.'

They watched him amble off.

Steph turned to Héloise, who was looking appalled by the duke's failure to grasp modern mores.

'Héloise is right,' Meredith threw in tactfully. 'I can't picture him on a stairlift. It'd be like seeing Errol Flynn with a walking frame.'

To their surprise, at one end of the enormous room there was a small area that looked almost cosy; that is, if you compared it with Buckingham Palace. The duchess had arranged a more substantial sofa and two large armchairs in front of an enormous marble fireplace adorned with statues of what looked like Neptune and Aphrodite, with a TV to one side and a roaring fire in the hearth.

'I can just see you curled up on that watching *Emmerdale*,' Steph teased Meredith.

'There are three bedrooms,' Héloise informed them, 'each with their own bathroom, and of course, a small kitchen. When there is a wedding taking place, if they are not needed, the duke and duchess can stay up here.'

'Don't they feel just a tiny bit imprisoned?' asked Steph.

'The upkeep of the château has to be met somehow!' was the crisp response. 'It could be far worse. Many châteaux have to open to the public and have people crawling over their bedrooms and opening their drawers to see what aristocrats keep in them!'

'Yes, I suppose you're right,' conceded Steph.

'Can I see the master bathroom?' asked Meredith. Steph and Jo exchanged a grin. Meredith was known for her extravagant taste in bathroom fixtures.

Héloise led them into a palatial room where the bath stood on a platform surrounded by silk drapes.

'Very Marie Antoinette,' commented Meredith drily. 'I like it, though, especially the view of the grounds and the river. I can just picture myself looking out with a glass of champagne!'

Steph glanced in surprise at her old friend. Bloody hell, she thought – she really seems to be serious about this.

'Now, *mesdames* –' Héloise gestured at her surroundings – 'I will leave you alone for a short while so that you can look around for yourselves. Would you like to join the duke, duchess and myself for a *petit apéro* at, say, five o'clock?' She swept out without waiting for an answer.

She had hardly shut the door when Steph rounded excitedly on her friend.

'Come on, then, Meredith. What's the verdict? Are you really going to try and buy it?

Five

David dropped one of his packages as he pushed open the door of the Café de la Paix. Steph had given him a long list of things she needed before she went gadding off looking at bloody châteaux and it had taken him all afternoon to find them. He was feeling hard done by, but as he found a seat at the long wooden bar he told himself he was being unfair. Her best friends were over, and seeing them had really cheered her up.

'I think you dropped this.' A sultry voice interrupted his thoughts. He turned to find a dark-haired woman of indeterminate age in a short skirt and a leopard-print blouse that seemed rather low-cut for this time of the afternoon. She was holding out the fresh coriander from Steph's list that he had visited three different shops to track down.

'Hi,' she continued, inching closer to him. 'I'm Suzi, Jackie Brown's friend. I'm sure we must have met before. We're both rather wicked to be drinking in the afternoon when good and honest citizens are at work, aren't we?'

She sat down next to David before he could offer any resistance, not that he was sure he wanted to. If Steph was having fun, wasn't he entitled to a little as well before he faced the bloody LeBruns and their son's diarrhoea?

'What are you having? Guillaume,' she called out. 'A large red for me and – what was it you said you wanted?'

'I didn't . . . but yes, OK, a *demi-pression* would be nice.'

Guillaume poured David's beer, directing an old-fashioned look at Suzi. She was only doing this because Jackie wasn't here. She wouldn't have dared otherwise, as they both knew perfectly well. Guillaume wondered if he ought to deputize for Jackie; but he was French, after all, and no enforcer of suburban English values. If two people wanted to have a flirtation in the afternoon, why should he stop them? Besides, business was business.

'You always seem to be such a good husband,' purred Suzi, making it sound as if this somehow made David a total failure as a man.

'It's not just about being a husband,' David replied, piqued. 'We run a business together, after all.'

'And very successfully too.' Suzi swiftly recovered her ground. 'I hear very good things about your B&B. But isn't it amazingly hard work?'

'Yes – but then, we came out here because we both love France and wanted to live here, and we couldn't have afforded to otherwise.' He looked round the characterful cafe with its old Ricard signs, a framed poster of Jean-Paul Belmondo in *Breathless*, Guillaume's famous moustache-twirling mirror, plus a reproduction of Toulouse Lautrec's cancan dancers at the Moulin Rouge – clichéd but still charming – and a series of atmospheric black-and-white images of Bratenac's vineyards during the grape harvest.

'And what will your wife think of you being in here at four o'clock in the afternoon?' Suzi asked provocatively. Jackie wasn't the only one who had noticed David's slightly guilty look.

'It's nothing to do with her,' he snapped back. 'We both need some time to relax. We work hard enough!'

'Quite. And you're much too attractive to put up with being told what to do by your wife.'

David looked at her with a slightly stunned expression. Was this woman . . . coming on to him? He sipped his beer, feeling flattered and slightly terrified in equal measure. She was quite attractive, when you really looked at her.

'Where is your wife? I suppose she's back at the ranch, slaving away?'

'As a matter of fact,' David replied, looking at his watch, 'she's been looking round a château with her old schoolfriend.'

'Did you know it's up for sale? Your wife's not thinking of buying it?'

David looked appalled. 'Good God, no!' They could hardly keep their current venture afloat. In fact, he'd been putting off having a serious conversation with Steph about their finances. 'Anyone who bought a heap like that would be out of their minds. Imagine how much it would cost just to heat it!' He thought of their own unpaid bills mounting up and felt slightly sick.

'Fancy another?' To his amazement, she'd got through her drink already.

'Well, I . . .' He really ought to be getting back. God only knew what chaos the LeBrun children, imprisoned by their sibling's illness, would have created.

His hesitation was enough encouragement for Suzi, whose long career of suburban seduction meant she understood husbands better than their wives. David was attractive, but had lost confidence in himself as a man. That meant he could be ripe for the plucking. And the best thing was, he didn't know it.

She avoided Guillaume's eye as she ordered their next round.

'Why don't we go and sit over there?' She pointed to a table in the corner.

At this, David experienced a twinge of uncertainty. It could be seen as innocent enough sitting at the bar, but sharing a table might look a bit odd. But now the drinks had come, and Suzi had already collected his packages and started to carry them to the table.

David got off the bar stool and followed her. At least there didn't seem to be anyone in here they knew. Thank God.

It seemed to David they had only got through about a third of their drink when Suzi suddenly got up, announcing that she'd just remembered an urgent engagement.

She took his hand. 'David, it's been a pleasure. I hope we can repeat it again soon.' With that she squeezed into a jacket that seemed to be several sizes too small, put on her sunglasses and departed, leaving David feeling completely mystified.

Guillaume caught his eye and shrugged. '*Les femmes. C'est un mystère.*'

Although in Suzi's case, as Guillaume well knew, it was less a mystery and more an obvious tactic for piquing the poor sap's interest. In fact, as his years behind the bar had shown him, men's behaviour was far less logical than women's. And this time the target had no idea what was headed in his direction.

'The duke and duchess await you in the orangery,' announced Héloise, trying to keep a smirk from her horse-like features at the thought of reeling in this rich British woman who, like so many of her compatriots who had settled here, apparently had more money than sense. No doubt this one thought it was all some happy fairy-tale fantasy.

The duke stood up at their entrance, flashing his trademark charming smile. 'Ladies, welcome back. May I offer you some of our *vin de noix*, which Liam, our *vigneron*, makes from the green walnuts picked in June? It is our most famous apéritif.'

Steph and Jo agreed but Meredith, instantly transforming from smiling tourist into hard-headed businesswoman, shook her head. 'I would rather we had the serious discussion first, if you don't mind. We may as well not beat about the bush, as we say in English. I am prepared to offer the asking price subject to the usual considerations. Legal searches of title—'

'The château has been owned by the de Savarin family for twelve generations, madame,' Margot, who had been intending to conduct the negotiations herself, interrupted with more than a touch of frost. 'I do not think you will find there is a problem with the title.'

'Consideration of any restrictive covenants, a structural survey naturally . . .'

'Madame, this is a thirteenth-century château, not a pent-house in Monaco,' snapped Margot, ignoring a warning glance from the duke that they were not dealing with some country solicitor. This woman knew what she was doing.

'Nevertheless, your grace—' Meredith tried to interrupt.

'*Nom de Dieu*, call me Margot, for goodness' sake!'

'Nevertheless, Margot,' Meredith continued, cool as a polytunnel of cucumbers, 'I would still wish to know that my thirteenth-century château was not about to fall down. And of course I would need to make *les vérifications nécessaires* – what we call due diligence. I imagine it is rather a lengthy process, but with the help of experts I would endeavour to speed it up as much as possible. Would that be agreeable to you?'

They both nodded, trying not to look suspiciously enthusiastic. Margot continued, 'I would also expect your goodwill, by which I mean giving an accurate guide to how the business is run. I am accustomed to advising banks, not brides and bridegrooms.'

'You will love every moment, madame!' the duke assured her with his most delightful smile. 'Weddings are happy events, *n'est-ce pas?*'

'He obviously hasn't been to the same weddings I've been to,' Jo murmured to Steph.

'And finally –' Meredith turned her face from the duchess and winked at Jo – 'I would want to consult my business partner here, Joanna Walker.'

Jo nearly dropped her glass of *vin de noix* in astonishment.

'*Naturellement, madame,*' agreed the duchess, wondering how the meeting had so completely got away from her.

'*Bien,*' Meredith announced decisively. 'Let us shake hands on this as a gentleman's agreement and I will get my people to take it on with you to the next stage.'

She delved into her large leather backpack and produced a bottle of vintage Krug, carefully chilling in its own little wrapper.

'To what I hope will be a happy business arrangement!' She popped the cork expertly as Steph and Joanna looked on in stunned silence. What on earth was Meredith up to with this *business partner* stuff?

As soon as they were outside the château walls, Jo grabbed her arm. 'What on earth was all that stuff about me being your business partner? Some sort of ploy to give you a way out if you change your mind?'

71

'Not at all.' A sudden smile lit up Meredith's brisk demeanour. 'I was entirely serious. Will you consider it? I can't run the whole operation on my own. I'm a businesswoman, not a wedding planner. But organizing events is your thing. Will you think about it? It might be a lot of fun.'

Jo took a deep breath. It was so tempting. Getting right away from Mark and Amanda and their horrible wedding – and worse, maybe even a baby – the thought made her feel sick. But there was Sophie to consider.

'I promise I'll think about it, but I don't know, Meredith. My daughter is my business partner . . .'

'Get her involved too,' Meredith replied, making it sound as if this were the easiest thing in the world. 'She probably understands all this social media stuff far better than we do. Héloise told me that's how brides plan everything now. She'd be a huge asset. Do you think she'd want to?'

'Well, it's rather come out of the blue. I need to talk to Sophie, though. I'll call her when I get back to Steph's.' Jo suddenly felt an overwhelming desire to say yes, to come and live in beautiful France. It felt like just the kind of adventure Sophie would recommend when her mother was feeling so down and depressed.

'My God,' Steph giggled. 'The Meads Girls would be back together!' She started to sing her own off-key version of 'The Boys Are Back in Town' at the top of her voice, with a suitable adjustment for gender.

'Stephie,' Meredith shook her head, smiling. 'It doesn't even scan!'

David looked irritably at his watch. It was after six and he'd just spent the last hour tidying up after the LeBrun children. Marcelline had phoned to say she had period pains – which seemed to be a perfectly acceptable excuse in France, where anything even vaguely connected with sex was held as sacred – so he'd ended up having to lay all the tables as well.

Then Monsieur LeBrun had suddenly appeared and announced that their son was better and they now wanted to stay an extra week to make up for the lost time.

He knew that Steph would make some excuse and refuse. 'That will be absolutely fine,' David had told him, smiling smugly. Serve her bloody well right. He heard the front door open just as the first guests were appearing.

'For God's sake, David,' Steph greeted him, 'aren't the drinks out yet? What have you been doing all afternoon, and where the hell's Marcelline?'

'Off sick.' David was too embarrassed to go into the specifics of Marcelline's indisposition. He knew he'd get it wrong and either be accused of not being sympathetic enough, or too sympathetic; it was hard to predict which.

'Did you get all that stuff I asked you to?' Steph asked shortly.

'Yes, Stephanie, I got every single thing on your extensive list, even though it took me about two hours.' Meredith noted the tone of irritated weariness she had picked up the other day and realized she'd done nothing about her own little scheme to help.

'Well, you didn't have anything else to do, did you?'

'Except find more diarrhoea medication for the junior LeBrun, or catch their bloody dog when it started chasing the deer belonging to our extremely touchy neighbour? By the way,' he added, 'they've asked if they can stay another week. I said yes, of course.'

He waited for the explosion, which duly came.

'What? Those bloody Belgians and their bloody dog? How could you?'

'I was under the obviously mistaken impression that we were running a B&B.'

'Well, you'll have to tell them you got it wrong.'

'No way!'

Steph ignored him and headed for the kitchen to remove the beef casserole that had been cooking on a very low heat all day and should by now be falling-off-the-bone tender from the oven – only to find that it had somehow been turned off.

'Sorry, I'm afraid that was me,' confessed David. 'I thought it was finished and was thinking of the planet.'

'Can't you even do the one thing you were asked?' Steph demanded furiously. 'So now our guests will have to eat under-cooked beef – just because you were incompetent enough to turn off the oven for some half-baked notion of yours?'

'Children, children.' Meredith decided it was time to intervene. 'I will finish laying the tables and assist Steph with anything last-minute that needs doing. I'm sure if you whack it back in the oven on high, it'll be done on time.'

'Thank you, Elizabeth David!' snapped Steph.

'I'll help too,' Jo offered, more than a little shocked at her friend's tone.

'Don't worry,' Steph replied, turning the oven back on irritably. 'Too many cooks. You go and finish unpacking and when you come down you can pour us a drink.'

'OK.' Jo decided it might be better to leave them to it. Besides, she had a lot to think about. 'See you girls in half an hour or so.'

She went up to her bedroom, wondering what she'd change into. People dressed up for dinner here and she couldn't decide what to wear.

She reached up for her suitcase, which she'd stored on the

top shelf of her wardrobe, to get out the last of her clothes, thinking about what she'd say to Sophie.

What was that funny shape in the front pouch? She put her hand in and withdrew a curious purple sculpture. Oh God! It was the Happy Rabbit. Liz must have slipped it in when Jo had gone upstairs to print her boarding pass.

Blushing furiously even though she was alone in the room, Jo wrapped the object in a scarf and tucked it behind her shoes. Surely not even Marcelline would start rummaging around in Jo's slightly smelly trainers.

She surveyed the small selection of clothes she'd brought with her and selected a cappuccino-coloured linen shift dress. It was old but highly flattering. She brushed out her hair, surveying her shoulder-length bob and realizing it needed tidying up, as usual, added earrings and a scarf and decided she'd pass. If Meredith really went through with this château purchase, she'd have to get Liz to send on some more of her stuff.

Almost holding her breath, she got out her phone and called Sophie. No answer after ten rings and no voicemail either. Maybe just as well. Jo couldn't begin to think how she'd explain things in a message. *Soph, you're not going to believe it, but Meredith's trying to buy a wedding château and she's asked us both to come and help run it!*

Well, no one could say life wasn't full of surprises.

When she stepped out into the hallway to go downstairs, Meredith was just coming out of her room as well. Jo hurried to catch her.

'Did you get hold of your daughter?' Meredith asked.

'Not answering her phone, I'm afraid. I didn't want to leave a message. I'll try again later. I wanted to ask what you thought about Steph and David. I'm not trying to be nosy, but speaking as someone whose own marriage collapsed . . . well, I'm a bit worried about them.'

'I'm not surprised,' Meredith agreed. 'In fact, I'm going to go down to the restaurant on the river tomorrow and look for that boy who works there. The other day, we heard him saying he wanted a job. If he could come and work here part-time, it'd give Steph a break. I might see if this Marcelline could come in and help more often as well. My little gift to them. How do you think they'll take it?'

'I think it'll be a huge relief – for David, at least. As long as you're diplomatic about it.'

'Me, undiplomatic?' protested Meredith, laughing. 'I spend my life dealing with cautious Chinese and sensitive Saudis. I could negotiate for the UN!'

A relative peace had been restored in the kitchen. The stew was cooked, the tables laid perfectly so that even Steph couldn't find anything wrong with them. David, looking more exhausted than Jo had seen him before, was busy filling glasses.

'Hello girls,' he greeted them, forcing himself to be genial, 'what's your pleasure?'

'A kir, please,' Jo said, 'but light on the cassis.'

David took a champagne flute, filled it three-quarters full with dry white wine and added a dash of cassis, the famous blackcurrant liqueur, recreating the cocktail created by Canon Félix Kir, Catholic priest and hero of the Resistance. When the Nazis invaded Burgundy and confiscated all the red wine, Kir had mixed cassis with the rough local white and produced a drinkable alternative – a delicious apéritif and a blow for freedom, all at the same time.

Just as she took her first sip, Jo felt her phone vibrate in her dress pocket and knew it would be her daughter.

She found herself a quiet corner, far away from the noisy

LeBruns and their boisterous dog. 'Sophie!' she almost squeaked. 'You're never going to guess!'

'Your rich friend Meredith's made an offer for a French château and plans to throw the most romantic weddings in France,' her daughter instantly replied.

Jo almost dropped her drink. 'How on earth did you know that?'

'Because she's already posted it on Instagram!'

'I hope that was wise; she's only just beginning negotiations. It could take ages.' But Jo was starting to understand that Meredith's business methods were highly unconventional. And yet, judging by her enormous success and obvious wealth, remarkably successful.

'The thing is, Soph,' Jo went on nervously, 'she's asked me to join her – be a partner and run the weddings side of it.'

There was a pause at the other end of the line before Sophie replied. 'That's amazing, Mum! What an opportunity for you.'

Jo smiled to herself. How like her daughter to be so unselfish. 'Not only that, she asked if you would consider getting involved as well?'

There was no hesitation this time. 'I love weddings!' Sophie enthused. 'I've been to about a million of them, and I always think how I could do it better myself. I've been feeling a bit stuck here,' she added. 'No boyfriend, and my friends are all getting married!' She laughed. 'Tell her yes, yes and yes! I'll come over and have a look as soon as this exhibition closes. It's been going really well, in case you want to know. Nearly all the paintings sold, and the gallery got a write-up in *The Times* as an exciting one to watch!'

Jo smiled, feeling guilty at not having even thought about the exhibition – and even more guilty about not having realized Sophie was feeling stuck. Maybe if Meredith's plan for the château came off, it would be just what they all needed.

Jean-Christophe pushed the irritating strand of long black hair out of his eye for the third time. Perhaps he should wear a ridiculous bandeau, like Rambo. He had once loved those old movies, and the shoot-em-up video games they spawned even more. He smiled, remembering how shocked his dad had been, because Jean-Christophe was such a gentle lad.

He went on chopping, using the knife Philippe had given him. It had originally been passed down from his grandfather, Antoine, who still lived with them despite his dementia. Philippe refused to consider putting Antoine in a home. Jean-Christophe sometimes wondered if that had been a factor in his decision to leave Paris and the restaurant so suddenly. But even though it was a long time ago, Jean-Christophe felt it was somehow more connected to his guilt at the failure of his marriage, even though it was a long time ago, and the need to come home and find meaning in a simpler life.

Jean-Christophe would never forget the moment his mother had come into his room to wake him up and tell him she was going and would always love him.

She had been a waitress when they'd married and perhaps Philippe had expected her to adore him, the great chef, like everyone else. But she was smart and ambitious and she wasn't prepared to live at the margins of his life, on the occasional crumb of time he tossed her. And so she'd left.

And then, two years ago, his father had suddenly appeared at home when he should have been at the restaurant and said to Jean-Christophe that he had been thinking about his life; that the restaurant had become an obsession that had cost him his marriage and was taking too much of his time away from his son. A year later they had arrived here, despite all the outcry and the protests and people telling Philippe he was mad, that no one threw away one Michelin star, let alone three.

'Have you seen my father?' he shouted to Marie, who worked for them prepping, supervising deliveries of the produce Philippe had ordered at the market and waiting on tables.

'Maybe he's gone fishing,' grinned Marie.

It was true Philippe often went fishing for trout, but he would hardly go an hour before they were due to open. Jean-Christophe went to check what had already arrived and started getting ready to assemble produce for the various dishes on the menu.

He was just trimming some duck breasts when Philippe appeared. He was unshaven, with what appeared to be two or three days' stubble, his eyes glassy and drooping, his clothes crumpled and stained. He made Jean-Christophe think of the walking dead. '*Putain!*' he breathed, staring at his father. 'Fuck me, you look rough!'

Philippe mumbled a single word. '*Grand-père.*'

No more explanation was necessary. Jean-Christophe put down his knife. 'Where did he get to this time?'

'A derelict barn over near St Lucien, on the Bratenac road. Covered in cow shit. I brought him home and showered him. Guess what he sang?' A smile cracked Philippe's face, which was full of sudden tenderness. 'That Jacques Brel song, "Ne me Quitte Pas" – don't leave me. As if I would leave him!'

'You've got a lot of patience with him,' Jean-Christophe said quietly.

'*En effet* I could have killed the old sod.' Philippe smiled wryly. 'I spent all night looking for him. I think he's getting worse. He took off his panic alarm and hid it in the postbox.' He noticed for the first time what Jean-Christophe was doing.

'I'd better get stuck in. You never know when the English women from that club are going to turn up.' He looked round him. '*Merde alors*, here is one of them now.'

Meredith was tapping gently on the window of the portacabin and making a 'Can I come in?' gesture.

Philippe elbowed his son in the ribs. 'Go on, see what she wants. Who knows, maybe she's having a party she wants us to cater. I think that's the one who's buying the château.'

'Not *our* château?' Jean-Christophe asked in amazement.

'So I hear at the cafe. No one's talking about anything else.'

'Excuse me,' Meredith enquired, 'but do you think I could have a couple of minutes with Jean-Christophe?'

'*Allez-y*,' replied his father. 'I'm sure he'd be delighted.'

Jean-Christophe put down the duck breast and beckoned her to come and sit outside by the river. 'Would you like a coffee?' he enquired, feeling excited that maybe she was going to offer him the job of chef at the castle. What a leg-up that would be for his career! 'I could make you one in two minutes.'

'I'm fine, thank you. Jean-Christophe, you know my friends who run the *chambre d'hôte* called Fleur-de-Lis?'

'*Monsieur et Madame Adams, bien sûr.*'

'I am looking for someone to come and cook dinner there three times a week. I know it isn't full-time, but I will pay an excellent rate and it's very near. I know you wanted something local.'

Jean-Christophe tried to hide his disappointment. On the other hand, if he made a good impression, she still might hire him when the château was up and running. This sounded like a temporary arrangement.

'*Certainement*, madame, I would be interested,' he beamed. 'Excuse me if I am very basic, but I am French, you know. What exact rate would you be paying?'

He almost whistled at her reply. It was far more than he would get at any of the cafes in Bratenac, where he had been about to look.

'*Très bien*, madame. What would you like me to do?'

'I just need to get the agreement of my friends to accept the arrangement.'

'You have not asked them yet, madame?' The British were strange people indeed. He glanced round at his father, who was smiling quietly as he chopped potatoes for the *pommes de terre sarladaises*.

Meredith followed his gaze, taking in Philippe's unshaven chin, crumpled clothes and bleary expression. The louche charm of the other day seemed to have vanished. Philippe looked up and met her eyes levelly. Fortunately, the cow shit was disguised beneath his chef's overall, or she would no doubt have called the *mairie* instantly and raised a hygiene complaint.

'Good night, was it?' she asked, raising a sarcastic eyebrow as she turned away.

'Excellent,' he muttered. 'You shouldn't always jump to conclusions about people, you know, madame.' The woman clearly imagined he'd spent the night drinking and carousing in some local hostelry. Funny, the other day he'd thought her rather attractive, and she must be very successful if she could consider buying the château. She'd made all her money in some place in the East, they said in the cafe – Singapore or Hong Kong. Funny how you could move on the world stage and still be small-minded. Pity.

She found his brown eyes fixed on hers in a disconcertingly direct gaze. And for once Meredith, the alpha female, could think of absolutely nothing to say.

Six

Meredith walked back through the small town of Bratenac, which was bustling with its Wednesday market, wondering what on earth Philippe had meant by that weird response. Why did he think she would care how he spent his drunken evenings? The vanity of the man!

Distracted by the sights and smells of fresh herbs and spices, rows of smelly cheeses and the inevitable jars of *pâté de foie gras* for which the area was so famous, she put him out of her mind. She passed a noisy scene with a British teenager accusing her parents of supporting disgusting cruelty – did they not know the poor ducks and geese were stuffed with food till their livers burst, just to make the stuff? – while the mother and father glanced nervously around them, imagining an international incident. This wasn't an argument she would ever have had when she was that age; *foie gras* was far too expensive a product for her own family to have tried while they were here.

'*Bonjour*, madame,' a cheery tone greeted her. She turned to find Guillaume waving from the door of the Café de la Paix. 'Congratulations about the château. I hope it will all go through, and you do not find – how do you say – bats in the belfry?' He smiled at his own mastery of the nuances of the barbaric English tongue.

'I imagine there will most certainly be bats in the belfry. Fortunately, we British are made of stern stuff. Thank you for your good wish; I hope my bid will be successful too.'

News certainly travelled fast. Was that Jackie standing behind him with what looked like an expression of triumph on her face? What did she know that Meredith didn't?

Meredith gave them a faint smile then turned back into the crowds, disappearing into a convenient cafe, only to find that there was a large black-and-white and extremely slobbery bulldog actually sitting on the chair of the only free table. The disgusting animal, she noticed, was accompanied by Jackie's friend Janine, who appeared to be in charge of it as well as about six others.

'Do you think you could remove your dog from the seat?' Meredith asked frostily.

'Oh, sorry,' Janine apologized. 'I didn't see her get up. Nelly loves seats, you see.'

She started to remove the large animal and as she did, Nelly put out a friendly paw to Meredith.

'There,' Janine laughed. 'She really likes you. She doesn't do that to everyone.'

Meredith was about to snap that the feeling wasn't mutual when she caught a glimpse of Jean-Christophe and Philippe two stalls away, buying cheese and laughing at some joke the stallholder had cracked. There really was a strong family resemblance, even if Philippe did look as if he'd slept off the night in a hedge.

'The thing is . . .' Janine was wittering on. 'Nelly may look scary but she's the gentlest dog I've ever looked after. You're an old softie, aren't you?' She caressed the dog behind its ears, producing an expression of utter bliss in the animal. 'The point is,' Janine the philosopher announced, 'I suppose you can't always judge a book by its cover.'

Meredith glanced across at Philippe and Jean-Christophe, tempted to admit that she did sometimes make snap judgements about people that turned out to be wide of the mark, and found Philippe's level gaze fixed on her. Despite priding herself on her brisk and decisive manner, Meredith experienced the oddest sensation. Was the man laughing at her again?

She walked back along the riverbank. The greenery all around her was almost dazzling in its intensity, especially after the urban smog of Eastern cities. A long, narrow expanse of pasture stretched close to the river, with cows peacefully grazing on it. Below her there was a bathing place with a small waterfall behind it. It was so reminiscent of her childhood that Meredith longed to tear off her smart city clothes to reveal the baggy elastic one-piece swimsuit of her ten-year-old self. The intensity of this longing made her forget everything except that precious moment in time.

Both Steph and David were in the kitchen when she arrived back at Fleur-de-Lis. She was glad to see that relative peace seemed to have broken out.

'Would you like a coffee?' David offered. 'We're just making some.'

'Thanks. That'd be perfect. Actually, I'm glad I've caught you because I wanted to have a word. Where's Jo, by the way?'

David and Steph exchanged significant glances. 'In the garden. With that winegrower chap, Liam. He brought over six bottles of the château's wine from the duchess, then asked her to show him the garden. We rather thought he wanted to be alone with her.'

Meredith tried to remember the man. All she could recall was that he'd worn workman's overalls and yet hadn't seemed to be the workman type. At least he wasn't a toyboy; and anything to take Jo's mind off that creep Mark had to be a good thing.

Meredith decided to take advantage of catching her hosts alone. 'The reason I went into town was because I wanted to drop in at the restaurant on the riverbank.'

'To make a booking?' Steph asked, puzzled. 'I'm sure we have their number.'

'No, to sound out that young chef, Jean-Christophe. Do you remember we heard him say he was looking for a job nearby?'

'Did we?' Steph's puzzlement was growing deeper. 'Oh, I see,' she finally decided, her brow clearing. 'You wanted to sound him out for the château! But you know, you may need catering companies rather than a single chef.'

'No, not the château. To see if he could come and make dinner here, say, three times a week.'

'But, Meredith,' Steph protested, 'there's no way we could afford it! We only survive by using our own labour. Marcelline's an exception because she's just a student, but even then we can't afford her as often as we'd like.'

David turned away, feeling sick. Steph didn't know the beginning of it where the money issues were concerned. He was going to have to stop running away from the truth and face it himself soon.

'It would be my gift,' Meredith said simply.

'Oh, Merry!' Steph threw herself into her friend's arms, hardly able to stop herself crying. 'You can't!'

'Of course I can. I can easily afford it. If I'm going to move halfway across the world, I don't want to have to see you two killing yourselves with exhaustion before I do! More importantly, do you think it would help? I mean, then you could actually get out and leave the place and have some freedom. Maybe Marcelline could come more often, too?'

David felt a wild impulse to admit then and there that the B&B had far more serious problems than their need for a bit of freedom; that he had an unpaid bill from Steve the builder they couldn't possibly meet, and another and bigger one for some tax he hadn't even known existed.

But Steph seemed wildly happy and was dancing round the room with glee. How could he spoil that?

Walking round the gardens, Jo suddenly felt herself stuck for something to say. OK, it was rare she ever found herself alone with an attractive man, especially one that had shown interest in her – but this was ridiculous.

'So, you're a winegrower in France but you're not French,' Jo found herself commenting at last.

Liam smiled, bringing an unexpected softness to his lean, tanned features. 'So it would seem,' he agreed. 'I'm from New Zealand. The North Island, if that makes any sense to you. A place called Palmerston North.'

'Called after Lord Palmerston, the prime minister?' she offered desperately.

'No idea, I'm afraid. Palmy North's claim to fame is that your very own John Cleese called it the suicide capital of New Zealand. "If you ever want to kill yourself and lack the courage," I believe were his exact words, "a visit to Palmerston North will do the trick."'

Jo grinned. 'Is it that bad?'

'We Kiwis have a certain black sense of humour. Good old Palmy North's reply was to name a rubbish tip Mount Cleese. Besides,' he added, laughing, 'it can't be that bad. It hosts the only museum dedicated solely to rugby in New Zealand.'

'That's OK, then,' giggled Jo, finally relaxing. 'And how do you New Zealanders differ from your neighbours the Aussies?'

'That old chestnut?' He took her elbow and steered her down the path in the direction of the river. 'We're the reliable, down-to-earth, boring ones. The Aussies are the party-loving fun types.' His mischievous grin belied the description. 'And anyway,' he added, 'who can call us dull? We invented the bungee jump!'

'So how did you become a winegrower?' Jo enquired, still smiling. 'Are there a lot of vines in Palmy North?'

Liam laughed. 'Not a lot. The only things that grow there are satellite dishes. But it's not far from Marlborough. You've heard of Marlborough?'

'Of course.'

'So I studied oenology.' He bowed, like a maestro about to conduct an orchestra.

'Is that a real word?' It suddenly struck Jo as wildly funny.

'Why would oenology not be a real word?' Liam did an excellent job of looking wounded. 'My dear girl –' he took on the cut-glass tones of the British upper class –'remember your ancient Greek. From *oinos* for wine, with the suffix *logia*, study of.'

'Of course,' Jo nodded, trying to keep a straight face. 'Silly me.'

'By that time, my folks had retired and bought a small winery near Cloudy Bay.'

'I've heard of Cloudy Bay,' nodded Jo.

'Not surprising,' he teased, 'since it's one of the most popular Kiwi wines. It's also one of the loveliest places on God's earth. Named by good old Cap'n Cook.' The laughter died suddenly from his face. 'It didn't last, though. My father got a little too fond of the product.'

'Couldn't you have taken over? You seem extremely competent.'

'Thank you. But the debts were bigger than anyone knew. I had to save something for my mother. So we sold. The big French champagne houses were sniffing around by then, terrified by climate change. We got enough for my mother's comfortable retirement back in Palmy North. To be honest, she preferred it there.'

'But you didn't,' Jo said softly.

'No, I didn't. So I came here. As far away as I could.' He looked out beyond Fleur-de-Lis' garden, already well in flower in the warmth of the south-western spring, to the Savarin River beyond. 'Not such a bad swap.'

'But not your own,' Jo commented, hoping she wasn't being too personal. The loss she could hear in his voice resonated with her own still-raw state.

He looked at her intensely for a moment. 'No, not my own.'

He suddenly stooped, as if he needed to change the subject. He had noticed a single early rose, already blooming, and handed it to her with a bow. 'At the risk of sounding clichéd – an English rose for an English rose.'

'Thank you,' Jo smiled. 'But should you be picking the only rose in the garden?'

'There'll be others. Besides, don't you believe in being bold?'

His meaning was so clear that Jo found herself flushing with anxiety that an attractive man should actually hint that she was desirable. How bloody stupid. What was the matter with her?

'Look at that!' He pointed to a pretty white flower with a bell-shaped bloom. 'Convolvulus. One of the biggest menaces in the garden. It'll strangle that rose if it gets the chance.' He pulled the plant out, roots and all.

'I'm afraid I'm not very good at flowers,' Jo shrugged.

'Bindweed,' he explained, laughing at her. 'You have plenty of that back in good old Blighty.' He suddenly changed the subject. 'Tell me about the English ladies who meet in the cafe. Are you in with that little lot?'

'The Bratenac Ladies' Luncheon Club? I've only just got here, but Steph says they're much too inclusive for us. Why?'

'Well, talking of bindweed – I glanced in there the other day, and it looked as if that Suzi woman was trying to wrap herself round your friend's husband. She should keep an eye on him.'

'Oh God,' Jo panicked. 'I thought David was the loyal type.'

'We men are very easy to flatter.'

'Does that include you?' Jo was shocked to find that she was flirting. But then, how long had it been since a man had come her way who wasn't married or a complete dick?

'Absolutely. As I said, we are poor creatures.'

'How long have you worked at the château?' she asked.

'Five years now. I would like to buy my own vineyard after this. Are you interested in wine?'

'Apart from drinking it?' she teased.

'I would say as well as drinking it.'

'As it happens, I am quite interested in the process of wine-making. I even spent a summer picking grapes when I was a student.'

'Did you, now? I'm impressed. And did you enjoy it?'

Jo smiled, remembering. It had been quite the fashion then to spend a few weeks earning a little money, getting free board and as much wine as you could drink, as well as meeting other young people from different nationalities. She could still recall the sunburn and horrible bites from the vine bugs, which brought pale English skin out in welts and put the kybosh on any thoughts of sneaking into anyone else's sleeping bag – something that had happened quite a lot in those happily promiscuous days, after the pill and before Aids. Not that she'd ever confess it to her daughter. It had all been great fun and would have seriously shocked Sophie!

'I had a fabulous time. Apart from those horrible biting bugs.'

'*Aouta*. They're vile little beasts, aren't they? You should put green tea on them. Works like magic.'

'I'll bear it mind. But I think my grape-picking days are over.'

'Not if you're still here, they aren't. Everyone gets involved. You should come and have a look round, especially if your friend is hoping to buying the château.' He obviously had no idea that she might be a partner.

'Would the duchess be all right with that?'

'Oh, they take no interest in the wines. Why not next week?' His smile was open and friendly. 'My house is on the property.' He grinned. 'Nothing like the château, just a small cottage. I'd be delighted to show you the vines. I might even cook you dinner.'

'Perfect.'

To Jo's relief, he didn't try to conceal his pleasure at her acceptance. If she was going to have dinner with a man, she didn't want one who played games.

As they turned back towards the house she suddenly laughed.

Liam looked at her, eyebrows raised, wondering what the joke was. 'It's just life.' Jo shook her head and grinned. 'It's so full of the unexpected.'

They walked back slowly, neither of them eager for the moment to end. 'Come in and say hello,' she insisted when they reached the back door.

Steph, David and Meredith were gathered round the big kitchen table, sharing a coffee. Steph and Meredith both looked delighted, but David's smile seemed to Jo to have a curiously forced quality. Did he disapprove of her getting to know Liam?

'Meredith's hired Jean-Christophe to come and cook here three times a week!' Steph told her excitedly. 'So David and I can finally have a date night! Can't we, David?' she asked her husband.

David nodded, still looking strained.

Jo was just wondering what to say when the LeBruns' boisterous red setter bounded into the room. She expected Steph to erupt in fury, but Steph was in such a good mood that she just shrugged.

Meredith stared at it hard. 'What's that it's got in its mouth? Not one of my Louboutin shoes, I hope?'

'Not unless they're purple,' Steph replied. 'It looks like some sort of purple statue. And it seems to be buzzing. What on earth is it?'

As if on cue, the dog dropped the object and it began to snake across the floor, buzzing loudly.

The ghastly truth dawning on her, Jo began to pursue it, but it was Liam who had the presence of mind to put out his foot and halt its progress. He bent down and picked it up, trying to suppress a look of unholy amusement.

'Oh my God,' Steph giggled, 'it's a vibrator! Whose is it, and how do you turn it off?'

Liam quietly examined the device, clearly fascinated by the rabbit's ears, which vibrated separately to give the owner maximum satisfaction. 'No wonder men can't compete with these,' he grinned as he expertly detected the switch and turned it off. He then placed it calmly on the table without passing any further comment, as if silencing vibrators were part of his everyday routine.

'Thanks, Liam.' Jo attempted neither to blush nor faint while she fervently wished she were anywhere else in the world but here. How pathetic he would think her! Reduced to having sex with a vibrator! 'It rejoices in the name of a Happy Rabbit. A gift from my friend Liz, who lives next door. It appealed to her sense of humour and I promise I've never used it.' Why the hell had she said that? It just made her look even more stupid. 'She slipped it into my luggage, for which I will happily kill her when I get back.'

But Steph had descended into hysterical giggles. 'I've just thought of the perfect murder for *Killing Eve*! She could stuff it down someone's throat and everyone would think he'd died happy!'

At which point Liam quietly said goodbye, leaving Jo entirely convinced she'd never hear from him again.

'God, that's the funniest thing I've ever seen,' Steph stated unfeelingly.

Meredith, aware that Jo really was upset, reached over to her. 'Here, you've got a rose behind your ear.' She handed it to her friend. 'If you ask me, he was amused rather than horrified. In fact, he seemed like a really nice guy.'

Jo smiled at her gratefully.

'Come on – it's at times like these we need a nice glass of Bergerac rosé. And from tomorrow, you and I had better do some serious thinking about weddings!'

'*Bonsoir, Grand-père,*' Jean-Christophe greeted his grandfather, Antoine. 'Would you like to watch some TV?' He turned on the giant screen. The news channel came on first, with an interviewer and three politicians.

'When will *le Géneral* be on?' enquired Antoine hopefully.

'He doesn't mean de Gaulle?' Jean-Christophe whispered to his father so that Antoine couldn't hear him.

'Probably. Though he loathed the man. An arrogant authoritarian, he used to always say, but he did allow de Gaulle to be a true Republican.'

'But he's been dead for forty years!'

'Not to Grand-père he hasn't,' grinned Philippe affectionately. 'As you see, he's expecting him on any minute. Anyway –' he raised his voice so that his increasingly deaf father could hear – 'you prefer *Astérix*, don't you Papa?'

Antoine nodded enthusiastically as Philippe inserted the much-used DVD featuring Astérix, the wily Gaul, and his big and slower-witted friend Obélix, as they outwitted the invading Romans once again.

Soon Antoine was happily roaring with laughter, actual tears falling down his lean and wrinkled face.

'It's new to him every time,' Philippe remarked. 'I'm almost envious.'

'Don't you ever get impatient with him?' If he were honest, Jean-Christophe sometimes resented the times he had to stay in and look after his grandfather. He even wondered if Antoine should go into a home, but Philippe wouldn't hear of it.

'He taught me everything I know in the kitchen. Making sure he stays in his own home is the least I can do for him,' his father insisted. 'He worked harder than any man I've known.' He grinned at his son. 'Even us.'

Jean-Christophe smiled back. 'You're a good man, Papa.'

Philippe shrugged, looking almost embarrassed at the compliment. 'I'm not sure your mother would agree.' He ruffled his son's long hair affectionately. 'Do you miss her still?'

It was his son's turn to shrug. 'Sometimes. But it's a long time ago.'

'I'm sorry, Jean-Christophe. I put success before everything. Maybe those bloody Michelin stars went to my head.'

'You threw them away easily enough,' his son reminded gently. 'To start again and look after Grand-père. Do you ever regret it?'

'Never,' his father replied without hesitation, then cut the seriousness with a grin. 'Well, not often. What I have here is far more important than what a handful of critics think. My family around me in one of the most beautiful places in France. Who could ask for more?' He looked at his watch. 'Saying that, I won't have a restaurant at all unless I get going. Can you sit with him till Amélie comes? She won't be long.' Amélie was the comfortable middle-aged woman who shared Antoine's care.

'Of course.'

'And congratulations on your job.'

'You're sure you don't need me? I know what hard work it is.'

'What, and have you under my feet with that awful music of yours?' Jean-Christophe's taste in rap music was a running joke between them. 'Can't wait to get rid of you! Besides, you'll be able to tell us what the *rosbifs* are really like.'

'Just like us, only speaking a different language, I imagine.'

'And with that he sweeps hundreds of years of wars between us under the carpet,' teased Philippe.

Jean-Christophe grinned. 'Best place for them in the twenty-first century. I was going to say we're all Europeans now, and then I remembered – they decided they're not!'

'Le Géneral would be outraged at the British stupidity!' suddenly piped up Antoine, taking them by surprise.

'He does that,' murmured Philippe. 'Has sudden moments when he's the old Dad, rational and argumentative.'

He hugged his father, then went to get his coat. 'See you later. Give my love to Amélie and tell her I'll try and be back by eleven.'

'*Papa*,' Jean-Christophe reminded him. 'It's Saturday night. You won't.'

'Amélie won't mind. Dad will have fallen asleep and she will have got him to bed and be deep into one of those *Miladi* books she loves, full of buccaneering pirates kidnapping French ladies in silken dresses and dragging them off to their cabins.'

Meredith had to go and take a phone call from the title expert she'd employed and Steph suddenly remembered that although Jean-Christophe might be coming to her rescue she still had twelve people to feed tonight and had better get on with it, so no one noticed Jo quietly slip up to her room.

She felt so bloody stupid. Worse, she felt a failure. Mark might be behaving like a shit and Amanda a silly and gullible young woman, but she was still younger and more attractive than Jo, and he had rejected Jo and chosen her. And now she was divorced. It was such a horrible word, conjuring up fast blondes in Noël Coward plays, and despite the statistics proving how common it had become, it still made her feel that she was on the scrapheap, no matter how many times she told herself she was a strong, independent woman. It was so exhausting filling your life with activity to stave off loneliness when as a couple you could just lie around, do nothing and enjoy each other's company. When she was half of a couple she had actually looked forward to weekends when they had nothing to do. Now she dreaded them.

She was standing at the window watching the early evening mist settle over the river, which was bathed in intense pink light from the sunset, when her phone rang.

'Hi, Ma, it's me! Just thought I'd let you know we've wrapped up the exhibition and it all went brilliantly!' A wave of guilt rippled through Jo at how, yet again, she'd all but forgotten about the exhibition and her life at home. 'They've paid us already, which must be a first, and I've settled with the caterers and the wine people for the private view. So it's all done and dusted, and I'm arriving at Bratenac on Monday morning courtesy of Ryanair!'

'Oh, Soph, that's wonderful!' Jo felt a sudden lifting of her spirits, like the mist clearing from the river in a burst of late sunshine. 'You do know the deal hasn't gone through yet?' she added anxiously. 'I do hope Meredith isn't being too ambitious. She's used to snapping her fingers and having things happen yesterday, but Steph says she hasn't encountered French bureaucracy yet. It normally takes ages to buy a French château and Meredith wants to start weddings as soon as possible.'

'Based on what you've told me, between Meredith and any system, I'd back Meredith,' replied her sensible daughter. 'Anyway, I'd like to know what we'll be in for if it does come off. And I'm not objecting to a quick break in the French sunshine. It's been the wettest spring here anyone can remember. Even the pigeons have umbrellas!'

Jo began to laugh, her sense of proportion miraculously restored, thanks to her lovely daughter. Her marriage hadn't been a complete waste of time if it had produced wonderful Sophie!

Steph and Jo had to admit that it was amazing watching Meredith in action. She had taken up residence in a room at Fleur-de-Lis known as the Library, although no one ever went there to read books. She produced all three of her phones – which she generally used for business transactions in Singapore, Hong Kong and Shanghai – and dedicated them to getting the job done.

Jo asked how it was all going.

'You won't be surprised to hear that the title, as Margot de Savarin so frostily reminded us, is impeccable. Some of the structure of the château, on the other hand, is worrying. There may have to be a negotiation. My ace negotiating skills may find a chink in the eight-foot walls where catapults and battering rams failed in the fourteenth century, and get something chipped off the asking price for repairs and building work.'

Jo grinned, imagining a modern-day jousting contest between Lady Margot and Lady Meredith. Even with all her friend's business savvy, she wasn't quite certain who would win – but it would certainly go viral on YouTube.

'You're looking more cheerful,' Meredith commented.

Jo gave her a brilliant smile. 'That's because my daughter Sophie's coming!'

'Excellent!' Meredith smiled back. She'd actually been quite concerned about Jo, but had never been very good at the touchy-feely stuff. No, that wasn't strictly true. At school, although she'd started off as prickly as a cactus with Jo and Steph, she'd learned to open up and even administer and receive the odd hug. When had she withdrawn again? She remembered how scary she seemed to some of her younger colleagues, and that she'd actually fostered that image, thinking it made her more effective in business. In business maybe, but not in life. She'd seen that since she'd arrived in Bratenac. Suddenly the words of that Paul Simon song drifted into her mind, about being a rock and an island. Was that what she'd made herself into?

To Jo's surprise, Meredith suddenly embraced her. 'Your friendship's incredibly precious, you know. Especially since I don't have a family. My friends are my family, and by that I really mean you and Steph.'

Jo hugged her back. 'And you're an important part of ours, even if we'd lost touch for a while. The Meads Girls are definitely back in action!'

Jo spent the next morning planning some nice things to do with Sophie. She was sure she'd love the Bratenac market; there were the famous prehistoric caves to visit; and perhaps they could take a trip down the river in one of the famous flat-bottomed boats. And of course, there would have to be some delicious lunches.

Naturally, Sophie would want to see the château. She must talk to Meredith about how to approach that, given their negotiations were still going on. That brought with it the thought of Liam and his dinner invitation. She had a feeling that after the episode with the purple rabbit, that might never happen. On the other hand, he had seemed to think it was funny. But was the laughter because he thought her a sad, pathetic woman? Someone of Sophie's generation might proudly proclaim their right to sexual satisfaction, whether it was achieved with a man or a machine, and, in fact, so might have Jo's younger self.

Come on, Jo, she reminded herself as she took a taxi to the airport to collect her daughter. You used to be quite a gal, back in the day. You weren't always so prudish.

Sexual freedom had been part of their credo as young women, along with equality and miniskirts; but that had been before life knocked the stuffing out of her. Somehow she had to get back some of that youthful optimism, even if she wasn't quite so youthful any more.

Idly she began to browse on her phone and, although she wouldn't have liked to explain quite how, came across an online article outlining the seven defining characteristics of the New Zealand male. These ranged from being stoical and blokey to independent and easy-going; a love of sport and loyalty to their friends; with their most defining characteristic being that they were 'bonded to the land'. Liam seemed to fit the Kiwi bill in most ways. But why, if he was bonded to the land, had he stayed here in France?

Stepping out of the taxi, she paid the driver and put her phone away to look out for Sophie. There was no chance of missing her because the airport was so tiny. In fact, it didn't even have a carousel for the suitcases; they were simply piled in a large and untidy heap in a semi-derelict hangar that looked as if it had been previously used as a cattle barn. Which is exactly what it had been, till the advent of cheap airlines. Neither was there a cafe, only a stall on wheels, and the loos were about half a mile away and consisted of that French speciality, the hole in the ground, where you took aim and hoped for the best then got your feet plunged into freezing water when you flushed, while the lights instantly went out to save on electricity.

She bought herself a cappuccino from the stall and sat down with it on a cool stone bench to wait.

Once the plane landed she didn't have to wait much longer. With her usual efficiency Sophie had paid for a seat in the first row and was therefore first off; and since her belongings were stowed in a smart leather backpack, she was able to stride past the trailer loaded with luggage and fling herself into her mum's arms.

'I have a good feeling about this,' she announced. 'A change will be good for you. For both of us. I can't wait to see the place. What's it like?'

'Your basic fairy-tale castle,' Jo grinned. 'Gorgeous golden stone, four turrets with pointy roofs like witches' hats – even a moat, for God's sake. And right on the riverbank. All it needs is a princess waiting to be set free.'

'Could she be you?' Sophie asked with a smile.

'Oh God, I'm too old for that sort of thing. A wicked step-mother, more like.'

'Oh, Mum.' Sophie hugged her. 'You could never be a wicked stepmother. You're much too nice.'

'Life has brought me to the conclusion that being nice is my problem. If I'd been tougher—'

'If you'd been tougher, you wouldn't have been you,' Sophie insisted.

'It *is* lovely to have you here. I've got lots of exciting plans.'

'We have to start with the château, though,' Sophie insisted. 'I'm dying to see all round it. I already have a scheme for the bridal suite. This château is going to be every bride's dream. It'll be booked up solid when I've finished with it!'

'Hang on,' Jo laughed, 'the negotiations are all still going on. Let's go drop off your bag and see what Meredith has to say. She's the businesswoman.'

Back at Fleur-de-Lis, Marcelline was busy clearing up from breakfast while Steph and David had gone into town to buy supplies. Meredith was in the library with her phones.

'I don't see why you shouldn't look round,' she agreed when Sophie suggested it. 'I've always thought how ridiculous it is that most of us spend longer choosing a pair of shoes than buying a house – and you can take shoes back! I think we're entitled to as many viewings of the château as we want. I'll call Héloise now.'

She had a brief chat, impressing them both with the fluency of her French, then put the phone down with a smile. 'Fine. Just call her and arrange a time that suits.'

'Now?' asked Sophie enthusiastically.

'I think that might look a bit *too* keen,' Meredith counselled. 'You have to keep the other side on the hop in business negotiations.'

'Come on,' Jo intervened, seeing her daughter's disappointment, 'we'll walk along the river and you can see it from the outside, and then into town for a stroll and some lunch. You can sample the delights of the region the locals like to call the gastronomic capital of France.'

'I don't suppose it'll go down too well that I've become a vegetarian, then,' Sophie grinned.

'Since when?' Jo asked, stunned. Sophie had always liked her steaks.

'Since I saw a TV programme about animal cruelty,' Sophie replied, slightly apologetically.

'I have no idea how vegetarians are catered for in France,' Jo commented. 'I was once told a vegetarian here is someone who doesn't eat horse.'

'Nothing wrong with horse,' Meredith chipped in. 'The Chinese eat everything – even chicken feet and fish lips.'

Jo glanced nervously at her daughter. Some of Meredith's comments could be red rags to politically correct bulls and she'd been so hoping for a lovely, peaceful time with her daughter.

But Sophie just laughed. 'Don't worry, Mum. I can see Meredith and I both like a good spat and I'm sure we'll have one soon!'

Meredith considered coming up with one of her famous put-downs, which had terrified fund managers from Beijing to Barcelona, but instead decided she liked Sophie. The girl had spirit and clearly wasn't cowed by Meredith, like so many of the people who worked for her. She might well be an asset to them.

Sophie dumped her bag in her allotted room, which was small but very pretty with a view right down to the river. 'Ooh, this feels like a free minibreak! How brilliant. Actually, let's hope it's going to be a maxibreak! Come on then, let's go and see your fairy-tale castle. I hope it's not a disappointment after all this build-up.'

They set off along the riverbank, feeling the heat of the sun on their backs as they took in the lush, fertile landscape. Ahead was an arched bridge of honey-coloured stone, its mellow tones reflected in the deep green of the river's smoothly flowing surface. All around them the birds were joyfully celebrating the arrival of spring and the return of warmth to the landscape.

And then, round the next bend, the château appeared, bathed in golden sunlight. Jo could just make out someone standing at the top of the sweeping stone staircase that led down to the terrace.

'Wow, it really *is* like something from the movies!' Sophie breathed. 'It just *oozes* romance. Look at that staircase! It's *made* for brides to come down. You just wait – if I get my hands on this place, every bride on Instagram is going to kill to have her wedding here!'

Seven

Sophie was charmed by the market and spent a good twenty minutes poring over the handbags being sold by the smiling trader from Senegal. Her favourite was a shoulder bag made of real leather and fake leopard. 'It may not be a genuine leopard,' the trader assured Sophie in the most sincere of tones, 'but it is still real fur.'

'You know, in this day and age with so many animals being threatened, you might sell more if you admit it's fake,' Sophie smiled back.

'You really think this?' The man looked at her as though she had just exposed him to a blinding revelation. 'In that case,' he smiled delightedly, 'I will tell the truth about all my products!'

They stopped at a charming pavement cafe and Jo introduced her to the local speciality of *vin de noix*. Sophie sipped it tentatively.

'What do you think?'

'On the whole,' Sophie wrinkled her nose, 'I think I prefer Aperol.'

They wandered through the half-timbered, medieval back

streets of Bratenac, past a cobbler's that looked as if it had been unchanged for hundreds of years, and stopped at an antique shop where Sophie lost her heart to an enormous oil painting of a young woman looking out of the window of a castle tower. 'Come on, let's get it! It'll be just right for one of the bridal suites I'm planning!'

'Slow down, Soph,' laughed her mother. 'We haven't even got the place yet!'

'We will. Meredith is an irresistible force, right? Just wait and see.'

'As long as Margot doesn't turn out to be an immovable object!' Jo replied.

By now it was lunchtime. Jo glanced into the Café de la Paix. 'Oh my God,' she whispered to her daughter, 'the whole of the Ladies' Luncheon Club is in session! I think we'll find somewhere else.' She quickly closed the door, but not quickly enough for Jackie, who was already out on the pavement.

'*Bon-jour,*' she said in her dreadfully accented French, somehow turning it into two words. 'Who's this?'

'My daughter Sophie, over from England.'

'Why don't you both join us?'

Sophie surveyed the ladies through the open door.

'That's very kind of you, Jackie,' Joanna said firmly, 'but I want to show Sophie the new pop-up.' The last thing she wanted was to be pumped for information about the château sale.

'Just an apéritif, then.'

'We've already had one, thanks. Enjoy your lunch!'

But Jackie wasn't so easily put off. 'How's it going?'

'At Fleur-de-Lis? Very well. We have a full house.'

'Up at the château!' Jackie replied impatiently.

'Oh, you know, nothing settled. My friend needs to be very sure before spending all that money.'

'I hear it's a very good business,' Jackie persisted. 'Pity to miss the opportunity.'

'Well, business is Meredith's expertise, so I expect she's well aware of all that.'

'While she's still alive,' Jackie added sarcastically.

'Come on, Jackie, you know that was a joke.'

'A pretty tasteless one.'

'Yes, well, humour's a strange thing,' Jo echoed Meredith, knowing she was on shaky ground. 'We really ought to be going.' She took Sophie's arm.

'What on earth was all that about?' Sophie asked.

'Apparently Meredith wound Jackie up a bit by claiming she was seriously ill – she says she did it because she hated how intrusive Jackie was being. Jackie fell for it, and it seems to have really annoyed her.'

'Certainly a bit strange of Meredith. Who was that other woman with all the dyed black hair and cleavage?'

'That's Suzi, Bratenac's *femme fatale*. Except that she's from Essex.'

'I know who she reminded me of!' Sophie grinned. 'Dorien from *Birds of a Feather*! You remember her; the ageing sex siren who could never keep her nose out of other people's business.'

'Sounds more like Jackie. Apart from the sex siren bit.' Jo couldn't help laughing too. Until she thought of what Liam had said about the bindweed he'd seen wrapping itself round David in the cafe. She had to hope that even if David was feeling a bit undervalued, he'd have more taste than to get involved with Suzi.

Except that taste wasn't always men's most obvious trait.

They walked through the back of the town until they came to the river path. The restaurant was already busy; Jean-Christophe gave them a friendly wave.

'*Salut*, Jean-Christophe,' Jo greeted him. 'This is my daughter Sophie, just arrived from England.'

'*Bienvenue en France*, Mademoiselle Sophie. But it is a French name, Sophie, *n'est-ce pas?*'

'Yes,' Jo nodded. 'It's even spelled the French way.'

'But then you will be very much at home in France,' Jean-Christophe smiled charmingly at Sophie. 'I will get you a menu.'

'The thing is,' Sophie explained, looking up through her lashes in a way her mother had never seen before, 'I am a vegetarian.'

Instead of the French reaction of shock and horror Jo had expected, Jean-Christophe beamed. '*Mais c'est formidable!* I am trying to persuade my father to try some vegetarian dishes, but he will only say that if people stop eating meat the land-scape of the France we love so much will all change!' He paused and added almost shyly, 'I have been thinking of testing a pasta with roasted peppers and our local Tomme Périgordine cheese, if you would like to try?'

'Like!' Sophie grinned. 'It sounds absolutely scrumptious. I usually just get offered a plate of veg!'

'What is scrumptious?' he enquired.

Sophie explained that it meant extremely delicious.

'*Bon!* I will get someone to take over as waiter and make this scrumptious dish for you.'

'Wow!' Sophie commented when he'd gone. 'He's a bit of all right, isn't he?'

'Sophie, you're sounding like a man! And what's all this looking up through your eyelashes stuff?' teased Jo. 'What happened to your feminist credentials?'

Sophie just laughed. 'I must have forgotten to pack them!'

The mention of packing brought back the painful memory

of her embarrassment with the vibrator again, which, thank God, Sophie knew nothing about. Liam still hadn't got in touch. Maybe that was a good thing. It was all right Sophie being a flirt at her age, but it was a different matter at Jo's.

Jo studied the menu. 'That sounds nice. Confit of duck and spring rolls in plum and hoisin sauce.'

'*Oui.*' Jean-Christophe had reappeared with the wine lists. 'My father has been experimenting with our local produce. Confit of duck is a famous product here.' He leaned down and added conspiratorially: 'Some of the old guard are in shock! To use our famous confit of duck like this . . . it could bring about *la fin du monde* – the end of the world!' He took Jo's order next. '*C'est tout?* Is that all you would like?'

Jo nodded. 'For now, yes. And two glasses of Bratenac sec, please.' She leaned over to Sophie. 'I'm assuming you're not thinking of becoming teetotal as well as vegetarian?'

'Don't be mean, Mum. Trying to imply veggies are disapproving non-drinkers.'

'And just to make your day,' she teased her daughter, 'Jean-Christophe is coming to cook at the *chambre d'hôte* three nights a week. It's Meredith's way of trying to give Steph and David some time off.'

'That's really nice of her,' Sophie sounded surprised.

'Yes. There's a heart hidden under that business suit.'

'Better not let on to the duchess.'

No fake flattery was required when her pasta arrived. It was one of the best things she'd ever eaten. Jean-Christophe beamed with delight when she told him so.

'Perhaps you could help me develop some more dishes for a *menu végétarien?*' he asked shyly. 'I am embarrassed at how little we address such things in France.'

Sophie replied that she was more than happy to do so,

ignoring the broad grin on her mother's face. 'Anyway,' she said sternly once he'd disappeared back to the kitchen, 'back to basics. Do you think we could go and look round the château tomorrow?'

When they got back to Fleur-de-Lis they found that efficient Meredith had already arranged everything. Héloise and the duchess were expecting them the next day at eleven. Sophie couldn't wait.

'It's lovely to see you so excited,' her mother smiled as they set out next day after a late breakfast of fresh fruit salad and croissants left over by the guests.

'I do love breakfast in France,' Sophie announced. 'So much nicer than my usual microwaved porridge!'

It was only a ten-minute walk and at this time they had it all to themselves. 'I've given up saying what a beautiful day it is,' Jo laughed, looking round at the landscape and river bathed in sunshine. 'Because round here every day seems to be beautiful!'

'Unlike home,' sighed Sophie. 'I adore the English spring, but this year it seems to have done nothing but rain.'

They turned away from the river and down a narrow path through the vineyards. Jo felt her nerves tighten like an over-wound clock at the thought of bumping into Liam round any corner.

'Are you OK, Mum?' Sophie asked. 'Only you look really weird.'

'There are often strange bugs in the vine leaves,' Jo lied unconvincingly. 'You know me and bugs!'

'Actually, I always thought you were pretty good with creepy-crawlies,' Sophie replied. 'I remember you picking up this absolutely ginormous spider when I was about two and throwing it out of the window. I thought you were the bravest mummy in the world!'

Jo felt a sudden wave of loss for that innocent time, when she'd thought her family life would go on forever. She put her arm round Sophie. 'Indiana Mum! That's me!'

When they arrived at the château they found Héloise and the duchess were already waiting for them in the Great Hall.

'Wow!' Sophie stared, amazed, at the twenty-foot-high fireplace surrounded by its ornately carved stone figures, all overseen by a stern medieval ancestor from his giant portrait above the chimney.

'Who's the snooty-looking gent?' enquired Sophie.

'That was the third duke,' Héloise commented approvingly. 'Famed for being cruel but fair. Now, I understand you would like a tour of the château?' She didn't wait for a reply but swept straight on. '*Bien, mademoiselle, venez avec moi.*' She exchanged a conspiratorial look with Margot. 'I will show you round while Madame *la duchesse* becomes a little better acquainted with your mother.'

Jo followed the duchess, feeling a little like a victim of the Spanish Inquisition, and was led into a surprisingly cosy salon where Margot indicated two chairs.

'So, Madame, er, Walker, is it?' the duchess began.

'Please call me Joanna,' Jo interrupted as politely as she could.

'And you must call me Margot. Now, tell me a little about yourself. Why do you wish to come and live here?'

'My friend Meredith fell in love with the château and wanted someone with experience she could trust to come and help her out. I already organize events professionally, so I seemed the natural choice.'

'And you? Why do you want to come? Are you in love with France like so many of your compatriots?' Margot uttered the words with just a hint of patronage. Jo wondered how much to divulge, and decided to jump straight in.

'I was looking for a new challenge, I suppose. My marriage ended three years ago and my husband is about to marry again.'

'A younger woman?' enquired Margot avidly before answering the question herself. 'Of course, a younger woman! *Là là, avec les hommes c'est toujours la même histoire.*' She nodded her startlingly auburn curls. 'With men it is always the same story. *Ma chère Joanna,* men are like chimpanzees – and who would expect a chimpanzee to behave with honour or delicacy?'

Jo tried not to smile at the idea of the courtly duke of Savarin as a chimpanzee. With Mark, it was easier to picture.

'And how about you, *ma chère* Joanna? As I always say, to get over one man you need to get under another. You are a very attractive woman. I noticed that our *vigneron* Liam was very eager to bring you the wine, and I am sure it was not for your friend the frightening Meredith!' Before Jo could respond, the duchess was away again. 'The way we deal with these questions in France when the husband is unfaithful is for the woman to have a little affair also. Since they have to marry chimpanzees, every Frenchwoman is entitled to her *jardin secret*, a secret garden where she has an erotic adventure of her own.'

It struck Jo that the only thing she did in her secret garden was to plant bulbs. No wonder Liz thought she needed the Happy Rabbit.

Jackie parked her car on a verge at the bottom of the drive behind the back of the château, and stepped out. There was a dense stand of trees between the edge of the château grounds and where she stood now, completely masking the building that was being erected here. Jackie had watched with fascination as it appeared over the last few days; she had read about houses like this in magazines, but had never actually seen one before.

The house was small, modern and unremarkable in every detail except one. This house had arrived pre-built in two halves, and had then been locked together until it was an entirely finished structure. Jackie was one of the few people who knew about it, since she had opened her curtains at three a.m. a couple of nights earlier and seen it arrive very discreetly on a trailer.

She looked at her watch. It was after midday, so any workmen would have stopped for their obligatory lunch and the coast should be clear. She peered in the window and had to marvel. There were four bedrooms, a large lounge, a galley kitchen with space for a kitchen table – even a fireplace with tasteful marble surround. There were russet tiles with a slightly Mediterranean look where the roof met the walls, and a front door with a small porch. The whole thing was like a toy house, only life-size.

No one British, who flocked here in their thousands to buy ruined *manoirs* and abandoned farmhouses, would ever understand that a lot of French people yearned for easy-care modern dwellings with absolutely no maintenance. After a lifetime of leaking roofs, no matter how historic, blocked pipes and damp plasterwork, they longed to simply turn their backs on history and embrace the contemporary. She also knew, since Guillaume's sister worked in the doctor's surgery, that the duke was actually quite ill and would soon need a carer, and the duchess had no intention of taking on this role.

Jackie peered inside and was just wondering if she dared try opening the door, when a voice made her jump.

'*C'est formidable, eh, madame?*' demanded a jovial man in blue overalls who looked like the gardener. 'Two days and she is built. *Pouf!* And let me show you the real magic. Come. *Entrez!*' He opened the front door as proudly as if it were his own home. 'It is the future, madame! For you and I when we get older!'

Jackie tried not to laugh. Next minute he would be carrying her over the threshold.

'See. Electric points up here!' He gestured at waist level. 'So the old person does not have to reach down. A ramp at the back for the *fauteuil roulant* – wheelchair, do you say?' He led her to the bathroom. 'This is the best of all! A *toilette* from Japan that needs no paper – is it not a miracle? I am sure you cannot now wait to be old!'

'And who are the lucky owners?' Jackie asked with a flirtatious smile.

The man leaned closer and simply gestured towards the château. '*Madame la duchesse* cannot wait to move in. She is hoping another one of your mad compatriots will buy the château and she can relax with *la télé*.'

Like hell she would. The idea of Margot leaving Meredith to get on with running the château while she watched TV was an absolute joke.

'But do not tell a soul, madame.' He looked suddenly anxious, as if he'd said too much. Jackie smiled to herself.

'Do not worry, *monsieur*,' she replied with a saintly smile. 'I will be discretion itself.'

'Mum, this place is amazing!' breathed Sophie when she returned with Héloïse. 'I can just see where the bridal suite would be in that left tower! The bride will feel just like a fairy princess!'

They said goodbye and headed back down through the vineyard, Sophie so bubbling over with enthusiasm that she could hardly get her words out fast enough. 'It's amazing! Do you know they don't let anyone actually stay in the château, even though they have all those bedrooms? It's such a waste! You'd get far more bookings if you offered a package. Dinner on the Friday, wedding on Saturday and then Sunday brunch for the whole wedding party and guests. That's what people want now. God, I should know; I get invited to enough of them!'

They turned to take one last look at the château. Sunlight glinted on the russet tiles of its towers, in harmonious contrast with the golden stone walls. Each tower had two weather vanes, starkly silhouetted against the bright blue sky.

From behind a row of vines, Liam suddenly appeared, literally barging into Jo as he looked up at the sky to gauge the next day's weather.

'I can hardly say "Ill met by moonlight, proud Titania," since it's blazing sunshine, can I?' he asked, with a smile of such unexpected sweetness that Jo's heart turned over. All at once she felt silly for having worried about the embarrassing incident. He was gorgeous, and she was feeling something again for the first time in years. That had to be good in itself.

'I've just brought my daughter Sophie to look round the château.'

'And what did she think of it?' He included Sophie in the smile, which was now one of polite formality. The sweetness had clearly been just for Jo, Sophie noted.

'So who's that?' she whispered as Liam disappeared once more into the neat rows of the vineyard. 'Quoting *Midsummer Night's Dream* at you in that flirtatious manner? You've never mentioned him, you dark horse. I thought he seemed quite keen on you.'

'I hardly know the man,' insisted Jo firmly, not fooling her clever daughter for an instant.

*

'Isn't it amazing of Meredith to hire Jean-Christophe to come and cook for us!' Steph enthused. 'What do you want to do next Wednesday when he starts?'

It was one of Marcelline's nights off, and she and David were laying the large table for dinner. 'We could drive into the cinema in Sarlat if you want? That's something we never get time to do.'

'For God's sake!' snapped David irritably. 'We can't just disappear like teenagers climbing out a window and leave the guy to it!'

For the first time in years, Steph did feel like a teenager climbing out of a window. The idea of going out at all felt exciting and slightly illicit after so many years of being tied to the kitchen and their guests. She couldn't understand why David didn't feel the same.

David, preoccupied by guilt about their increasingly precarious financial position, just grunted and disappeared into the kitchen to get the glasses. He knew that Steph had delegated the money side of things to him because he'd worked in the City and was supposed to know about these things. But the truth was, selling shares to high net worth individuals had done very little to prepare him for the ups and downs of running a B&B in France.

Then there was Suzi, whose invitations to share afternoon delights were becoming more overt. He should have been clearly rebuffing them, he knew – and he really had meant to – but instead he found them increasingly tempting, which made him feel more guilty than ever and hence even more short-tempered with Steph. His libido, which had been sleeping in a prehistoric cave, had started to wake up and roar but not necessarily for the right person.

Oh Christ, he thought as he polished glasses mindlessly,

I've got to *do* something. The trouble was, he couldn't decide whether to face the pain of Steph's anger when she discovered the truth, or hide away from reality in the overperfumed embrace of Bratenac's resident *femme fatale*. Even he didn't like himself for it, but he knew which tempted him most.

'Mmmm, not bad,' Philippe pronounced as he tasted Jean-Christophe's newest veggie creation, a roasted vegetable lasagne. 'Did you make the pasta yourself?'

'Chef,' Jean-Christophe teased his father with the formal title used in any Parisian restaurant. 'Am I your son?'

'As far as I know.' Philippe ruffled his son's hair. 'We appear to have the same hair, anyway, though mine is sadly greyer.'

'*Poivre et sel*, pepper and salt, as our English ladies would say,' pointed out Jean-Christophe. 'I would even say it suits you. Just grey and it would be creepy, like some sad 1960s rocker.'

'Hey, I happen to like sad 1960s rockers,' protested Philippe.

'Yes, but you don't want to *look* like one! Cadaverous Ronnie Wood or Keith Richards of *The Walking Dead*! You do look a bit zombie-like today, though. *Grand-père* again?'

'Don't ask,' shrugged Philippe. 'Into each life some rain must fall.'

'Quite a shower into yours,' Jean-Christophe said quietly. He stopped chopping and gave his father a hug.

'In the middle of the night when *Grand-père* wakes me, I worry that you must have missed your mother so much when you were young,' Philippe said softly. 'You needed a mother's love. I was always so busy. I didn't give you that everyday reliable love a child needs . . .'

'There are other ways of showing love,' replied Jean-Christophe. 'Love isn't some abstract thing. You got me out of bed in the mornings even though you had come back God knows when, and you left me dinner plus a different little note every single night to welcome me when Marie brought me home from school. In fact . . .'

He delved into his pocket, his mischievous smile looking so like his father's that an outsider would instantly have known their relationship without needing to ask. 'I still carry one of them in my wallet.' Again that impish grin. 'For when I get kidnapped by pirates and need to remember home.' He pulled out a crumpled piece of paper. '*Dear Son. Let us fish for the uncatchable carp on Saturday morning. Your unreliable father. X,*' he read, glancing up at Philippe with a smile. 'I always wished I was a musician, so that I could write a song called "The Uncatchable Carp".'

They both laughed, remembering the hours they had spent on the lake of St Savarin, staring into its green depths, waiting for the legendary fish that never appeared. 'Of course I missed *Maman*, but I was very young, and I wouldn't have had the relationship I've had with you if she hadn't left, would I?' He saw that his father's eyes had begun to water.

'Hey,' he teased, 'you're crying, you old softie.'

'It's just the onions,' lied Philippe unconvincingly.

'And you're a terrible liar, too.' Jean-Christophe was serious for a moment, his dark eyes fixed on his father's face. 'Besides, you trusted me with your most precious possession – your restaurant. What father could do more than that?'

'What stupid father would have a restaurant as their most precious possession?' Philippe replied. 'Besides, it isn't.'

'I know,' replied Jean-Christophe, his smile as wide and sunny as a brand new day. 'I am.'

Eight

When they all got down to breakfast the next morning, Meredith was busy opening a bottle of champagne.

'It's not your birthday, is it?' asked Steph. 'I thought that was in September.'

'Better than that. I've handed in my resignation.'

'Oh my God, Meredith.' Jo sat down, amazed at her friend's degree of self-belief, something she herself so notably lacked. 'But we haven't even signed anything with the château yet.'

The champagne cork popped loudly and Meredith began pouring into six glasses. 'The thing is, after spending time in this place, I just can't face all the hustle – and believe me, that's what it's like – of China and Singapore. Funnily enough, I've kind of lost interest in making rich people richer. Why not have wonderful weddings and make people happy instead?'

'Touching faith in the power of matrimony, I must say,' commented Jo wryly. 'So good, my husband did it twice.'

'Come on, Mum,' Sophie chided. 'Raise your glass to Meredith and wonderful weddings. I just know we're going to have such fun organizing them.'

Jo raised her glass, pushing aside her worries about their inexperience, their lack of skills in catering or hotel management, floristry or wedding planning. And about whether friends suddenly running a business together was really going to be plain sailing. 'To weddings, then. You'd better get on and sign the deal, Meredith.'

'Don't worry. If this doesn't work, France is littered with old châteaux, not to mention mad Brits turning them into wedding venues. We're part of a trend, girls.'

'That's a healthy attitude to have when negotiating,' commented David, raising his glass too.

Meredith smiled. She'd been a bit worried about him lately. He seemed quiet and subdued, not his usual caring self. She'd expected him to be a lot more upbeat, given her gesture with Jean-Christophe.

'I have been doing quite a lot behind the scenes to speed things along,' Meredith pointed out. 'As a matter of fact, I've got an important meeting tomorrow with a lawyer who's been recommended to deal with all the red tape. My specialists haven't been doing as well as I'd hoped. They've never come across anything like nitpicking French legislation. Jo, you'd better come too.'

Jo nodded, slightly aggrieved that Meredith had set all this up without even telling her. She'd have to sort out with Meredith exactly what it meant to be involved in this venture. She'd been a bit ditsy about the whole thing so far, without considering how her actual role would work in practice.

Time to wise up, Joanna, she told herself. And stop moping about Mark. If this venture only achieves that, it'll be well worth it.

*

The lawyer's office was in the old part of Bratenac, tucked down a tiny cobbled side street with a view of rooftops in every direction.

'*Bonjour, mesdames,*' a sleek middle-aged man greeted them. 'Please have a seat.' He held out a chair with the old-fashioned courtesy that seemed to be a watchword of the place. Jo couldn't imagine him ruthlessly pushing the authorities to hurry the process up, as Meredith had said she wanted.

'*Bonjour*, Monsieur Martel,' Meredith replied with her usual crisp efficiency. 'How are we doing?'

'We have made a lot of progress, but you must understand you cannot purchase a six-hundred-year-old château overnight. You must remember you have to deal with—'

'I know, French bureaucracy,' Meredith interrupted waspishly. 'So everyone tells me. How long do you think it is going to take?'

'At least six months, madame, to be realistic.'

'Too long.'

'Foreigners do not understand our system . . .' He looked out of the window at the rooftops, struck by a sudden thought. 'Perhaps that is what put the American gentleman off.'

Jo noticed Meredith instantly sit up. 'What American gentleman?'

'Did the duchess not mention him?'

'She certainly did not.'

Monsieur Martel grinned. 'Perhaps because he left her at the altar. Margot was thunderously annoyed.'

'By that you mean the negotiation was very far advanced?' asked Meredith.

'Ready to sign. But he telephoned to the château and cried off. His wife had apparently changed her mind. It cost them quite a lot of money. Americans –' he shrugged – 'they think they can behave the way they want.' He expected Meredith to be devastated, but instead she appeared to be thrilled.

'Do you know the name of this American gentleman?' she demanded eagerly.

He tapped his computer screen, searching for an email. 'Samuel Andrews. I understand he is quite well known in financial circles.'

'And is his wife Brazilian, called Elena – rather fancies herself as a decorator? I think I've met them and everyone's heard of him, of course. They call him the Sibyl of St Louis because he's so good at predicting the stock market. I may even have his card somewhere. I wonder what made him change his mind? It could give me some useful ammunition.'

'Maybe his wife saw the ghost,' grinned Jo.

'*Bien, mesdames.*' Monsieur Martel stood up and bowed again. 'You will talk to Monsieur Andrews, and we will push as hard as we can to move things along.'

Even Meredith with her expert contacts wasn't going to be able to dislodge the ancient edifice of French officialdom.

'I'm surprised Jackie didn't know all about that too,' grinned Jo as they walked back to the main square.

'Margot probably kept it a deep, dark secret,' Meredith replied. 'But I'm really keen to find out more.'

Most people would have been cast down to discover that a famous businessman had changed his mind about the château at the last moment, but not Meredith. As long as, of course, he hadn't discovered something disastrous.

It didn't take her long to unearth Sam's details, because she'd transferred them from the card he'd given her to her phone. Half an hour later they were sitting across the road from the lawyer's office in a quiet cafe, and Meredith wasted no time in calling him.

At first she only got through to his bossy assistant, but Meredith was skilled in the art of getting past bossy assistants. It only took the name of her company, plus the hint of an opportunity that the Sibyl of St Louis would hate to miss, and she found herself talking to the sibyl himself.

'Sam! Good morning. I hope it isn't too early for you but I remembered you start famously early, and I'm afraid I just told a white lie to your assistant,' Meredith told him gaily. 'I'm not in Shanghai but south-west France – the town of Bratenac, to be precise. Not to beat about the bush, Sam, I've made an offer for the Château of St Savarin, only to discover that you did the same and pulled out. I'd like to know why? Am I making a stupid mistake?'

Sam Andrews' throaty laugh reverberated merrily across three thousand miles. 'Not unless you've just been offered another château belonging to famous ballerina Louie Worth and all the remodelling's already been done, so you can move straight in and start business right away!'

'But Sam, you must have lost a lot of money pulling out! Surely the Sibyl of St Louis wouldn't approve of that?' she teased.

'Maybe not, but his wife did,' was his humourous reply. 'And I have to say, I would have loved to have seen the look on the duchess's face when we told her. If looks could kill, I imagine I'd be six feet under.'

'Sam, I have a little favour to ask . . .'

'You want a copy of all the documentation to speed up the slow wheels of château-buying?'

Meredith laughed delightedly. 'I can see doing business with you would be terrific fun. Almost makes me wish I wasn't giving it up.'

'To do what?'

'Hold glorious weddings at the château, of course.'

'I wish you great good luck! Of course, you'll now be a rival of my wife's. To be frank, I'd be happy if she abandoned the whole idea. It looks as if I won't see her during the wedding season unless I move in too – and I don't think I could stand all the bridal nonsense. Why women want to make all this fuss over weddings, I'll never understand. Men would just head off to City Hall.'

'Come on, Sam,' Meredith teased. 'Where did you get married yourself?'

'The fourth or fifth time?' he quipped back.

'Now, Sam, I know you're famous for having the same wife and living in the same place your entire life.'

'Which is why you can understand my reluctance to buy a château in France. Meredith, I look forward to meeting you when my wife drags me over there. Good luck with your wedding business. Naturally I hope it's going to be a big flop.'

'Thanks, Sam,' Meredith grinned. 'And the same to you!'

'I wonder what's taking so long?' Sophie asked Steph.

David put his head round the door. 'I'm just popping into town,' he announced briskly. Steph was so taken up with the meeting that she didn't even notice that this was the second day running he'd suddenly disappeared without any real explanation. 'That young man from the restaurant is here. Shall I send him in?'

They both got up, grateful for the diversion.

'Jean-Christophe, *salut*,' Steph greeted him. 'Can we offer you a coffee?'

'That would be delightful, madame.' He bowed with charming old-fashioned courtesy, while his dark eyes flashed amusement at his lack of Parisian cool. 'I thought it might be a good idea if I came and had a look round before I start tomorrow?' he explained. 'Then I can decide which implements to bring. I always carry my own knives anyway.' He gestured to a leather pouch tied to his waist under his light jacket.

He removed it with all the panache of a young Yul Brynner in *The Magnificent Seven*. 'My knife collection. Given to me by my father, who was given it by his father, who lives with us. He was a great chef. Sadly he now has dementia.'

Steph had just returned with the coffee. 'Yes, I had heard,' she commented sympathetically. 'That must be rough on all of you.'

Jean-Christophe shrugged. 'Mainly my father. As well as running the restaurant he has to go chasing off half the night trying to find Grand-père.' There was a sudden flash of humour in his dark eyes. 'No wonder my father sometimes looks like he has just come out of the grave! Last time Grand-père ran off he found him in a barn near Limeuil, covered in cow shit; *pardonnez-moi* for the language!'

'No apology necessary,' grinned Steph. 'Your grasp of the idiom is admirable! Oh dear, poor Philippe, and of course your poor grandfather. Is there not some kind of sheltered housing you could consider, or is that not a French concept?'

'My father would not hear of anything like that,' shrugged Jean-Christophe. 'Grand-père has a free spirit, he says, and he couldn't bear to see it crushed. How would I like it, he asks me, to be stuck in a home for old folks, dribbling in front of *la télé* all day long?'

Steph sighed. 'No indeed.' It was getting closer for them all.

Sophie had been silent, just listening. It was all so far outside her own experience.

'Mademoiselle Sophie.' Jean-Christophe suddenly smiled.

'Thanks to your inspiration I have been working on my *menu végétarian!* Do you know Pasta Norma?'

'The one with aubergines and tomato? I love it!' enthused Sophie.

'I have developed my own version which I think is very interesting using broccoli, red pepper and sweet potatoes. Like the original Sicilian version, I deep fry them in tempura batter before adding aubergines and tomatoes. I wonder if you would come and try some?' And then he added, almost blushing under his designer stubble, 'I would like to call it Pasta Sophie, if you are agreeable!'

Sophie laughed in delight. 'I would be most honoured,' she announced.

Steph proceeded to show Jean-Christophe round the kitchen and explain how the nightly menu worked.

'Would you mind if we added a vegetarian option?' he asked politely.

'Not at all. We probably ought to have done that years ago.'

'May I put it on the menu tomorrow, perhaps?'

'*Absolument oui!*' pronounced Steph.

'I think you've made a bit of a conquest there,' murmured Jo to Sophie as he left. 'You can be the inspiring older woman he'll remember all his life!'

'Excuse me,' Sophie pouted. 'I'm only a couple of years older than he is! I asked that woman Jackie, you know, the one who knows everything, how old he was and she said he was twenty-four.'

'That was a mistake,' Jo teased. 'She'll tell half of Bratenac, including him probably, that you've got the hots for him. She couldn't keep a secret if you offered her a million euro!'

'Anyway,' Sophie announced grandly, refusing to be riled, 'my name will live on in my pasta. That's enough for me.'

They heard the sound of a car pulling up in the driveway and peered out of the kitchen door to see Meredith and Jo jump out of a taxi, looking surprisingly cheerful.

'Congratulate us, girls, but I think we may have had a bit of a breakthrough. The lawyer told us an American businessman almost bought the château a couple of months ago and pulled out at the eleventh hour.'

'And why is that good news?' Steph enquired, mystified. 'Sounds ominous to me.'

'His wife found another château she preferred, but I called him and he's sending over all his documentation. I think this could really speed things up!'

There was a knock on the door and Jean-Christophe appeared. 'I will go now and see you later. By the way, if you would like some *déjeuner*, my father has sent a local quiche and some salad which I have left in the kitchen. Goodbye for now.'

'What a wonderful young man,' Meredith beamed, delighted with her own choice. 'Some lunch sounds perfect! He's going to be a real asset to the place! Where's David? Would he like to join us?'

'In town for something,' Steph shrugged.

Meredith caught the hint of anxiety in her tone and felt suddenly angry with the man. What was he doing that made Steph worry and spoiled this happy moment?

'By the way,' Steph visibly cheered. 'You know you mentioned bumping into Philippe looking like death after he'd been out on the town? Jean-Christophe explained to me and Sophie what he was really doing.'

'And what was that?' Meredith asked defensively.

'Chasing after his father, who has dementia and who he refuses to put into a home,' Steph announced with a certain satisfaction, which annoyed Meredith. 'The old man keeps running away in the middle of the night even when they lock him in. Last time he was in a barn covered in cow pats.'

Meredith took a deep breath. Shit. It might not be her best quality, but she didn't like to admit she was wrong – especially where people were concerned. 'I obviously deserve a gold star in character assessment,' she grinned, deciding not to take umbrage after all. In fact, she thought, she'd quite like to apologize.

After lunch, Sophie and Jo went upstairs so that her mother could give her a blow-by-blow account of what had happened with the lawyer.

'Meredith's really excited about it. I must admit, it's quite something to watch her in action.'

'It's all so exciting, Mum! It really is. I said you needed an adventure,' Sophie hugged her. 'And here it is!'

Jo looked out of the window at the sweeping view of lush green fields, broken up here and there by the neat tracks of the vines that grew all over the region. 'It certainly beats Basingstoke!'

After they'd gone, Steph realized she'd fallen behind with dinner and forced herself to get on with life. Where the hell was David? There was no answer to his mobile, so she sent him an irritated message and headed for the fridge to get out the meat.

Meredith decided that if she was going to apologize, there was no time like the present, and she might as well head into town. A walk along the river would do her good. When she arrived in Bratenac, she realized it was that quiet time in the afternoon when, despite it being the twenty-first century, small French towns always seemed to be closed. It couldn't have been more different from the high-tension hustle of Singapore or Hong Kong. She would have to kill some time before heading for Philippe's restaurant.

She made her way to a quiet cafe on the other side of the main square, bagged an outdoor table and ordered a mint tea as she watched the everyday comings and goings of the town.

By the war memorial, next to the boules pitch where the old men played faithfully all day in the shade of the poplar trees, she caught sight of that hideous bulldog. It was sitting on a chair again, wearing a ridiculous coat in the colours of the French flag. No doubt it was drooling as well. What was it called – Polly? Smelly? That would be appropriate, if unlikely. Nelly, that was it.

She paid the very modest bill, then set off across the square.

As she approached Janine the dog-walker, Nelly jumped off the chair and bounded towards her. The animal didn't even seem to be on a lead. She jumped up enthusiastically and placed her paws firmly on Meredith's thighs, stopping Meredith in her tracks. It was the strangest thing, though. If a dog could smile, Nelly was smiling at her, as if Meredith were her chosen goddess and Nelly a devoted worshipper.

'I've never seen anything like it,' Janine shook her head. 'The way that dog's taken to you. I just wish people weren't so narrow-minded. Because Nelly looks fierce they shy away yet, I kid you not, she is as gentle as a lamb, with the sweetest nature imaginable.'

A thought struck Meredith and she began to laugh. 'So I got you wrong too, Nelly!' And she began to fondle her ears. A look of total bliss settled on the animal's wrinkled features.

A sudden inspiration came to Janine. She looked hard at Meredith, trying to get the measure of her. 'The thing is, Nelly belongs to an old French lady who can't cope with a dog any more and the local charity can't house her either. It might be the end of the road for Nelly. Unless . . .' She paused, taken aback at her own temerity. 'You might consider having her?

She's had all her jabs, and now that it sounds as if you might be staying here . . .'

Meredith considered her new canine friend. 'Should I lose my mind and take you on?' Nelly smiled back engagingly. 'You could be a permanent reminder that I shouldn't make snap judgements about people.'

'Nelly could guard you up at the château,' suggested Janine, sensing a breach in Meredith's armour. 'Three ladies, living alone. A guard dog would be ideal!'

This time Meredith did laugh. 'She'd probably lick a burglar's hand!' She stroked the dog's ears again. 'Who's the old softie? Me or you? Meredith Harding, have you lost your marbles?' And Meredith, who had never wanted responsibility for anyone or anything, shrugged and accepted what had rapidly become the inevitable. 'All right. I will adopt Nelly. She's the only thing I'm likely *to* adopt, after all.'

'You can take her now, if you want. Madame Dufrais has gone into hospital again and I've been at my wits' end over what to do with Nelly. I could bring her stuff round later.'

The idea of turning up at Philippe's restaurant with Nelly suddenly struck Meredith as brilliantly appropriate.

'Fine. I should be back in a couple of hours.'

As she and her newfound admirer headed back towards the river, it struck Meredith that she hadn't raised the question of adopting a dog with Steph. Maybe they weren't allowed. Then she remembered the annoying red setter owned by the LeBruns.

And anyway, from what Margot had said, she and the duke had already found somewhere to move to and wanted to do so as fast as possible, so Steph and David might not have to put up with Nelly for long.

She took a route back down to the river to avoid too many

comments from surprised townspeople, through a narrow alley that led to a small green area on the riverbank, almost hidden by the branches of a weeping willow. There was a couple sitting on a bench who looked like lovers; the woman, with a mass of black curls, had her head on the man's shoulder.

Meredith decided to give them a wide berth but just as she was passing at a discreet distance, the man looked round and she almost gasped out loud.

It was David.

Meredith felt a flash of anger, not only on her friend's behalf but also because she had just gone to the trouble and expense of taking on Jean-Christophe to give him and Steph time to spend on their relationship. It looked as if it might be a bit late for that. She had stopped abruptly and Nelly rubbed up against her, puzzled at the diversion, causing Meredith to pause and rethink for a moment. Just as Nelly was the symbol of her rush to judgement, maybe she'd better slow down and think. Wasn't that the vamp from the Luncheon Club with him? Such an obvious type as Suzi had probably thrown herself at him and David, who she felt instinctively was a nice man, had just fallen for it all out of naivety. At least, she hoped so.

Her instinct was to slide quietly off, but then she decided it might be better all round if David knew she had taken in the scene as well as its significance. 'Hello, David,' she called out, making him visibly jump so that Suzi's head jerked off his shoulder in a satisfyingly comic manner like something in a TV cartoon. 'That's where you've got to,' she announced in her usual bracing manner. 'Steph was looking everywhere for you. You'll be in trouble if you don't get home soon.'

Then she walked briskly on across the narrow bridge across the river, not waiting to engage further in conversation. Judging by his startled expression, that would do quite well enough as a warning shot across the bows. She continued swiftly along the riverbank until she reached Philippe's restaurant.

From this angle the restaurant couldn't have been in a more stunning spot. The dozen or so tables were ranged right along the bank of the Savarin. In the background was an old arched bridge constructed of golden stone, adorned by an ancient market cross. Willow trees ran right down to its banks, reflected in the shining clear depth of the river, which dazzled like pink diamonds in the last of the afternoon's sunshine. A kind of deep peace emanated from the scene – belied, of course, by the bustle of business that would soon take over as the popular restaurant began to fill up. The good people of Bratenac had not been slow to appreciate it when Parisian quality arrived in their midst, apparently without Parisian prices.

The restaurant's kitchen was sited in a rather unprepossessing portacabin a few yards along the small quay and Meredith could see Philippe apparently engaged in the act of shining lamb bones, instantly noted with great interest by Nelly.

'For the *demi-glace*,' Jean-Christophe cheerfully informed her as she approached. He stopped and stared at the dog.

'Don't ask,' Meredith shook her head, laughing as Philippe looked up, equally startled. He was almost clean-shaven this time, his hair neatly brushed, his dark eyes unclouded by exhaustion and lit instead by twinkling good humour. The family resemblance between father and son and the obvious warmth between them struck her again. He had clearly been a good father.

'And who's this?' he enquired, handing Nelly a bone.

'My new friend Nelly.'

'I didn't have you down as a dog lover,' he commented, his head on one side, surveying the slobbering bulldog, who had forgotten to try and make herself engaging at the sight of the unexpected treat.

'Hmm, I'll think about that,' Meredith replied. 'You mean I'm a tough old bird who doesn't go soppy over furry animals?'

He shrugged. 'The British are dog-mad, we all know this, but you seem different, perhaps because you live in the East?'

'Where they eat dogs rather than pet them?'

'I imagine that is an outdated stereotype. All those terrible jokes – a dog is not for Christmas, you can make it last all year – yet when I visited Tokyo they dressed their dogs in baby clothes and wheeled them round in *poussettes* – how do you say that in English?'

'Buggies,' replied Meredith helpfully.

'We know that the British love dogs and gardens, *n'est-ce pas?*'

'Ah, but you see, the reason I have acquired Nelly is for a penance. She is going to encourage me not to accept stereotypes. When I first saw her I thought she was the ugliest and fiercest-looking dog I had ever seen. How would anyone on God's earth want to own a dog like that?'

'And?' Philippe and Jean-Christophe exchanged a grin. 'Why would they?'

'Nelly,' Meredith commanded, admittedly in a tone that would be recognized by conscripts everywhere as much as recalcitrant animals, 'drop the bone and come here!'

Nelly obeyed and trotted over. 'Paw for Philippe, Nelly.'

Nelly dutifully raised her paw, her sad and jowly features by some miracle suddenly rearranging themselves into an expression that was more human than animal.

'*Mon Dieu, c'est marrant!*' Philippe laughed. 'It's so funny! A dog that smiles! Where did you get her?'

'She belonged to an old lady who has gone into hospital and can't look after her any more.'

Philippe looked stunned. 'I am impressed.'

'As I am with you,' replied Meredith. 'That's why I came. To apologize for jumping to the wrong conclusion about you.'

'That I like to stay up drinking all night with the lads?'

'*Précisément,*' Meredith conceded in her perfect French.

'And I thought you were a cold-hearted Anglo-Saxon who was only interested in money,' Philippe smiled.

'Just as I jumped to the wrong conclusion about Nelly. I decided she was the ugliest, fiercest dog I had ever seen – and look at her now!'

Nelly had clearly decided that Philippe was a friend and had gone to sleep on his feet, an expression of blissful contentment on her unprepossessing features.

'Perhaps we should start our acquaintance again?' he suggested with a smile. 'Philippe Latignac – *je suis enchanté de faire votre connaissance.*' His formal bow wouldn't have shamed the duke of St Savarin.

Meredith held out her hand, dimly remembering that at Meads they had been taught that to reply 'Pleased to meet you' was somehow non-U and the correct reply was 'How do you do?' But to Meredith's ears that sounded like Eliza Doolittle trying to speak posh. Anyway, the French rules were probably different, and who gave a damn anyway?

'Meredith Harding,' she replied with equal ceremony. 'Delighted to make your acquaintance.'

She glanced round to see what Jean-Christophe made of this exchange, only to discover that he had tactfully taken himself off to lay the tables and leave them alone. She really liked that boy.

'One thing puzzles me,' Philippe added as he let go of her hand. 'What will you do with the dog when you leave? Have her shipped to the East by freight, or find some owner here?'

Meredith smiled slowly. 'I'm not going back to the East. I'm determined to buy the Château de St Savarin and with my friend Joanna we're going to turn it into France's most romantic wedding venue!'

'I've never met the *châtelaine* of a château before.' Philippe bowed again, the twinkle back in his dark brown eyes. 'Welcome to Bratenac. I hope you will be very happy here.'

Sam Andrews' documents arrived by scan the next day and were immensely helpful in speeding things up. And when the duke and duchess grasped that Meredith would be a cash buyer, things started to move surprisingly quickly.

Not long after, Meredith got a call from Monsieur Martel, the lawyer. 'Madame Harding, I have good news. The necessary permits have been agreed and the duke and duchess have agreed to your offer. We will soon be ready to sign the *acte de vente*. Perhaps you and Madame Walker could come to my office next Tuesday morning?'

Deciding that she really ought to look the part, Jo celebrated by buying herself a new dress from the rack for sale in the *tabac*. Only in France, she told herself, would the tobacconist sell frocks, and not only that, elegant smart ones at that. She chose a dramatic one in red linen decorated with soft circles.

Meredith sported the look she had honed to perfection: chic but businesslike. It had a lot to do with cut and colour. The cut was always strict and the colour always between caramel and cappuccino.

'Congratulations,' smiled Monsieur Martel, when the signing was over. 'You are now the distinguished owner of the Château de St Savarin!'

As they came out of the lawyer's office, Jo got a text that the others were waiting in the Café de la Paix with a celebratory bottle of champagne. For once the cafe seemed to be unencumbered by the Bratenac Ladies' Luncheon Club, though with Guillaume smiling and twirling his moustache behind the bar, the news would very soon be reaching them.

'To weddings!' Meredith raised her glass. 'Long may they flourish!'

'Not that we're the best examples ourselves,' giggled Jo. 'I'm divorced and you've never even married!'

'You don't have to practise something yourself to believe in it!' Meredith replied sternly, then started to giggle too. 'It's all still a bit of a surprise, to tell you the truth. And then I think of what my dad would make of me buying our château, and I just have to laugh!'

Jo raised her glass again. 'To Meredith's dad!' she toasted. 'Smiling down at us from heaven!'

'What's that, Dad?' Meredith made as if listening to a voice from on high. 'Stop drinking all this bloody champagne and get down to it?' She turned to the others. 'You heard what the man said, it's all work from now on!'

'Actually,' Sophie pretended to look superior, 'some of us have already started! It's staggering, if you ask me, that their wedding business exists at all when they hardly even use social media. That's how every bride plans her wedding now and their website's something out of the Middle Ages!'

'Did they have websites in the Middle Ages?' Steph enquired, trying not to laugh.

'Of course they did,' David suggested, looking a bit more cheerful than he had lately. 'Haven't you heard of Ye Olde Instagramme?'

'Anyway,' Sophie insisted, 'we're going to have to get a move on. The wedding season's well underway and since people plan their weddings so far in advance, we'll miss out altogether unless we get some soon. And we definitely need to feature some real weddings on social media.'

'Can't we mock some up?' Jo suggested. 'Soph, you'd make a beautiful bride and maybe Jean-Christophe would pretend to be a groom!'

For some reason, Sophie blushed and looked appalled. 'I'm not sure he'd agree to that – after all, he's a chef!'

'Maybe we should get him to mock up some food, then. And I've always fancied myself as a bit of a florist.'

'Madame Suzi is excellent at designing interiors,' Guillaume interjected, his face all innocence.

Meredith stared at him, wondering if he was being deliberately malicious, but he simply beamed out his usual good-natured benevolence. Maybe he hadn't noticed what was going on between Suzi and David. Or maybe it was just that he was French.

'I'm not sure that's a good idea,' David blurted, reddening.

'Why ever not?' Steph asked. 'Oh, you mean because she's such a frightful predatory woman?'

Meredith's eyes widened. Did Steph know too? And yet everything suggested she had no idea her husband was in any way involved with Suzi. 'Anyway –' she assumed her CEO tone – 'let's all try and think up some good ideas to get our wedding season off with a bang. Sophie, why don't you concentrate on social media; Jo, could you think about some kind of promotional video?' Jo nodded, conscious again of a slight resentment at the way Meredith took over so completely.

Meredith, supremely unaware of any ruffled feathers, bull-dozed blithely on. 'Steph, I know you're not directly involved, but would you have time to think about local caterers? Meanwhile I'll look after dealing with Héloise and the duchess and all the moving arrangements so we can take possession as soon as possible.'

They'd finished their champagne, and real life beckoned. Paying the bill at the bar, Meredith found David discreetly by her side. 'I just wanted to let you know that it's not what you think,' he said in a low voice, making sure that Guillaume was the other end of the bar. 'It hadn't gone as far as you probably imagined, and seeing you gave me the shock I needed.'

'Well, thank God for that. How did she take it?'

'Not well, as a matter of fact.'

'Let's hope that having cast herself as the *femme fatale*, she doesn't live up to it and become the harpy from hell,' Meredith commented, then elbowed David sharply to prevent him replying. Guillaume was fast approaching with her change.

'Congratulations on the château, madame,' he announced as he handed over the money. 'We are all relieved it has not been sold to some rich stranger who visits only once a year. Weddings mean good business for everyone in Bratenac!'

'Thank you, Guillaume. We'll try to bring as many as possible.' She was about to follow the others when she felt David's hand detaining her. He had stopped dead and was gripping her arm painfully. 'You don't think she'd try and tell Steph?'

'I have no bloody idea. You know her better than I do,' Meredith shrugged. 'Would she?'

'I'm sure she wouldn't,' he replied, sounding as though it was himself he was trying to convince.

Nine

'That's exciting,' Meredith informed Jo. 'We actually own the vineyard as well!' Was there a hint of knowingness in her smile? 'Would you like to take it on? I have zero interest in growing the stuff, only drinking it.'

The truth was, Jo was quite interested in the business of winegrowing, and not just because of Liam. The idea of planting, tending and harvesting grapes had always held a kind of romance for her since her stay in France all those years ago.

All the same, she didn't feel very comfortable about being in charge of Liam when her feelings were already so complicated towards him. 'I think you'd better do it,' she replied, not looking at Meredith. 'I'm great at day-to-day organization. Ms Sensible and Practical, that's me. But give me a long-term business decision and I'm hopeless.' The thought flashed into her mind that Amanda, for whom Mark had dumped her, was neither sensible nor practical, but he'd gone off with her all the same. Stop that, she told herself firmly.

'All right,' Meredith shrugged. 'I just thought you might want to, that's all.'

'Thank you, but no, if you're OK with it.'

'It appears there's an existing contract with Liam where we pay for day-to-day running of the operation and share the profits two-thirds to one-third,' Meredith continued. 'It seemed rather steep to me, but according to the duchess it's the usual arrangement round here, so I see no reason to try and change it. He seems very effective at what he does.'

'Do tell him soon,' Jo urged suddenly. 'I imagine he may be worried about his future with all this change in the air.'

Meredith smiled. 'OK, yes. I will put hunky but efficient Liam out of his misery.'

Back in her room, Joanna caught sight of herself in her bedroom mirror and paused to look properly. Was it her middle-aged appearance that had put Liam off, rather than the embarrassment with the rabbit? The face that looked back at her was a conventionally pretty one, hair a safe colour between blonde and grey, in an equally safe bob beloved by middle-aged women throughout the home counties. Maybe she should opt for a rebellious pink streak? She rather admired that in other women. *You may think I'm ridiculous at my age, but I don't give a stuff!* seemed to be the message, and Jo applauded it. For similar reasons, she even rather admired Jackie from the luncheon club; she might be an interfering old bag, but that was clearly her attitude to life too.

She hadn't noticed Sophie coming in until her daughter's face appeared behind hers in the mirror. 'Trying to decide who is the fairest of them all?' teased Sophie.

Jo sighed. 'Hardly. I was thinking I look so boring that it's no wonder Dad left me.'

'Mum!' protested Sophie in tones of genuine outrage. 'What's happened to your healthy anger? This is classic stuff. If you don't express your anger, it turns in on itself and becomes depression! You should be telling yourself you're gorgeous!'

Jo shook her head and started to turn away. 'OK,' she smiled at last. It transformed her face. 'I'm Joanna Walker and I'm absolutely gorgeous!'

If only she could keep believing it.

'Well, you can't say the old duchess isn't a woman of decision!' Meredith announced when they came down for a pre-dinner drink. 'She wants to move out of the château next week!'

'You mean it will be ready then for us to move in?' Jo asked. 'Won't it need a lot of work?'

'It's like anywhere you buy, I imagine,' shrugged Meredith. 'You think it's OK, then they take down their pictures and the whole place needs redecorating! But . . .' She smiled broadly at the revelation. 'The duchess has sold me a lot of the furniture at a very reasonable price. She's picked out the best stuff, naturally. Some of the pictures are very valuable and she's taking those, but we'll have enough to get along with. Steph can advise us on where to pick up anything to fill the gaps – and anyway, you have some ideas about bridal suites, don't you, Sophie?'

Sophie nodded enthusiastically, eager to put her design plans into practice. 'There you are, Mum,' she teased Jo. 'I knew we should have bought that huge painting. I wonder if it's still there?'

'Should we start doing up the bedrooms, do you reckon?' Meredith pondered.

'Absolutely!' Sophie insisted. 'Even if it's only a lick of paint. Staying in the château will be an important part of the package.'

Steph, who had arrived with a tray of drinks, felt a sudden pang. She'd got used to having them all here and was going to miss them so much! Still, they would only be a mile away. The thought struck her, painfully, that their presence had been a welcome distraction from an unwelcome truth: that she and David seemed to have lost the closeness she had valued so much. She had to ask him now for the little caring gestures that had once been spontaneous – the cup of tea in bed when they'd been up late working; the glass of wine in the bath he used to bring her before the evening onslaught.

When they'd all left, she would have to face up to it. Something was wrong.

'So where's the divine Margot moving to?' Steph enquired. 'A flat in Paris, with any luck, so the lovely old duke can get the care he's going to need. I can't imagine Margot changing any nappies when he gets senile.'

They all tried not to giggle at this unlikely prospect.

'No,' commented Jo, 'she'll be out tending her secret garden. That's a woman's right in France, so she told me. An erotic playground for her and her lover.'

'I think I'll stick to climbing frames,' Meredith grinned. 'Or maybe the odd slide.'

'I don't know, Meredith,' Sophie dared to add. 'Philippe's pretty damn sexy, in my view.'

'*Can* a man his age be sexy?' asked Jo, trying to fill the suddenly tense moment with an outrageous question.

'Mum!' Sophie reminded her. 'You adore Harrison Ford and he's about a hundred and you've always fancied Bruce Springsteen, and what about Jeff Bridges? Don't say you haven't got a soft spot for him! And what about the wine manager?' she added naughtily. 'He's pretty attractive too.'

Jo thought of saying she didn't know what Sophie meant, but that would be silly. 'Liam's going to be working for us, so that makes the question of whether he's sexy irrelevant.'

'Lady Chatterley didn't think so,' prompted Meredith naughtily.

'Meredith!' Jo protested, then remembered that when they were all asked by their English teacher to name their favourite fictional character among all the Elizabeth Bennets, Dorothea Brookes and Jane Eyres, Meredith had said Constance Chatterley and there had been a stunned silence. Meredith had not been asked, as the others were, to explain why!

'You haven't changed one bit,' accused Jo, laughing. 'You pretend to be this hard-headed businesswoman but underneath it all you're still this feminist rebel!'

'Why do you think I didn't get married?' Meredith smiled back. 'No compromise! Smash the patriarchy!'

'Poor Philippe,' Sophie murmured to Jo. 'He's got a challenge in Meredith all right.'

After that, the whirlwind of planning the move took them all over, with another visit to the château, this time with paint charts and measuring tapes in hand, all of them caught up in the excitement that moving always entails. Fortunately, a load of their stuff had arrived courtesy of Liz, and both Jo and Sophie finally had something new to wear.

'Which room are you having?' Sophie asked her mum as they looked round the spacious apartment at the top of the château, which had been the duke and duchess's residence.

Meredith – without consulting the others, naturally – had opted for their old bedroom with its massive canopied four-poster which looked as if it had last been slept in by Louis XIV, plus its canopied bathroom overlooking the river.

Sophie was delighted with a much smaller room that had a similarly lovely view but would give her some scope to imprint her own personality. Glancing round, she felt that sudden spurt of excitement creating an interior can give you: an empty palette for something beautiful to emerge.

Joanna had chosen one of the four towers. It meant the bedroom was smaller and a hard-to-furnish octagonal shape, but it made her feel like a princess in a fairy tale. 'But don't wait for a prince to come and rescue you,' Jo told herself firmly. 'This princess will find her own destiny!'

At least, she certainly hoped so.

Over the next few days Steph took great pleasure in introducing Sophie to her favourite *brocante*, where she found a perfect desk to adorn her new room plus a few modern touches to mix in with the antiques to create a more contemporary style.

'Sophie, you *are* clever,' her mother declared when she'd installed her new purchases. 'It suddenly looks like something from *Interiors!*'

'Thanks, Mum.' She sat down at the new desk. 'Perfect! Now I can get out my laptop and get on with it.' The first thing she did was listen to Meredith's advice and see what their rivals were offering. Sophie, used to the world of events management with plenty of competitors fighting for the big clients and exhibitions, was still taken aback at just how many châteaux were offering weddings. On top of that were the many websites, from *Tie the Knot in France* to *My Romantic Wedding* to *One Divine Day*. They offered the entire package, from wedding planning to supplying the cake. As one of them cooed seductively: *All the bride needs to do is choose her dress!*

Meredith, meanwhile, was drinking espresso and waiting for the decorators to arrive. Steve the builder seemed to be reckoned by almost everyone as the best on offer: efficient, good-humoured and fair. Her instinct had been to go for someone else, since he was married to the appalling Jackie;

but comparing prices, Steve appeared to be the best value, and Meredith was a businesswoman. So she was waiting, coffee in hand, looking out at the view down to the river and humming to herself. She'd been impressed by Sophie's bedroom and had decided to take the same approach with a number of other rooms, blending antique with modern. Some of the grander ones needed to remain unquestionably in character, but adding some clear, light colours in the darker dining room would bring it back to life and give it at the same time a more contemporary feel. And Steve, it seemed, was the man to do it.

She could see him now arriving at the side of the château, beginning to unload his ladders at 7.55. Impressive. She'd expected him to be a chatterbox like his wife but Steve, who turned out to be a giant of a man, seemed quietly humorous and a man of few words. Jackie would have to work hard at pumping him for the gossip at the end of the day. Meredith suspected Steve would simply say he hadn't noticed anything, which suited her perfectly.

'Good morning, Steve!' she greeted him. 'Can I make you a coffee?'

Steve smiled. It was a slow, sweet smile. 'Tea would be nice.'

'Let me guess,' Meredith laughed. 'Earl Grey or builder's?'

'I'll take a drop of Lapsang Souchong, if you have any.'

Meredith smiled appreciatively. 'And how about the others?' She gestured to the three young men who seemed to trail Steve everywhere.

'The lads bring their own. Funny generation, this. Don't drink tea and they bring their own lunches – strange things made of rice and whatnot, when I prefer a nice ham sandwich from the cafe. Where would you like us to start?'

Meredith led him into the dining room, then went to get his tea. Jo and Sophie didn't seem to be up yet.

'Duchess gone already, has she?' he enquired calmly when she handed it over. 'Well, she hasn't got far to go. That funny new Lego house at the end of your drive, Jackie says. Strange people, the French, I've seen it time and time again. The English come here and buy the old wrecks and the French, even the snooty ones like the duchess, can't wait to move into the new builds with all mod cons. I suppose they've had it up to here with the upkeep, and they are getting on a bit and, of course, the old duke isn't too well. She's got a carer moving in, Jack says. Can't say I blame her, but poor old duke. Not sure he'll like that. As long as she doesn't take away his daily bottle of Bordeaux. He always says that's what keeps him going.'

Meredith might have smiled at the sound of the friendly relationship between Steve and the duke of St Savarin, if she hadn't been so stunned by his other revelation: Margot hadn't moved into an elegant apartment in Paris, but a funny little prefab house at the end of their drive, where she could keep a beady eye on everything that came and went at the château. And there wasn't a thing Meredith could do about it.

She looked down to find Nelly grinning up at her appealingly with an expression that said 'That's all very well, but where's my breakfast?'

Meredith bent down and fondled the dog's ears. 'And the worst thing is,' she confided to Nelly through gritted teeth. 'I bet that wretched Jackie woman knew about it all along!'

Jo finished arranging all the clothes Liz had sent in her wardrobe and chest of drawers. Liz seemed to have thoughtfully packed practically everything she possessed! To think only such a short time ago she had been stuck in Basingstoke, dreading hearing about Mark and Amanda's wedding – and here she was living in a French château, thinking about how to organize other people's weddings! No one could say life wasn't full of surprises.

On the terrace leading down to the vineyard she spotted Nelly trotting merrily along, tail up, enjoying the beautiful morning. It was another of life's unexpected turns that Meredith, so chic and businesslike, should have succumbed to the dubious charms of a such a disgraceful animal, albeit one with a lot of winning ways. But what was Nelly doing out anyway? She very much doubted Meredith was even awake at this hour. She'd better dress quickly and go investigate, in case Nelly had somehow escaped without anyone knowing.

She pulled on jeans and an old shirt, not even bothering with make-up, and headed down towards the terrace. For some reason the door from the drawing room was open – maybe Steve had already started decorating, and that was how the dog had got out.

Realizing how heartbroken Meredith would be to lose her, Jo started to sprint down the front steps, through the neat rows of vines, bright spring green with new growth, towards the river. Thank God for all that bloody yoga, she said to herself, grateful that all that getting up early and sitting in draughty gyms had actually been worth it and made her fit.

The dog was now out of sight. Jo stopped for a moment to think, but there was no logic to the path of a frisky dog on a bright spring day, so she started up again and careered straight into the arms of Liam, who had bent down to examine a vine.

'And good morning to you too,' he greeted her with a disarming smile. 'Are you chasing the disreputable dog? If so, you can relax. I just returned her to the kitchen and gave her some chicken from the fridge. I left her looking appealingly at Steve the builder's bacon sandwich.'

'She would!' Jo blurted, to cover her embarrassment as

he let her go. 'And he'll give her some, too. You're starting early.'

'We Kiwis are early risers. That damn Protestant work ethic. It's our number one characteristic.' Again, the disarming smile.

'I thought it was being bonded to the land,' Jo replied without thinking.

This time he laughed outright. 'Been reading up on the seven characteristics of the New Zealander, eh?'

Jo blushed furiously. He'd realize she'd been reading it because of him.

'It's a very well-known survey and a load of nonsense,' he added with a grin. 'So much for Kiwis being stoical. I get man flu with the best of them. And I don't always start this early. It's a busy time with the vines.'

'So when does the winegrower's year begin?' asked Jo, grateful to be able to change the subject.

'The new growth cycle begins in March. The sap starts rising in the vine branches as they grow and oozes through any scars left by pruning. Look,' he leaned over a vine branch and showed her the sticky liquid. 'The French say the vine is weeping!'

'Very poetic,' smiled Jo. 'I didn't know sap did actually rise. It reminds me of all those English folk songs about maidens and young men heading out on midsummer mornings.' Oh God, how had she got herself back on shaky territory?

'Very romantic. Our job is a bit more down to earth. Removing any branches that might weigh down the vine unnecessarily. Believe it or not, it's called suckering.'

Jo grinned. 'Very Groucho Marx.'

'But I'm probably boring you with too much detail. The short answer is yes, we get very busy from now on right up to the harvest.'

'Which I remember only too well. I didn't get stung by all those vine bugs without it being imprinted on my memory!'

A moment of silence fell between them and he seemed to be studying her. This could be the moment she dreaded: when he asked her how long ago it was that she'd been grape-picking she'd have to admit to being older than she looked – and probably quite a lot older than he was.

But he surprised her by turning away and looking round him. 'I love this time of year, when the vines are suddenly green. I like the neatness of the rows.'

She considered him for a moment. How old was he? She reckoned mid-fifties. Not gigolo material, at least. She must have been smiling to herself without even knowing it.

'Feel like sharing the joke? Have I said something embarrassing and colonial?'

Jo almost panicked. 'I was just thinking about John Cleese taking the piss out of your birthplace. You know he comes from Weston-super-Mare, which for some reason I always find incredibly funny!'

And suddenly, ridiculously, they were both laughing unstoppably.

Her friends had only been gone a few days and were anyway just around the corner when they could have gone home to the UK, but Steph found she was missing them incredibly. As she took out the tray of croissants that had been warming in the oven, the thought struck her with horrible force that she was actually rather lonely. How ridiculous! How could she be lonely when she had a house full of people, and a husband she not only loved but worked with?

She burned her hand without even noticing as she realized why. It was *because* of the husband she loved that she felt lonely.

147

Something had definitely changed.

'For God's sake, Steph!' David's voice cut through her panic. 'Put the bloody dish down. You've burned your wrist!'

Two things struck her: that he sounded really concerned, and that her wrist hurt like hell.

She put down the dish while David turned on the cold tap and held her hand under it until it felt numb.

'Madame!' Marcelline burst in. 'Where are the croissants? That new lady who arrived last night is complaining about the service here!'

Marcelline, used to everything working like clockwork, clearly took this personally.

'She is also asking for the menu for dinner tonight.'

At least Steph could provide this. Jean-Christophe had dropped one in and told her he would, if she was agreeable, bring his own supplies for the moment and then they could work out the best way of doing it in the future.

'Come on, let me take over.' David was sounding a bit like the old solicitous husband she was missing. 'Take a coffee and go and sit down in the orangery. The sun's round there already.' His smile of concern warmed her more than any sun could. Maybe things were all right after all.

'Mum! Meredith!' Sophie burst excitedly into the salon of their shared apartment. 'I've had this really great idea!'

Meredith smiled to herself. She often encountered youthful enthusiasm in business back home – no, it wasn't home any more, she reminded herself with a slight shock, *this* was home now – and it usually had to be treated tactfully, since it tended to be unworkable or even illegal.

'To get the château noticed I think we should come up with

some kind of introductory offer. We could it give a clever name – I don't know, *Launched with Love* maybe . . .'

'You mean a cheap deal?' Jo enquired. 'Because if so, I think that would be a mistake. We need to have an exclusive image – "Your own château for a day", that sort of thing. To start pricing ourselves too low usually leads to a lot of problems in my experience.'

'And in my experience your problem is you're always too cautious, Mum.' Meredith could see Sophie's spark of resentment, swiftly extinguished.

'That's because I've had to learn to be,' flashed back Jo.

Clearly working with a mother and daughter was going to have its issues, Meredith noted. 'Come on, gals, bear in mind what the old duke said.'

'What did the old duke say? Apart from *Thank Heaven for Leetle Girls*?' Sophie demanded. 'No, sorry, that was just the way he looked at me.'

'We're in the happiness business, remember?'

Ten

Steph sat in the tiny cubbyhole off the kitchen and stared glumly at her screen. Summer bookings were definitely down on last year. She sipped her coffee, wondering what on earth they could do about it. Maybe Sophie, who understood the digital world of Airbnb and Booking.com better than she did, might have some bright ideas.

She was about to turn off her laptop when she noticed an email from her sister Veronica. What on earth was that about? Veronica never just got in touch with chatty news about the family. She must want something. Probably, knowing Ronnie, free accommodation.

Steph and Ronnie had a rather prickly relationship, partly because fifteen years ago her sister had thrown away a perfectly good husband on the pretext that he was too dull and wouldn't do anything or go anywhere – whereas she, Ronnie, was a colourful and vibrant creature who needed change and excitement and expensive holidays (mainly funded by dull Derek). Then, when Derek had quite quickly found a replacement in his doting assistant, Ronnie had done nothing but moan. She had been moaning about it ever since.

She also regularly harped on about how broke she was, although Steph knew – partly because Ronnie had asked her own husband David's advice, on the grounds he understood money and was completely trustworthy – that her sister's divorce settlement had been a very generous one.

And then, when Jo's husband Mark had cheated her of money that was rightly hers, Ronnie had announced that it was probably Jo's own fault for trusting him too much. And Steph had found herself resenting her sister all over again.

Reluctantly, she opened the email.

In typical fashion, instead of contacting Steph with the happy news that her daughter Nicky was getting married – though this was obviously the case – Ronnie banged on at great length about Nicky having the mad idea of holding the wedding at a French château because lots of her friends had done it. Ronnie shuddered at the expense, but Nicola had been quite determined and was spending hours looking at wildly expensive weddings on websites. Seeing as Steph lived in the place, did she know anywhere that might be prepared to do a deal?

Steph sipped her coffee thoughtfully. It was a supreme irony that of course she knew just the place, and also that Meredith and Jo wanted exactly this kind of wedding – one where they could do a kind of trial run to hone all the different skills they'd need, as well as using the photos and testimonials for their website. Nicky was a pretty girl, too. Rather a surprise, Steph thought bitchily, since Ronnie was a big woman and her husband Derek was certainly no oil painting.

There was just one drawback: the state of Steph's own marriage. Something was wrong between them, and Ronnie would sniff it out like a terrier after a rat.

Steph shut her laptop with a snap. She wouldn't think about

it yet, but would concentrate on trying to do something about the situation with David. As soon as Jean-Christophe seemed OK she would plan a really special night out and make sure they actually made love for once when they got back.

She smiled to herself, imagining some different scenarios.

'You look happy.' David's voice penetrated her fantasy.

'Do I?' she turned and smiled at him. 'Why wouldn't I, with a lovely husband like you?'

David tried not to look too surprised. 'Right. Oh. Of course. Perhaps, as your lovely husband, I should share the news that some of the guests are leaving and want to tell you they've had a wonderful time.'

'Tell them to put it on TripAdvisor.' Steph didn't feel up to facing guests at the moment. 'We could do with a bit of good PR.'

David's smile disintegrated. 'What's the problem now?'

'Bookings looking a bit thin in the summer.'

'But that's when we're always full!' exploded David, as if it were somehow her fault.

'I know. I'm as annoyed as you are.'

'Well, we'd better think of something.'

She could hear an edge of panic in his voice she'd never picked up from him before.

She leaned over and shut the door behind him so that they were both enclosed in the tiny space, no bigger than a lift. 'David,' she asked, dreading his answer, 'is there something you're not telling me?'

David knew this was the moment he should own up: that he had messed up their finances by not knowing about this stupid tax and spending far more than they could afford on extending the terrace by the pool. It looked terrific, but actually the guests didn't use it as much as they'd expected. And it still wasn't paid for. It was only Steve's surprising generosity in not pushing for payment that had kept them from disaster.

'Well . . .' he began. Then he stopped. There was so much fear in Steph's eyes that he felt like more of a failure than ever. It was his job as a husband to protect her from this kind of worry. He'd find a way. It wasn't too late. And he'd tell Suzi that, much as he liked her, it couldn't go any further between them.

Relief flooded through him. If he had to tell Steph about his involvement with Suzi, it might be the end of everything – their marriage as well as their business. This way, at least, he had a reprieve.

She was still waiting for an answer.

'It's just that our finances could do with a bit of a boost. Nothing to really worry about. But it would be good to find ways of encouraging trade, especially off-peak during the week. I don't know, cooking courses or art lessons or some such thing.'

Steph thought of her sister's email. It would help on so many fronts. The girls needed a wedding, and they needed more business. The wedding would mean guests to put up, and they were the nearest B&B. She'd never thought of it before, but a link with the Château St Savarin could be really good for Fleur-de-Lis. The immediate family might stay in the château but nearby B&Bs would certainly benefit from putting up their guests. Until now the duchess had only put far posher places on her accommodation list but now things would be changing, and they should definitely make the most of it.

Steph took a deep breath and dived in. 'There is one thing . . .' She explained about Nicky's wedding, and David started to get excited. Coming from a family with a lot of brothers, he'd always thought she complained too much about her sister's habit of sticking her nose in other people's business.

'This is just what we need!' he said earnestly. 'People are much more value-conscious now with all the different websites, and we're placed really well for wedding overflow!'

'All right,' Steph agreed reluctantly. 'I'll mention it to the girls and see what they think.'

'Great.' He seemed suddenly almost a different person. 'And let's go somewhere really nice when Jean-Christophe does his next stint.'

'Have you seen this email from Steph?' Jo asked Meredith at breakfast the next morning. 'Her niece is looking for a château round here for her wedding. Sounds heaven-sent to me. We could offer her an attractive rate if she'll let us make the thing into a bit of PR and get a photographer to take some glorious photos!'

'As long as she doesn't look like the back end of a bus,' Meredith commented in her usual outrageous manner.

'Meredith!' Jo tutted. 'I don't know how you survived all these years in the workplace with attitudes like that!'

'Oh, come on, don't be so drearily PC!'

'As a matter of fact, she's very pretty,' said Jo reprovingly. 'Both Steph's nieces are, so maybe you'll get the other one as maid of honour in a two-for-one deal.' The irony was lost on Meredith, she noted. 'So what do you think?'

'I think it's brilliant,' Sophie interrupted. 'We really need some content for Instagram. As long as it's not too far ahead. Some brides book their weddings years before. When does she want to get married?'

'Steph says sometime late summer, but she's pretty flexible.

She thinks people spend far too long planning and wants hers to feel more spontaneous.'

'Spontaneous, yet meticulously planned by someone else!' laughed Meredith. 'That's the kind of spontaneity I like.'

'Blimey, that doesn't give us long!' yelped Jo.

'I think we should definitely go for it,' Sophie enthused. 'We could get stuck in straight away.'

'What if she or her mother's a nightmare?' Jo protested, faintly remembering something Steph had mentioned about her sister.

'That's something we'll just need to cope with,' Sophie dismissed. 'We'll have lots of Bridezillas to deal with. Not to mention mothers of the bride from hell. Good practice. Come on, Mum, let's go for it!'

'I agree,' seconded Meredith. 'Best way of learning is on the job.'

'All right then,' endorsed Jo. 'Where do we go from here?'

Steph finished changing to go out to dinner with David and surveyed herself in the long mirror. She'd made more effort than she had in months, getting out a sheath dress that showed up curves she'd forgotten she possessed, and washing and blow-drying her hair. She sprayed her wrist with perfume, sniffing it tentatively in case it had gone off because she wore it so rarely. Behind her wrists, on her neck, down her cleavage. Even a bit on the bed to make it smell sexy. She had already turned it down and put on the bedside lights. With Jean-Christophe taking on tonight's dinner, she felt free for the first time in months.

She remembered something she'd bought on the spur of the moment in the *pharmacie*, away from the inquisitive gaze of the woman who ran it. It was called Sexy Lube. It had remained unopened in the back of the cupboard till now. Smiling to herself, she tore off the packaging and put it in the drawer of her bedside table. She was feeling naughty and adventurous tonight. Maybe it was time to finally use the stuff. Even though she wasn't quite sure what you did with it.

But before that, she needed to answer Ronnie's email. Yes, she did know of the perfect château, as it happened. It was a romantic dream and not far away from Fleur-de-Lis, right on the banks of the river. It had just been taken over by some friends of hers and they were very enthusiastic. How big a wedding was Nicky planning?

Her usual friendly instinct was to invite them both over, but she needed to sort things out with David before unleashing her terrier sister into their lives, so she left it there for now. She'd wait and see what their plans were.

She'd just switched off her laptop when David appeared, bearing a glass of champagne. 'Why don't you have it in the bath?' he asked, just like old times.

'Thanks, love. What a nice idea.' She didn't admit that she'd already had a bath, as well as shaving her legs and eliminating any straggly pubes.

After he'd gone she took off her dress and made sure she was wearing her sexiest underwear, sipping the champagne and smiling to herself. It was going to be all right between them, she knew.

In the bedroom of her small house in the oldest part of Bratenac, Suzi was also making a thorough inspection of herself in her mirror. Looking like this took a lot of hard work, and sometimes she longed to let go a bit – but you simply couldn't afford to at her age, not if you were alone. Although Suzi wasn't planning to be alone for much longer.

Probably it had been her own fault, but her life had been littered with bastards: charming bastards, bastards who used her – even one memorable bastard who spent the night with her and then, to her eternal humiliation, tried to charge her for it. For the first time she could remember, a decent man had sailed onto her horizon, and she wasn't going to let him go.

The difficulty, of course, was his very niceness – the thing that made him different and desirable. He was, she could sense, riven by feeling loyal to his wife, yet wanting someone who made him feel appreciated. Any other man would have jumped into bed with her already. Seduction was supposed to be all about signals, and she'd given him more green lights than the Orient Express. But he was still hovering on the brink.

So far, she'd respected it, understanding that affection was an important tool in landing him, instead of jumping on him and unzipping his fly with all the subtlety of a Russian hooker.

But she was beginning to lose patience. Soon she'd have to take drastic action.

If only she could think what action that should be.

And she'd have to keep under Jackie's radar, too. She added another layer of black mascara and gave the whole thing some serious consideration.

David had thought hard about tonight. Bratenac tended to have restaurants that were all about the food rather than an atmosphere of intimacy, but there was one he'd noticed in the old town that seemed unusually dark and candlelit, so he booked that. It was called La Pomme d'Amour – the apple of love – perhaps in some veiled reference to Aphrodite and the golden apple.

'What a lovely place,' commented Steph as she sat down

opposite him a little later. 'I've never noticed it before. But then I suppose I'm usually scurrying off to the market to buy exciting onions.'

'You work so hard,' David sighed, as if this was somehow his fault.

Steph reached out for his hand across the table, recognizing his comment as the olive branch it was intended to be.

'So do you.' She squeezed his hand affectionately.

'I'm not always sure you think so,' he smiled at her. She'd forgotten how attractive his smile was – in fact, how attractive he was altogether.

'I just get grouchy sometimes, that's all,' Steph apologized. 'You shouldn't mind me. You know I love you.'

'Do I?' The uncertainty in his voice took her aback.

'Yes. Let's get a drink.' She signalled to the waiter, who poured them both a glass of champagne. She held hers up. 'To us. We've been together a long time. Sometimes maybe we forget to appreciate each other.'

His eyes held hers with a sudden intensity and he knew that he had to tell her the truth about the business, even though it might spoil their evening.

He took her hand. 'Steph, there's something I need to tell you . . .'

To his surprise, Steph shook her head. 'Not tonight,' she said fiercely. 'I knew there was something going on. Is it over?'

'Oh . . .' he looked startled. 'Yes. How did you . . . ?'

'I'm your wife, David. I know you inside and out. Besides –' she smiled at him with a tenderness that tore his heart – 'you're a terrible liar. It's one of the things I love about you.'

He reached out and touched her face. 'The thing is . . .' He stopped suddenly, his eyes on the window. Suzi stood outside, staring in.

Seconds later, Steph turned round to see what had caught his attention. There was no one in the street except a disappearing figure in a leopardskin coat.

'Let's order,' David insisted, suddenly brusque. 'I think I need a large steak.'

'David,' she shook her head, laughing, trying to recapture the mood of moments ago, 'you always need a large steak.'

He couldn't tell her after all. They'd invested everything in Fleur-de-Lis. How could he confess that it was all down to his stupidity? And what was Suzi doing staring in like that? Oh Jesus, he needed to sort out his life or he might as well jump in the Savarin River. Maybe they could borrow some more from the bank. But he knew that was a fantasy, just like his answer that it was all over with Suzi. How had he let his life get in this stupid bloody mess?

Steph kept up a flow of bright conversation for the rest of the evening, but she knew something was wrong, and had no idea what. By the time they got back to Fleur-de-Lis everyone was in bed. The kitchen was tidy and immaculately clean. How wonderful, thought Steph. It usually took her hours.

There was a note from Jean-Christophe that all seemed to have gone very well. Even the vegetarian option had been popular.

'He seems quite a find, that boy,' commented David. 'I'll just go and lock up.'

Steph smiled. 'See you in a moment.' And then added softly, 'Don't be too long!'

She almost ran upstairs, undressed quickly and slipped into the sexy silk nightgown she'd bought in the market, which managed to look reassuringly Bond Street. The lighting was already low and flattering.

David arrived ten minutes later and for some reason undressed in the bathroom.

'Come on,' Steph murmured, holding the covers open invitingly.

David slipped in beside her. She began to caress him in the way she knew he liked.

He turned abruptly away. 'Stop, Steph,' he whispered, his voice full of anguish. 'I don't think I can . . .'

When she woke up the next morning Steph found a note from David on the bedside table that he had gone running, plus a cooling cup of tea. She knew she ought to get up and see to the guests, but for once she didn't have the energy. Instead she put her head back under the duvet and went back to sleep. She was roused not long afterwards by the phone ringing, and she reached out for it groggily.

'Stephanie!' The voice that greeted her dripped with reproach. 'Why didn't you tell me your friends had opened a château!'

Steph pulled herself up. Only her sister Ronnie was capable of such a finely honed tone of guilt-inducing reproof, especially when she'd just contacted her with this very information.

'Nicola picked it up on the internet!' Veronica continued unstoppably. 'Your friend's daughter Sophie's been doing a blog about launching a wedding château. Apparently it's going to be the most romantic wedding venue in France, and it's just next door to you. It's being run by your best friends and you didn't even tell me!'

Steph sat up and reached for her tea. She was going to need it. 'Don't you ever open your emails?' Steph asked impatiently. 'I sent you one yesterday telling you all about it.'

'Oh, well, I've been very busy with all this wedding stuff,' Ronnie replied unapologetically.

'They haven't actually opened yet, but in Nicky's case they're even prepared to give her a special deal, as long as she's happy to be their poster girl and appear in all the social media.'

'Have you met my daughter Nicola? She'd be in seventh heaven. She already spends half her life practising what her sister Lara calls her selfie face. Look, Steph, the thing is . . .'

Steph guessed what was coming next and considered diving back under the duvet.

'Could we pop over and see what it's like? I'm sure you could squeeze us in somewhere in your vast mansion. We don't mind sharing,' Ronnie offered generously. 'Though if there were a room each, it would be even better. Nicola's such a light sleeper.'

'I'll look at the bookings when I get up,' Steph agreed reluctantly. Saying no to Ronnie had always been like trying to scale Everest in stilettos: you might as well give up before you started.

'You're not still in bed, are you?' Ronnie persisted. 'You're forever going on about how much hard work it is running a B&B. What's happening to your guests? It's after nine, you know.' If *she* were running the B&B, her tone implied, she would be far more efficient.

'Marcelline is looking after them,' snapped Steph ungraciously. 'And David will be back from his run by now.'

'I didn't know David went running.'

'He does when he wants to think about something.' Damn, she shouldn't have even given that much away.

Ronnie instantly picked up the uncertainty in her sister's voice. 'You two are all right, aren't you?' she enquired.

'Yes, thank you, Ronnie. David and I are perfectly all right.'

'OK, OK, just asking. You'll let me know about the room? Soon.'

It was more command than request. Oh Christ, what was

she letting herself in for? 'Yes. Bye, Ronnie.' Steph put down the phone and closed her eyes. Maybe the girls could find someone else to have their wedding at the château.

She had just put her bare feet on the floor when her mobile rang. It was Meredith. 'Morning, Steph. Just a quick one. Jo didn't think we'd been clear enough when we saw you. We're all really excited about your niece getting married here. The timing sounds just right, and much better it's someone we know for our first time out. Especially if we can use the wedding pictures for promotional purposes. Do you think she'll go along with that?'

All Steph's thoughts about finding someone else sounded lame under this onslaught, even to her. 'Oh yes, she'll go along with that all right. I've just been talking to her mother. They both want to come over and have a look as soon as possible.'

'That's wonderful! I'll tell the others.'

Steph closed her eyes. She hoped she hadn't just made a mistake of epic proportions.

Eleven

'Wake up, *paresseux!*' Philippe nudged his sleeping son. 'Time to get up!'

Jean-Christophe opened his eyes reluctantly to find his father smiling down at him, several days' stubble blurring his chin as usual. 'Let's go and catch that uncatchable carp, shall we?'

He pulled himself upright and found a steaming black coffee thoughtfully placed at his bedside. 'I am not lazy,' he protested, sipping it as he pulled on his clothes. 'I was cooking for the English last night till gone midnight.'

'And how were they, the English, did they appreciate your efforts?'

'*Absolument*,' Jean-Christophe nodded. 'They ate everything, even the vegetarian choice!' He knew perfectly well there was only one English person who interested his father and she was tucked away up at the château, but he couldn't resist this dig at Philippe's reluctance to go veggie, at least for part of his menu.

He watched as his father packed coffee, a fresh baguette, hooks, sweetcorn, hempseed and raw minced steak into his knapsack.

'*Alors*, he likes steak tartare, this uncatchable carp?'

163

'He is French, after all,' grinned Philippe. 'Maybe not understanding this is why no one has succeeded in catching him.' He reached for two pairs of waterproof waders. 'Grand-père always talked of this monster fish when he took me out as a boy. Maybe he was related to our fish.'

'So how heavy is this monster?'

'They say thirty kilos.'

'Thirty kilos! That is more than a baggage allowance!' protested Jean-Christophe.

'If you flew with a carp in your luggage, *bien sûr*,' replied Philippe.

Jean-Christophe grinned and finished his coffee before getting up to dress. They both knew they didn't have a chance in hell of catching the carp. The venture was about bonding, because his father still worried that he'd screwed up his son's childhood through his own selfish ambition. So although it was still dark and cold and foggy, he pretended it was as exciting as a childhood adventure. '*Allons-y alors!* As long as no one sees me in this ridiculous garment.' He gestured to the rubber wader suit that went right up to his armpits. 'Not exactly John Galliano.'

'Don't worry.' Philippe ruffled his son's long hair. 'The fashion police aren't up yet. And you'll be glad of it when we meet our fish.'

By the time they reached the banks of the Savarin the sun was beginning to light up the sky with a faint pink glow reminiscent of the palest Provencal rosé, making the trees stand out against the lightening sky. A faint mist gradually replaced the fog, rising gently from the water and giving the morning a magical, mystical feel, as if it were completely out of time. Jean-Christophe felt grateful to experience it while having no desire to repeat it soon, though he would tactfully refrain from telling his father so.

Enjoy the moment was his mantra and he intended to, even though the moment he would have preferred would have been to stay tucked up warm in bed.

'Grand-père taught me to fish.' Philippe cast off the rod until the hook settled about four metres from the shore.

Jean-Christophe smiled and didn't say that he'd got the message: fishing for carp was a father–son thing, like learning football or going together to a bar. 'Can you fix the net under the water near the bank?'

'For when we catch the monster?'

'Of course.'

They both sat silently on portable stools, neither needing to speak, and studied the reflection of the light on the water. It was extraordinarily beautiful and eerily peaceful at the same time.

'Coffee?' Philippe asked, after almost half an hour had passed and the sun had risen above the treetops and was beginning to offer some welcome heat. 'It'll warm you up! According to Grand-père there are two useful things you can learn from fishing – to catch a fish you need first, patience and second, cunning!'

Jean-Christophe nodded as Philippe poured two small cups and smiled as he added a thimble of cognac. It was indeed warming. As he knocked it back, he caught a flash of movement towards the middle of the river. 'Look,' he pointed out, hearing the excitement in his own voice. 'There! Halfway across! It's a big fish!'

They stood up slowly. 'Careful not to let your shadow fall on the water!' Philippe whispered. 'The fish senses it.'

They stood silent as statues, eyes fixed on the water. There was definitely something large there. A sudden tug on the line told them that it had taken the bait.

'Wait –' Philippe's voice was suddenly urgent – 'sometimes they get the bait without the hook. Wait till we see him before you try reeling him in.'

In the intensity neither of them had noticed a slim figure, swathed in expensive-looking scarves and elegant Hunter boots, approaching along the riverbank with a large and slobbery black-and-white dog.

'You're up with the *alouette*,' remarked a vaguely familiar voice behind them, just as the dog began to bark hysterically and run along the side of the river, almost throwing itself in, so eager was it to pursue whatever was moving in the water.

With a flash of its powerful tail, the fish dived deep into the depths of the river, releasing itself in its fury from the hook buried in the bait, and disappeared.

'It's gone!' Jean-Christophe stated in anguished tones.

'Indeed it has,' agreed Philippe, through gritted teeth.

Meredith witnessed the split second when he almost lost his temper. She saw him struggle against shouting at her for not having the good sense to restrain her animal and force himself to exert some existentialist calm. It was clear that she had not only interrupted an important moment of father–son bonding, but also scared away the fucking fish.

'Good morning, Mademoiselle Meredith, you too are up very early,' Philippe greeted her ruefully. 'You almost witnessed my son here make his first catch.'

'Philippe, Jean-Christophe . . .' Meredith replied, looking pained. 'How can I apologize for Nelly's disgraceful behaviour? Not to mention that of her owner? Was it a big fish?'

They both shrugged in an inimitably Gallic manner, playing down the importance of their loss while still managing to convey that, yes, it had been a very big fish.

Nelly approached and lay down between them with paws

and ears flattened, the very portrait of abject abasement, until both burst out laughing and Jean-Christophe, clearly a secret dog lover, dropped to his knees and stroked her wrinkled fur. Nelly instantly rewarded him with one of her disarming smiles.

'I love this dog!' Philippe watched his son making lifelong friends with the disgraceful bulldog. Maybe he'd longed for a dog as well as a mother.

'I am genuinely very sorry.' Meredith knew better than to say that it was only a fish.

'It would probably have swum off anyway,' Philippe smiled. 'Do you walk her here every morning?'

'So that you can fish somewhere else?' Meredith replied.

'I was just thinking that it must be very pleasant.'

'It is. I can't tell you how life-enhancing it is to hear birds instead of nothing but traffic, as I did for so many years in Hong Kong and Singapore. Not that I didn't enjoy them greatly in other ways,' she added.

'It must be a very different life.'

'Yes. But then, you chose a very different life too.'

Philippe acknowledged this with another shrug. 'So how are things going up at the château?'

'Exciting. Scary. Good, I think. We are still in the middle of a lot of renovations.'

'And you have new neighbours, I hear.'

'Yes.' Meredith took a deep breath. 'The less said about that the better, I think.'

'Don't worry. Margot will have her hands full with her husband. He's really quite ill, I think.'

'I'm sure you're right,' lied Meredith. Margot, she suspected, would be out of the sickroom at the first sign of serious illness. As long as she wasn't back up at the château continually asking for a cup of caviar.

Behind them, Jean-Christophe was still staring intently into the water, with Nelly devotedly at his feet, looking up at him as though she'd just met the two-legged hero she'd been waiting for all her life.

'If it isn't too terrible a pun,' Philippe pointed out to his son, 'I think you're finally hooked on fishing!'

'Dad, look!' Behind them in the water there was a sudden flurry of movement and a definite tug on the line. 'It's him! I know it's him!' breathed Jean-Christophe.

Meredith was about to dive on Nelly and pick her up bodily, but with her new hero next to her she sat quiet as a lapdog in a handbag, giving every impression of a bored girlfriend at a cricket match who had no idea what was going on but was eager to give the right impression.

'Hold off for a few more seconds,' Philippe advised, almost as excited as his son. 'Now! Start to reel him in. Slowly now, don't jerk, or he might get off the hook. Easy, that's it!'

Resisting all temptation to wrest the rod out of his son's grip, Philippe watched with mounting pride and excitement as Jean-Christophe slowly landed the wildly struggling fish. The excitement even infected Meredith, who watched entranced.

'I'll get the net and put it under him. There!' Philippe closed the net over the fish and raised it out of the water onto the bank.

'I don't think it's the monster,' Jean-Christophe announced, studying it as it struggled.

'Maybe not, but it's pretty damn big!'

Carefully, Philippe undid the top of the net, and Jean-Christophe lifted out the enormous carp. Philippe delved into what seemed to be a bottomless knapsack for some hanging scales. 'Nearly nineteen kilos! It must be almost a record for the river round here!'

Meredith got out her phone. 'Here, I'll take the official photograph, shall I?'

Jean-Christophe stood proudly holding his prize carp as the fish obligingly sat in his arms, its round O of a mouth moving as it took in deep breaths of air, its small black eye fixed on its watery home.

Meredith took a whole selection, just in case. 'Come on, Philippe. One with the proud father!'

Philippe laughed and joined his son and the pair stood side by side, arms round each other with the fish in the middle, bathed in pride and sunshine. Then, just as suddenly, they both ran to the bank and tossed the gargantuan fish back in the river with a jubilant cry.

Oh well, thought Meredith, better than ending up on the menu, I suppose.

She glanced at Nelly, still looking up adoringly at her new hero. 'And you're no better than any other silly female. A sexy French smile and you'll follow him anywhere!'

She looked up to find Philippe's eyes on her. She dipped down to fondle Nelly's ears as she smiled back.

'So how are you getting on with that *vigneron* of ours?' Margot enquired. 'Sorry, of course, he's your *vigneron* now, silly me.'

Jo wasn't quite sure how it had happened, but Margot was sitting in their cosy kitchen drinking a cup of coffee.

The truth was, she had no idea. She and Liam always seemed to get on well, but he had never brought up his dinner invitation again. She had found herself watching him from her bedroom window that morning as he tended the vines.

Jo ducked the question and asked instead what was happening in the vineyard at the moment.

'My dear,' almost giggled Margot, 'I have no idea. I left all that to Liam. You must ask him. I'm sure he'd be only too happy to explain it to you. From that, I deduce that your relationship has not been flowering along with the almond trees outside in the garden. I love it when they blossom. It tells me spring is finally here.' She smiled out at the garden, imagining she still owned it rather than the tiny patch of grass in front of her new home. 'My dear, you will have to be more direct with him. You can flirt with a Frenchman, play a game of hide and seek that is very sexy and exciting –' she emphasized this with a rather scary wink – 'but with a New Zealander, no. You must make your intentions clear.' She paused as if considering whether to go on. 'Perhaps losing his wife has made him more nervous of playing his hand. But remember this.' She leaned forward. 'I have often noticed widowers who have had a happy marriage make the best husbands! They know what real happiness is, you see.'

'His wife?' Jo felt a jolt of surprise that he hadn't mentioned this. Poor man. Would that be better or worse than her own situation? At least he hadn't been replaced by someone else. She suddenly felt ashamed at making the comparison. 'I see. Well, thanks for the advice, Margot, but my intentions aren't even clear to myself.' That wasn't true, she realized as she said it.

To her relief, Nelly chose that moment to run into the kitchen and offer an appealing paw to Margot, whose response was to scream and drop her coffee cup, managing to scald Jo in the process.

'*Merde, alors*, this dog is wild and dribbling. I think it has the rabies!' she accused.

Nelly looked at her sadly.

'That's just Nelly,' Jo assured her. 'She dribbles a lot, but she's the most gentle animal.'

'I think it is time I left,' Margot insisted hastily. 'Before it bites me. I cannot afford to have the rabies just when I must be strong for my poor husband.' She adopted a noble expression which almost had Jo in fits.

'Goodbye, then, Margot. Thanks for the advice.'

At last Margot departed, leaving behind a cloud of Guerlain's Shalimar and a faint whiff of Gauloise, a heady mix that Jo imagined was rather how a Parisian brothel might smell.

Meredith arrived in the kitchen moments later to make herself a coffee. She sniffed the air. 'That wasn't Margot, by any chance?' she asked suspiciously.

'Who else wears half a bottle of Shalimar before breakfast?' Jo replied.

'The old witch. Snooping around, I suppose. What did she have to say?'

But at this Jo became curiously evasive. 'I must get back to my list of potential caterers,' she announced briskly. 'Most of the websites offer clients a choice of four for their weddings. Any news from Steph on the niece front?'

'Good, apparently. They want to come and see the château.'

Steph herself turned up half an hour later. 'My sister Veronica and her daughter Nicola want to come and meet everyone, if that's all right with you all,' she announced.

'Of course. All brides do that,' Jo agreed. 'I'm sure Soph will be fine with it too. Where is she, by the way?'

'Talking to Steve the builder about which shade of eau de nil among about two dozen options is the right one for the new dining room,' Meredith replied. 'She's good at that.'

Jo grinned at them. 'It is exciting, isn't it? Starting this whole new life running a château!'

Steph wished she could agree. Somehow lately she'd lost the feeling of loving her life and instead wondered what the hell had happened to it. And now she'd better go home and get ready for the arrival of her annoying sister, as well as coping with a houseful of demanding guests. She wondered if she should point out that dealing with Ronnie might be hellish rather than exciting, but somehow it didn't seem fair. She'd get back and have a large glass of rosé to take her mind off it. Dangerous, she knew, but effective all the same.

Meredith and Jo tracked Sophie down in the rather grand library she had adopted as her office. Sophie, the very essence of the modern young woman with her sleek laptop open in front of her, sat amongst plaster mouldings of mythical animals and several chandeliers that wouldn't have shamed the Palace of Versailles, with a vast fireplace behind her supported by two nereids. Caught up in what she was doing, she seemed oblivious to her surroundings.

'Do you know,' Sophie exclaimed irritably, 'Steve's just told me we need a new safety certificate for every single fire extinguisher in the château! And one of the caterers says you need a licence even to serve orange juice, let alone our wine for the wedding guests! French bureaucracy is an absolute nightmare. Mum,' she turned to Jo, 'you should really be taking on some of this. I'm in charge of décor!'

'Except that I didn't know about it either,' Jo replied defensively.

'Well, maybe you should have,' snapped Sophie. 'After all, this is a business now, not a holiday.'

Meredith stepped in tactfully. 'Look, we're all learning and as we do, we can make the roles we all take more clearly defined. OK?'

'Sorry,' Sophie apologized instantly. 'I shouldn't have snapped. It's just that I suddenly see how much there is to do.

By the way . . .' She put down her paint charts and gave them her full attention. 'What do you think of the idea of getting Liam to offer a wine tasting as part of the wedding package – Heloise said it was very popular. A lot of châteaux offer that, and then have their own wines with the meals. They often do a special Cuvée Brenda, or whatever the bride's name is. Isn't that cute? We should do that too, don't you think?'

She paused to take a breath while Jo and Meredith smiled to see her throwing herself so enthusiastically back into the fray.

'I'll take on the licences,' Meredith offered. 'And couldn't you get Steve to do the fire extinguishers? He's bound to have a buddy in the department; I promise you, Steve knows everyone.'

'But he doesn't even speak French,' protested Sophie, unconvinced.

'He has his own way of communicating, believe me. He just makes a joke about being a henpecked husband, and they all look at this great big bloke and roar with laughter, and after that he has them eating out of his hand. The real joke is that he *is* a henpecked husband!'

'Sophie, Steph's niece Nicola wants to fly over with her mother and have a look. Is that OK with you?'

'Of course. That's usual. At real weddings they show two or three prospective couples round on the big day.'

'What, at the actual wedding?'

'Don't worry, they don't pretend to be wedding crashers. They just look on from afar.'

'Sounds rather rude to me. Given how much people spend on weddings these days—'

'. . . or their parents,' cut in Jo tartly.

'I'm not sure that's true any more,' Sophie commented. 'A

lot of couples pay for it themselves, so they get control. Sometimes they actually charge their guests if they're getting accommodation too.'

'No!' Jo protested, scandalized.

'I've just been reading about it online. You wouldn't believe how many wedding websites there are now. And quite a lot of them are in France.'

'Should we be discouraged by the competition?' Jo asked anxiously.

'Nah,' Sophie grinned, brimming with youthful confidence. 'Our château's going to be the best!'

It had just struck midday and a few hundred yards away, at their new home, the duke and duchess of St Savarin were having their first drink of the day.

One reason Margot had been keen on moving to this single-storey residence was that at any time after one'clock in the afternoon, the duke had a tendency to fall over if not carefully watched. They both liked a drink, but the duke liked it more than most.

'So how are they doing up at the château?' he enquired.

'Ruining my décor, for a start,' replied the duchess tartly. 'Can you imagine? Introducing modern furniture into a seventeenth-century setting? Sacrilege!'

'Calm yourself, my dear, have another glass.' Margot watched him beadily as he topped up the mere half-inch she had consumed and more or less filled up his own.

'Louis! *Buvez plus lentement!*' she reprimanded. 'You will finish the bottle and it is only just midday. I could hear the Angelus sound from the convent in the village.'

The duke looked at the bottle with fascination, as if by some reverse miracle it had emptied itself.

The duchess sipped her wine and smiled. 'Mark my words, Louis. They are amateurs. They will make a mess of it, wait and see.'

'Margot, my love –' the duke held up his rapidly emptying glass as if in a toast – 'anyone who didn't know you better would think you sounded pleased.'

'I've been studying all our rivals' websites about catering and florists,' Sophie announced to her mother and Meredith as they all sat in the sunny orangery. 'Plus made one or two innocent calls pretending to be a blushing bride,' she confessed with a grin.

'I'm sure you made a lovely bride,' Jo teased her.

'The usual package seems to offer a list of caterers and one or two favoured florists. Sometimes the bride has her own favourite florist and occasionally, God help us, someone in the family wants to do it. The woman at Be Mine in France said they strongly discourage it but you get the odd person who has a fit at the cost of the flowers. They are a bit eye-watering, but I think that's the same at home.'

Jo nodded in agreement. 'Liz next door told me her daughter spent more on the flowers than the honeymoon. Whatever happened to little posies of wildflowers?'

Sophie shrugged. 'It's all part of the production these days. Weddings are more like Hollywood musicals now, starring Scarlett O'Hara in Vera Wang. On the catering front, I've had three sample menus in: one classic French, one very regional and the third a bit more Middle Eastern. That's all the vibe nowadays. Blame Ottolenghi. The fourth caterer decided he was too busy to pitch.'

'Let's see the menus, then,' Meredith requested. Sophie handed them over. 'Mmm. Scallops or lobster, followed by carré of lamb or pan-fried monkfish, crème brulee or mini pastries. That sounds nice. And rich. What's the local one?'

'*Salade Périgourdine*,' Sophie produced another menu. 'That's duck salad with a bit of fruit and nuts, basically. Very fresh and delicious . . . *Filet de boeuf sauce Périgueux*, with truffles, wouldn't you know? Then *tarte aux noix* or pastry with *Mara des Bois* strawberries. Have you tried them? They're amazing. Small and deep red, like rubies. The hip one is hot meze followed by lamb with roasted aubergine spiced with cumin and sumac. Dessert of Turkish yogurt with walnuts and honey, or mini baklava things.'

'What about the fourth?'

'They're the ones that dropped out. I did wonder . . .' She paused a moment.

'Yes?' prompted Meredith.

Sophie took a deep breath. 'Whether you might like to ask Philippe to pitch? It seems silly to have a famous chef on our doorstep and not ask him.'

'Not a good idea,' Meredith insisted, trying to move the conversation on.

'Why is that?' persisted Sophie, knowing perfectly well why. And if she didn't, the kick under the table from her mother would have reminded her.

'He's far too busy already. He says he left Paris for an easier life. I doubt catering for demanding British brides was what he had in mind.'

'What a pair you are!' Sophie said naughtily. 'Mum won't deal with Liam, and you think Philippe's too busy to cook for our weddings. Well, I have no such qualms with Jean-Christophe. I think he should definitely put in a pitch!'

Twelve

Liam inspected the new growth in the vines with care. The buds were beautiful: the blossom delicate and pale, patterned almost like lace. His task this morning was to remove any excess buds or branches that could add too much weight and lessen the quality of the grapes it produced.

The vineyard, with its neat rows, looked satisfyingly tidy. Soon it would be time to spray any weeds that the spring warmth had encouraged into wild abundance in the spaces between the vines. He would have to hire a special attachment for his small tractor, designed to be pulled along the two-metre gap. Many vineyards had changed to three-metre spaces so that normal-sized tractors and harvesting machines could fit, but St Savarin had stuck to the old width of the horse-drawn plough. The thought gave Liam a deep sense of satisfaction, that the château had kept this link with the past.

He thought suddenly of his wife Anne-Marie, with her enjoyment of all things connected to the past, and how she would have loved living here. How unfair it seemed that she had died before they had children. At least if they'd been able to do that, he would have had a part of her with him still: a small reminder of the vibrant personality who had shared his life.

He turned his face to the sun and closed his eyes. She had loved the sun so much.

He must stop thinking like this. She would not have wanted him to. 'You'll be fine,' she'd joked in the last days of her illness. 'There are plenty of desperate women out there, and you're actually quite attractive.'

She'd been right about the women, but none of them had appealed to him for long. None of them had shared his love of the land or had a trace of his wife's quirky sense of humour. Seeing Jo had given him an almost electrical shock because there was such a strong physical resemblance between them. And for a moment, when the dog had appeared with that ridiculous rabbit vibrator in its mouth, he had half expected her to roar with laughter as Anne-Marie would have done. Instead she'd looked mortified. He understood that, of course. Maybe even Annie would have been a shade embarrassed at something so personal, though he doubted it. Brits were hard to read and he had seen flashes of humour from Jo since. But then he'd heard about the château and realized she would, in a manner of speaking, be his boss. A fierce streak of ridiculous pride in him had made him baulk at that. What if it went further, then fell apart between them? He'd have to leave. 'Don't shit on your own doorstep' had always been his father's pithy advice. He suspected that in this, for once, Dad was right.

He caught sight of a few of the Blonde d'Aquitaine cattle he had introduced and smiled. Not only did they look picturesque in the landscape but, his practical Kiwi outlook reminded him, their dung was essential for the organic fertilizer he had persuaded Margot as his employer to use here, instead of the destructive chemicals used by other growers.

Employer – how he hated that word.

He shook himself, rather like Nelly would when she was wet. Being realistic was another quality Kiwis were supposed to possess. Hah.

Watching discreetly from her bedroom window, Jo smiled and wondered what was going through his mind, especially when his smile suddenly vanished. She had been studying him for the last five minutes while she should have been helping sort licences for the fire extinguishers. Maybe he was thinking about his wife.

She heard her daughter's footsteps coming upstairs, and turned away from the window abruptly.

Jackie scanned the members of the Bratenac Ladies' Luncheon Club suspiciously.

'Where's Suzi?' she demanded, looking keenly round.

'Not coming,' offered Mandy meekly, sounding as apologetic as if it were she who'd gone AWOL. 'I did pop round and knock on her door but she said she wasn't feeling up to it. Some kind of bug going round, apparently.'

'Yes,' Jackie snapped back. 'It's called guilt. Suzi is definitely up to something. She's been avoiding me as if I had the clap. And we all know why, don't we? She's got herself involved with David Adams from Fleur-de-Lis.'

'Oh, surely not, Jackie?' protested Shirley, the happy house-wife. 'I really don't think she would!'

'Guillaume saw them. And why else would she be avoiding me?'

No one had an answer to this. They studied their menus diligently as if the answer might lie among the *foie gras* and the *pommes sarladaises*.

'The question is,' Jackie persisted sternly, 'how are we going to put a stop to it before it gets out of hand?'

Since no immediate suggestions were forthcoming, she summoned Guillaume. 'Tell me the truth, Guillaume. Have you seen Suzi in here lately?'

The barman shifted from one foot to the other like an anxious stork. Even his moustache lacked its usual perky insouciance. 'Well . . . as a matter of fact . . .' he bumbled.

'Let me answer the question for you,' Jackie replied, stoking up her anger like a Valkyrie in leisurewear. 'The short answer is no, you haven't, which is very curious since she usually hangs about here every night until you, Guillaume, have to pour her into a taxi at closing time. So where exactly is she?'

She fell silent, lost in thought, while the others selected their starters.

'Right,' she concluded. 'Janine, your dogs are a perfect cover. I want you to start following her.'

'Don't you think that's a little bit over the top?' Mandy suggested bravely.

'No, Mandy, I don't,' Jackie replied. 'Suzi is at the dangerous age that tells her she can't pick up men in bars forever. So she thinks she either needs to find one for herself or be on her own permanently. The fact that he happens to belong to someone else is immaterial. Suzi does not consider the rights and wrongs of betraying the sisterhood. Suzi is not a woman's woman.' The Ladies' Club looked gratefully round at each other, relieved that they were women's women, with all the obvious and lasting benefits that this accrued.

'Jean-Christophe . . .' Philippe stopped chopping the shin of beef on the aluminium counter of their small kitchen. 'There's a mad idea I've been brewing that I really want your opinion on.'

Jean-Christophe looked at his father, flattered that his opinion counted. Knowing Philippe, it wouldn't be anything truly crazy. Though, of course, he had thrown away three Michelin stars to open a small restaurant in his home town, which a lot of people had thought completely crazy.

'A lot of the restaurateurs I knew in Paris were desperate for locally sourced meat, fish and vegetables with a provenance they can boast about on their menus.'

'Yes,' laughed Jean-Christophe, his dark eyes, so like Philippe's, sparkling with humour. 'I've seen that sort of menu: flank of beef, lovingly reared in Poitou-Charentes by . . .'

'Why don't we have a food festival here in Bratenac to showcase local producers? It would be early enough in the season to bring in tourists, too. We could take a stall. That is, if you run the restaurant while we do it . . .'

'But don't these things take forever to organize?'

'Usually, yes. But not if the mayor happens to be a good friend and keen to put Bratenac on the map – and annoy the mayors of Sarlat and Bergerac for good measure,' grinned Philippe. 'You'd be surprised how quickly things can happen then.'

'I suppose we could even move the restaurant to the festival for the duration. My friend Pierre has one of those Airstreams you see at rock festivals with a flap that comes down like an open-air bar. I'm sure he'd lend it to us for a small fee. We could serve from that. Where do you see it happening?'

'I thought on that large area near the river, but still close to the market car park, so the whole thing was manageable for producers.'

'Doesn't that belong to the château?' Jean-Christophe avoided his father's eye.

'Don't look like that, you cheeky bastard!' laughed Philippe.

'I'd hardly give up two weeks of my life just to be able to negotiate with the château, now, would I?'

'I don't know . . .' responded his son with a grin.

'Well, it's got nothing to do with it!' replied Philippe.

'Of course not. You haven't been going on any early-morning walks, I take it.'

'*Ça suffit!*' Philippe announced firmly. 'Or you might be needing another job sooner than you think.'

'As a matter of fact,' Jean-Christophe smiled back, 'I already have one at Fleur-de-Lis. So when do you see this festival happening?'

'Six weeks from now.'

'Not long, then.'

'Better when things don't take too long. You keep up the energy levels. It doesn't have to be huge. The mayor will love it. He can put it on their website and show what a vibrant little town Bratenac is. Much more interesting than Sarlat or Bergerac!'

'Ronnie's arriving tomorrow,' Steph announced to David as they prepared breakfast for the guests together.

'That'll be nice for you,' replied David tactlessly. He had just noticed a message from Suzi on his phone, even though he'd asked her not to contact him. It was three red hearts in a row. Oh God.

'I know you think I'm over the top about Ronnie. But you'll soon remember why, once she's here.'

'Is Nicola coming too?'

'Of course Nicky's coming. She'll be the star. If Ronnie will let her, that is.'

'Where are you putting them?'

'One good thing about the downturn in bookings is we can

give them each a room. Ronnie was terrified by having to share a bathroom. Probably needs all the space for her make-up.'

'Now, Stephie . . .'

'Only kidding.' She smiled at him. He still seemed jumpy and unlike his usual calm self. Who the hell had he got tangled up with? She knew it couldn't be very serious or the gossip would have reached her in such a small place. Marcelline, who came from a huge local family that had tentacles everywhere, would have found a way of dropping a hint over the dishwasher.

Sitting in the cafe near her house, Suzi took a forbidden bite of croissant. She hadn't eaten a croissant in ten years. Most of that *Why French Women Don't Get Fat* stuff was down to watching your calorie intake with the all the obsession of a closet anorexic. *Et puis merde!* She was only eating it, of course, because she felt miserable as well as powerless. David was avoiding her. He wasn't replying to her texts or messages, or even the cute little card she'd sent. She had to stop or she'd start to seem like a stalker.

She knew one thing for sure. She wasn't giving up the best chance she was ever likely to get at her age.

Across the road she noticed a large pack of dogs, some of them dressed in ridiculous coats even though the weather was pleasantly warm. Suddenly they paused outside her house. They were a comic lot, ranging from a large wolfhound to a tiny chihuahua. They were with Janine. She must have come to see if Suzi wanted to come out. Except that she'd hardly do that with a huge pack of dogs with her.

Of course.

Suzi smiled at the obviousness of the ploy. Janine had come

on behalf of the Bratenac Ladies' Luncheon Club, aka Jackie Brown, to see what Suzi was up to.

Well, they'd just have to wait. The only thing she could promise at the moment was that it wouldn't disappoint them.

'What a funny little airport!' Ronnie, wearing a typically subtle outfit in bright orange with blue chevron stripes, looked round the converted barn with a rather supercilious smile.

Steph, who had always thought rather the same thing about Bratenac's facilities, found herself jumping to its defence. 'We love it. In and out in ten minutes, and your bags may get wet but you never lose them.'

'Is there even a loo?' her sister demanded.

Steph thought of the deeply unattractive hole in the ground and the freezing water that gushed over your ankles when you flushed. Even she couldn't see a way of putting a rosy glow on the airport's *toilettes*.

'Maybe wait till we get home. It won't take long.'

'I can't,' wailed Nicky.

Steph surveyed her niece's white all-in-one jumpsuit with misgivings. Those things were hell to get out of at the best of times, let alone in a badly lit French toilet. She could already see how this trip was going to pan out.

But this time she was wrong. Five minutes later Nicky returned, all smiles.

'Mum, it was one of those loos Dad used to call dragons, you know where you expect a monster to come out of this hole in the ground and bite your bum when you're a kid! I decided maybe I could hang on after all.'

'Very wise indeed,' agreed Steph, warming to her niece by the second. 'Come on, let's get back to Fleur-de-Lis and have some lunch. It'll be mercifully empty of guests now!'

'How delicious. Isn't it rather weird having guests around all the time?' asked Nicky as they got into the car. 'Like a house party, only no one leaves on Sunday when they should do? That drives me mad.'

Steph found herself laughing. It was so true.

'You know the worst thing,' she confided. 'Apart from having to work twenty-four hours a day? You can never swim in your own pool!'

She realized she'd never told anyone that before. How funny.

'I thought you loved it,' accused Ronnie. 'You always tell me you do.'

'I do, most of the time. I promise. Anyway, it's like anything – a compromise. I want to live in the most beautiful part of France and I can't afford to unless I work. Besides, I thought working alongside my husband would be good for our marriage.'

Why the hell had she blurted that out? How bloody stupid.

'I mean, so many couples lead completely parallel lives,' she barrelled on.

'Mmm. Actually, Martin and I do that already,' mused Nicky. 'I do see your point.'

Martin. How interesting, Steph thought to herself. She'd hardly heard him even mentioned before. The lot of bride-grooms, perhaps.

'So when can we see the château?'

'Tomorrow at eleven,' Steph smiled. 'Meredith, Jo and Sophie will all be waiting for you.'

'I'm so excited!' beamed back Nicky. 'I know I'm going to love it!'

'Slow down, darling,' Ronnie counselled. 'It might be unsuitable. Or too expensive,' she added meaningfully.

Steph took them back to Fleur-de-Lis and showed them their rooms. Nicky loved hers but Ronnie, true to form, gave hers a cursory glance and threw her dirty-looking suitcase onto the pristine white cotton bedcover without making any comment. Biting back her irritation, Steph left them for a moment to prepare the lunch.

'How was it?' David asked her. He was chopping tomatoes and thin slivers of onion for a salad.

'Is that for us?' Steph enquired, touched that he was being so thoughtful.

'I thought you might need back-up,' he added with an engaging smile. 'And maybe a calming glass of Bergerac?'

'That sounds like heaven,' Steph laughed. 'Thanks for being so understanding. Actually, I think she's trying to behave. She's following my dad's advice: if you haven't got anything nice to say, don't say anything at all!'

She went into the dining room to find the table had already been laid. Before she had time to comment, David was at her elbow with a glass of white wine. He was obviously trying really hard. She decided not to dwell on why this might be, but she knew he still wasn't being honest about something. Well, it had better lie till Ronnie and Nicky were safely departed.

In the afternoon, to Steph's relief, they wandered into the town, only returning in time for a quick bath and tidy-up before coming down to dinner.

'Do we really all have to sit together?' Ronnie enquired in a loud whisper.

'It's part of the ethos in a *chambre d'hôte*,' David pointed out gently. 'People come to us because they like to meet other people. Almost like a big dinner party, as somebody said once.'

'I hate dinner parties.'

'Come on, Mum,' Nicky wheedled. 'You only hate them because you hate cooking. Tonight someone else is cooking and you can be free to chat to all these nice people.'

'Think of the Queen,' murmured Steph as she served drinks for David to distribute. 'She has to mix with all sorts of types and she always looks so gracious.'

'That's all very well,' Ronnie replied in a martyred tone. 'But a lot of these people are French!'

Thirteen

'Oh, Mum, it's absolutely perfect!'

Nicky stood at the top of the sweeping stone staircase that led from the château down to the terrace below. 'Can't you just picture me in my gorgeous Pronovias mermaid dress? Everyone will be blown away!'

'What?' gasped Ronnie. 'Those dresses from Barcelona that cost more than a Spanish holiday?'

'Everyone wears one these days,' Nicky shrugged.

'Not everyone, Nicola. I saw one from Zara in *Marie-Claire* for £39.99.'

'Maybe you think I should get mine in Oxfam,' flashed Nicky angrily. 'And save the world at the same time!'

'What a wonderful idea,' Ronnie replied without even a shade of humour.

'Don't worry,' Nicky told her. 'I'll get Dad to pay!'

'Good luck with that!'

Meredith, Jo and Sophie, who were standing by ready to answer any questions, tried to avoid each other's eyes in case one of them started to giggle and set the others off till they collapsed in a quivering heap. Definitely not good for business.

'Would you like a full tour?' suggested Sophie brightly. 'We could start in the dungeons, or *donjon* as the old duke calls them. This really is a medieval castle, you know.'

'To be honest,' Ronnie replied, looking bored, 'I'd rather just see the parts we'd use for the wedding.'

'Fair enough. Let's just run through the whole experience, shall we? Would you be wanting to have family staying in the château rather than a hotel?'

'Oh yes,' Nicky nodded enthusiastically. 'Except for Martin's family. They don't get on with each other, so they'd be better in a hotel.'

Jo suppressed a muffled giggle.

'As long as it's not too expensive,' added her mother predictably.

'How many guests are you planning to invite?'

'Eighty's the absolute minimum,' Nicky insisted. Everyone looked expectantly at Ronnie, but she was obviously too stunned to speak.

'The most popular package for French weddings is for the immediate family to arrive on the Friday and stay in the château and have a simple family dinner, while their guests stay in local hotels and B&Bs. Either on the Friday or very early Saturday, the florist arrives with the flowers—'

'Well, actually,' Ronnie interrupted, 'I'd rather like to do the flowers myself.'

Nicky shot her an anxious glance.

'I've always wanted to be like Mrs Dalloway.'

'I'm sorry?' Sophie looked blank.

'You know. The Virginia Woolf novel.' Ronnie cleared her throat dramatically. 'It starts, *"Mrs Dalloway said that she would buy the flowers herself . . ."'*

'But Mum,' Nicky asked tactfully, 'won't buying flowers in France be really complicated?'

'I'm sure Steph can organize it all for me. I'll just choose them online.'

'What about hair and make-up?' enquired Nicky.

Jo looked at Meredith. 'Good point.'

'We'll sort it out.' Meredith wrote herself a note on her phone. She could see it was going to be a long list.

'Now, you do know,' Meredith chipped in, 'that most couples don't actually get married in France?'

'Why ever not?' Ronnie sounded quite put out. 'I mean – what's all this expensive ballyhoo about having a French wedding, if you're not actually getting married here?'

'The thing is, one of you has to live here for three weeks,' Sophie continued patiently. 'So instead, most couples have a registry office ceremony quietly at home and come to France to exchange their own very special vows in a gorgeous, romantic setting.'

'Oh my God,' Ronnie looked appalled. 'You mean they make up their own vows? What happened to *for better or for worse, in sickness and in health*? I suppose *till death us do part* has gone out of the window. I hope it's not all that frightful Mind-Body-Spirit stuff!' She turned to her daughter. 'I ban you from using the word *soulmate*, OK?'

'I think you're getting a bit tired, Mum,' replied Nicky diplomatically. 'Maybe we could just whisk round the rest of the château?'

'Absolutely,' replied Jo, sharing a relieved glance with the others. 'We'll show you the salon where you may like to have your drinks reception, the dining room and the terrace where you can have tables outside. You just need to decide what arrangement you'd like. A top table? Lots of long tables, or round tables.' Jo remembered the advice she'd read from wedding planners – *If the parents had an acrimonious divorce, try and avoid a top table* – and felt suddenly tearful. When Sophie got married, would she and Mark be reconciled enough to share a top table?

Sophie saw the sudden change in Jo's expression and instantly understood. She slipped a comforting arm round her mum, and Jo almost wanted to cry more. Would the failure of her own marriage make it harder for her daughter to have a happy and successful one of her own? Sophie was so pretty that she'd never had any problems getting boyfriends, yet somehow they never seemed to last.

'For the wedding meal we will give you a choice of four caterers. I'll send you sample menus,' Jo made herself sound normal. Crying in front of a bride-to-be when she was planning her wedding was not exactly a good sales technique. 'And of course, a choice of wedding cakes.'

'Oh, by the way,' Ronnie dropped in nonchalantly. 'Gran wants to make the cake.'

'Oh God,' Nicky replied despondently. 'Gran's cakes are like medieval weapons. You could fire them at the enemy instead of cannonballs.'

'That's only her famous fruit cake. Ask for something else. Madeira or chocolate. She's quite good at those.'

'Would you like to have a wander on your own now?' Sophie suggested. 'We can always send you any more details afterwards. The important thing is for you to see the château.'

'One thing,' Ronnie demanded combatively. 'All this stuff sounds very lovely, but how much is it all going to cost?'

'You've heard what we can offer, now you need to decide exactly what you want and then we'll provide an accurate costing,' Meredith replied calmly.

'Well, one thing's clear,' Ronnie announced with a steely glint in her eye. 'Your father is going to have to bloody pay. There's no way I'm going to be able to!'

After they'd left, Jo took one look at Meredith and Sophie and announced it was time for a glass of champagne.

'What are we celebrating?' Meredith demanded irritably. 'I was just wondering why the hell I've bought a wedding château when it means I'll have to deal with the kind of people I've spent my life avoiding!'

'That's why we need a glass of champagne,' Jo insisted. 'To remind ourselves we're in the happiness business and be grateful that at least in this case we know what's coming in advance.'

'And we didn't even get to the part where I show them my bridal suite,' Sophie muttered plaintively. 'And it's so beautiful!'

'I must admit,' Meredith admitted, 'I couldn't help thinking, thanks a lot, Steph, for landing us with your ghastly sister!'

'You can't blame poor Steph,' Jo replied. 'She was being kind to us. She can't stand her sister either.'

'And you can see why,' Meredith said. 'I'll tell you one thing I've learned in business. Be very clear in advance who's paying!'

They went into the empty kitchen. Steve the builder's merry band had all taken their lunches outside, so they had it to themselves. Jo went to the enormous fridge and got out the champagne.

'We could always throw in the ghost for free!' giggled Sophie.

'And did you notice another thing?' Meredith pointed out, laughing too. 'No one even mentioned the bridegroom!'

'Of course they didn't, stupid.' Sophie raised her glass, her face alive with laughter. 'Weddings are all about brides. Even in this age of gender equality. Anyway – to the happiness business!'

Meredith put her arm around Jo and Sophie. 'Thank God one of us is an optimist!' She sipped her champagne. 'On the other hand, it's clear we've got to be practical and draw up a contract suitable for all our clients with a deposit to hold the booking. What kind of deposits do our rivals ask, Jo?'

'Thirty per cent seems pretty standard.'

'So, who's going to ask Ronnie for thirty per cent, then?' Sophie grinned.

'Hmmm,' was Meredith's response. 'I think we'd better talk to Steph about how to proceed delicately with this.'

It wasn't long before Ronnie herself was back in the château, Nicky in tow, brimming over with good humour. 'We bumped into this amazing old lady in the vineyard talking to a man out there. She said we could have a wine tasting as part of the wedding, and Nicky could even have a wine named after her. Cuvée Nicola! I think that's wonderful. Why didn't you tell us?'

'Bloody Margot,' murmured Meredith.

'Anyway, the nice man she was talking to said he'd set it all up for us to try tomorrow evening. Who is he, by the way? I thought he was rather attractive.'

They both looked at Jo.

'That's Liam,' she replied calmly. 'The château's winegrower. He's from New Zealand.'

'Jo, will you please go and see Margot,' Meredith requested, trying to keep her temper, 'and tactfully remind her that wandering about in our vineyard is actually trespassing? If I go myself, I might say something I'll regret.'

'I don't think that's very diplomatic,' Jo replied soothingly, 'seeing as she's our neighbour and it was her house.'

'It's precisely *because* of those things that we need to tackle her. If we're not careful, it won't be the White Lady who's haunting us but the duchess of St Savarin!'

'Is that who she is?' demanded Ronnie, impressed. 'I thought she seemed a bit grand. Maybe she'd like to come to the wedding?'

'No!' chorused Nicky and Meredith in unison.

'Right, you look for Margot,' Meredith suggested, 'and I'll talk to Liam. What time has he kindly suggested the wine tasting?' Nicky and Ronnie fortunately missed her ironic tone.

When Meredith set off to look for him, she found to her irritation that he was nowhere to be seen. The orderly rows of grapevines that ran in straight lines like cornrows on a holiday head, right down to the riverbank, were entirely empty.

The air was still and clear. Three in the afternoon always struck Meredith as the hottest part of the day, even in spring. She looked back towards the golden château with its broad stone terrace and four towers crowned by their russet tile roofs. 'It's all ours, Dad!' she murmured, turning round to find Liam only a few feet away, intent on tying up a vine to its trellis.

'The Chardonnay flowers have my favourite scent,' he commented. She suspected he was trying to cover for having heard her words and save her from embarrassment, which oddly made her twice as angry. 'Light and fresh, maybe a little citrus.'

'Liam, I'd welcome it if you'd run it by us first rather than set up wine tastings for our guests,' she told him firmly.

'Fine.' He stood ramrod straight, as if he'd once served in the army and she were the sergeant major. 'To be honest, I only did it to head Margot off. She was trying to get them to come back to her house and have a drink with her and the duke. I wasn't sure that was something you'd all welcome. Fraternizing with the enemy.' He grinned suddenly and his face transformed from its usual craggy lines into something almost boyish. Meredith could see why Jo found him appealing, but really, that was a complication they could do without.

'All right, let's have it on the terrace,' she suggested sharply.

He nodded. Was he suppressing a smile? Bloody man, he knew exactly what she was up to. Taking back control from an underling who'd overstepped the mark.

'Since the wedding season is quite short . . .' he began.

Meredith almost interrupted with a comment that they were looking at ways of lengthening it, but decided to listen. 'Yes?'

'You might consider wine tourism. It's getting pretty big now, especially if you get any of your wines recognized by the Hachette Guide. Most of the châteaux round here do it. It's a way of bringing in an income in winter.'

'I'll think about it, thank you.' Actually, it was quite a good idea, Meredith had to admit.

Back at the château, Ronnie and Nicky had departed and Jo had disappeared too.

'Gone to see Margot,' Sophie explained.

Jo stood outside the tiny new house, trying not to laugh. Fixed to its brand new Lego like outdoor wall was a smart sign, newly painted in gold lettering: *Domaine de St Savarin.*

On the minute terrace at the back of their new house, with its distant river view, the duke and duchess were on their second bottle of rosé. The duke somehow seemed to have aged dramatically since their first meeting, yet he still managed to get to his feet and scuttle slowly, like an ancient but beautifully coloured beetle, towards the kitchen to fetch a third glass and a fresh bottle.

'So, *ma chère Joanna*,' enquired Margot archly as soon as he'd left, 'how does your secret garden grow?'

'Still rather barren,' admitted Jo, then instantly regretted it. The last thing she wanted was Margot delving into her sex life. Or non-sex life. Anyway, she was supposed to be telling her not to wander round the château.

'I hope you won't mind me saying this,' Margot began ominously, 'but you need to do something about your style, my dear. You are . . .' She paused, looking for a suitably damning expression. 'So English!' She surveyed Jo's outfit. 'I mean, look at this . . .' She pulled the sleeve of Jo's cardi, one of her favourites, in fawn from H&M. 'What is this garment called?'

'A cardigan,' supplied Jo helpfully.

'Even named after a disastrous soldier!' Margot turned to her husband. 'Was it not this imbecile of a general who led all those young men to their deaths in the Crimea?'

'Yes, my dear,' replied the duke as he tottered back. 'The earl of Cardigan.'

'Only the English would name a garment after such a man. Or wear it! Come, my dear, take it off.'

'I don't like showing my arms,' protested Jo.

'If a man's interested in you, he will not notice your arms, will he, Louis?'

With a laugh, Jo removed her cardigan to reveal a lacy camisole.

'*Ah, c'est bien mieux, ça.*' The duke's approval was obvious, if not entirely appropriate.

Jo remembered why she'd come and pulled the cardi back on. 'Margot,' she announced briskly, 'we really need to have a word.'

'I know, *ma chère Joanna.*' Margot favoured her with a bewitching smile. 'You have come to pull wings off me . . . no, that cannot be right . . .'

A sudden image of a beautiful butterfly, its glorious shades

196

of purple, indigo and green, having its wings removed invaded Jo's mind, and she shuddered. 'I think you mean tear a strip off you,' she offered.

'I know, I should not wander on your land uninvited; but you must understand, it was my home for fifty years. I cannot just rip it out of my heart.'

'No, I see that,' accepted Jo, knowing that Meredith wouldn't see that at all.

'Besides, my suggestion was an excellent one. We always had much success with our wine tasting. Is the bride going to do it?'

'Possibly,' conceded Jo, not wanting Margot to go and boast to anyone who'd listen, which was most of the village, that she might have sold it to the mad British, but they still listened to her wisdom up at the château.

'OK, so who's going to have the conversation with Steph?' Sophie enquired brightly.

Meredith and Jo exchanged mystified glances. 'What conversation?' enquired Meredith.

'The one where we tell her we have a contract and need a thirty per cent deposit and actually would quite like to know who's paying?' Sophie shrugged. 'Unless, that is, we're doing the whole thing free for publicity? But given that the minimum cost for a château wedding is four grand – pounds, that is, not euro – rising up to forty with all the trimmings, it's quite an important question.'

'I will,' Meredith announced with her usual decisiveness. She looked at her watch. 'In fact, I'll go over there now. The breakfast rush should be over.'

'And David will have finished the clearing up,' Sophie said naughtily.

'And Steph will have pointed out that the table's still smeary,' Jo added. 'Are things any better since you got in Jean-Christophe?' she asked Meredith, feeling rather guilty that they were discussing their friend's marriage like this. But they all cared about Steph, and having just been through a horrible divorce herself, Jo certainly didn't want that for her friend. Especially since David had always struck her as being one of the good ones.

'I don't really know,' Meredith replied. The truth was, so far her scheme didn't seem to have had the effect she'd hoped.

'I hear we're all coming to your wine tasting tomorrow,' Steph greeted Meredith when she arrived at Fleur-de-Lis. 'Want a coffee?'

'I'd kill for one,' Meredith confessed.

'No need to go that far,' David smiled as he put the mats away, 'I'll make you one. Cafetière or cappuccino?'

'Either. Or even instant.'

'Meredith,' David replied in mock-shocked tones. 'This is France. They wouldn't even clear their drains with instant.'

'Cappuccino then, thanks. He is a gem, you know,' she pointed out to Steph as he left the room. 'I hope you appreciate it.'

'Delicate territory,' replied Steph quickly. 'Best avoided.'

Meredith looked at her friend searchingly. Did she know about Suzi? Was it really over between them, as David had said? Actually, Meredith had the strong impression it had never really started – but it easily could, if things didn't get any better.

'Back to Ronnie,' Steph said firmly. 'Knowing my sister, she may cancel if she thinks it's going to cost her a bomb. She'll insist Nicky forgets the silly vows in the romantic setting and goes for the registry office with a reception in the local pub. You have to persuade her she's getting an incredible bargain.'

Ronnie even tries to haggle in Poundland. Now you know what they want, cost it all out and then present it with a generous reduction for their co-operation in being a trial wedding and having their photos used for your PR. Once she's come down off the ceiling I'll phone Nicky's dad and explain it all to him. He's quite a reasonable type, despite the picture Ronnie likes to draw of him as a penny-pinching philanderer. Actually, he's rather a sweetie and more of a one-woman man. Unfortunately, since Ronnie chucked him out, that one woman is his faithful assistant. He'll see sense and I don't think the new wife will try and stop him coughing up. She's like him – nice, but dull.'

'Everything's hunky-dory, then,' Meredith announced.

'Let's hope so. And see you tomorrow for the wine tasting. I very much doubt you'll get Ronnie to spit hers out. Waste of a good perfectly good wine, in her view.'

'Fine.' Meredith paused fractionally, then added: 'Make sure David comes too.'

Steph looked at her curiously. Was this another shot in the Be Nicer to Your Husband campaign? 'You can tell him yourself. He'll be back with your cappuccino in a moment. In fact, what the hell's happened to him?'

'Can you just thank him and make my excuses?' Meredith said. 'I really need to get back to the château.'

'Fine,' Steph shrugged, 'I'll drink it myself.' She watched Meredith hurry down the terrace steps with her long, slightly masculine strides. There was something odd going on between her and David that Steph couldn't fathom. It was almost as if Meredith wanted to tell her something but kept deciding not to.

And then it suddenly struck Steph, like the clouds parting to let through a shaft of sunlight: David had been up to something, and Meredith knew what it was.

Fourteen

Liam had chosen a range of three white wines, two reds and a rosé for Ronnie and Nicky to sample for the wedding. He'd laid them out on a long table on the terrace, under a plane tree. It was a delightful spot, carefully chosen with a view down through the vineyard to the river, where the sun had just set, leaving a dusky glow all over the landscape.

He knew which wines were his own favourites, but he wasn't going to spoil the fun by announcing them. Taste in wine was an individual thing. He couldn't help feeling proud of them, almost like people felt about their children. You brought them up from babyhood and nursed them, not through croup and sore throats but by spraying, pruning and trellising, protecting them from mildew and natural disasters like frost in April or too much rain – or too little.

'How amazing. I love the labels!' Liam turned in surprise, since the wine tasting wasn't due to start for another fifteen minutes, to find Jo standing behind him wearing a beautifully cut black cocktail dress.

'You've dressed for the occasion,' he smiled.

'It's Nicky and Ronnie's last night. I thought it ought to be a bit special. Like you putting the labels on the bottles.'

'You'll also be trying our first crémant. I think it's pretty great.'

'Aren't we supposed to be the judge of that?' Jo realized she was sounding flirtatious, but what the hell. Why else had she deliberately turned up before the others, dressed like this?

'I was damn proud of it, as a matter of fact,' Liam grinned. 'The château's never produced a wine with fizz, so it's my personal Everest, if you like.'

'Aha,' teased Jo. 'Your Edmund Hillary moment. I wondered when we'd get to the list of famous Kiwis. I gather you're all pretty sensitive about that.'

He laughed. 'Only because bloody Westerners make us sensitive. Like drawing up lists to show there aren't any.'

'Oh, I don't know. Sir Edmund Hillary, Rutherford who split the atom, Kiri Te Kanawa . . .'

'Good girl!' His laugh was infectious. 'Have you been Googling that as well by any chance?'

'That's a bit vain,' Jo laughed. 'Why on earth would I do that? Just to impress you?'

He looked abashed. 'I'm sorry. Of course you wouldn't.'

Jo, who had been doing precisely that, gave in. 'Actually,' she confessed, 'I did!' Margot would be horrified at this failure to play the seduction game. 'I can even add a few more. Jonah Lomu the rugby player, although I confess I'd never heard of him. Sir Peter Jackson who made *Lord of the Rings*, Lorde the pop singer . . .'

'Flight of the Conchords, the comedy boys; and I'm afraid that's that.'

They were both still laughing when Nicky and Ronnie arrived with Steph and David. 'What's the big joke?' Ronnie demanded.

'Oh, nothing,' Jo shrugged. 'Just silly stuff about Liam being from New Zealand.'

Meredith and Sophie arrived moments later with some delicious snacks on a tray. 'Just some *foie gras*, olives and other nibbles,' Sophie announced, putting them down on a side table.

'OK, is everyone here?' Liam enquired. 'And which of you ladies is the bride?'

'I am,' Nicky smiled.

'I don't know if you've been to a wine tasting before, but we'll be tasting a range of different wines from a full-bodied red to a light rosé, so it's customary to swirl and spit. There's the receptacle.' He pointed to a long, narrow metal bin. 'It reminds me of the spittoons we used to have back home till surprisingly recently.'

Jo was impressed at the way he took such easy command of the situation, making them all laugh at once.

'Do you remember,' added David, 'how they used to have *Défense de cracher* signs on French trains? That means No Spitting!'

'Well, you're very much encouraged to spit here,' Liam smiled. 'I'll just fill you in very quickly about the background, talk a little about *terroir* and then we'll try the wines. OK?'

They all nodded obediently.

'We're at the far east of the Bordeaux region here, so we have hot, dry summers.'

'Great for a wedding,' Nicky commented.

'Yes, great for a wedding, although I must warn you we do occasionally have sudden hailstorms here, even in the middle of summer! Not so good for a wedding – but they are even worse for winegrowers, because they can ruin a crop in minutes. Thankfully they're pretty rare. Our clay and limestone soil provides ideal growing conditions. And excellent *terroir*.'

'What is *terroir* exactly?' Jo asked with genuine interest. 'I've always wondered. It seems to be so much at the heart of successful winegrowing.'

'I would say a combination of soil, direction of the slopes and climate. Oh, and fertilization. You've probably noticed our herd of Blonde d'Aquitaine cattle? They're very beautiful in the landscape, but we don't keep them just for decoration. Their manure is used to fertilize the vines.'

'I'm sure all this talk of cow shit is fascinating,' Ronnie interjected witheringly, 'but when do we get a damn drink?'

'Mum,' Nicky hissed furiously. 'You sound like an old soak!'

Liam laughed as though Ronnie's interruption was perfectly timed rather than the crass comment it actually was. 'You are absolutely right. It's time we all had a damn drink! Let's start with the reds.' He signalled to a young man standing in the shade of a large tree with a tray of red wine.

Jo watched him, increasingly impressed with his natural manner, right down to dealing with Ronnie the heckler. Did presentation just come naturally to him, or had he had professional training?

'Merlot is our main grape for red,' Liam explained, 'with Cabernet Franc and the famous Cab Sav for blending.' They tried both red wines, all dutifully swirling and spitting. Apart from Ronnie, who knocked back every drop.

'Who prefers the first?' Two hands went up. 'And the second?' Everyone else raised theirs. 'That was our St Savarin Classique 2016. You have good taste, as that was chosen by the prestigious Hachette Guide. Let's move on to the whites.'

This time there were three wines to sample.

Ronnie continued draining each glass.

'For God's sake, Mum!' Nicky firmly placed a plate of snacks next to her. 'Eat something, or you'll pass out.'

'Don't be ridiculous! I haven't even started.'

This time there was a division between the drinkers. 'As the *vigneron*, or winegrower,' Liam announced, 'my personal favourite is the St Savarin Sauvignon, but please take your time to choose. This is the wine your guests will consume the most, so do try as often as you like to make your decision. I would say the bride's choice is final. And now, the *pièce de résistance* –' Jo noted how French he sounded – 'our newest wine and our first fizz. The Crémant de St Savarin: Cuvée Nicola!'

He produced an elegant bottle with a silver foil cap and its own special label proclaiming the Christian name of the bride.

'How amazing!' Nicky looked as if she'd woken up in heaven. 'My very own wine. How cool is that?'

'She really loved the label,' Jo said quietly to Liam as he finished the presentation. 'It's a brilliant stroke.'

'Thank you. Maybe we could blend one for you, Jo,' he repeated softly. 'Is that short for Joanna or Josephine?'

'Joanna.'

'I'll have to see what I can do.'

The Bratenac Ladies' Luncheon Club was, for once, having supper instead of their customary lunch at the Café de la Paix.

'I don't like the evenings,' complained Shirley.

'That's because you want to be at home cooking a three-course dinner for hubby,' Jackie observed tartly.

'Why is it all men?' Shirley looked round at the crowded tables.

'After work drinks that end up in dinner. God, I miss those,' Janine sighed. 'It was the best thing about working.' She glanced round the crowded cafe. 'I expect the women are all at home cooking three-course dinners for their hubbies like you, Shirley.'

'That's a rather old-fashioned attitude,' Jackie observed.

'France *is* old-fashioned,' replied Janine. 'Round here anyway. We can't all be bossy old boots like you!' Her affectionate smile undercut the insult. 'Speaking of old boots, where's Suzi?'

'You were the one keeping an eye on her,' Jackie pointed out. 'What's she been up to?' She glanced round the cafe, as though Suzi might pop out from behind a potted palm.

'Nothing. Not even going out. I wondered if she was pining.'

'Suzi? Pining? She doesn't know the meaning of the word. Are you sure there isn't anyone in there with her? David Adams, for example?'

Janine shook her head vigorously. 'As a matter of fact, her curtains are all pulled and she doesn't answer the door or her phone when I ring. Actually, I'm quite worried about her.'

'Right, that's it,' announced Jackie. 'I'm going round there now.'

'But Jackie, it's almost ten o'clock. She's probably in bed with one of those sexy Mills & Boons she loves,' Janine protested. 'The ones with strong independent women and sizzling red-hot lovers. Suzi thinks they're all about her.'

'Then I'll wake her up. She'll probably think I'm a red-hot lover and be sorely disappointed.'

Ten minutes later, Suzi sat up in bed when she heard the doorbell, her heart leaping. Could it be David?

The last person she was expecting was Jackie.

'Hello babes,' Jackie greeted her cheerily. 'Me and the girls have been worrying about you. Can I come in?'

'Well . . .' Suzi hesitated.

Jackie tried a diversionary tactic. 'How fascinating. You even wear make-up in bed.'

Suzi grinned. 'I even frighten myself without it, I look so old. Come on then.' She pulled her shiny pink kimono a little tighter round her. 'Fancy a drink?'

Jackie grinned back. 'When have I ever refused that offer?'

'It's only supermarket plonk. It's cheaper than milk at Carrefour.'

'I'm not fussy.'

Jackie glanced round. Suzi's taste could best be described as Istanbul bordello with a touch of French rococo. Her sitting room sported three daybeds piled with velour cushions in exotic designs, cheek by jowl with embroidered spindly armchairs that looked as if they'd collapse if you sat on them.

They sat on a daybed each. Jackie struggled not to disappear into the cushiony depths and had to perch on the edge as Suzi poured her a very large glass of red. 'Come on then, Suze. Spill. What's happened to keep you housebound?'

Suzi hesitated, then stuck out her chin mutinously. 'I'm in love.'

Of all the possible answers, this was the one Jackie had least expected. As far as she knew, Suzi didn't possess a heart, in the romantic sense at least.

'Who with?'

'That's the problem. He's married to someone else.'

'Suze! It's David Adams, isn't it?'

'Yes indeed, it's David. And I'm pretty sure he loves me. The thing is,' she embroidered, 'he has a lot of money worries he hasn't told his wife about, and he doesn't feel he can leave till he sorts them out.' She was adding her own fantasy to the reality, since David had never talked of leaving Steph.

'What kind of money worries? I thought their place did pretty well. It always seems full.'

'He owes money for a tax bill he wasn't expecting. And the other person he owes money to is Steve.'

'Steve?' Jackie repeated, astounded. 'Not my Steve?'

'Yes. Quite a lot, as I understood it. He's amazed Steve's being so patient about it.'

'So that's why we can't afford a bloody holiday!' Jackie fumed. 'He told me things were too tight this year! Silly sod.' There was affection in her voice, though. Even a touch of pride that he'd shown so much generosity, though of course, in business terms it was crazy. 'But Suzi, how can you be so sure he'll leave Steph? How many women have waited their lives out for some married shit – and when he finally does leave, he goes off with somebody else? I've seen it time and time again.'

'But David isn't a shit. That's the difference.'

'Oh, Suze, sweetie; if he isn't a shit, he won't leave her. Look, come and have a hug.'

Like most men's women, Suze wasn't the huggy type, Jackie knew. Still, she let herself be enveloped in Jackie's pneumatic embrace and burst into operatic tears.

'Oh God, Jack, you mean he's just stringing me along?'

'What has he actually said?'

'Just that he enjoys my company and loves it that I don't criticize him all the time like his wife does.'

'No actual mention of leaving her, though?'

The tempest of Suzi's tears redoubled until she had deep runnels of mascara blackening her face. Jackie delved into her bag for a tissue, spat on it and wiped Suzi's cheeks clean. It was a slender enough premise to build a fantasy on and Jackie suspected it was just that. Though obviously she wasn't going to say so.

'OK, you haven't asked my advice, I know, but I'm going to give it to you anyway. You've got to get on with life, Suze. It's like anything. It's more likely to happen if you live your life the way you always do. That was what attracted him in the first place.' Jackie thought for a moment. 'You should find something to do with yourself.' She didn't add 'instead of hanging about in bars', but it was implicit in her tone.

'What you mean, a hobby?' was the withering reply. 'Learn French? Join a choir? Walk bloody dogs like Janine?'

'Maybe you could help Guillaume behind the bar?'

'Rather than hanging round embarrassingly in front of it?'

'Come on, have another hug. It'll work out. These things do.'

Suzi reluctantly submitted to her embrace. Jackie was surprised at how thin and bony she seemed, despite the boobs that were so often on display. Fragile, almost. Not a word she would ever have applied to Suzi.

'Yeah, usually with the other woman losing out.'

Jackie thought of the predatory bitch who'd walked off with her first husband and begged to differ. She shouldn't feel too sorry for Suze. She was obviously getting soft in her old age.

'Anyway, come on, join us girls again from tomorrow.'

'If you say so, Jackie.'

'I do.' Whatever happened, she'd better be around to clear up the fall-out.

'Come on, everyone,' Ronnie wheedled, the orange lipstick that had at the outset of the evening perfectly matched her vintage orange kaftan now smeared around her mouth like something from a horror movie. 'Just one more little drinkie!'

Steph cast a half-angry, half-despairing glance at David.

'Well, I'm going to bed,' announced Nicky firmly. 'Our flight's at eleven tomorrow and I've got to pack. What time do we need to leave?' she asked Steph. 'And can I print up the boarding passes on your printer? I usually use my phone, but I doubt that airport could deal with anything beyond the nineteenth century.'

'Very wise. Breakfast at eight thirty, leave about nine fifteen? It's only ten minutes to the airport. We'll print up the passes in the morning. I have to get up at seven anyway for the guests.'

'Thanks for everything, Auntie Steph,' Nicky said. 'It's been really amazing. I'm dying to tell Martin all about it!'

Steph smiled, touched at Nicky's obvious delight, even though she still couldn't help wishing the whole thing would go away.

'OK, Ronnie, I'll join you,' David weakened, even though he looked tired too. 'But just one, mind. I'm not up for a session, and you have to get up for your flight, remember.'

Steph threw him a grateful glance. He was a kind man and she knew she could sometimes be a bit shrewish to him. 'See you soon. I'll do breakfast.'

David led Ronnie into the guests' sitting room, where there was a table at one end with drinks and an honesty box. It was untidy, with empty glasses strewn around and a whiff of stale cigar smoke, jarring Ronnie into a sudden sense of what hard work it must be to run a place like this with almost no backup.

David poured them both a cognac.

Although he could see exactly why Ronnie drove her sister mad, there was something about her he admired. Maybe it was her energy, a kind of life force that exhibited itself in her over-the-top clothes and exuberant personality. On the down-side, she could certainly be a world-class moaner.

Ronnie suddenly pierced him with her heavily mascaraed gaze. 'David, I'm worried about you two,' she announced bluntly. 'There's something going on neither of you are facing up to. And the thing is, you're not allowed to split up. I rely on you both too much.' She smiled at the outrageousness of her own remark. 'So spit it out. For once, I promise to be discreet.'

David felt his own defences begin to collapse. He'd tried so hard to battle this thing out on his own. Maybe it had been a mistake.

'It's mainly about money,' he admitted, looking away. 'There are other things, but the money's the key. We're in debt to a builder and the taxman and I haven't dared tell Steph. I thought I could sort it out, but I can't. And Steph tells me our summer bookings are down, when I was relying on them to rescue us. We're always full in the summer!' There was an edge of desperation in his voice she had never heard before. 'The thing is, Ronnie, if things don't pick up, we could lose everything!'

Ronnie took his hand and squeezed it gently. 'Look, Dave . . .' That made him smile despite the stress. She never called him Dave. 'You're going to have to tell Steph. Tell her tomorrow. Wait till we're out of your hair. Take her away from the B&B. For a drive, maybe. I don't know why, but it's easier to be honest in cars. Or a walk, at least. And just tell her.'

'I expect you're right, but Jesus, I'm dreading her reaction. She'll blame me for everything. And she'll be right. I'm the man . . .'

'Oh for God's sake, David, what century are you living in?' Ronnie demanded. 'Isn't modern marriage supposed to be about facing things together, and all that crap? Knowing my sister, she'll probably be more pissed off with you for not telling her than for getting into difficulties in the first place.'

'You're probably right,' sighed David. 'I'll tell her when she gets back from the airport. The guests should be out by then.'

'Good lad. Do you know –' she yawned and stretched – 'even

I think I'm ready for bed.' She got up, then held out a hand to pull him up from the depths of the cushiony sofa. '*Courage, mon brave*, time to grab the bull by the horns and other clichés. I'm sure you'll feel better afterwards.'

Fifteen

'Thank you *so* much, Auntie Steph, for all you've done!' Nicky flung her arms round Steph. 'The château is so absolutely perfect. I can't wait to get married!'

Nicky and Ronnie were waiting at the tiny airport and had even managed to procure a coffee from the pull-along stall that looked as if it would be happier at a rock festival. Their suitcases had been taken and their tickets checked by a lady in a t-shirt with the cheery slogan COME FLY WITH ME.

Nicky left them to check her phone and Steph looked round for somewhere to sit other than the hard benches. They seemed to be the only takers so far for the UK flight but no doubt the French would arrive, as usual, at the last minute.

Ronnie, who considered this an indecently early hour, wrestled with her conscience. She had promised David she would be discreet, but she couldn't help recalling how tough Steph could be with her husband. She had occasionally winced at some of her sister's comments. She was conscious of a guilty pleasure that their marriage wasn't as perfect as Steph liked to portray it, but she still wanted them to stay together in case at some point she needed them.

'Stephie . . .' she began.

'Yes?' replied Steph suspiciously. This humble and tentative tone was not one she recognized from Ronnie.

'It's about David. I think there's something difficult he wants to talk to you about. Don't be too hard on him, Stephie. In my experience, husbands don't come much better than David.'

What the hell was Ronnie going on about? Had David been having an affair after all, and confided in her sister? A wave of humiliation washed over Steph. Was that pity she'd picked up in Ronnie's voice? She was the strong one, the one with the successful marriage. Ronnie was the one who had messed up her life. Steph realized with a shock that while still loving her sister, she'd enjoyed her superior status – and now Ronnie sounded as if she were sorry for *her*!

'They're calling our flight, Mum.' Nicky was standing next to them.

'Right.' Ronnie stood up and picked up her carry on bag. 'Thanks for everything, Steph.' Again, in an uncharacteristic gesture, she enveloped Steph in a hug. 'See you soon and thanks for setting it all up.'

One more wave, and they were gone.

By the time Steph got back to Fleur-de-Lis she was boiling over with resentment and didn't notice that David had been to extra trouble to leave the kitchen and breakfast room immaculate.

'Everything clean when I get here,' commented Marcelline admiringly. 'Monsieur David, he work hard.'

'Where is Monsieur David, Marcelline?'

'I think out on the terrace maybe.'

Steph stepped out into the bright sunshine. The terrace was mercifully empty of guests. David was sitting at the far end in the shade, laptop open in front of him. He looked up anxiously. 'All go well with the send-off?'

'Fine. Except that Ronnie told me you had something diffi-cult to discuss with me and that I should be kind to you, which obviously she thinks I'm not normally.' Anger battled with fear of losing him, and anger won. How bloody *dare* he do this to her? 'I assume you've been having an affair? OK, spit it out. What's been going on?'

Her whole body stiffened as if expecting a blow while she waited for his answer.

'Actually, nothing like that. Well, not quite nothing, that's dishonest – but no, I'm not having an affair. An involvement, perhaps, which I regret; but I felt like you just didn't value me.'

'And the fact that I tarted myself up like a Soho stripper the other night to get you into bed, that didn't occur as a sign I needed you?' The anger in her voice lashed at him and he hung his head.

'Maybe it was too late,' he replied softly. 'Stephie . . . this isn't about sex. It's money. I'm afraid I've been hiding things from you. I thought I could sort them out – after all, I'm supposed to be the one who understands money. But it's gone beyond that. We have two bills we can't pay.'

'Who the hell from?'

'One from the builder for the swimming pool. We spent much more than we meant to. And the other from the French revenue. They changed the way they calculate local tax and I hadn't kept up.' She could tell he was close to tears. 'I'm so sorry. I hoped we could borrow and pay back from the summer rentals, but when you told me they were down, I knew things had got out of hand. Steph . . .' He reached out a hand, but she couldn't bring herself to take it. 'I don't know what we're going to do.'

'I know exactly what you're going to do.' Steph could hear the hardness in her voice. 'You're going to pack your things and move out right now. I can cope with money problems but this is different. You didn't trust me. Marriage is based on trust. If you didn't trust me, our marriage means nothing.' She turned away before she started to cry as well. 'I can't talk to you any more about this now. Sorry. The hotel near the station is meant to be clean and cheap. Goodbye, David.'

'But Stephie . . .' The anguish in his voice nearly halted her steps, but she pressed on.

'No, David. It's too late.'

She set off down towards the river, forcing herself not to look back. When she got to the bank she instinctively turned left, but that way was towards the château. She really mustn't go there. Meredith would offer to bail them out, and she couldn't let her.

Not even checking to see if there were any other walkers approaching, she found a patch of pasture between the path and the glittering waters of the Savarin River, half hidden by reeds, and threw herself onto the ground. She curled her whole body into the foetal position in a cry of vulnerability that no one would hear, especially the husband she still loved back at Fleur-de-Lis.

'*Alors, c'est super!*' Philippe had received a formal letter from the mayor's office, not only approving the food festival but announcing that they would take care of the necessary licences and help with all the arrangements. '*Putain!*' Philippe swore, laughing at the same time. 'That wily old fox, the mayor, has somehow got me on the morning show for Radio Sud-Ouest to talk about it!'

Radio Sud-Ouest was the most listened to show in the region.

'I thought you despised Radio Sud-Ouest?' enquired Jean-Christophe, poker-faced. 'Pap aimed at middle-of-the-road morons, you said.'

'I don't mind addressing a few middle-of-the-road morons if they come to our food festival!' flashed back Philippe, laughing. 'We'd better start signing up some contributors.'

'What, like Fromages de Savarin, the baker on the corner, Foie Gras of Bratenac?'

'Exactly,' confirmed Philippe.

'Done already.' Jean-Christophe grinned. 'Every time I've been into town since you mentioned the festival idea, I've had a word.'

'*Formidable!* You really are my son!' He began chopping an onion with such amazing skill and speed that it almost seemed a magic trick.

'You should do that at the festival, you know. A demonstration of knife skills would go down really well.'

Philippe laughed.

'Tell them that thing you told me,' Jean-Christophe insisted. 'The sharper the knife, the less you cry! Anyway. When's the interview?'

'Next week.'

'Then isn't it about time you went up to the château and asked if we can use that bit of their land?' Although he was trying to keep a straight face, laughter lit up Jean-Christophe's eyes.

'*Petit con,*' responded his father rudely. 'Perhaps I will go this very afternoon.'

'Meredith?' Sophie always knocked before entering the amazing boudoir Meredith had created, adapting some of Margot's fixtures with new things of her own. The ten-foot gilded mirrors remained, plus the elaborate chandeliers and wall lights, magnificent swagged curtains and canopied bed, on its own platform so that the occupant had a view of the river in the distance. In the bathroom she had added some art deco panels and Japanese prints of ladies in kimonos under cherry trees laden with blossom, which looked exactly right.

The only questionable touch was sitting bang in the middle of the pale green silk-covered four-poster, smiling at Sophie in a decidedly superior manner.

'I thought dogs weren't allowed on the furniture,' Sophie said mildly.

'Nelly's not a dog,' Meredith replied. 'She's a reincarnated wise woman. Look at those eyes!'

Nelly turned her face obligingly towards them. Her eyes were round, large and almost black in colour. 'Can't you see the wisdom of ages in that look of hers?'

'I can see a very clever dog who's wrapped you right round her not-so-little paw.'

Nelly's eyes took on a distinctly wounded expression.

'I must admit,' Sophie conceded, 'she does seem almost human.'

'Superior to human,' corrected Meredith.

'Anyway, I'm not disturbing you just to argue over human versus dog evolution. Philippe from the restaurant is downstairs wanting to talk to you.'

At the mention of Philippe, Nelly jumped off the bed and bounded towards the door.

'I rest my case,' Meredith laughed and followed her downstairs.

Philippe waited by the fountain in the courtyard in a shady spot looking out towards the horizon, where the sun was beginning to set, bathing the whole landscape in the soft light of evening.

Nelly rushed straight over and threw herself at his feet. Meredith followed, holding a tray with two glasses of the palest pink rosé. 'Before you admonish me for not drinking local, try my discovery,' she said by way of greeting. 'As pale as the palest Provençal and yet produced just beyond the Savarin River. Try.'

She waited, expecting the inevitable put-down. She watched him run the wine round in his mouth. As usual his jaw was covered in days' worth of stubble, giving him the look of a slightly untidy gangster.

'Delicious,' he pronounced to her amazement. 'Expensive?'

'Eight euro,' she grinned.

'Keep it yourself and buy as much as you can.' He was being so nice; clearly he wanted something. 'I apologize –' he even managed a faint look of embarrassment – 'I did not come dressed for an *apéro*.' He indicated his work clothing.

'No, I see you didn't,' Meredith agreed. His sartorial short-comings didn't seem to worry Nelly, who still lay adoringly at his feet.

'It's amazing how that dog has taken to you.'

'I'd like to say it was mutual, but I do prefer elegant grey-hounds to bulldogs, even charming ones.'

'Shhh! She'll hear you! Besides,' Meredith raised an appraising eyebrow at his ensemble, 'I'd have thought you were the type to see through the vanity of appearance.'

'And why is that?' he asked with a challenging glint in his eye.

She cast an appreciative eye at his two-day stubble. 'You concentrate so very little on your own that you set the rest of us an example.'

'Ouch. So, Mademoiselle Meredith Harding, the ice-cold money manager, can get out her claws! If this were a romantic novel, I would stride over and take you in my arms at such provocation.'

'Nah,' commented Meredith scathingly, wrinkling her nose, 'you're not the romantic type. Which is just as well, because I'd have to slap you.'

'As it happens, I didn't come to trade verbal insults – or even physical ones – enjoyable though that may be.' He looked straight into her eyes, and once again she knew he was laughing at her, though perhaps this time it was *with* her.

'What did you come for, then?'

'To put a business proposition to you. I am organizing a Bratenac Food Festival to showcase local producers, from winegrowers to cheesemakers, plus a few local establishments like the cafe, who wish to broaden their appeal.'

'And how does this concern us? Do you want us to take a stand?'

'I would like to hold the festival on that field.' He pointed to a field beyond the edge of the last row of vines. 'It's very convenient for parking for traders, they can then use the main car park just out of sight.'

Meredith looked thoughtful. 'We might take a stand, as it happens. Good publicity for our weddings business. Maybe Sophie could dress up as a bride.'

'Not you?' he countered.

'Too old,' she stated baldly.

'How ridiculous.'

'It would be.'

'Are you ruling it out, then, ever being a bride?'

'This is a very stupid conversation,' she stated crossly.

'That's why it's so enjoyable. And people sometimes say very revealing things in ridiculous conversations. Such as, would you care to have dinner with me one of these days? Not in my own restaurant, I promise.'

Even though Meredith wanted to accept, an instinct stopped

her. Somehow he would be winning in the way men always won. 'I think we should get back to the details of this festival,' she said sternly. 'How long will it last? I assume there will be a fee for the château, and most important, will the land be cleaned up afterwards?'

'The mayor's office is taking responsibility, but I can at least tell you the fee.' She was quite impressed with the figure he mentioned, given the small scale of the festival.

'I see no major problems, then,' she said. 'What will happen to the restaurant while you are organizing it all?'

'My son has had a clever idea. He is going to run the restaurant from a van, as they do at music festivals.'

'That sounds fun!' Sophie had just arrived to tell Meredith she was needed inside. 'I love the food at festivals!'

Philippe smiled at her and bent down to fondle Nelly's ears, while she looked up at him adoringly. 'I am sorry, Mademoiselle Nelly,' Philippe apologized to the animal, 'to have insulted you earlier. You are the most charming creature I have ever met.'

'Don't listen to a word of it, Nelly,' Meredith advised tartly. 'That's what they all say at the beginning!'

'But *Mademoiselle* Meredith . . .' Was he deliberately stressing that *mademoiselle*? 'Some of us say it because it is what we actually mean.'

Steph pulled herself up, conscious not just of a stiffness in her knee, which she recognized as an inevitable part of getting older, but a pain that seemed to engulf her whole body and mind. David had been her rock for thirty years. Not having children had felt like a tragedy at first, but as the years unfolded it had seemed somehow to draw them even closer.

And now he had gone. Sent away by her.

As if to reinforce her sense of loss and helplessness,

darkness was falling fast around her. The birds were twittering in their evening chorus, which tonight struck her as sounding like a dirge – the death knell to her marriage.

She tried to shake herself back into some feeling of normality. Even without David, life had to go on. Thank God that tonight Marcelline and Jean-Christophe would be looking after the guests, even if they were wondering at the same time what on earth had happened between their employers. But, mercy of mercies, Ronnie would be safely back on the other side of the Channel. She was grateful to be spared her sister's superficial sympathy and barely hidden sense of glee that Steph's perfect marriage had come unstuck. Maybe she wronged her sister. Maybe she wronged everyone, David included.

Stop, she told herself as she made her way back along the riverbank. Or you'll go seriously mad.

David had betrayed her trust. The sudden realization dawned that chucking her husband out had not solved her problems. Far from it. The money issues that had so worried him were still there, waiting to devour the business – maybe even take the house.

Steph paused a moment. She was feeling physically sick. She saw how much she had leaned on David and how lightly he had carried the burden of her dependence. Although she had seen herself as the practical one, the everyday organizer, she had simply assumed he would sort out the big stuff. And she had never thanked him for it.

But then, he'd screwed up, and done it without telling her. She speeded her step, trying to hang on to that sense of injustice, as if it were a shield that could ward off the intense, searing pain of knowing he had actually gone.

*

'I've had an idea,' Sophie suggested brightly as they sat down to dinner.

She had left it for an hour because it struck her that Meredith was rather distracted, perhaps even angry. If she were going to attempt a bit of agony auntery, she'd guess that Meredith was angry with herself rather than anyone else. Perhaps because she was attracted to Philippe, but wouldn't admit it to herself for complex Meredith-style reasons to do with patriarchy and always having to win.

'What's the idea then?' Jo asked, since Meredith still seemed rather silent.

'About the fourth caterer. As you know, I spend ages on Instagram and Pinterest, not to mention all those wedding websites, looking at trends in wedding ideas. You know, dresses, food, flowers, what the bridesmaids are wearing . . . and there's one word that comes up all the time.'

'Love?' prompted Jo with a smile.

'You must be joking! That's the last thing your average bride's thinking about. No. Festivals. They all talk about not wanting a conventional wedding, but more of a festival.'

'What, like Glastonbury, you mean?'

'Well, not quite that scale,' Sophie smiled. 'But that kind of vibe. Relaxed. Unconventional. Though of course, they still want some of the conventional aspects, like the vows, and that moment when someone announces "Mr and Mrs Smith!" and everyone goes wild clapping, as though exchanging vows is the only possible thing that matters on this planet.'

'Don't be cynical, Soph,' her mother teased. 'You're too young. Wait till you're my age.'

'So what's your idea?' Meredith finally gave them her full attention.

'You know I mentioned Jean-Christophe as a possible caterer – well, now he's got the use of an Airstream for the food festival, I think we should definitely go for him. It could be really popular.'

'What food festival is that?' Jo enquired.

'Philippe has roped the mayor into backing a Bratenac Food Festival in a few weeks' time,' Meredith explained. 'He just came to see me about renting that field of ours down by the river to hold it on. It's out of sight of the château and they've promised to pay and tidy up after, so I agreed. Hope that's OK?'

Sophie picked up the crackle of tension between them over another decision made without consultation, and decided distraction was the best policy. Things would come up that really mattered, and this wasn't one of them.

'I adore street food, and it'd fit right into this festival feel the websites keep mentioning.'

'Brides with burgers,' Meredith mused. 'Not exactly chic, as images go. I wouldn't want that one on Instagram. Ketchup smeared all over the girl's face like Zombie Bride Rides Again.'

'It's not just burgers now, Meredith,' Sophie pointed out. 'More Lebanese lamb with sumac and Mediterranean spices. Really quite sophisticated.'

'OK, OK,' conceded Meredith.

'And we know Jean-Christophe can really cook.'

'Do you want to speak to him?' Meredith suggested. 'Get him to come over and see the facilities and we can discuss details. If he has time to take this on. He's still doing Fleur-de-Lis three nights a week.'

'Yes, but that's midweek,' Jo countered. 'Weddings are still usually at weekends. And he's young and strong. I'm sure he'd be up for it.'

'You're making him sound like a stud from a porno channel,' Sophie protested.

'Sophie!!' chorused Meredith and Jo, choking on their *carbonnade de boeuf*.

'The other thing we need to sort out,' asserted Sophie, 'is staff for here, since Margot is kindly taking hers with her. Though what they're going to find to do in a Lego house, heaven knows. We'll need at least one cleaner, preferably two, and some help with bedrooms, plus an everyday cook wouldn't go amiss.' She grinned at her mother who had produced the *carbonnade*. 'Then you'll have more time to relax.' She almost added, 'and wander round the vineyard' but sensibly thought better of it. Perhaps they'd gone with Héloise, who had announced grandly that she intended to retire to Cannes and sunbathe.

Suzi sat at the rather ridiculous, if pretty, table she used as a desk, with its pink marble top and feet like lion's claws. It hadn't really mattered that it was impractical when she'd bought it, because she'd never really used it for anything functional. But now, as she tried to fit a large glass of wine, her diary and the new A4 notebook she'd just bought and carefully inscribed with the words SUZI'S NEXT STEP on the table at the same time, she almost gave up. It might be all right for Madame de Sevigne writing down her *pensées* for posterity, but she probably passed on the vino.

Suzi took a large sip. The list she'd started was pretty brief:

Help Guillaume behind bar at cafe
Estate agent? [except I don't speak French]
Start yoga group [except I've only done basic yoga and can't tell my Hatha from my Ashtanga]
Interior designer

There was a loud knock on the door, almost making her spill her wine. Who on earth could it be at this time of night? Probably Jackie, back to spy and patronize.

She pulled her dressing gown a little tighter so that it revealed less of her slightly saggy bosom. It was a silk kimono covered in blossom and exotic birdlife in a rather startling bright pink, which she'd bought in Bratenac market and decided would be suitable for entertaining gentlemen callers. She'd loved it at once because it had reminded her of a similar, though rather classier, version she'd worn with jeans when she was eighteen and determined to cut a dash back home in Basildon. Unfortunately, there hadn't been a lot of gentleman callers lately, but she wasn't going to dwell on that. She was going to find a job.

She opened the door and almost had a heart attack. David was standing on her doorstep, looking pale and stressed and carrying a suitcase.

He found his mouth full of her hair as she smothered him with kisses, just as he was attempting to explain that he wasn't moving in – that his stay was only temporary, because both of the local hotels were full for a conference.

Sixteen

'Have you heard the news?' Janine arrived at the cafe without her usual canine accompaniment, yet still managing to look like a dog with a very juicy bone.

'Heard what?' Jackie went on admiring Guillaume's artistry in producing the perfect heart of froth on her cappuccino. The challenge was how to drink it without destroying his painstaking creation.

'About Suzi? David Adams moved in with her last night.'

'Blimey!' In her shock at the news, Jackie accidentally speared the foam heart with her spoon. 'My God – I was round there the other night and Suzi was in the Gulch of Lost Souls. In such a bad way that I ended up giving her a pep talk. Swore David Adams was such a nice man, he'd never leave Steph.'

'Maybe he didn't,' Shirley suggested, looking smug. 'Maybe she chucked him out!'

'Over Suzi? She's mad if she did,' Jackie snapped, trying to hide her irritation at not being the first to know of this seismic shift. 'Suzi was sure he'd stay. Steph should have let sleeping dogs lie.'

'Not everyone could live with a spouse who was unfaithful,' Shirley preached. 'I know I couldn't.'

'I don't think he technically *was* unfaithful, from what she told me, though there was clearly something going on,' Jackie replied, secretly wishing Shirley's husband might run off with his secretary.

'Knowing Suzi, she'd have done all she could to get him.'

'Well –' Jackie shook her head at the stupidity of the world – 'she's got him now. But Steph's made a big mistake.' She necked her cappuccino and disappeared to see whether Steve had heard anything up at the château, where he was busy with all the refurbishments.

She found him up a ladder in the east battlement, replacing some loose tiles.

'You shouldn't be up at that height without even a harness on, at your age!' she scolded. It really did look quite high.

He climbed down to see her. 'Much you'd care if I topped myself,' he scoffed. 'You could get yourself a younger model.'

But marriage suddenly seemed more precious after the news about Steph and David. Jackie reached up and gave him a kiss. 'I prefer 'em with a few miles on the clock.'

'OK,' Steve grinned back. 'What's up, then?'

'I just wondered if you'd picked anything up at the château about David and Stephanie Adams?'

'What kind of thing?'

'They seem to have split up. He's moved in with Suzi.'

'That man-eater? He must be off his rocker. I suppose he found running that B&B too much. He was always dashing round like a blue-arsed fly whenever I went up there and she didn't half order him around. I suppose he decided he'd had enough.'

'So you haven't heard anything, then?'

'Not a thing.'

'Well, keep your ears open and let me know if you find anything out.'

'Yes, Sergeant Major. Will do.'

Jackie patted him on the bum. She'd been going to give him a bit of a bollocking about their unpaid bill, but perhaps she'd better take more care of him after what he'd just said about Steph. Marriage was a precarious business.

Sophie stood proudly surveying the almost-completed bridal suite, which was not only stunningly beautiful but, thanks to her skill in finding bargains at the *brocante*, had been achieved at a remarkably low outlay.

After much deliberation she had placed the white-canopied bridal bed in the tower, and she was convinced it really worked.

'What bride wouldn't feel romantic and loved-up when she's a princess in a tower?' she told herself as she lay down on the bed. 'If only I had a handsome prince . . .' she murmured out loud, her thoughts straying to a dark-eyed young chef.

'Don't suppose I'd do?' Sophie jumped up to find herself confronting Steve the builder, shirt stripped to the waist, tanned beer belly peeping out above the belt of his baggy blue jeans.

'Thanks for the offer, Steve,' she grinned. 'But I just came up to admire your handiwork. You've done a really great job up here.'

'Thank you. I'm a bit old for this bath in the bedroom caper –' he pointed at the freestanding bath at the end of the bed – 'but you young people seem to really go for it. As long as there's somewhere private to take a piss, I tell them, cos there's nothing romantic about seeing a man point Percy at the porcelain!'

Sophie could think of no suitable reply to this earthy assertion.

'I suppose you all know the talk going round the village about your friends up at Fleur-de-Lis?' he enquired.

Sophie looked even more dumbfounded at this. 'No – what?'

Jackie would be so jealous that he was the one who got to break the news, thought Steve. 'It's Mr Adams. He's only gone and moved in with that tart Suzi. It's more Mrs Adams I feel for. She's a nice lady. Men will be men, I suppose, but at his age he ought to know better than to be led by his ding-dong, don't you reckon?'

'Excuse me, Steve, I'm afraid I've got to dash. Something urgent to discuss.'

'I'll bet there is,' Steve murmured under his breath as she left the room. 'Like why your friend's husband's been such a damn fool. Still, it might make Jackie a bit nicer to yours truly.' There was plenty of scope for that. For a start, she could stop making it clear she preferred the dog to him.

Sophie found her mother and Meredith walking round the orangery, inspecting the new paint. Now that it had been furnished and the cracked glass replaced in some of its panes, it looked truly spectacular. It would be a perfect space for pre-wedding drinks, especially in spring before the weather got really hot.

'Are you all right?' Jo asked at once. 'You look like you've seen the ghost! You haven't, have you?'

Sophie shook her head. 'It's the news Steve the builder just told me. Apparently it's all over town. David Adams has moved in with that ghastly Suzi, the one who hangs round the cafe with her boobs out. Oh, Mum!' Sophie was close to tears.

'What's the matter with men?' It was obvious who she was thinking about. 'Can't any of them be trusted?'

Jo swept Sophie into her arms. 'Of course they can, darling. There are lots of good men out there.'

'Oh God, this is awful.' Meredith intervened looking genuinely stricken, and suddenly older. 'I saw them together. They were on a bench down by the river. She had her head on his shoulder. At first I thought they were some old married couple . . . and then I saw it was David. With that woman.'

'Oh God, Meredith,' Jo sympathized. 'How horrible. Did he see you?'

'Yes. But he also told me they weren't having an affair. The thing is . . .' Meredith delved into the depths of her memory. 'There was something David said. What was it? Me and my bloody memory! Sometimes I think I'm getting dementia.'

'You've got one of the sharpest brains I know,' Sophie asserted, shocked.

'I still forget things. Just don't get old, Sophie. I know! He once said he hoped they had a bloody good summer up at Fleur-de-Lis. They needed it. I was quite surprised, because I'd got the impression the place was flourishing. I wonder if this is actually about money?'

'Only one way to find out. Shall we ring her? Go round?' Jo suggested. 'Whatever we do, we're going to have to be extremely tactful.'

'You bet. Look, Jo,' Meredith asked seriously, 'please don't be offended – but would you mind if I went on my own? If money is the problem, I might be able to help her work something out. I mean, money's my thing. Unlike me, you're great on sympathy and hugs and she'll need those in spades, but just now, maybe money might be the answer. I'll call you as soon as I've seen her and maybe you could pop over then?'

Sophie went off to work on one of the amazing lists she was devising of exactly how a wedding package should work, from the bride-to-be's arrival with her mother and brides-maids, with every last thing that ought to happen listed next to the name of who ought to be responsible for making it happen. So far, it came to about ten A4 pages. And growing. But with less than three months to go, they'd certainly need it.

The modern wedding, it struck Jo, with all its Pinterest and Instagram and Snapchat and its drone aerial photography, was more like a Hollywood production with one of those funny cast lists featuring gaffers and best boys (whatever they were) than anything she really recognized. It would be heresy, of course, since they were in the weddings business, to wonder if it had all been better before, when a wedding took place in a village church with a marquee in someone's garden.

But then, as any modern bride would tell you, back then the whole day belonged to the parents. Weddings might be expensive and elaborate now, but they were exactly what the couple wanted. And with a little help from the château, Jo reminded herself, the whole thing could be magical.

It was early afternoon by the time Meredith pulled her hire car into Fleur-de-Lis' small parking area. She was going to have to get one now that she was staying. The whirlwind of buying the chateau had pushed all those dull details of everyday living – cooking, cleaning, transport – out of her head. Fortunately, down-to-earth Sophie was talking to a staff agency who had promised to supply them. Meredith looked round. There was only one other car in the car park, which was a relief. Steph's guests must be out sightseeing.

She walked in by the garden entrance and found her friend

deadheading roses. 'Hello. I didn't know you were into gardening.'

'I'm not,' replied Steph, who had washed her hair and applied more make-up than usual, like protective armour in battle. 'Deadheading's different. I love it. By taking off the bloom that's died you ensure the appearance of another, and that makes it extra satisfying. Plus the rose bush looks better, too.' She glanced at Meredith. 'You know about David, don't you? I'm surprised it's got round that quickly. Does somebody's son or daughter work at the hotel?'

Meredith stared. Oh God, she obviously didn't know where he'd gone. Shit.

'What's the matter? Meredith?' Steph stared at her. 'Meads honour. You're bound to tell me. What don't I know?'

'He seems to have gone to stay with someone, rather than book in to the hotel.'

'Who?' Steph sounded genuinely puzzled. 'Not you lot, obviously, or you'd have said.' She racked her brains for David's friends and acquaintants, but couldn't think of anyone. She was the one who made all the new friends.

The awful thought suddenly broke into her consciousness like a stalactite being stabbed through her brain. 'Not . . . the woman he's been seeing? I knew there had to be someone. Oh God, the silly sod. Who is she? Not some teenager, I hope.'

Meredith felt Steph's eyes bore into her as she waited for the answer.

'I gather she's one of the ladies from the Bratenac Luncheon Club; you know, Jackie's lot from the cafe.'

'Oh, perfect. My fucking husband leaves and moves in with a crony of the biggest gossip in Bratenac!'

'Did he leave?' Meredith asked gently.

'You mean, did he jump or was he pushed? Does it really

matter? He betrayed my trust – not just with this woman, but about our livelihood.' Steph turned away towards the river in case too much emotion was showing on her face.

Meredith waited a moment, thinking how best to handle the situation. Steph was proud and her pride was stopping her from confiding, which had the effect of leaving her alone and scared. Somehow Meredith needed to break through that pride and offer her support.

'Steph, you know we love you. We've all known each other so long and life has done different things to all of us. But the one thing that's helped is having each other. Why don't you just tell me about it from the beginning?' She glanced round to make sure they were alone. 'Go and sit over there in the shade. I'm going to get us a bottle of wine. I'll be right back. All right?'

When she got back Steph was staring straight ahead. 'I was sitting at this table with David only about twenty-four hours ago,' she announced bleakly, sounding almost as if he had died rather than left.

'Are you missing him?'

'Yes. I'm missing him. I woke up missing him, having his body next to me, and I missed him all morning. The house seemed empty even though Marcelline and a couple of guests were here. I missed him at lunch when I ate alone, and I'm missing him now.' She looked Meredith in the eye. 'Is that enough of an answer?'

'Yes, Stephie,' Meredith replied, keeping the emotion out of her voice, because she could sense sympathy was the last thing her friend wanted at the moment, 'that's enough of an answer.'

'I suppose it started when I told him a week or two ago that bookings were down in the summer and he wildly over-reacted.'

'You hadn't noticed anything before then?' Meredith was thinking that the encounter she'd interrupted on the riverbank was longer ago than a week or two.

'OK. Yes, I had. He had been behaving strangely at times. Out a lot during the day. Once or twice I thought he'd been drinking. To be honest, my fear was that he was becoming a drinker, not wrecking our business and having an affair.'

'How exactly was he wrecking the business?' Meredith enquired quietly.

'He'd hidden two big bills, just hadn't dared tell me about them.'

'Who are these bills from?'

'Ironically one from Steve, your builder. I'm amazed he hasn't taken us to court for payment. Instead he's been very good about it.'

'And the other?'

'From the tax authorities. Some rule had been changed and he hadn't kept up.'

'The French tax system can be very Byzantine. I wonder if he's tried appealing against it or at least for more time. I think you need a good *notaire*, a local lawyer who really understands this stuff. I'll ask around and find you someone and if you raise the question of payment, I may have to hit you with my handbag, OK?'

Steph smiled for the first time. 'Did you ever see that episode of *Father Ted* where the two housekeepers go out to tea and both want to pay the bill? They end up on the floor walloping each other with their handbags. I wouldn't want to upstage Mrs Doyle.'

'Excellent. I'll get on the case. One more thing.' Meredith hesitated and found Steph's gaze scanning her. She must have sounded weird, and maybe guilty. Very unlike her usual confident self.

'Yes?'

'I don't think he was actually having an affair with this woman.'

'And how would you know something so personal?'

Again a hesitation. This time Steph was concentrating one hundred per cent on her answer. 'I came across them sitting on a bench. And then David found me and told me it wasn't an affair. This woman just had a way of building his confidence.'

'And I didn't.' Steph hung her head so that her hair drooped all round her face, completely hiding her features. A few seconds later, it shot up like a punchbag. 'You mean you knew something was going on between them and you didn't tell me?'

Meredith sighed again. 'I thought from what he said it was all over and it would hurt you more to know about it.'

'Well, you got that wrong, didn't you, since it's her he's gone to? I think you'd better leave. And forget about the lawyer. I wouldn't want to keep Fleur-de-Lis on without David. It might as well go bankrupt.'

'But you love the place,' Meredith blurted.

'A bit late to think of that now. Goodbye, Meredith. Say hello to the others.' Reluctantly Meredith stood up. 'Steph . . .' she tried one last time.

'Go!'

As soon as Meredith was out of sight, Steph filled her glass to the brim and took it off to sit next to the swimming pool, where she stared into its Hockney blue depths. Funny; it was the swimming pool that had partly done for them. They could never use it when the guests were around and despite all they'd spent on it, hardly anyone swam in it anyway.

In the distance she could hear Meredith's car start up. The

thought occurred to her that now she'd lost her friends as well as her husband.

Next it would be her home and the business.

She downed her wine in one long gulp, stripped down to her bra and pants and dived into the beckoning blue beneath her, not even noticing how deep the water was.

Seventeen

'You were back late last night.' Philippe went on chopping without looking up. It always surprised him that such a good-looking boy as Jean-Christophe didn't seem to have a girlfriend. He'd thought he'd seen a spark between Sophie and him, but nothing seemed to be happening. Maybe Jean-Christophe was too shy.

'You must have been in bed early, then,' his son replied.

'Quiet evening in the restaurant, and I'd had a rough night before with Grand-père.'

'Not running off again? You should have called me.'

'No. He just wouldn't go to bed, that's all.'

'To be honest, it was a strange night up at Fleur-de-Lis.' He'd suspected something was wrong last night when there had been no sign of either of his employers when he'd arrived or, more disturbingly, when he'd left. Of course, they might have just taken advantage of his presence to go out to dinner.

'Strange how?' asked Philippe.

'Normally I see David or Stephanie when I arrive and quite often both of them later on. Sometimes, of course, they are out and I finish before they get back.'

'So what was different this time?'

'Tu penseras que je suis complètement fou . . .'

'Why will I think you have gone mad?' his father asked.

'Because it was just something in the atmosphere. Something cold, I don't know.'

'Wasn't there anyone you could ask about it?'

'Marcelline, who helps out as well, but she didn't know anything.'

Philippe was about to suggest he ring Meredith, when Jean-Christophe's phone buzzed. By the time he put it back in his pocket he looked genuinely upset. 'That was Marcelline. She's just gone in and there's still no sign of either of them.'

'Ring the château. Here is Meredith's mobile number. That may be the quickest.'

Jean-Christophe nodded and dialled the number. 'Mademoiselle Meredith? I am very sorry to trouble you. It's Jean-Christophe. I'm a little worried about your friends at Fleur-de-Lis. I did not see them when I left last night, even though it was later than usual, and Marcelline has just telephoned me to say they are still not back. Do you think there could have been some accident?'

Meredith hated clichés like being rooted to the spot, yet she stood, phone in hand, entirely still for almost a minute as she fought against panic and decided what to do. Where had Steph gone to? Should she go and get David from Suzi's? Yet it might make things worse if Steph had just checked in to a hotel herself and was about to walk back in at any moment. But that didn't feel convincing.

She'd better get up there herself and see if there had been any developments.

Philippe had the same thought on behalf of his son. 'Come on. I'll get the car. You and Marcelline can staff the place for the moment. At least that will seem less strange to the guests.

And we can look around the property at the same time. Marie can get on with prepping lunch here.'

By the time they reached Fleur-de-Lis, Meredith, looking less than her usual cool and calm self, was already standing outside on the steps with Marcelline.

'Have you looked all round the house?' they heard her ask the girl anxiously.

'Of course, madame.' Marcelline, suddenly flushed with embarrassment, added: 'I knew about Monsieur Adams and could see that Madame Stephanie was very upset ...' A hideous thought suddenly struck Meredith about where Steph was headed when she'd last seen her.

'OK, Jean-Christophe – why don't you go behind the reception desk in case any of the guests are wondering what's going on?' Meredith suggested. 'And could you possibly cook again tonight? Until we find out where Steph is?'

'Of course.'

'I am at your service also, if there is anything I can do,' Philippe offered. He had almost been tempted to quietly withdraw, feeling he might be in the way, but there was something disconcerting about Meredith's manner. He sensed that she was genuinely afraid for her friend.

Meredith had almost forgotten Philippe was there. 'I've just got to go and look somewhere . . .' she began.

'I will come with you,' stated Philippe. 'And do not worry, after that I will disappear.'

For once Meredith didn't protest but smiled gratefully as she set off down the path towards the swimming pool.

'Is it not quite wonderful, the things people do for love?' Margot smiled into space, as misty-eyed as her mascara would allow, no doubt imagining the two lovers entwined as in some magical Chagall painting. How she had even dared to just walk into their salon and plonk herself down on a sofa after their discussion the other day was beyond Jo.

'No,' Jo replied with spirit. 'I think it's sad and selfish and sordid, as a matter of fact. But then, given my own circumstances, you'd hardly expect me to bang the drum for late middle-aged encounters, would you?'

'Now, *ma chère*,' Margot replied with the kind of patronizing smile Jo had come to expect, 'don't sound bitter. Bitterness is not attractive.'

'Sod attractive!' Jo scoffed. 'It'll never last anyway. I'm sure Steph and David do actually love each other.'

'You English are so funny!' Margot shook her red curls. 'You understand nothing about marriage. Loving someone is not enough. You must *show* them you love them, all the time. Every day. That is the way to make a marriage work. And this Suzi. I hear that she understands this.'

Jo almost laughed out loud, thinking of how Margot treated her own husband. The poor duke was like the runt of a litter who never gets near the teat, however hard he tries.

'Let me tell you about one of the happiest marriages I have encountered,' Margot wittered on. 'I have a friend. He is the ugliest man you would ever see. Yet every day his clever wife says to him: "Julien, you are the handsomest man I know. Even at seventy you could outdo Alain Delon, the great Belmondo, even these young lions like Vincent Cassel and Brad Pitt. You would always get my golden apple." And they have been together for fifty years.'

'And one day she'll get up in the morning and stick a knife in him!' countered Jo.

'Joanna!' Margot looked as shocked as if she had produced a knife then and there. 'Where do you get thoughts like this? Perhaps you should talk to someone?'

Jo just laughed. 'You get thoughts like that if you don't let your healthy resentments out. Speaking of healthy resentments, Margot, I am very fond of you, I really am, but you can't just keep wandering into the château – or the vineyard for that matter – as if they still belong to you. I know you say it's hard to let go, but you do see my point, don't you?'

Margot gathered her skirts around her with all the contained contempt of a vitriolic Jeanne Moreau. 'I will remove my objectionable presence from your sight at once and not trouble you with it again,' she announced grandly and hobbled out on her ridiculous heels, leaving Jo feeling both faintly guilty and reasonably certain Margot had no intention of carrying through the threat.

Meredith, usually the first to face any difficult situation, walked across the terrace of Fleur-de-Lis, bathed in sunshine and over-hung with fragrant blossoms which today she didn't even notice, past the table where they had sat and drunk wine and talked about David's departure, towards the arched opening with its iron gate that led to the swimming pool.

She stopped there for a fraction of a second, terrified of what she might find. After a moment's thought Philippe slipped an arm around her, in a gesture that was clearly meant simply to be supportive. 'Shall we go through?' he asked gently. 'In fact, would you rather I went ahead and had a look round?' It was equally clear that he understood the nature of her fear.

'No, thanks,' Meredith replied. 'Just come with me.' She pushed open the gate.

Steph's towel was still spread out on the wooden sunbed, now damp with dew. Meredith forced herself to stare into the pool, scanning the entire length, then let out a deep sigh of relief. 'She isn't there!'

'No.' His arms closed round her for a moment, holding her in a close embrace that was more friend than lover, for which she was deeply grateful. He glanced around, his eyes fixing on the pool house at the far end.

'*Allez* . . . we should take a look in there.'

The pool house was new and made of wood, a large cabana, still smelling of pine and wood preservative. It was empty, but at the far end a kind of baffle had been erected to separate an area where the sunbed cushions were stored. Philippe strode over. 'Come!' he commanded gently. 'Take a look.'

Meredith's shoulders drooped in gratitude at the smile in his voice. She ran across to join him.

Steph lay on a pile of dark blue cushions, sleeping like a baby, beneath a covering of smart towelling robes also in dark blue, piped with white, that seemed brand new. 'She looks like a babe in the wood,' whispered Meredith.

'Or an advert for Galeries Lafayette,' grinned Philippe and squeezed her hand before he removed his arm and took a step back.

Meredith, still watching her friend, was conscious of an unfamiliar sensation – not the loss of protection, she'd never needed that, but of solidarity perhaps, a moment of something shared. She knelt down next to the sleeping figure.

'Steph,' she said softly, 'time to wake up.'

Steph's eyes flew open, filling with a sudden sense of reality. 'Is it all true?' she asked.

Meredith stroked her hair back from her face, which was drenched with sweat. 'It's true, but you've got us. You're not alone. We're just down the road. Besides,' Meredith smiled at her tenderly, 'now that I've bought a château next door you can't abandon me and bugger off back to Blighty! How fair would that be?'

Philippe, standing back in the open doorway, heard the shared laughter and smiled. Silently, he turned round. Time to leave them to their moment. Friendship like theirs would pull them through.

As he headed back towards reception to tell his son the good news, he thought how sad it was for men that their friendships lacked the depth of feeling and trust he had just witnessed between Steph and Meredith. Football and fishing were all very well, but they couldn't rescue you from life's toughest moments.

Then he laughed out loud. He had plenty of friends who would argue that was exactly what football could do.

Of course, all of them were men.

David contemplated the small mountain of perfect-looking French fries Suzi had heaped on his plate next to an enormous T-bone steak and felt slightly defeated. It seemed hardly a moment since she'd provided a full English breakfast. This must have been how poor King Harold had felt, still tired from marching nearly two hundred miles from another battle when suddenly faced with the overwhelming forces of William the Conqueror at the Battle of Hastings.

Suzi, he had discovered, had certain unshakeable beliefs. First was that the way to a man's heart was through feeding him gigantic meals. Second was that Men Like Steak. And cheese. And red wine. And pudding. Indeed, anything guaranteed to raise your blood pressure sky-high.

David had for the last few years cut most of these things out of his life and almost become a pescatarian, something

Suzi assumed must be his star sign when he attempted to explain it to her.

Then there was her attempt to settle him into her home, ignoring the fact that he had insisted he would only be staying two days until the hotels emptied.

Pysching himself up, he managed as much of the steak as he could, accepted a slice of runny Brie so small that she insisted it wouldn't feed a mouse and retired as soon as he could to the bedroom.

This, he was soon to learn, was a tactical error. No sooner had he got into his pyjamas and switched on *The World Tonight* – which he listened to largely for the reassuring British voices, ignoring any scary content – than Suzi got there first, wearing a skimpy nightgown, and climbed into bed.

'Come on, sailor.' She patted the bed archly. 'What are you waiting for?'

David felt a sudden temptation to bolt for the door. Maybe tomorrow he'd check once more whether any rooms had become free at the hotel.

Meredith found herself faced with a dilemma.

She had been trying to decide the best way of communicating to Philippe that she had changed her mind and would very much like to have dinner with him. Should she call, WhatsApp, or drop round in person to the restaurant with Nelly to break the ice? As it happened, she felt like a stroll and decided to put the whole thing out of her mind. Nelly at least would be happy about it.

It was a glorious evening. The air felt clear and heady, and she decided to climb the steep ridge on the far side of the river which led up to a *causse* or limestone plateau typical of the region. Clambering to the top was harder work than she'd expected, especially in shoes that weren't intended for serious walking. Nelly, who took the climbing as a personal affront, had to be pulled all the way up.

No wonder Meredith was quite out of breath by the time she got to the top. Maybe she wasn't as fit as she'd thought.

Once there, she stared down at the Savarin River. The blues and greens were so intense they reminded her of an enamel brooch her mother had owned, which she'd always admired. What had happened to that? How strange life was, the things, the experiences, the people who made up part of it. Now there was Philippe and for the first time in years, she actually felt something for a man. And it scared her.

'Dad, lovely Dad . . .' She found herself half praying, which was crazy, since she didn't even really believe in God. 'I'm not really sure what I should do next.'

Unfortunately, there were no signs from on high. No flashes of lighting, burning bushes or even swooping white birds – only Nelly smiling up at her.

'I got you both wrong, didn't I?' She remembered part of the reason she'd taken the dog on in the first place was because she'd been wrong about Philippe. 'You've worked out pretty well.' She sat down next to the dog and stroked her soft ears. 'Maybe that's the sign I've been looking for.'

After the disastrous attempt at lovemaking, David was rather hoping Suzi might let things lie, if that wasn't too ghastly a metaphor, for a little while.

But he didn't know Suzi.

Sex was Suzi's major weapon in her battle to win him and she was going to wield it like Cleopatra. Last night she had deployed a range of tricks he had no idea existed outside a

Bangkok brothel, and all to no avail, he was still as soft as a limp handshake.

He'd been thinking about it half the night. Getting it up had never been one of his problems; in fact, he'd often been eager for sex when Steph pleaded either exhaustion or wanting to watch the next episode of some box set. Lately, his libido seemed to have disappeared.

His startling conclusion was that he hadn't been able to do it last time with Steph because of guilt over money, and he couldn't do it with Suzi because of guilt over Steph.

His first mistake was to murmur, 'I'm so sorry about last night,' on waking up together, adding: 'I promise it was nothing to do with you.'

To Suzi, this was the equivalent of throwing down the sexual gauntlet. Of course it was nothing to do with her! Her guiding principle had been learned from supermodel Cara Delevingne's great-aunt Doris, a dazzling siren of the Thirties, that 'there was no such thing as an impotent man, just an incompetent woman.' Winston Churchill had once told this racy beauty that she could bring a corpse to orgasm, and Suzi certainly wasn't giving up on David. It might only be eight a.m., but she smiled with all the seductive allure of Great-Aunt Doris as she began to remove her nightdress.

'Actually . . .' David sounded feeble even to himself. 'I don't suppose there's any chance of a cup of tea?'

'So how are things going with the food festival?' Jean-Christophe asked as they packed up their things for another fishing trip.

'Excellently, as a matter of fact,' beamed Philippe. 'People are falling over themselves to take stalls. We may not even have enough room in the field.' After their success with, if not the uncatchable carp, then still a pretty big fish, he put some high-quality minced steak into his fishing bag with the usual hemp seeds, tiger nuts, sweetcorn and bread from last night's table.

'And when's the big radio interview?'

'Tomorrow,' Philippe grinned. 'I'm very honoured, apparently. I'm going to be interviewed by the famous Françoise Gilbert.'

'Wow!' Jean-Christophe whistled. 'Even I've heard of her.'

'She does their morning show, the one with the big audiences. I'm amazed. With a little story like ours I thought I'd be on in the middle of the night.'

'Don't forget, you're famous too!'

'*Was* famous. Anyway, I'd hardly call myself that.'

'Tsk, tsk, Papa. Chefs are the new rock'n'roll stars, everyone knows that.'

'I always thought they should be concentrating on their cooking. Anyway, *petit paresseux*, if we don't get moving, the fish will have gone back to bed.'

Meredith woke up and stretched. Nelly was right in the middle of the bed. No wonder her back ached a little. She was almost dangling over the edge.

'How did you manage to get away with it?' she asked the dog. 'I've always thought people who let their dogs on the bed were eccentric loonies. You aren't even one of those stylish French bulldogs with the cute ears!'

Nelly looked back with an endearing expression, as if to say, 'Dogs like that trade on their looks – with me it's all personality!'

'All right, all right, come on – let's get up and go for a walk along the river before it gets hot!'

Nelly cocked her head.

'And don't look at me like that. Yes, I know there's a chance he'll be out fishing, but it's not much of a chance. And think how stupid I'll look if he is!'

She pulled on some slightly less smart than usual clothes and ran downstairs, Nelly at her heels.

In the kitchen Sophie sat at the table, wearing her pyjamas and a pair of slippers like furry ski boots. Her hair was standing on end, reminding Meredith of a particularly pretty cockatoo. With her laptop open in front of her and a mug of black coffee, she had the air of a naughty eleven-year-old who'd sneaked out of bed to watch children's television.

'Not working already?'

'Just catching up with posts on Instagram.'

'Jo still upstairs?'

Sophie nodded. 'Probably lying in bed watching Liam longingly as he disbuds the vines, or whatever winegrowers do!'

'You're well up on the lingo,' Meredith grinned as she made herself a quick coffee.

'The modern world is all about getting the technical terms right, Meredith. Forget the actual content!'

'Anyway, your mum and Liam, is it as bad as that? Her lying in bed looking longingly?'

'She'd much rather look longingly at him *in* bed,' Sophie shrugged. 'But how to accomplish it? I'm sure there's a vibe between them but she's a bit shy, and still hurt by the Dad thing, and he's a rugged Kiwi who's probably better at talking to didgeridoos than people.'

'I thought a didgeridoo was that weird instrument played by Rolf Harris.'

'Kangaroo, then. Wallaby. Antipodean animal.'

'Rather sweeping colonial attitude there, missy,' Meredith

laughed. 'I'm surprised at you!' She paused a moment. 'By the way – the Dad thing, as you called it. Are you OK yourself?'

'Well, you know . . .' A look of pain flashed into Sophie's eyes. 'It does rather put you off men. Sometimes I think, why am I spending my life organizing lovely weddings when they all end in bloody disaster?'

Meredith slipped an arm round her. 'Plenty of them don't, you know. Plenty are ordinary and long-lasting. As my old nan used to say, they haven't come up with anything better yet to make two people happy. Unfortunately, there just isn't any recipe about how to make it work, despite what all those agony aunties say.'

'Is that why you haven't tried it yourself then, Meredith?' teased Sophie.

'Clever brat!' She ruffled Sophie's hair. 'And how do you know I'm not still considering it?'

Nelly was waiting impatiently at her feet, beginning to whine mournfully. 'You have to learn,' Meredith told her firmly, 'humans first, dogs after. OK?'

'You're bonkers if you think she buys that,' laughed Sophie. 'Nelly knows perfectly well it's the other way round, don't you, Nell?'

'Go on, cast off now!' Philippe instructed patiently. The last two attempts had either got stuck in the branches overhead or been a long way short of the mark.

Jean-Christophe repeated the gesture for the third time. The hook and bait landed in the perfect spot. 'Don't forget, Papa, it was me who landed the big fish last time.'

'*Ah oui, c'est vrai*,' Philippe acknowledged generously, 'with just a little bit of help from me.' He sat down on his low-slung canvas seat and placed his hands behind his head to relax. It was a glorious morning. Not as early as last time, so no mists evaporating in the tree-tops along the riverbank; just a brilliantly clear blue sky decorated with a few fluffy white clouds that served to point up the intensity of the blue without threatening any change of weather. In the distance he could see a figure with a dog. He sat up, bracing himself for another incident where the fish was frightened away.

As the animal got closer he saw, to his surprise, that it was indeed Nelly. But this time she was firmly on a lead and walking in a dignified manner, as if the last thing on earth she would dream of was indulging in feverish barking, running along the bank, jumping up and down or frightening the fish into instant departure.

'*Bonjour*, Meredith,' he greeted her with a smile. '*Bonjour*, Nelly.'

Meredith began to giggle helplessly.

'Why are you laughing?' Philippe enquired, mystified. 'Have I said something funny?'

'It's your pronunciation of my name. Nelly sounds just like Nelly. But Meredith is *Mey-rey-dites!*'

'*Eh bien oui!*' Philippe agreed, joining in her laughter. 'Meredith is a difficult word for French people to say. But we have a Nélie in French. One my favourite museums in Paris was started by the painter Nélie Jacquemart!'

'There you are, Nelly, you've upstaged me already.'

'Ah,' Philippe bowed politely. 'But when it comes to beauty . . .'

'I should bloody well hope so,' Meredith replied in mock outrage. 'Since you said Nelly was the ugliest dog you'd ever encountered!'

'Excuse me, *mes enfants*,' Jean-Christophe announced sternly, 'but all this juvenile behaviour is frightening the fish!'

'We will take ourselves away from the serious fisherman,' Philippe announced. 'I am sure we would both hate to disrupt his sport.'

He clasped Meredith's elbow and led her away.

'How's your food festival progressing?' she enquired.

'Amazingly! We are running out of space!'

'I'm really pleased for you, and for Bratenac. It's a delightful place and deserves much more publicity. Though I suppose this means you may be too busy to spare an evening for dinner, with your commitments to the restaurant as well.' She looked away modestly, bringing another smile to Philippe's lips.

'I would always find time to have dinner with so lovely a woman.'

'Right.' She looked him straight in the eye. 'You can cut all the crap about how gorgeous I am, and just message me some dates!'

This time it was his turn to laugh helplessly. 'I love British women. So direct. In France, flattery is considered an art form.'

'I prefer my art in galleries.'

'I'll try and remember that.'

'Good. Come on, Nelly, time to go home.'

Philippe watched her turn and walk to the nearest bend in the river before he returned to his smirking son. 'Don't say a thing,' Philippe counselled. 'You don't want to frighten the fish.'

Just round the corner, safely out of sight, Meredith dipped down to her knees to fondle Nelly. 'Not bad, eh? We achieved what we wanted, didn't we?'

Nelly fixed a mournful dark brown eye on Meredith. Her eyebrow, such as it was, seemed to be raised questioningly. The message was clear: 'I wouldn't count my *poulets* if I were you.'

*

Philippe looked round the studio at Radio Sud-Ouest. It was surprisingly small and crowded for a programme with such big audiences.

Françoise Gilbert, extremely glamorous and exceptionally thin, sat behind a microphone with a comical foam cover that made it look as if it were auditioning for Red Nose Day. There were three other microphones set up, each with identical red foam covers. A huge bottle of water stood beside each. Françoise and her guests also wore huge black headphones. She read out her introductions from a large laptop on the table in front of her. In another, separate glass box, the producer controlled the running order of items from another laptop.

Philippe had done a little radio and television in Paris, so he didn't feel at all nervous, just rather fascinated at this intense, nervy, concentrated world.

'My next guest,' Françoise said with her wide, warm, welcoming smile, 'is now a local, living in Bratenac, right in the heart of the Savarin region. But not so long ago he was a Parisian running a highly successful restaurant with not one, not two, but *three* Michelin stars. We are honoured, *mes amis*, to welcome Philippe Latignac to our humble programme!'

Back at the château, Meredith, Jo and Sophie all pretended to be busy at different tasks while tuning in to the radio. So did Margot in her Lego house. In the Café de la Paix Guillaume had placed his radio on the bar and the entire Ladies' Luncheon Club, except for Suzi, sat in a row attentively. At Fleur-de-Lis, Jean-Christophe and Marcelline stopped chopping vegetables for dinner and listened too.

The first thing anyone heard of Philippe was his very engaging laugh. 'Come now, Françoise,' he responded merrily. 'You are the famous one, not me!'

'Well, now,' she contradicted, her voice full of answering

laughter, 'to run your own restaurant in Paris and get three stars makes you pretty special in my book. Why did you give it up? Don't you miss Paris?'

'Those are very different questions. I am the third generation of chefs in my family, but the biggest influence on me was my father, who taught me everything I know. Now my father needs someone to look after him, so I came home and opened a small restaurant on the banks of the Savarin – *tout simplement*.'

'Lucky father, to have you!' Françoise commented.

'She is flirting with him!' declared Margot to no one in particular.

'He comes over well, doesn't he?' Sophie commented, not looking at Meredith. 'He's a natural.'

'And as for missing Paris,' Philippe continued, 'how could I live in the most beautiful region of France and go to work on the banks of the Savarin River, and not be grateful for every single day of my life? Besides,' he added confidentially, as though they were simply chatting, 'I love to fish. Two weeks ago my son Jean-Christophe, who is also a wonderful chef, caught the biggest fish in the river for years!'

'Congratulations to your son. I have to tell you, ladies, since this is radio, that Philippe is a very attractive man. Does your son look like you, Philippe?'

'A much handsomer version.'

'What do you think, ladies – don't you agree with me that when Philippe and his even handsomer son go fishing, the poor fishes stand no chance? They will come to you and surrender!'

'This is outrageous!' Margot declared, listening even more attentively.

'But enough about me,' Philippe deftly turned the subject. 'It's the Bratenac Food Festival I am sure people will be far more interested in. Three weeks from now. Come and try all our wonderful foods and wines. We will give you all a proper Savarin welcome!'

'If you ever need a job,' Françoise Gilbert confided once the interview was over and some music was being played, 'forget all this cooking nonsense. You'd be a brilliant broadcaster. If we didn't have an hour more of this programme to run, I'd invite you to lunch.'

Philippe smiled, relieved nevertheless to escape the over-whelming personality of the south-west's leading radio star and get back to Bratenac.

In a minimalist loft conversion at the top of an old factory on the outskirts of Bordeaux, Lucille Latignac stared unseeingly at her copy of Charles Baudelaire's *Fleurs du Mal*.

She had a class in just over an hour with her group of mature students, but she didn't know if she would be up to it. She hadn't heard her husband Philippe's voice in fifteen years, and the sudden sound of it had felled her almost as if she had been struck by lightning.

But it was the mention of his handsome son, Jean-Christophe, that had made her memory flood with the pain she thought she had left behind her in Paris when she'd walked out that night.

At first, she'd intended to fight for shared custody. But she was herself the product of an acrimonious divorce, fought over by two warring parents, used as an emotional pawn, sent from one house to the other where she was ruthlessly quizzed about the other parent's lifestyle – and based on all of this, she had decided it would be better for Jean-Christophe to stay with Philippe. If she were honest, it also gave herself the chance to reinvent herself in the way she really wanted, but self-awareness was not one of Lucille's strengths.

Suddenly the image of father and son, now a grown-up man, catching fish together, filled her with jealousy and regret at what she'd lost.

And Philippe himself had sounded so different! Instead of the peremptory chef/waitress tone that had characterized their relationship, and which she had found so hard to take, his voice now held both humour and humanity.

When he'd talked about leaving his starred restaurants in Paris to look after the father who had taught him everything, it could have been just a good story, but she could hear the genuine emotion in his voice. Sitting here in this fashionably sparse setting, in the new life she had created for herself, she remembered his feelings for that irritating old man and almost cried. Men who could love were not so easy to find.

Without really meaning to, she found herself checking online for details of the food festival he was organizing. And what a strange coincidence it was that as well as teaching mature students literature, she had spent so many years of her life running Street Taste, a small charity that helped refugees earn a small income by using their culinary skills. She wondered for a moment if the trustees would pay the fees for Street Taste to take a stall – and, more importantly, whether it would be a good idea if they did, after she had spent so long convincing herself that that chapter of her life was firmly closed. How would her ex-husband and son feel if she walked back into their lives without warning?

Eighteen

In the rare luxury of the taxi back to Bratenac, paid for by the radio station, Philippe got out his phone and called his son.

'Could you hold the fort at the restaurant next Friday or Saturday if I'm otherwise engaged?' he asked, being careful to keep the excitement he was feeling out of his voice.

'Aha,' Jean-Christophe replied, in a knowing tone that made Philippe want to clip him round the ear, 'and let me guess where you will be going. Flushed with the success of your radio debut, are you finally inviting the *châtelaine* of St Savarin to dine?'

'*Ta gueule!*' replied Philippe good-humouredly. 'I think I preferred you before you came out of your shell!'

Instantly he realized his mistake as he imagined a shadow passing over his son's handsome face. At his mother's departure Jean-Christophe had changed from happy to tongue-tied; it had taken all of Philippe's skill and energy to coax him back into confidence over the years. A process that, to his delight, had accelerated since they had arrived in Bratenac.

'So where are you taking the lady?'

'Nowhere in Bratenac, that's for sure,' Philippe laughed. 'Certainly not to the Café de la Paix, where all those British busybodies gather!' He almost added, 'Why don't you follow my example and invite out the lovely Sophie?' but fortunately he had the good sense to see how insensitive that would be. If he wanted to, Jean-Christophe would get round to it in his own time.

The British busybodies were, in fact, at that moment gathered round the bar of the cafe, having just listened to Philippe's interview at the insistence of Guillaume.

'Wasn't he wonderful?' Shirley pronounced breathlessly. 'So caring about his father.'

'I thought he sounded really sexy,' pronounced Janine, trying to persuade a particularly overweight basset hound to get off her foot. 'That Françoise woman was flirting with him as if they were in some online chat room!'

'And you would know, Janine,' slipped in Mandy slyly, then quickly changed the subject. 'Is that why you called us all here, Jackie? Because I'm going to be late for this lunch I'm catering if I don't go soon.'

'Ladies of the Luncheon Club,' Jackie announced portentously, 'it is not. I summoned you here to this special meeting with only one thing on the agenda. How are we going to get David Adams away from Suzi and back to his lawful wedded wife?'

'Gosh,' Janine replied. 'Isn't that rather a Victorian attitude?'

The others quaked at this outbreak of revolution in the ranks.

'No, it is not. I am a great believer in marriage, especially long marriages where you have negotiated tough times together, and particularly when I happen to like the parties involved.'

'And also because some little bitch pinched your first husband,' murmured Janine mutinously.

Jackie turned a face to her that wouldn't have shamed the god Mars in its warlike ferocity and replied, 'There is that too.' She suddenly grinned. 'But look, we all know it's not going to work between them. Come on, girls: ideas!'

They all fell silent, including Guillaume, who seemed to have elected himself an honorary member and was twirling his moustache thoughtfully. '*Parler comme un homme*, speaking as a man, I would try and examine the reasons why he left. Was it just for sex with Suzi or something else?'

'How are we going to find that out?'

'I think –' he stood back a pace, bracing for an explosion when he finished his sentence – 'you should consult the lady up at the château. The one who is *très élégante*.'

'You mean Margot? The duchess?'

'Pah! The duchess is *grand guignol*! Something from a horror show! The other lady, she is the big friend of Madame Adams. I have seen her pass on her way to their house many times.'

The others looked on, awed, realizing he meant Meredith, whom Jackie considered as pretentious as her name. It was a rare occasion when Jackie Brown was lost for words, but this was one of them.

'I think Guillaume's right,' Shirley announced bravely. 'I've never thought Mr Adams was the philandering kind. I think it's all a ghastly mistake.'

The object of this intense discussion sat at the sunny table outside Suzi's house contemplating an enormous pile of rather stodgy-looking pancakes and feeling distinctly queasy. If he couldn't find the nerve to tell her he wasn't staying, his stomach might well take the initiative.

They had already had breakfast a couple of hours ago – croissants and *pains au chocolat* – but Suzi had brightly insisted they should have brunch in the garden.

In even a couple of days he had realized how very different their daily lives were. David's had been strictly ordered by the demands of running a B&B, whereas Suzi's life was exactly what she made it, which seemed to mean eating, drinking (a lot) and catching up with British soaps on TV. David hadn't liked to admit that the last time he'd watched *Coronation Street*, it had featured Ena Sharples.

He also couldn't help wondering how Steph was getting on. As he waited for Suzi to return with coffee (she had refused all offers of help) his mind wandered back to when they'd first bought Fleur-de-Lis all those years ago.

Everyone back home had thought they were mad. But to them it had been like a magic trick. Take your safe suburban semi and – *ta-da!* – by some amazing economic sleight of hand, you suddenly owned a large house in a French village. OK, it had a septic tank that was forever overflowing, twelve crumbling bedrooms to do up, twelve baths to install, a boiler that had been there since Napoleon. And then, when it was all done, you couldn't live like the lord of the *manoir*; instead you led the life of a skivvy, exhausted and permanently on call.

So why the hell did he miss it?

'Hot chocolate's ready,' chirped the permanently cheerful Suzi, 'plus golden syrup and cream for the pancakes. Yum!'

David smiled tentatively, trying to prevent his stomach from heaving out the contents of last night's steak and chips plus this morning's croissants with Nutella all over the snowy white tablecloth. 'Suzi,' he finally psyched himself up to begin, 'I told you my stay was temporary because the hotel was full—'

'Oh, pooh,' she cut in. 'Why would you move to a hotel when you've got me to look after you?'

'So can I go ahead and sign Jean-Christophe up as the fourth caterer?' Sophie enquired. Meredith was sitting at her desk with such a look of concentration that Sophie had hesitated to interrupt her.

'Yes, go ahead, certainly,' Meredith replied. Sophie was more in touch with the tastes of young brides than she was, and if she felt queuing up and being served from a trendy van as if you were at a music festival was what young women wanted at their weddings, then Meredith was willing to trust her instincts. 'But remember, Steph may be leaning on him more than usual at the moment.'

'He only has to come up with sample menus at this stage, so it shouldn't take him that long,' Sophie replied.

Jo had been listening in, sitting at the delicate seventeenth-century escritoire she had adopted as her own. 'Oh God, Merry –' in her concern for their friend, she reverted to the schoolgirl nickname – 'what's going to happen to Fleur-de-Lis without David?'

'I really don't know,' shrugged Meredith. 'I'm not at all sure Steph has the heart to go it alone. But, for starters, she needs a good lawyer. Who would know of one, do you think?'

Jo thought. 'You know, funnily enough, I think Margot might. She's quite a tough cookie. Otherwise maybe your *bête noir*, Jackie.'

Meredith looked horrified. 'Are you crazy? We can't ask her, because Steph and David owe her husband quite a lot of money. They might get scared and decide to pull the rug out.'

Jo thought about it. 'Actually, I think if you appealed to her better nature, she might be quite helpful.'

'If she had a better nature,' Meredith replied scathingly.

Jo shrugged. 'OK, Margot it is. I'll hop over and see her this afternoon. God, it's beginning to get hot!' She blotted her brow with a tissue. 'Pity the château doesn't run to a pool. Maybe if things go well we should put one in.'

'Let's walk before we can run!' Meredith grinned. 'I agree a luxury venue needs a pool, but Steph told me (a) it was the pool that almost bankrupted them and (b) as the host you can never use the pool yourself – which must be mega-irritating. It looks unprofessional, apparently.'

'That must be torture when it gets really hot,' Jo replied.

'Which it does,' Sophie supplied. 'I've just been Googling, and in August it can get to forty degrees. Last year they had a *canicule*, a heatwave, and it got to fifty!'

'I think I'll also ask Margot where you can swim in the river,' Jo laughed.

'*Swim?*' Margot demanded. 'In the *river?*'

She sounded as horrified as if Jo had suggested she ride naked through Bratenac like a French Lady Godiva without the long hair.

'*Ma chère* Joanna, the river is no doubt full of algae, and pesticides from the greedy farmers, not to mention overflow from the *toilettes* of the whole region. You would be mad to swim in it. *Voila, c'est tout.*'

Fortunately, she was more helpful with the question about lawyers, providing a list of three so that Jo didn't have to head back completely empty-handed. As it happened, there was no chance of that anyway.

'You must request some grapes from your own hothouse!'

Margot insisted, smiling wickedly. By the time Jo had worked out what she was up to, she was dialling her phone.

'The *vigneron* will have them ready in five minutes. You have met the *vigneron*, I believe?' she asked in a voice laced with irony. 'His name is Liam.' She paused and produced an even more outrageous smile before shooing Jo off towards the vineyards.

The expression on Liam's face as he walked towards her with the grapes was one of barely concealed irritation. He had clearly been in the middle of something important when Margot called.

'I'm sorry,' she greeted him as he came towards her, bearing a large bunch of grapes. 'I'm sure you've got better things to do than go grape-picking for me.'

His irritation seemed to melt away at the sight of her. 'It isn't you. It's the duchess ordering me about. I don't work for her any longer – I work for you!'

There was something in his tone Jo found highly revealing. So that was part of the problem! It hadn't been anything to do with the Happy Rabbit, or not being attracted to her. He found the idea of getting involved with someone who was technically his boss difficult. And so he should, Jo realized.

A silence fell between them. Should she broach their professional relationship head-on? She had a feeling that wasn't the best method. Instead she completely changed the subject. 'There was one thing I was going to ask you, though. Do you happen to know if there's any kind of beach or swimming spot in this reach of river?'

Liam laughed. 'Tell you what, if you can wait five minutes while I get my stuff, I won't tell you, I'll show you!'

A few moments later, Liam was leading her down a narrow path between the vines and a high stone wall that marked the end of the property. The river dazzled and sparkled ahead in the bright sunshine, looking cool and inviting.

'I can't swim right now, I'm afraid,' Jo apologized.

Liam instantly understood. 'No cozzie? Wear your shred-dies. I won't look!'

'Shreddies?' laughed Jo. 'We have them for breakfast back home.'

Liam fell about with laughter. 'That's Kiwi for underpants!'

'Look at the river, then,' Jo instructed. 'It's beautiful today.'

'I prefer the view a bit nearer,' Liam laughed.

Jo found a convenient shrub and ducked behind it to strip down to bra and pants. Thank heavens they were matching. Taking a deep breath so that her stomach flattened, she emerged and headed for the water, but Liam caught her arm. 'Hey! With that pale skin you'll burn in five minutes. We Kiwis learn to take the sun seriously.'

Before she had time to reply, his hands were on her shoulders, rubbing in sun cream in firm but gentle strokes. Relieved that she was facing away from him, Jo closed her eyes. The physical shock of his touch rooted her to the spot with the realization that she hadn't felt a man's hands on her body for longer than she could remember.

'*Félicitations*, Philippe!' congratulated a message waiting from the mayor of Bratenac. Apparently appearing on Françoise Gilbert's programme had led to a slew of applications for stalls at the food festival, and it was rapidly turning into the big attraction of the summer.

The mayor had attached all the new messages.

'At this rate,' Philippe announced to his son, 'we will definitely need to rent that extra bit of land that adjoins the car park.'

He glanced through the messages, stopping at one from an organization called Street Taste applying for a stall. There was something about the name that was faintly familiar, but he couldn't place it. Maybe it would come to him.

'You were really good,' Jean-Christophe congratulated. 'I thought that woman was going to ask you to marry her, she seemed so keen! Grand-père listened to it with Marcelline and he said marriage wasn't what the host lady had in mind.'

Philippe roared with laughter. 'He can be the sharpest tool in the box when he's in the right mood! Do you know, I think this festival might be rather a success. Hard work, though. Are you sure I haven't railroaded you into it?'

Jean-Christophe shook his head and grinned. 'Contrary to your assumptions, I enjoy hard work.'

Philippe looked serious for a moment. 'How is Stephanie getting on without her husband?'

'Not brilliantly,' Jean-Christophe shrugged.

Philippe sighed. 'I was never unfaithful, but I certainly wasn't the best husband, so I don't think I should cast the first stone.'

'Don't worry. I'll throw yours for you. Our generation is determined to be different.'

Philippe studied his son for a moment. He was thoughtful, considerate and empathetic, yet not at all soft. It was wonderful to watch. He wished their generation a lot of luck with making themselves a different kind of men than those who had gone before.

Perhaps they would even do it.

'I'd like to call a meeting,' Sophie suggested to Meredith.

'What time? I'm pretty free this afternoon. What about Jo?'

'What about her?' Jo replied, coming in through the garden door. Her hair was damp, an attractive sprinkling of freckles had appeared on her nose and the top of both her shoulder blades were beginning to acquire a gentle tan.

'Oooh, you're going brown, Mum!' pointed out Sophie.

'I know, it's getting really hot out there.' Jo smiled a soft, secret smile.

'You wait,' grinned Meredith, remembering childhood summers where she'd stayed in the sun all day. 'The climate here is weird. It can be blazing hot and then suddenly, just like that, there's a hailstorm and it takes every grape off the vines in five minutes.'

'Oh goodness, Liam mentioned that at the wine tasting,' Jo exclaimed. 'Sounds awful for the winegrowers. I hope it doesn't happen often.'

'Oftener than you'd think,' Meredith decreed.

'Anyway,' Sophie reminded. 'Back to work, girls.' She went over to a large Louis IV cabinet and opened it. 'I've made a chart,' she announced proudly, indicating a flipchart blu-tacked to the inside of the door, 'of everything that has to be done between now and the day of Nicky's wedding.'

'Oh, brilliant!' Jo announced gleefully. 'Once Sophie's got a chart you know things are going to happen.'

'Right, let me explain.' Sophie indicated three neatly item-ized columns. 'There is one for each of us, listing everything we have to do – and there's a column at the end to tick when the job's completed. I'll make one of these for every bride we get. As soon as Nicky's beautiful wedding becomes the envy of each bride in the Western world, we'll need millions of them! One other thing.' She looked serious for a moment. 'I've also estimated all the costs more accurately than before. The quote covers all the elements of a château wedding – venue hire, accommodation, family dinner, wedding feast with champagne reception, hair and make-up, photography, flowers and entertainment . . .' She named a figure.

Jo whistled. 'That much?'

Sophie nodded. 'At least. That's cheap by comparison with most places. In fact, we should do more research before we launch properly. Sixty per cent of the cost of a château wedding goes on venue and catering, so it's crucial we set the right fee for hiring the venue.'

'Good idea,' Meredith agreed. 'Why don't I make a comparison of four or five other châteaux to make sure we're pitching it right?'

'We need to face the tricky question of Nicky's deposit. Normally it would have been paid months ago, so it's way overdue even in this special case. Who's going to remind her and Ronnie?'

Meredith sighed. 'We can't expect Steph to get involved, given all that's been happening.' She thought about it and came to a decision. 'OK, I'll take that on.'

'Good luck,' Jo acknowledged. 'Oh, and have you heard about our local hero? Margot was bending my ear about him for hours.'

'No, who?' Meredith tried not to sound irritable at this distraction from the important discussion they were having.

'Philippe, of course! He was a real hit on the radio talking about this food festival. Everyone's raving about him, saying how good he was and what a success the festival's going to be.'

'Oh, right.' Meredith wondered if the piece of land she'd agreed to rent him would be large enough. She'd assumed it was going to be little local affair. If it was going to be big, it might also turn out to be a headache, with much more hassle and clearing up.

She glanced down at her phone to find a message from Philippe himself. No doubt he wanted to talk about the festival, fresh from his hit on the radio, and she felt a flash of irritation. She didn't want it to start taking up a lot of her time when she had the wedding to concentrate on. Sophie's chart had had the effect of crystallizing her mind.

When the others had gone back to their various tasks, Meredith wandered out onto the terrace and returned his call.

'I hear you're quite the celebrity,' she greeted him drily. 'So, what can I help you with? Only I am a bit busy, you know.'

'I will try not to take too much of your valuable time,' Philippe replied with a laugh in his voice. Everyone else might be impressed with his instant fame, but not Meredith. 'As a matter of fact this isn't a business call. I'm ringing to invite you out to dinner next Saturday night. Of course,' there was a hint of challenge in his tone, 'you may be far too busy to waste your time on a purely social occasion.'

For a moment even the poised and unfazeable Meredith was temporarily silenced. She took refuge in prevarication.

'But what about the restaurant? Surely you can't leave that on a Saturday night? Or are you inviting me to dine with you there?'

'Of course not!' She was annoyed to hear him laughing at her again. 'That would hardly be a very romantic invitation, would it?'

There was an embarrassingly long pause during which Philippe wondered if he should rescue them both with some polite social cliché. Clearly this had been a mistake.

'Thank you,' Meredith replied at last, wondering why she felt the temptation to sabotage even something she had been half hoping for. 'That would be delightful.'

Philippe whistled as he chopped the onions, giving his already impressive technique an extra flourish, making Jean-Christophe laugh out loud. 'You should have been one of those TV chefs, then you'd have been really famous.'

'Then thank God I wasn't!' replied his father. 'I already got mobbed in the *boulangerie* for my modest level of media exposure. Madame Demarchelier from the *blanchisserie* even asked for my autograph!'

'Go on, you love it!' teased Jean-Christophe.

'The good thing is, the mayor's delighted. They've been deluged – his word, I expect he means five or six – by new applications for stalls.'

That name, Street Taste, flashed into his mind again. Why was it familiar? Had he read about it in the paper? He'd have to look it up when he got a moment. Some chance. He was so busy with the festival and all that needed to be arranged for it, as well as running this place, that he hardly had time to take a leak, let alone Google anything.

'At least it'll impress the *châtelaine*.'

'*Tu plaisantes!* It takes more than a stupid radio experience to impress Mademoiselle Meredith Harding!'

But it wasn't to Google that Philippe resorted later on when he finally got ten minutes for a coffee break, but to his own wallet.

Buried there among the receipts, parking chits and bills was a small, rather crumpled black-and-white photo. It was of his ex-wife, Lucille. She'd always preferred monochrome photographs, saying they had more drama; but borrowed drama was not something Lucille needed. Her face was startingly beautiful, with shoulder-length black hair, dark eyebrows and arresting blue-green eyes.

She had been so young when they'd met, and he had been on the crest of his own success. Maybe she had been right that he'd thought he was a young god who could demand anything of anyone. He'd certainly behaved like one.

It had taken him years to stop blaming her for leaving and understand why she might have done it; at the time, all he'd felt was blazing anger. How could she simply abandon her husband and ten-year-old child – disappear from their lives as if by a wave of a bad fairy's wand?

Lucille had been the love of his life. Deep down, in the depths of his unconscious, did he want her to return and find out how much he had changed? And what had happened to her? Where had she gone?

He was going to find out a lot sooner than he imagined.

Nineteen

———————

'Meredith!' Jo arrived in Meredith's adopted study just as she was getting ready to go and see one of the local lawyers about Steph's tax problem. 'Someone rather surprising to see you.'

'Who?' demanded Meredith. She was already running slightly late, which she abhorred, and didn't want any further delays.

'Me,' announced Jackie, 'just in case you were about to say anything rude.' She turned to Joanna. 'Speaking of being rude, I don't suppose there's any chance I could speak to Meredith alone?'

'Fine.' Meredith pointed to the salon. 'Come in here for a moment.'

'Sorry about that,' Jackie grinned. 'Outrageous, I know, but look – I've got a proposition to put to you and I wanted to do it alone. I know you're the one who really runs things round here.' Meredith was about to protest. 'Oh, I'm sure you're pretty fair to the others and they're important in their way, but in the end you're the majority owner so in my book you're the boss.'

'Look, honestly, I have a meeting with a lawyer in town and I really am going to be late . . .'

'Don't worry.' Again, that infectious grin. The woman actually expected Meredith to like her! 'I'll drive you. Which one is it, Madame Petit or Monsieur Gelignac?'

'Madame Petit, as a matter of fact.' Meredith tried not to sound actively rude. How did this bloody woman know everything that happened round here when she wasn't even a local?

'Good choice.' Jackie opened the passenger door of a disreputable-looking Honda Civic. She moved what was clearly her butcher's delivery off the front seat and into the already cluttered back one. All the seats, Meredith noticed with a shudder, were covered in dog hair. Meredith brushed hers off, grateful that although Nelly wasn't the most beautiful dog in the world, at least she didn't shed.

'Sorry. I helped out my friend Janine when her car wouldn't start. She's a dog-walker, you know.'

'And part of your little lunch group?' Meredith found herself enquiring.

'Yes. There's myself and Janine; and Shirley – she's happily married, amazingly; then there's Mandy, she caters lots of expat events; and finally—'

'And you're all British?' interrupted Meredith, not wanting to get to the subject of Suzi.

'Yes – sad, isn't it? Though Guillaume gives us French lessons, so we do try not to be your fish'n'chip Brits.' She turned from the bumpy château drive onto the deserted main road.

Ten seconds passed before Meredith realized they were on the wrong side and screeched at her.

'Oops, sorry,' Jackie grinned unapologetically. 'I do that sometimes. Steve says I'm making an unconscious statement that I want to go home.'

'And do you?' Meredith couldn't resist asking. Jackie was probably one of those ghastly expats who called the locals Frogs and said they only stayed here because there were so many immigrants back home that you couldn't tell it was England any more.

'No, actually. I love it here. Bunch of bloody racists back in Essex. I love the weather and I love the French. Guillaume's my best mate – apart from Steve, obviously.'

Meredith found herself wondering what it would be like to consider your husband your best mate, and smiled for the first time.

'You've got a lovely smile,' Jackie commented, looking at the road ahead. 'Pity we don't see more of it.'

Before Meredith could think of a suitable put-down they were parking outside the lawyer's office.

Jackie switched the engine off and turned to Meredith. 'OK, here goes. You're worried about your friend Stephanie up at Fleur-de-Lis, aren't you?'

Meredith picked up the strong impression that despite all her own preconceptions about Jackie, the woman was genuinely trying to help.

'Yes, very.'

'Well, so are we.'

'Your friend Suzi isn't exactly helping.'

'No. And we're worried about her, too. I think she genuinely feels something for him, and maybe he does for her, but they're hopelessly unsuited. I mean, can you imagine Suzi thinking of David as her best mate, like I do with Steve?'

'No, probably not. But isn't that rather a high bar?'

'Making each other laugh. Protecting each other from the bad stuff that comes with ageing. That's what matters at our age, and I don't think Suzi and David can offer each other much of that. It was with your friend Steph he had all that. Well, used to, anyway. I used to see them laughing like kids in the market sometimes.'

'They seemed to lose that. Part of the problem, I suspect. And what's your proposition?' Meredith was going to be late for her meeting, but this was too intriguing to miss.

'You give Suzi something to do up at the château, maybe advising on interior design – she's got quite a good eye, actually, apart from in her own home. You wouldn't need to pay her much, she's quite well off. Boyfriend who was in hedge funds gave her some investments before he buggered off. And in exchange, Steve and I will write off your friend's debt. Amen and goodbye.'

'But how will that help? Even if I could do it.'

'You could do it.' Jackie fixed her with the beady eye of an exceptionally determined parrot. 'A job is what Suzi needs, not David. They're chalk and cheese. I give it a month, less if she keeps wanting sex – but that may be too long for your friend's marriage. Now I know you're a rich lady and you could just pay off this debt, but you see, your friend's too proud for that. She'll feel patronized and that'll be the end of your friendship. It's different with me. I can say he got the books wrong and apologize. If Suzi's got something else to think about, this whole thing'll fizzle out. The risk is to your friend's husband. It's up to him to prove to Stephanie he's worth having back.' Jackie sniffed. 'As a matter of fact, I think he is. But obviously that's up to her. I'll leave you to make up your mind.'

She reached over and opened the passenger door.

'You've really been thinking about this, haven't you?'

'I have indeed. That Italian chap's got nothing on me. What's his name now?'

'Machiavelli?'

273

'That's the dude. Steve says I should have been born a Borgia. I don't think I'd have liked it, though. Women got pushed round even more than they do now. No wonder they resorted to poisoning people. I can think of a few I'd like to poison myself.'

Finally it was Meredith's turn to grin. 'You're a one-off, Jackie, in any age, if you ask me.'

'Steve says a good thing, too. I hope you don't think I'm interfering.'

'Friendship sometimes involves a bit of interfering. Look, I'll have to consult the others, but I'll let you know as soon as I can.' Meredith held out her hand. 'And thank you, on behalf of my friend Steph. Though if she knew about it, she'd probably kill us!'

'Have that woman Suzi working for us here?' Sophie's face was a picture of horror. 'I thought next to Margot she was your arch-enemy!'

Meredith burst out laughing. 'You make me sound like a character in Agatha Christie! As if I've got wax dolls of Jackie and Margot to stick pins in.'

'And Suzi!' Jo added. 'Don't forget Suzi!'

'Well, I haven't,' Meredith insisted. 'Now listen to the deal Jackie's proposing and see what you think.'

They both listened patiently.

'OK, let me see if I've got this right. The lawyer says the tax was wrongly charged and they can claim a rebate; and Jackie says she'll write their debt off and convince Steph it was her fault, that she accidentally overcharged them,' Jo paraphrased. 'Won't that sound a bit suspicious? I mean – they built a swimming pool and spent too much money on it. How could that just be a mistake?'

'You don't know Jackie. She'll manage. Lucrezia Borgia could take lessons from her. The difference is, she's got a good heart.'

'And she thinks this will mean Fleur-de-Lis will be saved and David will go back to Steph and everything will be happy ever after?' Jo enquired drily.

'What happens if we take Suzi on and David doesn't comply with Jackie's plan?' countered Sophie.

Meredith thought. 'Then we'll have to sack Suzi. I'm sure we'll be able to find a reason.'

No one said anything for a moment, and then Jo spoke up.

'Speaking as someone who's been royally dumped – sorry, Soph, he's your dad after all . . .' Her throat closed up with emotion and she had to stop for a moment. 'I think it's worth a try. I don't think David's like Mark, though God knows he's behaved badly enough. But we've all seen how Steph behaved to him. Sometimes I had to leave the room, it was so painful to watch. So you see, the difficulty in all this is Steph herself. I'm prepared to give Suzi a go for Steph's sake, and because I don't want her to suffer any more than she has to. But how are we going to solve the problem of Steph herself?'

'Oh, Mum,' Sophie launched herself bodily at her mother and held her in a breathless embrace. 'You are amazing. I think the only person who could help Steph is you. On the other hand, you're hurting as well and it's an awful lot to ask.'

'If you both think it would really help, I'll do it,' Jo agreed. 'Though God knows when or how.'

'But this is ridiculous!'

Back in Basingstoke, Ronnie had just read the email from Meredith that had been sitting for the last three days in her inbox. 'How can a wedding possibly cost that much? Ours was above a pub and everyone had pints and pasties and the whole thing cost less than a grand!'

'And look how that turned out!' Nicky protested. 'Martin and I want a romantic wedding in a wonderful setting with all our friends round us to treasure forever!'

'That's all very well, but who's going to pay for it?'

'Dad is.' Nicky had been working up to telling Ronnie that her father had agreed to meet the entire cost with no argument.

'But that means he'll be there. With *that woman!*'

'Of course he will, Mum. You can't expect him to pay for the wedding and not come? Anyway, the split was years ago, and you did throw him out, remember?'

Nicky knew her father was rather a dull man, but as she grew older, dull didn't seem such an insult as it once had. She had, over the years, spent time with Bill and Maureen at their home in Penge. She hadn't, as some people in her position did, fallen in love with her little brothers and sister, but she had found them perfectly nice people.

'Well,' said Ronnie dramatically, 'I've just read on this website that the person people look at most after the bride is her mother. So I'm just off to choose my outfit.' She swept out, clutching her laptop.

'Yeah,' Nicky murmured, with a kind of bitter acceptance born of experience, 'thanks for being interested in what *I'm* going to wear!' But at least it meant her mum was accepting that the wedding was actually going to take place.

There was one advantage to Ronnie's self-obsession: Nicky didn't need to consult her or put up with her saying 'You're going to spend *that* much on a dress?' or point out again that she could have a honeymoon for the same money. This was going to be a wonderful wedding, and she'd happily settle for a honeymoon in the Isle of Wight if it meant she could have the dress of her dreams.

Nicky wasn't the only person who wanted to find the right dress to make an impression. Meredith was standing in front of a long pearl-embellished mirror that had belonged to Margot and before her, countless previous ladies of St Savarin over hundreds of years, getting dressed for her date with Philippe.

The trouble was, she was used to dressing mainly for work and her wardrobe reflected this fact. She had a couple of dresses she'd worn to the opera, but they seemed too formal. What if Philippe had chosen some pop-up, like his own place? Or planned a picnic on the river, or some hip little joint where you had to queue to get in? Being overdressed was a worse fashion faux pas than being underdressed. What made her uneasy was not knowing, not being in charge.

Come on, control freak, said a voice in her head, *let go for once. You might even have fun.*

Then she remembered the twenty-five-euro linen dress Steph had persuaded her to buy from a stall in Bratenac market, and pulled it out of the back of her wardrobe.

It was both chic and dressed-down. The vibrant green might be a shade more typical of Ronnie than Meredith, but actually, it worked.

She slipped down to the kitchen and poured herself a glass of champagne, hoping the others wouldn't notice the indulgence, then slipped quietly back upstairs. She ran a bath in her eau de nil bathtub with lion's-paw feet that stood on a pedestal, swagged by floaty curtains, looking out towards the river.

Aren't you making a bit too much of this? asked that familiar voice in her head.

No, she thought. For once, I'm going to bloody well enjoy myself and not worry about anything else at all!

Down in the kitchen, Sophie held up the bottle of champagne with the missing glass and grinned. 'Come on, Mum, let's have one too!' She poured out two glasses. 'To Philippe and Meredith on their first date! Good luck to them. God, I hate first dates. All that stress wondering if you're actually going to like each other. Though in this case I suspect they know already!'

Lucille Latignac sat looking out over the rooftops of Bordeaux and reading through the application she'd sent to the Bratenac Food Festival, which started in less than a week.

Why had she done it? Was it simply because it would be good for Street Taste?

It was a source of great pride to her that her charity taught immigrants to use their cooking skills to produce and sell street food. She and a friend had put two and two together when they'd witnessed how many new arrivals there were in France, particularly from North Africa and Senegal, due to the country's colonial past – at the same time noticing the sudden leap in interest in street food. Street food had become hip and chic. Why not help refugees use their skills to cook? And it had been a big success.

The charity awarded small loans, taught basic skills in bookkeeping and general marketing awareness, and provided backup when necessary. It was fairly small-scale but it had attracted a fair amount of attention, especially since it empowered women in very male-dominated societies, and with that had come extra funding. It could grow a lot bigger if they had more time, but Lucille and her partner in the charity needed to earn a living.

After she'd left Paris, Lucille had managed to win a place at university. It had been a hard slog, since she'd funded it through waitressing, but her degree had led to her present job teaching French literature to mature students on part-time courses; hence her passion for Baudelaire.

It had been a strange life compared to her previous security, but that security had come at a price. She relived for a moment the loss of leaving her ten-year-old son, who, despite her saying goodbye, had not understood that her departure was permanent. She was suddenly aware of tears falling on her laptop and wiped it dry.

What would Jean-Christophe be like now? A young man of twenty-five. She wondered if he looked like her at all. He certainly shared her eye colour, but face shapes changed. His hair, too, was black like hers. Maybe he'd dyed it blond, maybe his beautiful young skin was covered in tattoos like so many of the young people she saw in the streets. Or maybe he looked like his father.

The man she'd heard on the radio had sounded nothing like the easily riled, temperamental, unappreciative husband she recalled, who'd treated her like a waitress in life as well as at work. Could someone really change that much?

She looked down at the form again. Are you doing this for Street Taste or for yourself? she wondered, but no answer presented itself. She might be beautiful, but she was getting older – and although she'd had serious relationships, none had lasted since she'd left Philippe.

'Oh shit, I don't know,' she said out loud.

There was only one way to find out.

'What would you like to drink? A *gin-tonic*? Champagne?' asked Philippe as they sat down in a small restaurant, nestled among russet towers, next to the church in the hilltop village of Loubressac.

'I didn't think champagne was local,' Meredith quipped, remembering how he had insisted on her ordering a wine that came from the region. How long ago was that? It seemed so long, but was actually quite recent.

'You are right, of course,' Philippe grinned. 'Champagne has to come from the Champagne region, but they've probably got a nice local *crémant*.'

'That sounds delicious,' Meredith replied.

They looked out over the valley and for a split second Meredith couldn't think what to say. What had happened to her famed social skills? 'Well, here we are,' she heard her own voice finally produce, 'on that awkward first date. At our age, too!'

What the hell was she thinking?

But Philippe's response was to laugh. 'Indeed. We could start with that old cliché, "Tell me about yourself."'

'Sounds like a seminar. Or a therapy session. I remember a business thing in Singapore where we had this guru type who said "I want to know just one thing about each of you that you wouldn't dare tell anyone else!"'

'*Bon!* What is the one thing you would tell him?'

'I'm scared.'

Where the hell had that come from?

'You?' Philippe raised his eyebrows in surprise. 'You seem one of the least scared people I have met.'

'Well, there you are. It's the château. I'm in uncharted territory. In a normal business I know how to cost every last thing. But this is about fantasies, dreams, happiness. How do you cost those? And I've dragged my friends into it, too.' She looked him in the eye. 'Your turn now. What would your one thing be?'

'I'm scared too. But for my son. He is the best thing in my

life. But will he find love, the deep fulfilling love that can last a lifetime?'

'That sounds more like a woman's question than a man's,' Meredith commented wryly.

'And now we have the gender bias in reverse,' replied Philippe with a smile.

'Do you think everyone's scared?' Meredith found herself asking. 'Just of different things?'

Before either could answer, the waiter arrived. '*Bonsoir, monsieur et madame, vous êtes prêts à commander?*'

They had a delicious meal of hot *pâté de foie gras* with white grapes, followed by capon cooked in different ways, the thigh as a *confit* and the breast served in roast spiced aubergine, followed by the most delicious chocolate mousse she'd ever eaten. And all accompanied by a red Bergerac wine.

'What makes you a good chef?' she suddenly asked him.

Philippe thought for a moment. 'I'm a bit of a maverick. I hate the alpha male nonsense in the kitchen. My wife – sorry, my ex-wife would be surprised to hear that, because it's something I've had to learn.'

Meredith registered the words with an almost physical jolt. Of course there had to be an ex-wife, or how could there be a Jean-Christophe? But she'd never heard her mentioned before. It was crazy, but Meredith felt the old thing her grandmother used to talk about – a ghost walking over her grave. How ridiculous! It must be all the rich food.

'I can't bear all that Stalinism in the kitchen,' Philippe persisted. 'Some of the famous chefs in Paris actually demand silence. They run their kitchens like military operations. I believe cooking should be enjoyable.'

As he spoke, a strand of hair started to fall over one eye

and he lifted his arm to tuck it behind his ear, revealing as he did a neat criss-cross of fresh burns.

'From the oven,' he laughed. 'You never seem to learn!'

At the sight of the red weals in the tender flesh, Meredith dipped down and without even realizing she was doing it, touched them with her lips.

As she sat up he reached for her arm and copied the exact gesture. She tried not to register the electrical volt that ran right through her and simply return the pressure of his hand.

'A very memorable evening,' Philippe said softly as they finished their coffee. 'A pity it has to end here.'

'Does it?' replied Meredith evenly, remembering in the same moment that she no longer lived on her own but in a château with two others. She could invite Philippe back, of course, but her instinct for privacy prevented her.

Philippe read her thoughts. 'Sadly I share a home with my father, and you and I are a little old for shenanigans in the car.'

'It would probably put my back out,' conceded Meredith.

'Next time we will have to think ahead,' he grinned.

'I'll live for the moment,' she replied, regretting that the words sounded arch and flirtatious when she'd never been more serious in her life.

Next morning, Meredith sat staring at her laptop. She was supposed to be producing an analysis of all the costs of hiring the other châteaux in the area, but all she could think of was last night. How could she, Meredith, the least touchy-feely person she knew, have suddenly kissed his scars? And then – just like some suburban sixteen-year-old – suggested they spend the night together?

And she wasn't sorry!

'Are you OK, Meredith?' Jo's voice penetrated her reverie.

'Have you got a moment for a coffee? I'll go and make some if so.'

'Do I look like I need a coffee?' Meredith grinned. 'Actually, I'd love one. Come on; I'll come to the kitchen with you and we can chat on the way.'

It was actually quite a squash with them both squeezed into the small room that passed for a kitchen in the apartment. Given the grandeur of the rest of their accommodation, it had surprised Meredith at first. Then she realized that any entertaining Margot did would have been provided by caterers. Like Meredith, Margot was not a cook.

'Ooh, those biscuits look nice,' she commented, helping herself to one as soon as Jo laid them out.

Jo glanced at her in surprise. Meredith never ate biscuits.

'What did you want to talk about?'

'Steph. I could hardly sleep last night, worrying about how to approach her over David.'

'Hmmm. Yes, it's tricky. Why don't we see if Suzi takes the bait first – otherwise, there's no point trying to persuade Steph that she wasn't always the sweet and put-upon wife she likes to think she was. Do we have a number for Suzi, I wonder?'

'I doubt it. I think your choice is either to go round, or ring David and ask to speak to her.'

'That'll give him a heart attack,' grinned Meredith. 'But I think I'll try speaking to him.' She looked at her watch. 'A bit early yet. Let's have that coffee.' Without noticing, she hummed as she heated up the milk.

'You're in a good mood,' commented Jo. 'Sorry, that was crass of me,' she added instantly.

'Very crass,' agreed Meredith. 'But yes, I did have a fun evening with Philippe; and yes, I do think I like him.'

They were still laughing when Sophie joined them, her hair

standing on end like a ghost in a zombie film. But before she had a chance to ask what the joke was, the doorbell chimed down on the ground floor.

'Who on earth could it be at this hour?' wondered Meredith.

'Well, it is nine o'clock. That's probably quite late in the country,' Sophie replied. 'Do you mind if one of you goes? I don't want to frighten the locals in my nightie.'

'Not to mention your hair,' teased her mother. 'I'll go.' And she disappeared down the magnificent Aubusson-carpeted staircase.

Twenty

A moment later, Jo returned with a very excited-looking Steph. 'Morning all,' Steph beamed. 'You'll never guess what's happened!'

'Jackie came round and told you your debt's all a mistake,' Meredith was tempted to suggest. Instead she replied: 'No, what?'

'You know that frightful woman married to Steve the builder? The one who made so much of your admittedly tasteless claim to be on your deathbed?'

'The leading light of the Ladies' Luncheon Club?' prompted Meredith innocently.

'Exactly. Well, she suddenly appeared last night. It seems there's been a mix-up. Her husband got the money we owe them for the swimming pool wrong. Some mix-up over accounting methods. And the upshot is, we hardly owe them anything!'

'That's terrific, Stephie,' congratulated Jo, trying not to catch Meredith's eye. 'I'm so pleased for you.'

'And thanks to your lawyer, we might even get a tax *rebate*!'

'So things are looking much healthier financially?' prompted Meredith.

'Absolutely. We won't have to sell Fleur-de-Lis after all!'

Noting the fact that she still said 'we', Jo dared to ask another question. 'Have you heard from David at all? He must be relieved too.'

The temperature in the room instantly dropped. 'Not a word. Safely tucked in his love nest, stupid fucking idiot!'

This was definitely not the moment to broach the topic of Steph's own contribution to the situation, Jo decided. 'Have you got time for a coffee? We've just made some.'

They took their coffee out onto the balcony of the main salon. Although it was only nine o'clock, it was already hot. 'You wait,' Steph warned. 'This area's deceptive. In spring you think it's like England, all green and pleasant land, and then round about now it heats up almost overnight and it's forty degrees!'

'I wonder how hot it'll be for Nicky's wedding in August,' mused Sophie.

'Very hot, I imagine,' said Steph. 'Now, I need to get back to my guests. Marcelline's English isn't quite up to the requests we get about where people can go swimming, find a burger, buy laxatives . . .'

She embraced them all merrily.

'Nice to see her in such a good mood,' Sophie commented once she had gone. 'Funny life she leads, dealing with all those guests all the time.'

'Takes her mind off missing David, I imagine,' suggested Meredith. 'Talking of which, I'd better have a go at our side of the bargain and get hold of Suzi.'

She went across to her desk and dialled David's number. 'Hello, David,' she greeted him cheerily. 'Meredith here.'

'Meredith, hi.' David sounded both defensive and deeply nervous. 'What can I do for you?'

'Can I have a word with Suzi, please?'

'Why on earth?'

'I'll explain it to her.'

'I'm not sure . . .'

'Come on, David. I haven't had a contract taken out on her, I promise.'

David forced a laugh as he reluctantly handed over the phone.

'Suzi, hi. Meredith here.'

'And what do you want?' Suzi screeched. 'I'm not giving him up, no matter what the old bags of Bratenac think.'

'Of course you're not. Ignore the old bags. They've got nothing better to do than gossip. As a matter of fact, I'm calling to offer you a job – well, actually, more of a consultancy.'

Suzi couldn't have been more astonished if Meredith had been offering her the Miss World title.

'What kind of job? I'm not prepared to be a cleaner!'

'Certainly not,' soothed Meredith in her best client-smarming tone. 'Both Jackie and Guillaume have commented to me on your exceptional eye for décor, and that's just what we need to give our weddings the style of the moment. Take a look at some weddings on Instagram and you'll see what I mean. Do you think you might be interested?'

Suzi, who had been primed to refuse any offer from Meredith in the deadliest put-down tone she could muster, found some quite different words coming out of her mouth. 'I must admit, that sounds right up my street. How much money are you offering?'

Meredith took a deep breath and named a very generous hourly rate. After all, what price could you put on helping out a friend?

'When do you want me to come in?' was the instant reply.

Meredith decided she might need some time to prepare the others for the onslaught of this tornado. 'How about tomorrow afternoon?'

'See you then,' replied Suzi, in such a honeyed tone that it was clear she believed she'd won.

Meredith just hoped this crazy scheme of Jackie's would finally pay off. And how they were going to explain it to Steph, she hadn't yet worked out.

Philippe whistled as he opened the latest email from the mayor. It was strange to be Bratenac's blue-eyed boy. Everyone kept saying hello to him in the street, and bookings had gone up in the restaurant. He liked the second thing but wasn't at all sure about the first.

'Morning, superstar,' Jean-Christophe greeted him. 'I don't need to know how it went last night. I can see it written all over you.'

Philippe grinned. 'That's just the sprinkle of stardust you get from appearing with Françoise Gilbert.'

'Hmm,' challenged his son, 'not sure that's all there is to it. So how did you get on in Loubressac, eating *foie gras* and watching the moon?'

'*Merci, mon fils*, it was a wonderful evening. Once you break through the frost with Mademoiselle Harding, there is much warmth beneath.'

'I can see that it's still having an effect.' He looked serious for a moment. 'I'm glad for you, Papa,' he said. 'You've been alone for a long time.'

'I probably deserved it. Men can behave like complete shits without even beginning to accept it.'

'I wouldn't know about that, but I can tell you one thing. You aren't any more.'

'Thank you, *petit*, that means a lot to me coming from you. Now I suppose I'd better get back to organizing this food festival, or it'll turn out to be Bratenac's very own complete disaster.'

'David Adams, I'm David Adams . . .'

It sounded crazy even to him, but David was having to repeat his own name because he felt his entire world had turned on its head; and of course, it was his own bloody fault. He was the one who'd sat drinking in the Café de la Paix with Suzi, knowing full well it wasn't entirely innocent, lapping up all her flattery as if every word were true – when all the time he knew he was a perfectly ordinary guy with an almost-happy life. Almost, but not quite. Steph had played her part too. She had belittled him, sometimes publicly, and whatever he did to make her life easier, it had never seemed enough.

And yet. He was the one who hadn't told her the truth about their financial difficulties – hadn't *trusted* her with the truth, in her own words.

Sitting here, repeating his own name to try and grasp onto his identity, just made him realize one thing: he missed her. He missed the ordinariness of their days. When Suzi had come onto his horizon he had persuaded himself he deserved something more. Excitement. Passion. A bigger canvas.

But in a funny way, the canvas had turned out to be smaller.

It was as though Suzi had Googled *What makes men happy?* and was desperate to fulfil it: as much as possible of food, sport, sex. And yet the only time he'd seen her looking genuinely content was sitting, as she was now, with a moodboard, creating romantic room sets for the château.

Suzi, he'd discovered, didn't want to live in the real world.

And Steph did. But what the hell he was going to do about this discovery, he had no fucking idea.

'Oh God,' groaned Jo. 'Ronnie's asking if she can come back and stay in the château for a couple of days to line up some florists.'

'But she only went home to Basingstoke a couple of weeks ago!' protested Sophie.

'Can't she do it online like everyone else?' Meredith demanded. 'And why not stay with her sister?'

'She wants to drink in the atmosphere of the venue so that she can get the mood of the flowers right,' giggled Jo.

'And drink in quite a lot of our wine at the same time! Oh my God: Ronnie *and* Suzi here at the same time.' Meredith shook her head. 'I think I might book a flight to Singapore. It's quieter there.'

'At least Steph seems more cheerful,' said Jo.

'Yes. That's step one. But how the hell do you pull off step two?' shrugged Meredith.

'Remind me of step two.'

'Getting Steph and David back together.'

Philippe stood in the field adjoining the château with the event organizer hired by the mayor, trying to work out how to fit thirty stands into the available space.

'Not possible,' asserted the organizer. 'You will have to expand into the next field, plus you may have some late applications. You'd be surprised how often that happens. Now, where are you going to put the WCs?'

Philippe was beginning to grasp the scale of the organization needed for an event like this. 'Can't people just use the facilities in the car park?' he enquired.

'Not for this many. You'll have to hire portable toilets. Next to the entrance booth would be best.'

'Do we need an entrance booth?' asked Philippe.

'You have to stop people just wandering in without paying. How do you see that working, by the way?'

'I thought we'd charge a flat entrance fee, then give them a glass and plate, and they can sample all the food and wine included in that.'

'Sounds good.'

'Then we distribute the profits among the stallholders.'

'Right,' the organizer sounded surprised. 'So it's not designed as a moneymaking venture?'

'More of a community idea.'

'We'd better get going. It'll take a while to put your stalls up and all the rest of it. Here comes your mayor by the look of it.'

'*Salut, Philippe, et félicitations!* You are doing such an excellent job, and my office is happy to give you any backup you need.'

'That's music to my ears, *monsieur le maire*,' Philippe replied, grateful. 'There is much more organization involved than I had realized.'

'Important question,' the mayor interrupted. 'Who would you like to declare the festival open? In the past at events like this, it has usually been the duchess.'

Philippe smiled to himself. 'May I suggest a change?' he enquired boldly. 'Invite the new *châtelaine*, Mademoiselle Meredith Harding.'

'I wonder how Nicky's getting on with the guest list,' Sophie speculated. 'I hope to God she's put a closing date on the invitation and didn't leave the whole thing open, or we'll have no idea how many we're catering for!'

Jo stopped to admire her daughter's chart and the lists she had already prepared. Sophie really was a powerhouse when it came to organization. With skills like hers, perhaps she should be doing something more demanding than organizing exhibitions and weddings. She could do anything, Jo thought proudly, and then remembered that as a parent her opinion on such matters would not be welcome unless specifically requested. 'When is Ronnie actually arriving?' she asked the others. 'I hope she's lining up florists herself and not expecting us to do it.'

'No idea, dearest Mama,' grinned Sophie. 'I'll leave the delicate chore of dealing with Ronnie to you.'

'Thanks a lot,' protested Jo. 'It wasn't me who said she could come.'

'It wouldn't have made any difference who made the decision,' Meredith pointed out. 'She would have come anyway. More to the point, does Steph know she's coming?'

'Oh, my God! I hadn't thought of that,' Jo exclaimed. 'She'll be furious if she doesn't.' She fell silent for a moment. 'A hideous thought has just struck me. Ronnie does know about Steph and David, doesn't she?'

They looked at each other and shrugged. Given the complicated relationship between Steph and her sister, this was in no way a foregone conclusion.

'Good heavens!' Meredith had turned back to her laptop. 'I've had an extraordinary invitation!'

'Who from?' Jo and Sophie gave her their full attention.

'The mayor of Bratenac!'

'And what does the mayor of Bratenac want you to do?'

'Only to officially open the food festival!'

'I wonder who gave him that idea?' teased Sophie.

'I can't begin to imagine,' seconded Jo.

'Shut up, the pair of you.'

'We'll both have to come along and watch you cut the ribbon,' Jo smiled.

'And you know who'll be absolutely furious?' Sophie giggled. 'Our next door neighbour Margot. She's used to being the *grande dame* round here.'

Meredith dropped her head into her hands. 'And to think when I bought the château I was expecting the deep rural peace of France!'

'I don't think peace is something the French go in for; and certainly not if you're running a wedding château!'

'And certainly not today,' Meredith added. 'I've just remembered that I asked Suzi to come in this afternoon.'

'What exactly is she supposed to be doing?' Jo enquired frostily.

'Interior design advice. Don't worry – just as a consultant.'

'But that's my role!' objected Sophie. 'And I've been really enjoying it.'

'It's only a sham, Sophie. Just have a go at pretending to listen. For Steph's sake.'

They were interrupted by tapping on the French window and Liam came into the room. As usual, despite his workman's clothes he still managed to look like a rugged model from a country clothing catalogue.

Sophie watched her mother trying not to look at him, and had to hide her smile.

'Hope I'm not disturbing you, but I wondered if you all had a moment?'

'Hang on,' said Sophie, whose experience of these words usually meant impending disaster of one kind or another. 'Don't say you're going to leave!'

'It's about this food festival,' he reassured. 'What about

taking a stall to show the château's wines? I've always thought we should get into wine tourism in the off-season, when the wedding business dies down. As I mentioned before it's getting really popular and most of the châteaux round here are climbing on the bandwagon.'

'Have you got time?' Meredith enquired, ever the business-woman. 'You always seem very busy in the vineyard.'

Sophie tried not to grin. Her mother could vouch for that. She spent long enough looking out at him.

'I can always get help from the village. Wine's in the blood round here.'

'OK, why not?' Meredith agreed, then realized she ought to consult the others and looked at them enquiringly. 'That is, if it's not too expensive to take a stall.'

'They end up paying you,' Liam reassured. 'But I would get through plenty of wine in the tastings – though if you're not planning to market it, that makes quite a lot of sense.'

'Go ahead, then.'

'Thanks.' He smiled round at all of them, his expression friendly but not intimate, and then went back out through the French windows.

Sophie watched him thoughtfully. 'You know, Meredith –' She stopped, realizing she was acting as if Meredith were in charge. 'And Mum. What he says about the wine tourism makes a lot of sense. If this festival is a success, why don't you ask him to look into it properly? I mean, people only really get married in spring and summer.'

'I was hoping to roam round the château naked when the season finishes, and swim in our own pool!' laughed Meredith.

'You can still do that if we do wine tourism,' Sophie pointed out. 'Well, the pool bit anyway!'

'What do you think, Jo?' Meredith enquired in neutral tones.

'Well, obviously I'm a bit prejudiced,' Jo conceded. 'But Liam's a very bright guy and I think we all acknowledge bright people should be given a shot, so I agree with Soph.'

'Come on,' Meredith suggested. 'Let's have lunch out on the terrace. I picked up some delicious charcuterie and salad from the market and some really crunchy *baguettes*. And no one correct me and tell me the thin ones are called *ficelles*. To me, they're all *baguettes*. And a nice bottle of white won't do us any harm either.'

They all sat, bathed in sunlight, looking down towards the Savarin River. Meredith raised her glass. 'A toast: to having survived this far!'

'Nonsense,' Sophie amended. 'To the most romantic wedding destination in France!'

When Suzi arrived promptly at two p.m., it was clear she had taken great care with her wardrobe in her new stance as Professional Woman. The boobs were nowhere to be seen. Leopardskin had gone back to the jungle. Instead, Suzi was a symphony in beige: a knee-length beige suit, beige silk blouse, high-heeled beige court shoes. She had even somehow acquired a beige briefcase, which she opened to reveal a huge sheaf of images that she proceeded to spread out all over Meredith's desk.

'I printed these out from the internet. This one's my favourite. The theme is Turkish Delight and they did the whole venue up like a harem, with cushions spread out all over the floor.'

'Fascinating for a smaller wedding,' agreed Meredith, trying not to sound appalled, 'but perhaps a bit impractical with so many guests.'

'Especially in the hot weather,' seconded Sophie. 'People do like to be outside.'

'This one's just gorgeous,' Suzi went on. 'It's a recreation of Princess Diana's wedding. Look, she's even got that wonderful Cinderella dress with the amazing train. I thought, seeing as this is a château, you could have a Marie Antoinette bride – you know, with a dress like a shepherdess and a straw hat with loads of feathers on it?'

'Lovely idea,' Meredith agreed. 'Except that brides obviously come to us with very clear ideas of their own.'

'And Marie Antoinette did end up on the guillotine,' Sophie murmured.

'Tell you what,' Meredith suggested brightly, 'why don't I take you on a tour of the château?'

Suzi got out her phone and proceeded to take photos of every room they passed through. Clearly they would be in for a great deal of advice on how to make it more Pinteresting. But it was the bridal suite that attracted her particular attention.

She looked round at the sunlight-filled room with its own round tower, in which Sophie had placed a pretty French bed draped and swagged in simple white muslin.

'Oh no,' she pronounced, shaking her head. 'This is all wrong! That tower is much too poky, and the bed isn't nearly dramatic enough!'

Meredith glanced behind her, grateful Sophie had pleaded an urgent appointment.

'You need one of those four-poster beds you can pull the curtains round. When it's your wedding night you want a bit of fantasy. You might be saying *I do* to Brian Boring from Burnley, but you have to imagine it's George Clooney or Jamie Dornan, or maybe David Beckham, except I can't stand all those horrible tattoos, carrying you into bed and—'

'Absolutely!' Meredith decided to close the curtains of the

imaginary four-poster with a snap. 'I have to say, Suzi, you have a very fertile imagination.'

'Thank you, yes, people do tell me that.'

'And thank you for your input. I'll be in touch about the next consultation. Did you bring your car, or would you like me to call you a taxi?'

'Oh, I've got my car, thanks. Is that all you want? I'm bursting with ideas.'

'No, that's terrific for today. It's just an inspiration we're looking for, then we can go off and see how it fits in with what we're offering.'

Meredith just hoped Steph and David found a way of reconciling soon before one of them told Suzi the truth about her taste in decorating.

'How did it go?' David asked when Suzi got back.

'Brilliant,' she replied with a dazzling smile. 'They loved my stuff! Meredith said it was an inspiration! At last I feel appreciated. All my life I've been looking for approval from men and now I realize what I needed was a fulfilling career! In fact, I'd really like to get back to it now. Do you think you could shop and cook today? I really don't have time now I'm working.'

David experienced a feeling of relief that the focus was no longer so slavishly on him, together with the revelation that Suzi's real preoccupation was with Suzi. The flattery, the promise of a sexual garden of Eden, even the endless feeding up, had all been part of her determination to get a man – probably any man.

But he wasn't criticizing her. She was a lonely woman who didn't want to spend the years ahead on her own.

He was the one at fault. He had felt a failure at home and sought the solace of the offered embraces without putting up a fight. He had wanted to feel wanted. But it had been as much an illusion for him as it was for her.

Now he just had to break the news that he was moving out.

Philippe sat surrounded by lists in the small kitchen, making sure the produce orders were done for the restaurant while at the same time keeping an eye on the progress of the food festival, now due to open in two weeks' time. Thank God for the help from the mayor's office. They had been absolutely brilliant as backup, taking on all the dull and official aspects of the event, sorting out all the licences, indemnities and parking challenges that French bureaucracy loved to impose. He was already thinking about how he might thank them at the end – a meal here, perhaps, for the whole department?

But mostly, his nimble brain was preoccupied with deciding where to invite Meredith for their next dinner. He had come across a romantic-looking restaurant with rooms in the adjoining valley, which seemed more appropriate than a hotel with all the assumptions that would entail. They might both like to spend the night together but Meredith, he suspected, would find it insulting if it were assumed to be a foregone conclusion. Whereas he wouldn't mind at all, he grinned to himself; in fact, the sooner the better!

He would message her now, before he lost his nerve. But should he mention about the rooms so that she could come prepared to stay? Meredith might seem casually groomed, but his experience of women told him that they liked to bring their stuff.

Success belonged to the brave. He would simply be open about the possibility of staying. He laughed as he poured himself a coffee. It wasn't what Humphrey Bogart would have done. But Bogey didn't live in the tricky twenty-first century!

Twenty-One

'I'll pick up Ronnie,' Jo offered bravely.

'Are you sure?' Meredith looked up, feeling pleased with herself that the approval had finally come through for licences for all their ninety-three fire extinguishers. 'Isn't it amazing, Dad?' she'd asked her father silently. 'We own a château that needs ninety-three fire extinguishers!' She knew it was crazy, but in her mind he owned it too, and the thought gave her immense delight. 'We could easily order her a taxi.'

'Mum's trying to get away,' Sophie grinned, 'in case Suzi comes in and tells her the hire company she's using for Nicky's wedding is crap and chairs with little skirts on are *so* last decade.'

'Thanks for that, Soph,' her mother replied. 'I was actually trying to be helpful. And anyway, Suzi would be more likely to criticize me for *not* having little skirts on the chairs!'

Meredith had to laugh, remembering Suzi's reaction to the simplicity of Sophie's bridal suite; thank God Sophie hadn't been there. So far, she'd seen absolutely no sign of this 'good design eye' Jackie had promised. Unless Jackie liked chairs with skirts on, too.

'Right,' said Jo. 'Important question. Has anyone found out if Ronnie knows about Steph and David's split?'

'Surely she must,' Meredith replied uncertainly. 'I mean – they're *sisters*.'

'That's exactly why I'm not so sure,' argued Jo. 'There's quite a lot of rivalry between those two. I think Steph quite enjoyed being the one with the successful marriage.'

'But surely,' replied Sophie, who was an only child, 'her sister's the first person she'd turn to for support?'

Jo shrugged. 'Families aren't always as straightforward as they seem.'

'Well, we'll soon find out,' said Meredith. 'And anyway, why is she asking to stay here rather than at Fleur-de-Lis?'

'Maybe she likes our grand appointments,' Jo gestured round at the rococo décor of the salon. 'It does rather suit Ronnie's personality.'

'Well, I hope she's not planning to stay for long,' pronounced Meredith crossly. 'I find a little of Ronnie goes a long way!'

The usual morning rush was over. Marcelline had taken to staying on an extra unpaid half hour to make Steph a cup of coffee, which she knew was a gesture of solidarity even if tact wasn't exactly the girl's strong point.

'You must be missing Monsieur Adams very much,' Marcelline stated loudly. 'He was always such a helpful man, so considerate, always trying to make things easier for you. You would never find a French man like that!' Marcelline's opinion of men in general was not high, but she had made an exception for David. 'You look very tired now he has gone. I could work a few extra hours, if you wanted?'

Steph made a polite reply, but she felt the familiar panic rising. She had no real idea if they could even afford a little extra for Marcelline. She knew she needed to get to grips with the accounts, but that had been so much David's job. Hers had been the domestic side of the *chambre d'hôte*.

She felt suddenly overwhelmed with anger at David for leaving, even though she was the one who had chucked him out. But was Marcelline right? Was it partly her own fault for not appreciating what he was doing for her? She looked away, not wanting Marcelline to see that tears were close to the surface.

'*Un petit cognac* is what you need, madame!' counselled Marcelline, getting to her feet. In the midst of her life falling apart, Steph smiled at this universal French panacea.

'No thanks, Marcelline, but thank you for your support.'

She stared out over the beautiful landscape stretching out in front of them. Lush pasture with cattle grazing peacefully, the neat lines of the vineyards, grapes ripening in the sun, and beyond that the silver snake of the Savarin River. The landscape that had brought them here all those years ago. But today it brought her no peace of mind.

She had to talk to someone, to share with someone this burden of pain and grief. Of course, she could ring one of her friends at the château, but it all felt too devastating and personal to begin explaining. For a moment, she imagined ringing her sister Ronnie and for once being listened to and helped. She smiled bitterly. The chances of that were zero. Ronnie would simply talk about herself.

Even so, she got out her phone from her bag and stared at it for a moment. Could you be a real sister, Ronnie, and help me with this? She dialled the number, but after five rings it went to voicemail.

She didn't leave a message.

*

It would have been hard to miss Ronnie even if she'd been arriving at an enormous airport like Heathrow, let alone the tiny barn that served as Bratenac's terminal.

She was last off, marginally before the passengers who'd asked for special assistance, apparently in no hurry to disembark, and her outfit could only be described as eye-catching. Red and orange psychedelic-patterned wide-leg trousers paired with a contrasting lime-green top and lime-green stripy socks with high-heeled sandals. To finish the ensemble, her hair was tucked into an orange and green turban.

'Hello, Jo. It's kind of you to come and meet me.' She noted Jo's slightly stunned expression. 'I decided to brighten up my outfits, since the world around us seems so depressing.'

'Well, you certainly succeeded,' conceded Jo, her eyes fixed on the sole suitcase left in the Arrivals hall. It was huge. How long was Ronnie planning on staying?

'I never was any good at travelling light,' Ronnie remarked casually. 'So how's it all going here?'

'Great.' Jo had to resist adding, 'Just the same as when you were here about five minutes ago!' as she grabbed the suitcase and put it on the trolley. 'The refurbishment's going really well and Sophie has drawn up terrific charts of what we all have to do between now and the wedding. How about your end?'

'Bill, my ex, is going to come up with the money, so that's a relief. To you lot especially, I imagine. Though it means he and his tedious wife, Maureen, will have to be invited, I suppose.'

Jo looked at her in amazement. Had she seriously been thinking of not inviting the bride's father? You never knew with Ronnie.

They took the short walk to the car. 'Nicky's been a bit annoyed with her bridegroom Martin for not entering into the spirit of things, but maybe that's natural.'

'I expect Martin feels it's all a bit much. A lot of bridegrooms do.' Jo opened the car door for Ronnie. 'I hope it's all right, but I've set some meetings up for this afternoon. We thought you'd want to get the flowers sorted out quickly so you could get home,' she hinted gently.

The hint was lost on Ronnie. She pushed her seat back as far as it would go and stretched luxuriously. 'Don't worry, I'm in no hurry. A bit of French sunshine's just what I need.'

Terrific.

Philippe sat in his tiny office with his phone in his hand, willing himself to call Meredith. For God's sake, he kept telling himself, you're not some adolescent trying to fix a first date; you're a grown man!

'*Bonjour*, Meredith,' he finally greeted her, stressing the syllables of her name to recall the joke they'd shared about it.

After some inconsequential chat, he got straight to the point. Meredith, he knew, was a woman of decision. 'Are you free for dinner again one of these nights? I have found a delightful little restaurant in the hills a few miles away.' He paused, then added, 'It is a restaurant with rooms.'

It was the laugh in his voice that won Meredith over. With engaging subtlety he managed to convey that he was in no way assuming she would accept, and yet he very much hoped that she would do so. It was a hard course to steer, and he did it brilliantly.

If she were French, Meredith would have pretended to hesitate now, enjoying the cat-and-mouse game of flirtation; but being Meredith, she had no time for such time-wasting tricks. 'I would very much enjoy that,' she replied instantly. 'On both counts.'

'I am delighted to hear it – and a little relieved.'

This time, they laughed together.

After he'd said goodbye Meredith stood in front of the long mirror in her boudoir holding up an expensive-looking silk nightdress and smiling to herself. Her body wasn't too bad for someone her age but she'd feel more confident covering it up, at least at first. Older bodies were like expensive gifts. The more wrapping they came in, the better.

She glanced down at the ever-faithful Nelly and found the animal fixing her with a pathetic, imploring gaze.

'Yes, Nelly. Maybe I've finally found a man I could really like; and no, Nelly, you are not coming on our dirty Wednesday. At least, I hope it's going to be dirty.' She put her arms round Nelly's soft, wrinkled neck. 'Oh, Nelly. I feel ridiculously excited, and a bit scared at the same time!'

Nelly reached out a paw in female solidarity, as if to say that she knew exactly what Meredith meant.

'I've been doing quite a lot of research into buying flowers,' Sophie announced.

They had taken Ronnie into the new eau de nil dining room so that Meredith would have the peace of the salon to get on with her own work. 'Flowers will be part of our wedding package, so I need to know about them anyway. There are four main suppliers. If you want it simple, there's a very good florist here in Bratenac.' She produced a printed leaflet and handed it to Ronnie. 'A lot of the weddings round here use a van from Bordeaux, which has a wider choice. Then if you want flowers on a really big scale, there's a wholesaler in Bordeaux. Or, obviously there's the internet. Do you have any kind of theme in mind?'

'Absolutely. I want the flowers to look like those Dutch Old Master paintings, you know – huge displays of really bright flowers, blowsy roses, delphiniums, dahlias. Often with witty touches like birds or butterflies and branches of out-of-season blackberries!' Ronnie got so carried away that she knocked over the glass of rosé Jo had poured for her.

Sophie could picture these creations all too well. Beautiful, but more suited to a Paris fashion show than the relaxed festival feel Nicky seemed to want. 'And is Nicky on board too? I mean, they sound quite . . . eye-catching.' What she really meant, of course, was over the top, but the nuance was lost on Ronnie.

'They'll be the talk of the wedding,' enthused Ronnie. 'Nicola'll be fine. She's not really interested in flowers anyway.'

'But you have discussed the bride's bouquet, at least?' Jo asked her nervously. She couldn't quite imagine Nicky going down the aisle with a bunch of flowers tastefully adorned with blackbirds and Red Admirals.

'I'll send her some samples when it's all ordered,' was the tart response.

'If I were you,' Sophie suggested hopefully, 'I'd run it by her before you make the order definite.'

'You don't know Nicola,' Ronnie dismissed. 'She can never make up her mind about anything. I'm doing her a favour.'

'Excuse me, ladies.' Steve the builder appeared, looking red-faced and sweaty; the heat had increased noticeably over the previous few days. 'Only there's someone here to see you.'

'Hi girls,' Steph burst in, her attention on the cake box she was carrying so that she didn't at first notice who was there. 'I've got us some *religieuses* from the bakery as a little treat. You know, those eclairs with topknots stuffed with café crème, the ones that look like nuns. They're terribly bad for you and absolutely delicious. Ronnie!' She almost dropped the box in her amazement. 'What the hell are *you* doing here?'

'Oh, hi sis,' Ronnie replied, as though it were the most

natural thing in the world for her to have appeared here from across the Channel in the company of Steph's best friends, without having the good manners to tell her. 'I've just nipped over to choose the flowers and I didn't want to put you to any trouble.'

'I can't think why not,' Steph replied with deadly calm. 'It doesn't usually stop you. So were you planning to come to France, stay with my very best friends and go back without even telling me? You know, Ronnie, I make a lot of allowances for you, but it doesn't stop me sometimes thinking you're a complete bitch!'

Sophie exchanged a telling look with her mother. 'You know, Mum,' she whispered, 'I'm really looking forward to this wedding!'

Jackie sat in the Café de la Paix contemplating everyone who went past the window. So far, so bad with her plot. OK, Steph was no longer going to lose her B&B – but Suzi and David were still living together.

David must surely have realized by now that Suzi never thought about anyone but Suzi. She might have imagined briefly that she loved David more than herself, but that would be wearing off by now. Loving someone was hard work.

Jackie put the question to the rest of the Ladies' Luncheon Club. How could they get Suzi to show her true colours and come back to join them – the friends who understood her and could put up with the selfishness – and let David go? She was already producing designs for the château, and that was a start.

'Another man?' suggested Mandy.

'And where would we get one of those?' Shirley protested.

'You can probably order one online from Amazon,' giggled Janine.

'Make David ill, so she has to be a carer for a bit. She'd run a mile,' suggested Mandy.

'And just how would we do that?' snapped Jackie. 'Creep in and put poison in his porridge? This isn't *Miss Marple*, even if Bratenac is a French version of St Mary Mead.'

'I know,' Janine suggested. 'A Birkin bag.'

They all looked at her in complete mystification.

'What has a bag got to do with anything?'

'Suzi's completely obsessed with them. She keeps a scrapbook of all the different versions and gets alerts whenever one comes up on eBay.' Janine leaned forward. 'She told me she wanted one more than anything else in her life!'

'What exactly *is* a Birkin bag?' asked Jackie, whose sense of what was fashionable had stopped developing when Biba went bust.

'It's a handbag,' repeated Shirley.

'I know that,' Jackie replied impatiently. 'But what makes it so special?'

'They're hand-made by Hermès, sometimes in lizard and crocodile skin, and people like Victoria Beckham own them,' Janine enlightened. 'They come up for about 35,000 euros. Suzi told me about one that was 70,000, but that was ostrich.'

'Why are they called Birkin bags?'

'They're named after that singer who had an orgasm on the record that got banned by the Pope. And no, Jackie, we don't want you to exercise your acting skills and give us a demonstration!'

'I keep my orgasms for my husband, thank you very much!' Jackie pretended to be offended. The truth was she didn't get many orgasms these days, public or private, but heigh-ho.

'But how are we going to get hold of one of these ridiculous things?' Jackie asked.

'The reason I thought of it was because there's a fake one in the window of the charity shop in Sissiac,' Janine announced triumphantly. 'I went in and had a look and it's really good. You could only tell it wasn't real if you were some kind of Hermès handbag expert. Why don't I buy it and then offer it to Suzi for some huge amount – which we won't actually take, obviously– and then let David find out what she's agreed to, and he'll see just how crazy she really is!'

'I don't know if that'll work.' Jackie shook her head.

'Come on, it's only fifty euro – if we all give ten,' Janine encouraged. 'It's worth a try.'

'That'll make forty,' Jackie pointed out, unconvinced. 'No wonder you're always losing dogs, Janine. You can't count.'

'I'll put in the extra ten,' replied Janine with a wink. 'And maybe Jane Birkin'll throw in a free orgasm. Now all we have to do is decide how much to charge Suzi!'

Philippe and the mayor walked round the site of the food festival together. Some early birds had already arrived and were setting up their stalls, eager to get the best pitches.

'It's going to be wonderful!' enthused the mayor. 'Every town and village had their annual fair in the Middle Ages. It was a really big occasion – people looked forward to it all year. And here you are, organizing ours. *Merci, mon fils* – I hope you don't mind me calling you son? I had a son of my own. He died young, a defective heart, but I hope he would have been someone like you. Energetic, clear-eyed, valuing the things that matter in life. Not everyone here can afford to eat in your restaurant but everyone knows the story, how you gave up your three stars in Paris to make a home in Bratenac, and they feel a little bit proud.'

Philippe, completely unprepared for this sudden endorsement, took the mayor's hand and held it in a tight and reassuring handshake. If it hadn't been for the immediate physical gesture, he knew he would otherwise have cried.

'And your *châteleine*? Has she agreed to open the festival?'

Philippe thought of Meredith and how he was seeing her tonight and felt a leap of excitement and anticipation, spiced with a healthy sprinkling of fear that she might not like what she saw. What seemed so natural, so unaffected, so *unimportant* when you were young took on a different tinge at this age. Both of you brought so much history and experience as well as expectation which might be different from the other person's. On the other hand, you had tasted all the chocolates, and made up your mind which ones you liked. He wondered what Meredith would choose and found himself smiling in a sly and sexy way. Whatever the outcome, he hadn't looked forward to anything as much as this for a very long time indeed.

'I don't know what you're doing after this,' commented the mayor, taking in Philippe's expression, 'but I can only say I envy you enormously.'

Lucille Latignac looked at the rooftop view and opened her notebook. It felt very strange to be going to a food festival organized by her former husband.

She didn't regret leaving. Even after all this time the memory still stung of being treated like the waitress she was, but she did miss her son and, sometimes, the security of the family unit. She had built a successful career. She was an independent woman and proud of it, especially when she saw how much the people she helped through the street food venture appreciated her.

309

But still. Sometimes, in the middle of the night, she longed for another body next to hers. But was it Philippe's? She knew she was still attractive, she'd had enough relationships to prove that and yet none had lasted and here she was, still alone.

Lucille made herself concentrate on the job at hand. She needed to organize transport for the three women who had signed up for Street Taste, eager to introduce the good people of Bratenac to the delights of *tajine*, cooked in its familiar conical hat to keep in the juices, vital in desert regions where there is little water; Tunisian *chakchouka* made of onions, pepper and tomatoes fried in a skillet with eggs thrown in to poach at the end; and *harira*, from Algeria, a stew of lamb, beef or chicken spiced with ginger, cinnamon and turmeric. Her favourite, *mechoui* – a whole lamb rubbed with cumin, coriander and thyme and either roasted on a spit or cooked in a pit – would probably have to wait till the final night, when there was often a celebration.

And then there were all the cooking utensils, mobile gas hobs, bamboo cutlery, paper plates, glasses and napkins. Plus the challenge of payment methods. Should it be cash only? The trouble was, so many people didn't have cash any more, so she would need to sort out some means of electronic payment.

All this organization fortunately left little time for fruitless speculation on the past. Even still, a rebellious part of her brain reminded her that Philippe would certainly be in evidence.

How was she going to feel when she saw him – and her son?

'I see you've shaved,' Meredith smiled at Philippe as they drove up the narrow, winding road towards the restaurant. 'I'm flattered.'

'But of course, *mademoiselle*,' he laughed, his eyes firmly on the road. 'You have commented several times on my unkempt appearance.'

Meredith felt a prick of embarrassment that, early in their acquaintance, she had dismissed him for drinking all night when he had actually been looking for his runaway father. And now she had Nelly as a permanent reminder of how misleading superficial judgements could be.

The view all around them was stunning. Rich green pastures rising up the hillside, occasionally wooded, with small farms and tiny villages half hidden in the valley below. But Meredith found her glance drawn not by the landscape but Philippe's face. He really was a very good-looking man.

'Tell me about where we're going,' she forced herself to say.

'Small château. Typical of the region. In fact, here it comes now.'

They arrived at the top of the hill and found themselves in a doll's-house-sized square with a war memorial and a viewing platform where you could stand and see the whole of the Savarin valley falling away beneath you. It was breathtaking. In one corner was a golden stone building, its four towers half hidden by vines and ivy. The kind of mini-mansion you could imagine actually living in.

'Do you want to see the church?' Philippe enquired. 'It's famous for its gargoyles of devils poking the depraved and ungodly into vats of boiling oil.'

'Charming,' giggled Meredith. 'The Church does like you to pay for your sin.'

'We'd better make it worthwhile, then.' His eyes held hers for a moment.

Meredith looked away in case she gave away too much of what she was feeling. The medieval words for it would have been 'unbridled lust'.

She was right about the château. Inside it managed to feel cosy and welcoming with its deep sofas and small tables dotted with shady lamps. The art on the walls seemed full of light, unlike the usual dark oils and faded tapestries of similar houses. Jugs of roses from the garden filled every room with the heady scent of early summer.

'*Bonsoir*, Monsieur Latignac.' The woman at the reception desk smiled at him flirtatiously. 'I have given you the Pigeonnier – it is our best suite, separate from the hotel in a dovecot in the grounds. You can be alone there.'

'Apart from the pigeons,' Meredith added, laughing.

'Don't diss the pigeons,' Philippe replied as he signed the register. 'Pigeon shit was highly sought after. Only the nobility could own a pigeonnier. We're in good company.'

'*Je suis désolée, Monsieur Latignac,*' the receptionist announced, turning her whole body seductively towards him, 'but there is only one sitting of dinner during the week.'

'And what time is that?' Philippe enquired.

'Seven thirty.'

Meredith's practical brain did a quick computation. Not enough time for sex. Sometimes, in her experience, it was better to get the first time over with and then, with the tension defused, subsequent lovemaking was far more enjoyable.

Stop it, Meredith, she told herself. This isn't some business event that needs to be organized. Just go with the flow.

The room was indeed lovely. Understated and modern, with the odd antique lamp or piece of furniture added. The most significant feature was the bed. It was a beautiful example of the French classic *lit bateau* or boat bed, in polished oak with scrolled ends.

'It makes me think of Peter Pan,' Meredith commented as she put down her overnight bag. 'Second to the right and straight on till morning.' She turned towards him, smiling mischieviously. 'Except that I hope it won't be straight on.'

Philippe's reply was to laugh. 'Mademoiselle Harding, you are a joy. A French woman would never be direct. She would hint. She would accidentally touch you with her body. She might imply that she couldn't possibly stay.'

'What a waste of time,' Meredith laughed with him. 'I have learned in business that you have to know what you want. If I didn't want to stay, I wouldn't have come.'

'Impeccable logic. And now we must go and eat.' He glanced round. 'Unless you'd prefer to stay here and order room service?'

'I don't think eating in bed is sexy at all. Let's go to the restaurant.'

'I am in your hands.' Again, that slow sensual smile, tinged with humour that said it wasn't taking itself too seriously. It was a killer combination.

The restaurant was more traditional, with comfortable curved armchairs. Each table had a crisp white tablecloth and its own individual lamp. The food was some of the most delicious Meredith had tasted since she'd been here.

'Well, I am a chef. I could hardly take you to MacDo!'

After four courses with *amuse-bouches* before and *petits fours* afterwards, they sat back to have a rest and enjoy looking at each other in pleasurable anticipation.

Until Philippe's phone buzzed. He ignored it at first, then quickly checked the caller. 'It's Jean-Christophe. I left him in charge at the restaurant. I'm sorry – I'd better just take the call. He wouldn't ring for no reason.'

Meredith looked on. He was a workaholic like her, and workaholics could never completely switch off.

She could see from his face that it was serious. Philippe ran through various options in rapid French, but clearly Jean-Christophe had already tried them all.

Meredith asked herself what she would do in his position, and the answer was undeniable: she would go and sort it out. She was on the point of standing up to accompany him to reception, when he put his phone back in his pocket and smiled.

'No gas and thirty covers to feed.' He shrugged. '*Ça arrive, ces choses-là*, these things happen. Jean-Christophe will find a solution.'

In the end it was he who stood up, but not to leave. He held out a hand to Meredith. 'Shall we go up?' Meredith could hardly believe it. He was prepared to risk a complete disaster at the restaurant in order to spend the night with her.

Suzi examined every zip and pocket of the black suede bag. She stroked it, checked all its different features and then sighed with suppressed longing.

The relationship with David had proved more problematic than she'd hoped. He seemed to approach life in a diametrically opposite way from her. She'd always been more of a spender than a saver, and he was the other way round. Sometimes she wondered if he regretted the whole thing.

She studied the bag again, remembering a cartoon she'd seen of a saleslady consoling a female shopper: '*Hello, madame, I've got the perfect shoe for a disappointing marriage.*'

This was the perfect bag.

'It's gorgeous. Utterly divine,' Suzi sighed. 'Exactly the one I've always wanted. I can't believe it's actually for sale here in Bratenac – and for only five thousand euro.'

Janine gulped. Could she even pretend to ask for five thousand euro?

A sudden inspiration came to her. She was supposed to be selling the bag on behalf of a rich but conveniently anonymous acquaintance. 'You're a good friend and it's a lot of money, Suze. Why don't you take it home and be sure you really like it, before you hand over the dosh?'

'Your friend won't mind?'

Janine looked coy. 'No, because I won't tell her.'

'You're a pal, Janine.'

'So how's it all going with David?'

Suzi turned away. 'Do you mind if we don't talk about it?'

So Jackie was right. Things weren't hunky dory. Janine had heard Suzi moan about how cautious David was with money, and wondered what he would make of Suzi spending five thousand euro on a handbag. Or whether Suzi intended to tell him.

Meredith rolled over sleepily to find the space next to her empty. She opened her eyes wide. Where was Philippe, and what the hell time was it? She scrabbled about on the bedside table. Ten a.m. She never woke late like that. Admittedly she had been a little more busy than usual in the night. A slow smile spread across her face just as the door opened and Philippe appeared, clean-shaven and fully dressed, carrying a tray bearing a teapot, milk jug and two cups.

'Room service, madame,' he beamed. 'I know how you British like your tea in bed.'

Meredith sat up, wondering how she looked and trying not to think about it.

He handed her a cup.

'Amazing,' she pronounced with a smile. 'How did you get fresh milk? They never have it in France. Only that horrible long-life stuff.'

'I milked the cow myself,' he smiled seductively.

'Liar! Anyway, why didn't you wake me?'

'I had the crisis at the restaurant to deal with. We couldn't afford to lose another day. In fact, Jean-Christophe had a stroke of genius. No gas, so my clever son buys three barbecues from the hypermarket! *Formidable!* We still need to get the gas back, though.'

He took away her cup and saucer and kissed her.

'Hey,' she protested, 'what if I want another cup?'

'You'll have to wait.' He took his clothes off in record time.

'You've done this before,' she accused teasingly. 'Only a lunchtime lover could get undressed as quickly as that!'

'*Actuellement*, it's because I go to the gym.'

'What if the chambermaid comes in?' she protested, laughing.

'This is France. She will think, *Bon!* The couple in No 6 are making love. I will come back later. Now stop raising ridiculous arguments, and kiss me.'

David stared at the handbag, and then at Suzi. Admittedly he didn't have much of an eye for these things, but the bag seemed perfectly ordinary to him. A bit unpleasantly showy, perhaps, and rather too large. In fact, he preferred the one Steph had bought herself in Debenhams.

'Is this some kind of joke?' he asked, trying to be patient and understanding but genuinely bewildered. 'You aren't seriously considering paying this woman five thousand euro for a handbag?'

But Suzi's face had a rapt quality, like someone who'd just seen a vision and didn't expect anyone to believe her.

'But it's *cheap*! A real bargain, in fact. They can go for seventy thousand euro.'

David shook his head. He knew that he and Suzi were different; in fact, different didn't begin to encompass how separate were their worldviews.

'Come on, Suzi, see sense!' he protested. 'No bag could be worth that much! I'm not going to say think of the starving millions, but you must be able to see what a stupid symbol of the capitalist system it is! Brands are bad enough. But brands that charge people that kind of money are outrageous!'

Suzi looked at him, bewildered. He just didn't get it. 'But David,' she explained patiently, 'it's a Birkin bag made by Hermès. Even Victoria Beckham has one!'

'Stop humming, we all know you had a highly satisfactory encounter with Philippe,' commented Jo drily. 'Any minute now you'll break into dance. Have you looked at those figures for the different florists yet?'

'Do you mind,' protested Meredith. 'It was romantic! He brought me a cup of tea in bed!'

'A chambermaid could have done that. I hope you got more than PG Tips?'

'Stop fishing. It's creepy.'

'Nonsense,' Jo grinned. 'You can practise sixty-nine hanging from the chandeliers as far as I'm concerned, as long as you look at the floristry figures!'

'Mum!' Sophie made a face. 'Too much information! Honestly, your generation . . .'

'. . . had a lot of fun!' Jo completed her sentence.

'And ruined the planet. And bought all the cheap housing. And refuse to accept you're getting old and should move over because it's our turn,' Sophie announced.

'And your generation pretends to be liberal and all-accepting but is actually quite judgemental!' retorted Jo, piqued.

'Now, now, people. Peace in our time!' Meredith started opening the post. 'Oh, look, isn't that sweet?' She held up a card of a bridal couple with the message: *Marriage is finding someone who loves you – even though they know you!*

'She wants to remind us that it's only two months till the wedding. And that she's really excited. God, is that right? That really is quite soon!' marvelled Jo.

'It's only what I've been putting on the charts you both laugh at so much for weeks now,' Sophie pointed out with a trace of exasperation.

'I'm sorry, darling,' Jo apologized. 'Here, come and have a hug!'

'Mum,' Sophie reminded her. 'We're at work, remember?' And then, remembering her mother's jibe at her generation's narrowness: 'Come on then, just a quick one.'

'And don't forget tomorrow, girls, it's the launch of the food festival,' Meredith said. 'And I'm cutting the ribbon, hilariously! There'll be lots of opportunities for us to mingle and promote the château.'

'And avoid bumping into Margot,' Sophie reminded naughtily. 'I bet she was the empress of opening things!'

'Yes,' Meredith grinned back. 'But we all have to retire from ribbon-cutting at some point.'

'OK, Nelly,' Meredith enquired of her faithful friend the next morning. 'What do you wear to open a food festival when you are the grand lady who owns the château? Country or chic?'

Nelly, who was looking distinctly mournful at being left behind, replied with a baleful stare. In the end, Meredith decided that Kate Middleton with a touch of Joan Collins seemed about right.

'Nelly says that for the queen of taupe, you're looking

surprisingly colourful, and she's wondering what can have happened to make you suddenly want to show off?' asked Sophie when she appeared downstairs.

'Tell Nelly she can mind her own business,' replied Meredith crisply.

It was true she was looking more eye-catching than usual in a burnt orange jacket over her pearl grey sheath dress, paired with a large orange flower in her hair and lipstick to match. It was indeed a much bolder look than she normally wore.

'Nelly also says, watch out that Margot doesn't grab your scissors and stick them into you,' warned Sophie.

But as it turned out, any danger to Meredith's future happiness was not likely to come from Margot, duchess of Savarin, but from another direction altogether.

Twenty-Two

Meredith caught the red ribbon firmly between both blades of the enormous scissors she had been provided with. '*Je vous souhaite très bon chance avec votre festival!*' she pronounced in her excellent French accent. 'I wish you very good luck with your festival!' – and she cut the ribbon to tumultuous applause.

'I could get used to this,' she murmured to Philippe as they strolled through the field together.

'I'm surprised,' replied Philippe. 'I'd have thought you were far too spiky to enjoy adulation.'

'Ah, but now I own the château I'm becoming a *grande dame* and rather liking it.'

'You weren't behaving like a great lady the other night,' he reminded her softly, his eyes on hers.

'But, *monsieur*,' Meredith replied in shocked accents, 'surely you know that great ladies are the biggest sluts of all!'

She looked around her. There must be thirty stalls at least, the majority featuring food or wine. They passed some stalls festooned with local cheeses alongside one from the organic bakery. Next, several vintners peddled their wines. They stopped to taste at the one belonging to the famous vineyard of Clos d'Yvgne. Another couple specialized in the sweet dessert wine, Monbazillac, that Philippe had made them try with their *foie gras*. How long ago that seemed! Before I began my new life, Meredith thought, and smiled to herself.

Two or three *foie gras* stalls clustered together next to others specializing in huge wheels of cheese made on nearby farms and sold together in a cooperative by cheery farmers' wives.

Already queues were forming as people piled their plates with tempting samples from each stall, washed down with wine in the special tasting glass they had picked up at the gate. It was all looking like a big success.

They had almost done the rounds when they bumped into Guillaume, his moustache waxed for the occasion into perfect curlicues either side of his mouth. 'Guillaume,' Meredith congratulated, 'if there were a contest for best moustache, you would definitely win it.'

'He's aiming for lounge lizard, but he ends up more bounder or brothel creeper, if you ask me,' said a voice from behind the stall.

'Oh hello, Jackie,' Meredith greeted her. 'Are you helping out?'

'Just trying to drum up a bit of business for the cafe. Can we tempt you with a cocktail?'

'What do you fancy?' Meredith asked Philippe. 'Or are you not allowed to drink on duty?'

'This is France, as I keep reminding you,' he smiled back. 'It's your duty to drink. Perfect timing for an apéritif before we head for Jean-Christophe and the Airstream to get some food. He's parked it in a good spot, just by the entrance.'

Guillaume mixed the cocktails while Jackie studied Philippe and Meredith with interest. Their obvious attraction for one another, tempered by a slight awkwardness, told her that they must have just got together. How fascinating. She couldn't wait to share with the girls the news that Philippe had managed to melt the ice on Everest. Jackie had never taken to Meredith, but even she could see that she was visibly softening.

There were just a few stalls left now, round the corner in the annexe. They must have applied late. They all seemed to be selling North African street food. A small speaker blasted out Moroccan music, bouncy and infectious, with its hand drums, tambourines and the lute-like *oud*.

'Want to try a little?' he invited Meredith.

'Congratulations!' suggested a deep female voice, not at all the kind of voice that pimped unwitting tourists into mediocre restaurants. 'Why don't you start with the Moroccan? You'll find it delicious.'

Meredith turned, struck by something strange in the speaker's tone that she couldn't put her finger on. Behind the stall stood a striking woman with almost black hair, cut to a stylish shoulder length, arresting blue-green eyes outlined in black to make them more noticeable, and an ironic expression.

She was one of the most beautiful women Meredith had ever seen.

'Hello, Philippe,' she said coolly. For a moment her eyes held his as if there were no one else on the planet. 'How are you keeping these days?'

Philippe stopped as if he'd been shot. 'Lucille,' he gasped. 'What are you doing here?'

'I run Street Taste.' She gestured around her to the various stallholders. 'It's a charity.' To Meredith's sharpened gaze, the newcomer seemed to be revelling in the moment. 'Even waitresses don't stay waitresses forever, you know.'

'Meredith.' Philippe turned to her, still looking stunned. 'This is Lucille, my ex-wife. Jean-Christophe's mother.'

Jackie, only a few feet away behind the stall, was watching Meredith's face. Behind the confident exterior, fear flickered momentarily in her eyes. She was clearly wondering why his wife had made a sudden reappearance, and what it would mean for her new relationship with Philippe.

Expecting to feel smug satisfaction, Jackie instead found herself experiencing a pang of sympathy. This Lucille might be doing it for a good cause but there was something stagey and fake about the way she had arrived, unannounced, and waited for such a dramatic moment to reveal herself.

Bitch, thought Jackie. No, in fact, something far more lethal: a genuine *femme fatale*, combining extraordinary luminous beauty with complete self-absorption. Not like poor Suzi undoing her top button – this woman was a genuine threat. Why hadn't she even noticed her own son? She must have known Philippe was organizing today and planned the whole thing. She'd probably heard him on that radio show and decided to stage a comeback. And of course, rumour had it he'd made a pile when he'd sold up in Paris, and that would have certainly added to his attraction.

Meredith made herself approach one of the smiling stall-holders and request a taste of their wares, glancing at Philippe's face as she passed. To her immense relief, bewilderment tinged with slight discomfort seemed the emotions most in evidence, rather than barely suppressed delight.

'Where have you been living? What are you up to?' he finally blurted, rather incoherently. 'Obviously you run a charity, as you've just told me.'

'I live in Bordeaux. I teach mature students French literature, specializing in Baudelaire. Street Taste is just what I do as a sideline.'

'That's amazing! Congratulations.'

'Yes, I thought you'd be surprised.' Again, that challenging smile.

Meredith pretended not to listen, but she was taking in every nuance. Philippe's wife might have left many years ago, but it was clear that she still wanted his approval.

'Have you seen Jean-Christophe?' asked Philippe. 'He's running a mobile outlet of our restaurant.'

'So he became a chef. Like his father.'

'Except that he's nothing like his father, thank God.' He could have sounded as fake as she did, but there was genuine humility in his tone.

'I hear you gave up the life in Paris?'

'Yes. I realized what it had cost.'

'A pity you didn't learn that a little earlier.' Whatever bitterness she still felt was cleverly disguised behind a slightly arch friendliness.

Meredith decided on a little subtle intervention of her own.

'It's a really impressive idea,' she broke into the conversation. 'To celebrate different cuisines by helping new arrivals use their skills like this. Congratulations.'

Lucille turned a frosty stare on her. 'And you are?'

'Lucille –' Philippe seemed boyishly shy in her presence – 'this is Meredith Harding. Meredith has just bought the Château de St Savarin.'

Lucille's glance turned from chill to permafrost.

'Yes, I'd heard the British were buying up the whole of Bratenac.'

'Well,' Meredith drawled, not allowing herself to be insulted by this deliberate attempt to get under her skin, 'not quite the *whole*.' She could feel her dislike and innate distrust for the woman rising by the moment. If Nelly were here, Meredith decided, she'd bite her.

'I must see my son now,' she announced dramatically.

'You'll have to queue,' Philippe shrugged. 'There's a long line of people waiting.'

'I can wait.'

After all, Meredith wished she could add, you've waited fifteen years.

Lucille approached the Airstream and stood at the back of the queue.

'Is that a good idea?' asked Meredith quietly. 'Just going up to him without a word of warning? I mean, poor Jean-Christophe. He's already stressed, poor lad. Shouldn't you try and stop her?'

But Philippe was still looking as if he'd been struck by an asteroid.

'Come on. You ought to be there as well.' She started walking towards the van with Philippe in her wake. They arrived just in time to see Jean-Christophe, pan in hand, turn to the queue. '*Et pour vous, madame?*' And then the tiniest pause before he dropped the pan, scorching his other hand as he did so, and exclaimed, '*Maman?*' in tones of anguished surprise.

'*Bonjour*, Jean-Christophe.' She reached across to touch the wounded arm, making Jean-Christophe shudder as if he'd been burned again. 'I know this isn't a very good time . . .'

'*Ah oui, madame,*' endorsed the man in the queue behind her rudely. 'We are waiting to order here!'

'Look, here is my number.' She handed him a card for Street Taste. 'I'd really like to hear from you.' She turned and walked away.

Jean-Christophe looked through the crowd till he found his father. 'Are you OK, Papa?'

'I think so,' replied Philippe. 'Are you?'

Jean-Christophe suddenly ducked away from the service

opening and emerged at the side of the van, rubbing the red weal on his arm. He ignored the angry gentleman who was eager to give his opinion on the service. 'Fifteen years without a word, and now this?'

'I suppose the reason she didn't get in touch might have been because she felt a clean break would be easier for you,' Philippe attempted.

'You're a good man, Papa, but can I tell you something?' Jean-Christophe went on rubbing his injured arm. 'It wasn't.'

'Come here.' Philippe moved towards his son until they were both locked in a tight embrace.

Behind them Meredith, usually so practical and cynical, found herself rubbing away a tear. It could hardly have been Lucille's intention, but by leaving her husband and child for what, Meredith had to admit, might have been perfectly valid reasons, she had prompted them to form a bond strong enough to face anything.

Jo and Sophie suddenly materialized out of the crowd. They slid their arms through hers. 'Come on, Merry,' they announced, sensing that this was a moment for some moral support. 'Time to get back to the château for a glass of fizz!'

'What a complete bitch!' Jo's venom had been sharpened by the news from her neighbour of bumping into Mark and Amanda poncing about as a newly married couple. 'How bloody dare she?' Jo fulminated. 'That woman Lucille thinking she can walk back into their lives after fifteen years just because she's lonely!'

Even the beauty and peace of sitting out on the terrace outside the orangery, looking down at the silver river, couldn't calm Jo's indignation.

'How do you know she's lonely?' enquired Sophie.

'No one volunteers for a charity unless they're lonely.'

'Mum!' Sophie tutted. 'You can't go around saying things like that.'

'Why not, if it's true?'

'You don't know it's true.'

'Well, let's see what happens next, shall we?' Jo persisted.

'Let's just talk about the wedding, shall we?' Sophie tried to steer the subject away from Philippe and Lucille, guessing how painful it must be for Meredith. But before they could return to the subject of Nicky's wedding, there was rap on the ornate glass window of the orangery. Sophie went to see who it was.

'Evening, girls,' Steph greeted them all. 'What glorious weather. You all look a bit glum. Don't tell me Nicky's cancelled the wedding?'

'Nothing so drastic,' Sophie replied. 'We'll tell you about it another time.'

'Thank God for that. I've had my mother on the phone non-stop asking me what I think of different recipes for the cake!' She got out her bag – the very one from Debenhams, as it happened, that David preferred to the Birkin. 'There!' She produced a page torn out of a women's magazine. 'My mother doesn't hold with the internet. She thinks it's run by robots with malicious intentions.'

'Granted Jeff Bezos looks a bit like an extra from *Star Trek*, but that's a bit harsh,' giggled Jo.

'She prefers to get her news from her weekly visit to the hairdresser. No doubt that's where she pinched this.' Steph held the photo up so the others could see it. It was a glossy chocolate cake shaped like a castle. 'Ours is going to be shaped like a château, obviously. *This* château, in fact, so she says can someone email her a very good photo showing all the towers and turrets. She's already bought those ice-cream cones shaped like witches' hats to make them.' Steph shook her head and sighed. 'I told her it would make far more sense for her to stay with me and make it – or even do it here – but she insisted she had to do it in her own kitchen with her own oven and then drive the thing across France. Madness, if you ask me, but that's Mum for you.'

Sophie grabbed the photo and held it up, glowing with excitement.

'Do you know, this cake makes it all seem real.' She held up her glass of fizz. 'To our very first château wedding!'

To everyone's relief, by the next day Meredith seemed back to normal. Whatever worries she had about the sudden arrival of Lucille Latignac had been submerged in getting on with the job.

The first recipient of Meredith's renewed energy was Steve the builder. Why had he not completed the bedrooms on the first floor? And did he consider the quality of the paintwork to be up to standard? Because she didn't.

After years of being married to whiplash-tongued Jackie, Steve took this criticism in his stride. 'As a matter of fact,' he replied mildly, 'we've been working on the second floor at the same time. If you'd like to inspect it up there, I'd be happy to show you.'

One of Meredith's strengths, her teams in Hong Kong and Singapore would have attested, was to know when she was behaving unfairly and admit it. That's what she did now.

'Sorry. It's been a demanding week.'

'That's all right,' Steve acknowledged with a cheeky grin. 'I was almost ready to believe the duchess up at the Lego house that you were the Queen of Bitches for a moment there. *Who does she think she is? Just because she's bought a château she thinks she's got the status to go with it?* I got a right old ear-walloping when I went up there to help her out with installing a new plug socket, I can tell you!'

'You can tell the duchess I don't give a toss about status!' Meredith replied waspishly, then thought better of it. 'No, don't say anything. It'll only make it worse. What am I supposed to have done?'

'Declaring this festival open, when apparently she should have done it.'

'I thought so. Hopefully it'll blow over. At least she's stopped lurking about in the vineyard.'

'Only because Liam told her she was trampling on the vines.'

Meredith smiled. 'Yes, he's got a knack for handling Margot.' She wished he had one for handling Jo. Nothing much seemed to be progressing there, when it had looked so hopeful. Pity – Meredith liked the man. There seemed to be something solid about him, unlike the ghastly Mark.

Walking in Steve's wake, she surveyed the succession of rooms in different shades of green. It reminded her of being on holiday, when the sea changed colour according to the depth of the water.

When they put the furnishings back, plus the new antiques Sophie had picked up here and there, the rooms would look exceptionally elegant. A small flare of excitement penetrated the sense of anxiety that Lucille's reappearance had created. It really wouldn't be long now until Nicky's wedding when the world, as well as the bride, would see what an incredible place the château would be to have your own romantic wedding. 'Thanks, Steve. It looks terrific.'

Steve ambled off, looking quietly delighted.

Meredith found herself staring down at the Savarin River below.

'Oh Dad,' she whispered into the empty air, 'at last I'd found a man I might be able to love, and now this. I shouldn't care, but she's got this luminous bloody beauty and I'm not even young any more. In fact, under all the hair dye and make-up, I'm almost old. Help me, Dad, help me decide what to do. I just can't let myself get hurt, not at my age!'

She shook her head at her own stupidity. Her dad was dead and she didn't believe in God so how could she appeal to – what? – a spirit? Some enduring angel? She was getting worse than the poor deluded souls who swallowed self-help books whole.

A noise behind her made her turn.

It was Sophie. 'Philippe's here,' she announced, being careful not to imply anything in her tone that might make things worse. 'He's brought a bottle of your favourite rosé. I put him out on the terrace. Mum's gone to get a couple of glasses. She says would you like some snacks?'

Meredith almost laughed out loud. Here she was in the middle of a life crisis being offered snacks. 'No, I don't want any snacks, but thanks for asking. Tell him I'll be down in a moment.'

She headed for her bedroom and looked in the mirror. Whether she was going to end the relationship or decide to wait and see, with competition like Lucille she needed to look her best.

The face she saw reflected in the mirror did not fill her with confidence. The new-found glow of happiness had visibly dimmed, leaving her looking drawn and grey, the bags beneath her eyes suddenly more prominent. *You look like what you are,* Announced her inner voice – *an almost old woman!*

What's wrong with that? countered her rational self.

Meredith stared back. *Everything,* she challenged it, reaching for her make-up bag.

330

There are times in life when the expenditure on Yves St Laurent primer, Touche Éclat concealer and Le Teint foundation are worth the ridiculous outlay. This was one of them. Five minutes later, with the final addition of a slash of red Chanel lipstick, Meredith was ready to face her future.

Twenty-Three

Philippe stood up when she arrived. Behind him the sun blazed over the lush green landscape. Bees buzzed in the heat and Nelly lay panting adoringly at his feet. 'I see you've put the warpaint on,' he smiled tentatively. 'Are we at war?'

'I don't know,' replied Meredith. 'Are we?'

'I'm not,' he replied with feeling. 'You have to believe me, Meredith, I had no idea Lucille was going to pull something like this and turn up here.'

'And has she gone?'

'Yes, back to Bordeaux.'

'And is she planning to stay there?'

He paused for fractionally too long.

'I see,' Meredith replied in a colourless tone.

'She wants to see Jean-Christophe, that is all.'

'And she will start turning up at the restaurant, where you will be as well.'

'Meredith, you are not being fair!'

Meredith knew this already, but her protective instincts had sharpened in readiness.

'Would you like a glass of wine?' Philippe had remembered

his father's advice when out carp fishing. Learning when to leave the fish alone was just as important as knowing when to pursue it.

'No, thank you,' Meredith replied. 'I have too much work to do. But feel free to sit and enjoy the view. Nelly seems happy to look after you.'

'I would prefer it if it was you,' he stated simply.

Meredith almost softened.

'Another day, perhaps, when you are sure of your priorities.'

'For God's sake, Meredith.' He got to his feet, almost losing his temper. 'I am perfectly clear about my priorities now!'

But Meredith was already disappearing into the orangery. He watched her, suddenly seeing that although Lucille might once have seemed the love of his life – and he had even flirted with the idea of a reconciliation – Meredith was the woman he really wanted to be with.

'*Merde, alors*, Nelly, what do I do now?' he enquired of the adoring hound.

Nelly, sensing his frustration, got clumsily to her feet and placed a comforting paw on his pale linen trousers.

'Thank you,' Philippe replied. 'I am trying to be patient but perhaps I should ignore all this disdain and carry her off to the bedroom! What is your view, Nelly?' He studied the dog's mournful expression. 'You think that attitude does not ring with the times? You are a modern dog. Perhaps you are right. Besides, it's time I got back to the restaurant and started cooking.'

There are many different ways of dealing with heartache, and Sophie and Jo soon discovered that Meredith's was working like a demon.

'So has Jean-Christophe agreed to be our fourth caterer?' she enquired briskly the next morning.

'We left it to see how he got on at the food festival,' Sophie replied, wishing she didn't have to raise that distressing topic.

'And how *did* he get on? For some reason, I didn't notice.'

Jo could hear the pain behind the self-deprecation and wanted to hug her friend, but Meredith was in the wrong mood.

'Very well, I think. There was always a long queue, but he seemed to handle it really well.'

'Let's go for him, then. He offers a different choice to the others and from what Nicky was saying, it's what some brides want.'

'Are you sure?' Jo asked gently. 'I mean, Jean-Christophe may be around quite a bit then.'

'Reminding me of his father? I expect I'll cope.' She got out her laptop to consult her notes. 'Right – Nicky needs to make some final decisions about the wedding, especially the caterer. We're already incredibly late. Steve is confident the new rooms will be ready soon. Jo, you might check that Ronnie's still on top of the flowers, find out where she's ordered them from . . . oh, and ask about the cake too. How is it going to be transported, or is the grandmother making it here? The new guest kitchen will be ready if she wants to use it.'

From then on, they seemed to be busy all the time.

David sat holding a card the postman had just delivered and staring out into the sunny garden. It was from his niece Nicky, and it was an invitation to her wedding at the Château de St Savarin.

Nicky had scrawled a message on the back in her large, schoolgirlish writing.

Please come to my wedding, Uncle David. I know you may not want to, but it won't be the same without you. And let's be honest, you're the best person on the planet at handling Mum's outrageous behaviour! Besides, I love you, and with our weird family set-up that counts for a lot. It wouldn't be the same without you. Do come. Nicky.

David had tried so hard not to look at the past since he'd left Steph, but this appeal had unlocked the floodgates of memory, and now all the happy and poignant moments he'd suppressed were streaming out and threatening to pull him under. He tried to get up and find some distraction, but it was as if he'd been glued to the spot.

Without warning, he felt Suzi's arms snaking round his neck. He jumped as if he'd been stung.

She let go abruptly. 'What the hell's the matter with you?'

'I was just reading something private, that's all.'

'What kind of thing?'

'An invitation to my niece's wedding at the château.'

'Which you will decline, naturally, because I can't go with you for obvious reasons.'

'Which I will accept, because my niece means a lot to me.'

'I see.'

'Yes.' There was a long silence, which neither dared to interrupt. Finally it was David who spoke. 'You're a lovely woman, Suzi . . .'

'So lovely you're about to dump me,' she stated brutally.

'The thing is, we're entirely different people who like different things. The bag is a metaphor, maybe . . .'

'You're not leaving me over a bloody Birkin bag! I won't buy the sodding thing. Metaphor! Yes, that's where we're different, maybe. I believe in real things, not airy-fairy concepts like *metaphors*. Food. Pleasure. Indulging yourself a bit. You're a dreamer, David. That's probably why the B&B got into trouble.'

Her words cut into him like a surgeon's knife. Maybe she was right.

'I'm moving into the hotel for a while.'

'Make your bloody mind up!' she shouted. 'Are you leaving or not?'

'Yes, I'm leaving. Sorry.'

'Well, good riddance! I'm going out. I don't know where. I assume you'll be gone when I get back.'

She stormed out and off down the street, almost tripping over one of Janine's pack of dogs, which were coming down the pavement from the opposite direction.

'Hi, Suze, everything all right? I mean, you look kind of upset.'

Suzi longed to tell someone her problems, but certainly not a member of the Ladies' Luncheon Club.

'Fine, thanks. Just a few tech issues.'

'Oh, I do sympathize,' Janine nodded. 'There's nothing like tech problems to really screw up your day. My server went down on Tuesday and . . .' But Suzi was already disappearing in the opposite direction.

I wonder, thought Janine, if something's really up. She tied the dogs to some convenient railings, went into the cafe opposite Suzi's house and ordered a large *café crème*. Before she'd finished drinking it, David emerged carrying a suitcase.

'Aha,' smiled Janine. Now she'd really have something to tell the others at lunchtime. She untied the dogs and headed

336

home, powered by the forbidden delight of seeing someone else's life falling apart while your own was going averagely well.

Sophie was busy photocopying a large shot of the château to send to Nicky's grandmother, the cake maker.

'Look at it,' she said to her mother. 'It really does look like something out of Disney. She'll have no trouble finding someone online who'll tell her exactly how to make the cake. That's what I love about the internet, it's such a community.'

'A community of people who don't actually know each other,' commented Jo.

'OK, sourpuss, what's the matter with you?'

Jo grinned. 'You know me too well. A message from Bill and Maureen, Nicky's dad and stepmother, asking if they can stay in the château.'

'And you don't think Ronnie will be happy?'

'I don't think Ronnie will be happy at all, but Bill is paying for the whole show so I don't see how they can say no.'

'And Nicky will have to be the one to decide,' Sophie concluded. 'Eek. Poor girl. That's really tough.'

Five minutes later, her phone rang. It was Ronnie. 'Have you heard from Bill at all?' she demanded, without even saying hello.

'Yes, as a matter of fact, we have.'

'Asking to stay at the château?'

'Yes,' Jo replied in as neutral a voice as she could.

'Well, obviously they can't.'

'Is that what Nicky thinks too?'

'I haven't asked her.'

'Don't you think you should?' Jo suggested firmly. 'After all, it is her wedding.'

The answer came via Nicky's WhatsApp: *Yes. My dad and stepmother can stay at the château. End of story. Nicky.*

Jo and Sophie exchanged a look.

'Don't you love a wedding?' Sophie laughed as she dropped her head into her hands.

David hardly noticed that the hotel he'd booked himself into was both small and shabby. His overwhelming sense was one of relief.

Staying with Suzi had felt as if he had an exotic cat permanently camped on his chest and it was stopping him breathing. 'And I'm allergic to cats!' he kept telling Suzi in his mind, but she wouldn't listen.

He unpacked his bag and sat on the bed. He'd really screwed things up. Suzi wasn't a bad person, just entirely different to him. And OK, Steph didn't tell him he was wonderful all the time – but plenty of people had to put up with a lot worse than that.

He stared out of the window at the dusty car park. There was no way he could expect her to take him back, but he felt he owed her one thing, at least: to save Fleur-de-Lis.

Of all the ways of communicating with her the modern world offered, he decided email would be best. If he rang, it might be awkward, especially if she didn't want to speak to him, or if he ended up speaking to Marcelline. So he opened his laptop and began to write.

'Since Steve says the rooms are all ready, let's pick some flowers and take a bottle of fizz and go and christen them!' Jo suggested, thinking this might cheer Meredith up in her newly fragile state. 'We could do a bit of a test run.'

So Jo spent a happy hour wandering round the garden

picking roses of all colours, deep blue delphiniums, pale pink cosmos and, for contrast, some fizzy green euphorbia.

'You want to watch yourself with that,' said a voice behind her.

She turned to find a hardly recognizable Liam, masked, gloved and visored for spraying the vines. 'The stuff in the stem can really irritate your eyes.' He pointed out the white milky substance that leaked from the stem of the euphorbia plant. 'Here, I'll take it. But only handle it in gloves. I'll put it in a sink somewhere.'

'Thanks so much – put it over there, if you could? We're probably going to use that outhouse for arranging the wedding flowers, if it isn't too hot.' Jo pointed to the last of a row of flat-roofed buildings at the rear of the courtyard.

Liam took all the flowers out of her arms.

Watching him go, Jo felt a small leap of happiness. She felt cared about, looked after. Modern women weren't supposed to need looking after any longer. The Sleeping Beauty of today was supposed to rescue herself by her wit and savvy, not wait for some imaginary prince. Jo wouldn't tell her daughter, who was firmly of the 'save yourself' school, but Jo still longed to be rescued. If any princes fancied sweeping by on their steeds and scooping her up, she realized rather shamefacedly, she was all for it.

Especially if they happened to be Kiwi.

'It all looks fabulous, Sophie!' Meredith said.

Sophie had arranged the rooms with her usual style, placing the right cushion there, a polished candlebra there, filling the vases with flowers Jo had picked, and even supplying music on her phone to add to the atmosphere.

'You really do have a gift for interior design,' her mother agreed. 'You could take it up properly when you go home.'

'Thank you,' Sophie bowed. 'It's funny thinking of Basingtstoke as home. It's really started to feel more like home here.'

They toured round their new bedrooms, all en suite, plus the spanking new kitchen for use of the bride and groom's families during their stay. Each of the rooms was slightly different with their own individual touches. 'I have to say,' Sophie confessed, 'I took a lot of inspiration from Fleur-de-Lis and went to Steph's favourite *brocante*. They have lovely stuff there, it just needs a bit of love and attention.'

'Don't we all?' laughed Jo. 'You've done a brilliant job, darling. I wouldn't mind moving in here myself.'

'When the wedding season finishes, you can always move into the bridal suite!' Sophie teased her mum.

Meanwhile, Meredith, back in the library, had opened the bottle and was giving out glasses. 'To our beautiful château!' she toasted.

'Hey girls,' Sophie announced. 'An important moment. We've had two enquiries for a wedding here next year!'

'That's fantastic!' replied Jo.

'And the pace is heating up – I've had six emails from Nicky today.'

'Good God, what about?' asked Meredith.

'That's nothing, Sophie,' Jo laughed. 'Be warned. I talked to the woman who runs Be Mine in France and she says most brides send her about a hundred! Oh, and the other good news –' she deliberately didn't look at Meredith as she spoke – 'Jean-Christophe is delighted to be on the catering list. Which is just as well,' she added, laughing, 'since Nicky's just decided it's him she wants to do the food for her wedding!'

'Sophie!' Meredith thundered. 'You didn't offer him before you'd checked he could do it?'

'Sorry, yes; that was a bit of a slip-up,' confessed Sophie.

'A slip-up hardly covers it.' Meredith still sounded furious.

'Look, Meredith,' Sophie replied tensely, 'I have just apologized.'

'It didn't sound like much of an apology to me. Am I supposed to check that you've ordered the table and chairs, or the DJ she wanted? These people get booked up for months. Years, even.'

'Of course I've checked,' flashed Sophie. 'And just because you're upset about this Lucille, you don't have to take it out on us! You're not our headmistress, you know. We're all in this together!'

Meredith's face changed from expensive beige to blotchy red. 'Except for one thing. I happen to be the major shareholder!' She picked up a file from the table and held it against her like a medieval shield as she pushed her way out of the room.

'Oh God!' Sophie was already regretting her tactlessness. 'How could I have said that?'

'Because Meredith, who famously doesn't believe in losing her temper, just lost her temper,' reassured Jo. 'On the other hand, it was a little outrageous of you. I wish we could think of something to do to help.'

'I know,' Sophie looked as if she might cry. 'Jean-Christophe's coming in this afternoon. Do you think we dare talk to him about it?'

'Don't mention anything about Philippe. Just ask him about the mother and see what he volunteers,' Jo suggested.

'Mum, you are so wise!'

'Am I?' Jo didn't feel wise at all, but compliments like this were rare enough to be squirrelled away and brought out in the bad times.

In her sparsely furnished loft in Bordeaux, Lucille Latignac was staring at a crumpled family photo and considering her next move. She hadn't been sure until she'd been to the food festival and seen her son and ex-husband together. Their closeness had made her feel both jealous and excluded. Their life in Bratenac, which she'd expected to find suburban and dull, had instead seemed a garden of Eden.

And she, she well knew, was the serpent. But then, she'd always felt the serpent got a bad deal. After all, she wasn't trying to bring evil to the world – only to get a little happiness for herself.

Philippe, always attractive in a crumpled sort of way, had mellowed into a rounded human being. Just as the salt and pepper in his beard had softened his almost superhero jaw, his new attitude had softened his personality. Some people became more rigid as they aged, but Philippe seemed the opposite. At its most basic, she had seen the strength of the love between him and their son, and feeling excluded from that was almost physically painful. There was also the fact that Philippe was rumoured to be really quite wealthy, and she was fed up with scrambling for the rent every quarter and looking for cheap holidays on Airbnb.

Lucille became even more determined to get her family back.

Twenty-Four

Meredith, Jo and Sophie sat on the terrace waiting for Jean-Christophe to arrive.

'Phew!' Sophie fanned herself with the Moleskine notebook she always carried. 'Getting hot!'

They looked out at the ripening vines in their neat lines, the soil between the rows now a rich baked brown.

'Well, it's the beginning of July. Poor Steve has been telling me how much he hates the summer heat,' Jo remarked.

'Then why did he come and live here?' asked Sophie.

'Jackie wanted to! Why else?'

The doorbell jangled and the tall and smiling figure of Jean-Christophe appeared. With his long, almost black hair, eyes the colour of black olives and fashionable designer stubble, he could somehow only be French.

Meredith, who'd been staring down the valley thinking of her father, turned and experienced a physical shock. Even though she'd been expecting him, encountering Jean-Christophe, who was so much the image of Philippe, hurt in some deep and hidden part of her.

Noting that Meredith was oddly silent, Jo took the initiative.

'Hello, Jean-Christophe. Let's just run through what Nicky's requested, shall we?'

He produced a wafer-thin laptop from his rucksack to take notes.

'They would like dinner for about twelve people here on the Friday night. Martin's family don't get on, so they won't be coming,' explained Jo.

'But they are coming to the wedding?' asked Sophie.

Jo nodded.

'Happy families,' Sophie grinned. 'Don't you love them?'

Jo tried not to wince as Sophie turned to Jean-Christophe. 'Nicky's requested something simple for the Friday night. She doesn't want a lot of fuss. Could you come up with some menus? Oh, there's the wine tasting as well, we mustn't forget that! Liam will be organizing it and they'll choose which wines they want for the day.' She tried not to catch her mother's eye. 'Liam will provide them at the right temperature. Can you liaise with him about how to keep it cool?'

'Of course,' he agreed.

'And for the wedding day itself, we will order croissants and pastries from the *boulangerie* for the family breakfast. Why don't you get out your list now, Sophie, and talk us through it?'

'Delighted,' beamed Sophie. 'The moment I've been waiting for!' She produced a printout from her folder. 'The exchange of vows is at one o'clock, followed by the photographs, but they want their guests to have a drink while they wait. The official reception is at two and they'll need canapés as well, so can you suggest a variety of those? The actual meal follows at three thirty.'

'Is the celebrant booked?' Meredith enquired, softening the

request with a smile that acknowledged her previous bad temper.

'Of course,' replied Sophie smoothly.

'What kind of tables have they chosen?' Jean-Christophe enquired. 'Just so I can tell my servers.'

'Round,' replied Sophie with a smile. 'The favourite choice when there's been a difficult divorce. No top table.'

'Except that, speaking as an ex-wife,' Jo pointed out before she could stop herself, 'the ex-wife always knows which is *really* the top table. And that she's not on it.'

'What have you got in mind for the wedding meal?' Sophie dived in quickly. 'Nicky keeps saying she wants it to feel like a festival. I don't think she wants to go for the conventional safe chicken option.'

'Let's go for the spiced lamb with warm salads of rice, aubergine, red pepper and pomegranate seeds. It could even be roasted whole on a spit, if you want it to feel like a real festival.'

'I'll check with Nicky.'

Jo had stopped listening and was watching Meredith, who sat, still uncharacteristically quiet. Jo recognized the look on her face: it was the same look she'd had herself when she'd learned about Mark and Amanda.

'Jean-Christophe,' Jo said suddenly. 'Are you all right? I mean, this sudden reappearance of your mother. Does it make you happy?'

Jean-Christophe put down his laptop. If he was taken aback at this sudden change of topic, he didn't show it. 'It is wonderful, of course, in some ways. But you must remember, I always had my father. We developed a closeness I do not see in other families. It is for him I feel, not myself.'

Jean-Christophe, a sensitive young man, who seemed to know that Meredith would be listening to his every word, came to a halting conclusion. The question hung in the air as to exactly *how* his father was reacting to the sudden reappearance of Lucille in their lives.

It was Sophie who spoke next. 'The bride will love that,' she announced brightly.

He shot her a look of gratitude. 'Will you be having a wedding cake? And will that be the dessert, as in France – or will people take it home, as I think you sometimes do in England?'

'Oh my God, I'd forgotten Granny's chocolate château!' Sophie confessed. 'Yes, we will be having cake – for the dessert. Nicky's grandmother is bringing it all the way from England. We may need cream to go with that.' She noted it down on her list. 'I'm sure there'll be a million other things, but I think that's it for today. Thank you very much for coming.' She got up to show him out.

'*Avec grand plaisir,*' Jean-Christophe smiled. He wondered if he should mention the madness of driving a chocolate château for hundreds of miles in the middle of summer. 'And thank you for adding me to your list. It's a great honour.'

Sophie stopped for a moment and almost said she'd like to add him to more then her catering list, but for once her nerve failed her. What if she'd got the signals wrong? There was a reserve about Jean-Christophe that made him hard to read.

She found his dark eyes fixed on hers as she opened the vast front door for him. But neither of them broke the slightly awkward silence.

'Come on, girls,' Jo announced when she got back. 'Time for a restorative glass of our very own rosé. So what if it's only five o'clock? We're just doing a bit of quality control. We wouldn't want to give our guests something we hadn't tested ourselves, now, would we? And this wedding's coming up pretty bloody soon!'

Sophie drank her glass and disappeared back inside. Jo glanced at Meredith and decided to take the plunge.

'Don't you think you're being a bit hard on Philippe? It would have been difficult for him to just send Lucille away. After all, she was his wife and Jean-Christophe's mother.'

'You don't need to remind me of that!' flashed Meredith bitterly. 'Sorry, Jo, I shouldn't take it out on you. I'm the sort of person who has to act, and I feel I'm stuck in limbo, powerless to do anything.'

'Then do something! Be yourself. That's why he fell for you, after all. Tell him how you feel. Sometimes you have to be explicit, even if it does involve a risk.' Margot's words, giving her the same advice, suddenly came back to Jo. She hadn't exactly practised what she was preaching. All the same, she was sure Meredith and Philippe had been happy before all this.

'OK, you're right. I will!' Meredith looked at her watch. 'No time like the present. Before I lose my nerve!'

It was a glorious evening, so she decided to walk to the restaurant along the riverbank. Should she take Nelly? The dog, sensing the chance of a walk, was already on her feet and looking up at her mistress hopefully. 'Come on, then. You can give me some moral support.'

The riverbank was deserted at this hour. Most sensible people would be at home preparing dinner, and that meant she had it all to herself.

She had only been walking for about ten minutes, admiring the stillness of the water and the shapes reflected in it, almost like an impressionist painting, when Nelly began to bark madly.

'Sshh, Nelly,' Meredith called out. At least there were no fish to frighten. And then she glimpsed a movement from inside a small fisherman's hut a few feet from the bank. This was what had attracted Nelly's interest. It was probably just an angler gone to change his rod or look for different bait. Then she heard a faint groan and decided perhaps she ought to investigate.

Behind the door, lying on the bare wood, was a rumpled figure of a man singing quietly to himself. Meredith thought she recognized the words of Charles Trenet's famous song 'La Mer'.

'*Bonsoir*,' she attempted. '*Tout va bien ici?*'

'*Non, madame*,' was the faint reply. '*Je crois que je me suis cassé la jambe.*'

Meredith rushed forward, realizing that it was Philippe's father lying here with a possible broken leg.

'*Je suis desolé*, madame,' he apologized. 'But I think I have lost my telephone.'

Meredith instantly produced hers, but Antoine was too confused to remember the number.

'Don't worry,' Meredith reassured. 'I can call the restaurant.'

Nelly decided this was the moment to offer not suspicion but reassurance, so she sat herself down by Antoine's side and produced her most engaging smile.

Meredith dialled the number and waited anxiously, feeling faintly relieved that the old man had stopped groaning and was smiling back at Nelly. '*Quel drôle de chien*,' he announced, stroking her neck.

Philippe answered on the fifth ring. She could hear the sounds of the kitchen behind him. 'Philippe, it's Meredith. I'm afraid it's your father.'

'*Mon dieu!* Where is he this time?'

'In a fishing hut just below the château. He thinks he's broken his leg.'

'Thank you, Meredith. Can you stay with him?'

'Of course.'

'I will come at once. I should be no more than ten minutes.'

Meredith sat down next to the old man. 'Philippe's on his way.'

'He will be angry with me. He will say stupid old man.' He smiled at Meredith. 'I *am* a stupid old man.' He winced suddenly as he tried to turn his leg.

'Sing "La Mer" again,' Meredith suggested as a distraction. 'It was my father's favourite. He said nothing made him think of France like that song.'

'He had good taste, your father.'

'You would have liked him, I think. He used to bring me here every year as a child. We camped on the riverbank. He was happier here than anywhere else in the world.'

Antoine began to sing again about the sea under summer skies with clouds like white sheep in the sky. Quietly, Meredith joined in. As they finished their third rendition of the song, Philippe appeared.

'A customer gave me a lift on his scooter,' he explained. 'I have already called an ambulance.'

Not long afterwards, they heard the siren approaching.

'*Merci, jeune femme*,' Antoine smiled at Meredith, 'and thank you for the dog.'

'Did I hear "La Mer"?' Philippe tried to distract his father from the pain as they lifted him onto a stretcher.

Antoine nodded and closed his eyes.

'He used to sing me to sleep with that when I was a kid,' he smiled at Meredith. 'And thank you also from me.'

Meredith hesitated about whether to confess that she had

been on her way to see him, but the ambulance man called to ask if he was coming with them.

'Goodbye.' She pressed his hand, hoping to convey the message through touch and look.

'Goodbye. Bye-bye, Nelly. Look after your mistress.'

And they were gone.

'Janine,' Jackie ordered – there was no other word for her tone – 'go and see Suzi and get her to join us for lunch.' They were enjoying a morning coffee at Jackie's modern bungalow. Just like the French, she had no desire to acquire an old wreck even if she was married to a builder.

Jackie, in fact, was celebrating with a Mimosa because Steve had finished up at the château and they would soon be in the money. Meredith, she was sure, was a prompt payer – unlike their friend Steph. This line of thought took her back to Steph and David. If David had left Suzi, that was a start. But had he gone back to Steph? And if not, why not, and how could she make him?

Janine looked appalled. 'I can't. I've got six dogs to walk.'

'Take them with you. They'll break the ice.'

'Suzi hates dogs.'

'Then tell her you and the dogs aren't budging till she agrees to come.'

Meredith's enquiry about the celebrant reminded Sophie that she had been asked to check on Ronnie and the flowers.

Ronnie, she discovered, seduced by their glorious website, had gone for Fleurs Romantiques, by far the most expensive supplier around. They provided flowers for the luxurious châteaux and boutique hotels in the area at extortionate prices.

She wondered if she ought to try and talk her out of it, but suspected talking Ronnie out of anything might be too much of a challenge. Besides, it wasn't really their problem. They had specified that all contracts had to be direct with the supplier, so it would be Ronnie who got lumbered with the enormous cost. Or poor Bill, her ex-husband.

Sophie decided instead to do what she was really good at: refining all her lists of what needed to happen when and who was responsible for what, in order to make Nicky's wedding run like clockwork.

'Right!' Jackie took over, as she always did. 'Get Suzi a large glass of red.'

Janine scuttled off, climbing over a small mountain of dogs to place the order with Guillaume.

The glass appeared and was placed in front of Suzi. Suzi, her face so gaunt that even thick layers of make-up couldn't disguise her distress, didn't even notice.

This was serious.

'So what actually happened?' Jackie enquired gently.

'I tried really hard to think of everything he might want,' Suzi replied in a tortured tone. 'I kept remembering that Jerry Hall saying that to keep a man happy you had to be a maid in the living room, a cook in the kitchen and a whore in the bedroom. And I was! But he kept on going on about how different we were.' She turned towards her embarrassed audience for greater effect. 'You're not going to believe it, but what really seemed to get to him the most was me buying that handbag!' Suzi raised anguished eyes on which a whole bottle of black eyeliner had been expended, giving her the appearance of Lady Macbeth as the face of Rimmel. 'I mean, I ask you!'

Shirley, Janine and Mandy all looked at each other guiltily. Jackie was made of sterner stuff. 'Relationships don't end over handbags,' she insisted, ignoring the fact that they had all contributed to the purchase of the Birkin bag in the hope of achieving just this outcome.

'Perhaps he was right,' suggested Janine, whose kind heart was melting a little. 'Maybe you *were* just too different.'

'But I don't want to be alone!' wailed Suzi.

'We'll look after you. Won't we, girls?' Janine insisted.

Even Jackie wasn't immune to that universal female cry – perhaps not even female, but definitely universal.

'Absolutely!' the others chorused, equally grateful they all had partners and making a mental note to be nicer to them, so they didn't end up alone like Suzi.

'So tell me about *l'anglaise*,' enquired Antoine of his son when he came home a few days later, his leg in plaster with two new crutches on which he hobbled proudly round, waving them in the direction of anything he required and swearing noisily if he encountered any obstacles. 'You two seemed to know each other pretty well. You should bring her home. I liked her. Time you settled down again, don't you think?' he added with a roguish look.

Philippe repressed a smile. No doubt Grand-père had heard about the reappearance of Lucille. He had never liked her, and the fact that she had simply disappeared without her ten-year-old had naturally reinforced his opinion. 'She was only ever out for herself, that one,' was his constant refrain on the subject whenever he found anyone who would listen.

Happily for Philippe, Jean-Christophe arrived before he had time to reply to his father's question. 'I'll stay with him for a bit,' he offered, seeing his father's look of exhaustion. It was hard to decide which was more tiring: having Antoine at home on crutches, or chasing round the countryside looking for him.

Jean-Christophe glanced at his father, wondering if he were any nearer to resolving the much more crucial dilemma: did he want to give Lucille another chance, or continue his relationship with the lady from the château?

Sophie had been busy emailing Ronnie with a list of all the different uses for which flowers would be required: most importantly, the bridal bouquet, but also buttonholes for the ushers and bridegroom, table centrepieces and suitable blooms to deck the wedding pavilion where the happy couple would be exchanging their vows. At the moment the château garden was a riot of flowers that could be pressed into use, but by the date of the wedding they would be past their best. She suspected Ronnie would not be a reliable provider of the right flowers, but she could only do what she could.

Sophie closed her eyes and mentally decorated the château as if for her own wedding. A glorious vision appeared of Sophie dressed entirely in red, with a bouquet of blowsy red roses and a red rose arch to walk through on her way to the wedding pavilion. Red might be thought an unusual colour for a bride, but naturally Sophie looked sensational in it. Suddenly the tall figure of Jean-Christophe in a chic black suit introduced himself into Sophie's fantasy. 'Really, Soph,' she told herself sternly, 'pull yourself together. He hasn't even asked you out!'

She opened her eyes from this pleasurable interlude to find that Nicky had finally sent her the guest list.

Twelve family members were to stay in the newly refurbished château, while Martin's family – Sophie grinned at the memory that they didn't get on – were lodging at various hotels round about. Then to the guest list. This numbered eighty people: a nice neat figure that could be divided up into ten tables of eight or, perhaps better, eight tables of ten.

Nicky had helpfully added a line of description beside each name. Sophie ran her eyes down the guest list, not expecting to recognize anyone, then stood suddenly as still as a statue. Halfway down the alphabetical list of names were Mark and Amanda Walker, described as 'friends of Martin's from work'.

Shit, shit, shit!

What Nicky clearly hadn't taken in was that Mark Walker was Sophie's father, and that while Sophie and Jo had been in France, he'd gone ahead and married Amanda the airheaded sales exec, and here they were on the guest list.

Jean-Christophe looked in the mirror above the fireplace and attempted to comb his luxuriant curls into a semblance of order. He was meeting his mother for lunch and, without quite understanding why, had given more thought than usual to his appearance. It wasn't as if she were going to love him more because he'd dressed carefully. All the same, he was aware of wanting to look his best and had selected a smarter outfit than usual of black turtleneck and black jeans.

'*Nom de Dieu!*' commented a voice behind him rudely. 'Where are you going? You look like a waiter at a Parisian funeral.'

He turned to find his grandfather surveying him with the gaze of a malicious gargoyle.

Jean-Christophe considered ducking the question but knew his grandfather would find out. '*En effet*, I am meeting my mother for lunch.'

'Oh, *her*.' His tone couldn't have been more withering. 'What do you want to waste your time on doing that for?'

Jean-Christophe suppressed a smile. His grandfather had

never taken to Lucille and, like the rest of the world, had only condemnation for a woman who was prepared to leave her own child, no matter what the motivation.

'Be careful, *mon petit*.' The old man's voice rang with sudden tenderness. 'Ask yourself why she suddenly wants to come back into your life. Was it really an accident of luck, or has she planned the whole thing?'

'Sophie, are you OK?' Meredith asked. 'Only you look as if you've seen a ghost. The White Lady isn't out and about, I hope?'

'No,' Sophie covered her face with her hands, 'this is all too real, I'm afraid. I've just got the guest list from Nicky.'

'And? Has she asked double the number you expected?'

'I could handle that. It's just that Martin, the bridegroom, has invited my father and his new wife. Apparently they know each other through work. I remember Nicky saying something odd, that Martin didn't have a lot of friends. He'd have to be scraping the barrel to invite my dad.'

'Shit. What a disaster.'

'What are we going to tell Mum?' Sophie, normally the calmest of people, fought back tears as she raised an anguished face to Meredith's. 'Oh God, Meredith, why do men always seem to leave women?'

Meredith opened her arms. She always told herself she'd never missed having children, but there were times when Sophie almost felt like a daughter. 'Come on, have a hug.' She folded Sophie into her arms.

'Maybe if I asked him not to come,' she blurted into Meredith's shoulder.

'Asked who not to come? Sophie, darling, what on earth's the matter?'

They turned to find Jo standing in the doorway.

Sophie decided the truth was the only option. 'Mum, I'm so sorry. I've just got the guest list, and . . . Martin's invited Dad and Amanda. I assume he has no idea of the connection with us.'

For a split second Jo seemed as if she might collapse. And then a furious sense of dignity came to her rescue. She was damned if she'd be pitied over this. 'Oh well,' she announced, a smile creeping across her face, 'he'll only make an arse of himself on the dance floor, so we've got that to look forward to.'

Sophie launched herself across the space between them. 'I love you, Mum. And I think you're absolutely wonderful!'

Jackie looked at her shiny kitchen surfaces with satisfaction. Everything about her modern bungalow was easy-care, from the gleaming white worktops to the neatly stacked modern dresser. Apart from Steve, that was. He still managed to lounge on the small sofa, draping his large frame over its edges like whipped cream oozing out of a Victoria sandwich, and throwing discarded garments onto the nearby armchairs. He had the knack of being relaxed wherever he was. He could probably, Jackie thought with grudging affection, have made himself at home in a medieval dungeon.

'Are you quite comfortable?' Jackie enquired. 'Fancy a cup of tea? A cool beer?'

'What's the matter with you?' he asked cautiously, waiting for the trap to close if he gave the wrong answer.

'I wanted to talk to you, that's all.'

Instinctively he moved his feet off the arm of the sofa and lumberingly pulled himself upright, like a great beast surfacing from a watering hole in a David Attenborough programme.

'What about?' he asked suspiciously.

'Have you got anything more to finish up at the château?'

'Mostly finished. This was only stage one, obviously. We'll do the rest over the winter. It looks a lot better, though. On time and under budget.'

'No wonder you're so popular with all the Brits.'

'They thought about a swimming pool but decided it was too expensive. Maybe next year. I've got a few tools to pick up still. Why?'

'I want you to go up there and let it slip – very naturally, of course – that David, their friend's husband up at Fleur-de-Lis, the one that left her for Suzi, has moved into a hotel. I don't know which, but there are only two in Bratenac, so it shouldn't be too hard to find out.'

'You're a born stirrer, Jack.' Steve shook his head. 'Always interfering in other people's business. What are you up to now?'

'I just think life needs a little nudge now and then, that's all.' Jackie smiled innocently.

'I always thought he was a mug to leave her in the first place,' Steve conceded.

'Maybe she'll have learned to appreciate him. Speaking of which . . .' She suddenly leaned down and kissed Steve on the lips.

'Blimey, what was that for?' he asked.

'Maybe I thought I ought to appreciate you a bit more myself.'

'I'm up for that,' he grinned. 'And where's that beer got to?'

Jean-Christophe sat at the window table of the small restaurant in the pretty square surrounding the town well. He had arrived early so that he could prepare himself mentally. He ordered some sparkling water to calm his nerves. Why the hell was he feeling apprehensive at the prospect of meeting his own mother?

Behind him was the comforting buzz of old friends talking in quiet voices, punctuated by the occasional burst of companionable laughter.

Suddenly the laughter stopped. Jean-Christophe turned to find an old lady elbowing her companion sharply and nodding towards the door.

He followed her gaze.

Lucille stood framed in the doorway, looking round with the mysterious smile of a fallen Madonna that somehow characterized her. Her dress was simple and beautifully cut in coffee-coloured linen, which she had teamed with bronze leather shoes and a tightly belted trench coat in some light and filmy fabric. She looked as Parisian as an ad for Chanel No 5.

Jean-Christophe waved, suddenly unsure what to call her, and got politely to his feet.

'You don't need to stand for me,' she told him, in her soft voice that somehow floated like her trench coat. 'I'm your mother!'

Fortunately for Jean-Christophe, his initial period of embarrassment was lost in the discussions of what they would like to eat.

'You are a chef too,' Lucille smiled. 'What would you recommend?'

Jean-Christophe studied the menu. 'The *quenelles de brochet* look good.' But the thought of pike made him think of Meredith and that morning by the riverbank with Nelly. He liked her and he knew that his father, unmoved by any woman for years, did too. Yet something had happened between them since his mother had reappeared in their lives. 'Or the tartare of salmon. I will have that and then the beef fillet with the Perigueux sauce.'

'And I will have the same,' Lucille smiled. Jean-Christophe wondered if it was designed to flatter him. Maybe she just liked to follow suggestions.

She leaned in and offered him her melting smile. 'So tell me all about yourself. I want to know everything.'

He had the oddest feeling that she expected him to be flattered by her interest.

'After you left, we stayed in Paris and Papa looked after me with the help of various au pairs. But we were different to other people.'

'You know your father was impossible,' Lucille suddenly interrupted. 'He thought because I was a waitress and he was the great chef, that I should always stay like that. But I needed more.'

'One favour you did us –' Jean-Christophe attempted a smile – 'that also made us different to other people – we got to be good friends, not just *enfant et père*.'

'And how about your grandfather,' Lucille interrupted as if she didn't want to hear any more details of their close relationship, 'that wily old bastard, how is he?'

'It was for him that Papa sold up in Paris and came back here. He said he didn't want to give everything to his work any more.'

'A pity he didn't learn that a little earlier.' He was surprised at the bitterness in her tone, sharp enough to pierce and wound, though he didn't know whom.

'And who is this woman, this blonde with the unpronounceable name?'

'Me-re-dith.' Jean-Christophe smiled without knowing it.

'See, I have learned how to say it like a *rosbif*. She used to come here as a child and stay at the campground by the river with her father. It was their special place. He used to tell her he would buy her the château one day. And now she has bought it for herself.'

'Ah, a rich bitch, *hein?*'

'Not at all!' Jean-Christophe bristled on Meredith's behalf. 'They were very poor. It was just a joke between them. But he made sure she had a good education and when she was older she made a lot of money in the East – Shanghai, Hong Kong, Singapore. And then he died and she saw a picture of the castle one day in a magazine and came to stay with her friend near here, and they heard the château was for sale, *et voilà* she bought it.'

'You know a lot about it,' Lucille commented acidly.

'She is a good friend. She got me a job with the people at Fleur-de-Lis and now they have asked me to be on their list of caterers for the weddings. I am doing their very first wedding there!'

'Sounds like a fairy story to me,' Lucille shrugged. 'Good for PR.'

Jean-Christophe attacked his food, uncomfortable at Lucille's obvious hostility.

They had just finished their steak and were relaxing over a glass of local red wine when she suddenly looked fixedly at her son. 'How do you think your father would feel if I came back?'

'To live with us?' Jean-Christophe, who had so longed for this moment as a child, suddenly wasn't sure. He also saw that, as his grandfather had hinted, it wasn't him she was really interested in at all.

The remembered pain of her first leaving ran suddenly through him like molten lead until he wanted to scream.

'I'm afraid you'd have to ask him that yourself.'

'I will.' She smiled her fallen-Madonna smile. 'And Jean-Christophe . . .'

'Yes?'

'If you suddenly need any extra staff at this wedding you are catering, remember me. I would be happy to help.'

Twenty-Five

Meredith went out onto the terrace to find Steve the builder with Jo and Sophie, sharing a drink to mark the end of his work here. Steve, jovial, bear-like and slightly pink from the sun, turned and smiled as she approached.

'Steve just came to get a ladder he'd left behind,' Jo informed her, 'so we thought we'd have a bit of a celebration.'

'Aren't we supposed to have all the workmen, and their wives, all dressed up to the nines like in *A Year in Provence*?' Meredith enquired.

'They were probably French,' Steve replied deprecatingly. 'My lads are from Bradford.'

'Well, thank you, Steve,' she said. 'You've done a terrific job.'

'Glad to be of help. Oh, and Jackie wanted me to tell you ...' He broke off suddenly, blushing like a teenager telling his girlfriend that he was very sorry but he had the clap. 'Oops, I shouldn't have mentioned that it was from her.'

'We'll be discreet,' Jo giggled. 'What did Jackie want you to tell us and pretend it wasn't from her?'

'Oh well –' Steve downed his wine, hoping for Dutch courage – 'here goes. It's just that your friend Stephanie, the

362

one who owns the B&B . . .' He seemed to run out of nerve and petered out.

'Yes,' Meredith supplied reassuringly, 'Stephanie Adams. It's her niece, Nicky, who's going to be our first bride here.'

'OK. Well, you know her husband left, nice man, done a few jobs for him.'

'David, yes. What about David?'

'He went to stay with Jackie's friend, Suzi. Mad bird, if you ask me. And a bit desperate, like. I always kept well away from her, to be quite frank. Jackie thought you should know he's moved out of her place. He's gone to a hotel in town.' He looked at them all nervously. 'Would you mind not telling Jacks that I told you, you know, about her not wanting me to?'

'Our lips will be sealed,' Meredith promised, trying to keep a straight face.

'Me and my ladder'll be off then. I'm glad you like the rooms. And cheers for the drink. Call me any time for jobs that need doing, no matter how small. Since you're new here you probably don't know that French builders all stop for the summer, but being from Bradford, my lads keep going.'

'We will,' promised Sophie. 'Lucky we found you!'

They waited till he'd gone and then looked at each other. 'Right.' Meredith took control as usual. 'What are we going to do with that information?'

Sophie suddenly reached out a hand to her mother. 'Mum, what do you think? You've been married to a man who was unfaithful. Should we tell her he's left Suzi?'

'I'm not sure it is the same, though,' Meredith intervened. 'I saw them together, there's no getting away from that, and she was obviously after him. But he told me they hadn't slept together and that he was giving her up.'

'Men in that position often lie,' said Jo after a moment's hesitation. 'Mark told me that Amanda was just a colleague!'

'Oh, Mum.' Sophie squeezed her hand. 'I thought you were feeling better.'

With an immense effort, Jo forced herself to smile. 'I am. Don't worry, darling. I really am. Of course we should tell Steph. It's up to her what she does with the information after that.'

'Bloody love,' shrugged Meredith, thinking about the reappearance of Lucille and the impact it was having on her and Philippe. 'You can never get away from it!'

'I know.' Jo reached out her other hand to her friend, feeling suddenly light-hearted. 'But what would we do without it?'

At Fleur-de-Lis, Steph finished tidying the kitchen after the guests' breakfast and sighed. She was furious with herself because the truth was, she missed David like hell. On one level it was practical – she'd had no idea quite how much her husband had quietly taken off her shoulders – but it was more than that. She missed the closeness, the unspoken communication in a thousand small ways. The truth was, life with David had been a more enjoyable, richer experience.

She tried to remind herself of the reasons she'd chucked him out, but somehow they didn't seem so important now. 'What are you?' she attempted to ask herself, 'a pathetic doormat who puts up with anything?'

But it didn't work. If David could hear her describing herself as a doormat, he'd burst out laughing, she knew.

She glanced up at the clock. Five past one. The list of tasks still stretching ahead of her was endless, but at least if she started planning dinner now, it might take her mind off David.

In fact, a welcome distraction arrived in the form of an

email from Ronnie reminding her that it wasn't long now till the wedding. Steph felt a sudden reckless impulse to pour herself a glass of rosé, take it upstairs and spend a stolen half hour trying on outfits for the big day.

She settled on a floaty green number she'd loved because it made her think of tea dresses from the Thirties, and a little grey jacket that had been her standby on countless posh occasions. Would hats be worn? she wondered. Screw fucking hats! she told herself, collapsing on the bed, overtaken by worry at whether Nicky, her favourite niece, was making the right choice. After all, it seemed so very easy to get marriage completely wrong.

Margot looked out at the vineyard at the bottom of her garden and wondered how they were doing up at the château. It seemed a complete *folie* to her that they were only having one wedding this year, but of course, she hadn't exactly encouraged any enquiries she'd received before she'd left. She'd had to be discreet because of the terms of the contract, of course, so she'd just told the potential brides that her husband was ill and the future was uncertain rather than actively putting them off. The good thing was, it seemed to have worked. Apparently they were going to use this year as practice, which seemed weirdly extravagant to her, but maybe Madame Meredith was actually Madame Moneybags. If Lucille Latignac got what she'd come for, at least Meredith would have nothing but the château to concentrate on.

Margot found her collapsible stick – ridiculously, the doctor said she must have a support when she walked anywhere! – and headed out. Maybe Liam knew more. She liked Liam, not just for his looks, though handsome men always cheered her up, but because he understood her need to roam a little on the land that had been hers until very recently. His family had lost their land too, so he could relate to the elemental feelings that tied her to this place. He also turned a blind eye to what Madame Meredith would no doubt label nosiness when she had a peek into the orangery and the ground-floor salon.

Today Liam was busy thinning out the leaves on the side of the vines that faced the sunrise so that the newly budded grapes would achieve maximum exposure to the warming rays. He didn't at first hear Margot's approach because he had music on, apparently coming from some device he carried in his jeans.

Margot, about to tap him on the shoulder, stopped instead, smiling.

Liam was listening to the warm and heartfelt tones of American singer Scott Walker. When she realized which song he appeared to have on repeat, Margot held back a moment.

'*I can't forget*', he sang along with Scott, '*the one they call Joanna . . .*'

In an unusual outbreak of tact, Margot turned round and headed back to her little house. Let him enjoy the music.

She just hoped he wouldn't leave it at that.

Steph sat down, fighting the wave of exhaustion that hit her in the late afternoon. All the changeovers had been done, beds made, bathrooms cleaned and the dinner ingredients assembled. Thank God tonight it was Jean-Christophe who would be cooking them.

She decided to take advantage of her rare moment of freedom by nipping up to the château. She took a box of cheese straws she'd made for the guests from the top shelf of the pantry. They wouldn't miss what they didn't know about. No need to take wine, since the château had plenty from its own vineyard.

She found Sophie, the list queen, trying to discover when all the family members would be arriving next week.

'Good luck with that!' she laughed. 'Organizing Ronnie is like herding cats. She'll tell you she's arriving by Eurostar at six p.m. and then grab an Easyjet and turn up at four!'

'Thanks for the warning.' Sophie took a deep breath. 'At least I know when the bride's coming! Nicky messaged me that she's booked a seat for herself and another one for her wedding dress.'

'What about the bridegroom?' asked Jo, who'd just joined them. 'He is quite important to the proceedings.'

'I suppose she could get married to herself,' Steph giggled. 'People have actually done that in America, you know!'

'Nicky's not the type,' Jo smiled. 'Now if we were talking about Ronnie . . .'

'I think the groom is coming separately. Staying in a room at the Pomme D'Amour. As far away as possible from his family. What's he like, by the way?'

'Martin?' Steph replied. 'I don't know him very well. Quiet type, but seems nice enough. Where's Meredith, by the way?'

'Here I am.' Meredith appeared, holding a tray of apéritifs. 'Hello, Steph!' she said, making them all suddenly conscious of Steve's revelation earlier. 'There's quite a breeze outside. Let's go and sit in the orangery. Right, now who's having what? I can offer a G&T, gin & It, white or rosé – or a glass of our own crémant.'

'How about a Kir Royale?' asked Steph.

'Fine, but I don't think we have any Royale.'

'I think there's a bottle of cassis in the kitchen somewhere,' offered Sophie. 'Though I can't vouch for how old it is.'

'I'm sure it only gets better,' Steph replied.

'Let's all have one, then,' suggested Jo. 'We can die together. Not a bad fate.'

'Excuse me,' Sophie protested. 'That might be OK for you old broads, but I'm only twenty-four!'

'Just stick to the crémant, then.' Meredith began to pour as soon as the ancient cassis was produced. 'Smells OK.'

'Oh, go on then,' Sophie said, weakening. 'After all, we're in this together!'

'To weddings! May they be many and plentiful!' toasted Meredith.

'Guess what I did this afternoon?' Steph said.

A silence fell as they all wondered who was going to tell her.

'What's the matter with you lot? I tried on my wedding outfit, that's what!' she continued.

Meredith, conscious that she usually took the lead, looked meaningfully at Jo.

'The thing is . . .' Jo began, then faltered to a stop.

'The thing is –' Meredith picked it up – 'Steve the builder has just told us that David's left the ghastly Suzi. He's gone to stay in a hotel.'

To her shame, Steph felt a sudden soaring of hope. Maybe things were going to be all right after all. And yet, why hadn't David been in touch?

She realized they were all waiting for her reaction. 'How long ago, do you know? And which hotel?'

'I'm not sure.' Jo looked at the others, but they just shrugged. 'I got the vague idea it must be fairly recent and I don't think Steve knew which hotel.'

Steph felt some response was called for from her. 'Stupid shit,' she commented. None of them were convinced by this, least of all her, but they felt the less said the better. This was something she and David had to work out for themselves.

*

In the days that followed there was little time to worry about the state of Steph's marriage, because wedding fever descended on the château.

Nicky seemed to be in touch almost permanently with requests, reminders and demands that made Sophie fear she was already undergoing that unique wedding metamorphosis, from nice Nicola into Bridezilla. Could Sophie make sure there were sufficient options for veggies at the wedding feast (of course); could Sophie supply a non-allergenic pillow, as Nicky suffered from hay fever (no problem); could they have pale pink tablecloths on the round tables, as Nicky particularly liked that shade of faded pink they had in some restaurants (OK, although quite a challenge); would it be possible for Sophie to supply sleep-inducing tea, as Nicky could never sleep when she was nervous (OK . . . but couldn't Nicky bring her own bloody teabags?).

Sophie had to give herself a lecture on remaining patient in the face of this transformation and be relieved it was she who was dealing with it rather than Meredith, who would probably have cancelled the entire nuptials. Lots of brides were a nightmare – if they were going to run a wedding château, they would just have to get used to that fact.

'Tout ça va, madame?' Marcelline enquired the next morning. Steph had been standing over a bowl of egg white waiting to be beaten into meringue for at least five minutes.

He's got to make the first move, not you, she told herself for the hundredth time. She had found herself accidentally driving past the two hotels yesterday evening, convinced that it would be fate, and therefore OK, if David came out, but weak of her to actually go and enquire if he was staying there. Such was the crazy logic of the heart.

'Sorry, Marcelline. In a bit of a daze.'

Marcelline, as it happened, knew exactly why this was, since her cousin worked on reception in the Hôtel Clos des Lilas and had reported that a Monsieur David Adams had just checked in, and wasn't he Marcelline's ex-employer? The one Marcelline had always said was so nice and considerate?

She also hoped for David's return because when he was around the B&B had been better run in a hundred small ways you took for granted. Toilets were magically unblocked, drains didn't smell and the swimming pool was never a suspicious green. And – better than anything else – Stephanie looked a lot happier.

As if in evidence of this, a Mademoiselle Signac, who was staying in the Oriental Room, their very best bedroom, burst dramatically into the kitchen.

'There are ants everywhere!' she screamed hysterically. 'They are all over the bed and the pillows! I cannot stay another moment. I am allergic to ant bites and I may die!'

'Oh my God,' Steph murmured to Marcelline, sounding almost hysterical herself. 'If only David were here. He'd know how to deal with this!'

Marcelline debated with herself. Her cousin had told her not to divulge this information, since Mr Adams had informed the hotel he particularly wished to remain private. She might lose her job.

She looked at Steph again. Well, Madame Adams might lose her mind. Which was more important? Marcelline took a bold decision. 'He is staying at the Clos de Lilas, madame, in case that is useful information.'

Clearly, it was.

'Right. I'm going to look for him. Take out the *îles flottantes* in ten minutes. And move Mademoiselle Signac to Room Six.'

And with that, she was out the door.

Twenty-Six

'Which room is Mr David Adams in?' Steph, still out of breath from the dash to make it, enquired of the receptionist.

'*Je suis désolée* but I cannot tell you, madame,' replied the young woman.

'What do you mean, you can't tell me? This is a hotel, isn't it?'

'*Oui*, madame, but it is what the guest requested.'

'How bloody ridiculous!' Steph insisted. 'I am his wife!'

Since the girl also happened to be Marcelline's cousin and had instantly worked out who Steph was, she added in a low tone that a lot of the guests were in the garden enjoying an *apéro* before eating. Marcelline, she knew, would expect no less.

The receptionist watched Steph departing and silently wished her luck. She'd just got engaged herself, and still believed that marriage was for life.

The Clos des Lilas was a small and rather charming hotel built around an inner garden sporting a famously ancient lilac tree. There were tables and chairs dotted at intervals under the trees. Steph scanned them, looking for David, but there was no sign of him anywhere.

She was about to give up, imagining the receptionist must have got it wrong, when she caught sight of a small table at the far end of the garden, almost buried in woodland. David was sitting at it, reading a book and nursing the last of a drink.

She rushed past the other guests until she reached the bottom of the garden.

David looked up. At the sight of his wife, he almost jumped to his feet.

'Steph! What are you doing here?'

Part of Steph wanted to tell him the truth – that she loved him and she missed him, and she had never appreciated all he did for her. But he had trampled on her heart and after all they had been through together, he had got involved with another woman.

'We've had an ant infestation in the Oriental Room,' she blurted instead. The things are everywhere, all over the bed, and the guest is allergic to ant bites. She's absolutely hysterical! I don't know what to do!'

'So that's why you're here?' His voice was barbed with bitterness and the expression in his eyes changed so swiftly from excitement to contempt that she could hardly bear to look at him. 'So that I can rescue you from an ant infestation?'

Steph knew instantly she'd blown it; that anything she said now would sound fake.

'Well, you do still own half the place,' she added limply.

'I suggest you go on Google,' he replied in a voice drained of all emotion. 'There's bound to be a twenty-four-hour service that deals with such things. I'm afraid it doesn't happen to be me.'

He picked up his book and began studiously reading as if she wasn't still standing there two feet away from him.

It wasn't your heart that hurt, Steph realized, in a situation like this. It was your stomach that wanted to throw up and your bones that wanted to crumble beneath you. She turned sadly away and walked back towards her car, unable to think of anything beyond putting one foot in front of the other.

As anyone who has been involved in planning a wedding knows, they have a habit of turning into monsters that eat up all the participants' time, energy and finances. Yet the fantasy of the perfect wedding is not to be resisted.

As the big day approached, all Sophie, Jo and Meredith found themselves doing was talking to coach and minibus drivers, negotiating with the chosen DJ and the string quartet who would play during the drinks reception, following up on lighting effects, double-checking equipment hire, reassuring the celebrant that the bride and groom were busy writing their vows, fixing an arrival time for the hair and make-up artists . . . not to mention dealing with videographers, photographers and a drone specialist.

Welcome to the modern wedding.

The one thing Sophie still had no idea about was the flowers. What exactly had been ordered and when were they due to arrive? Since she could get no answer from Ronnie, Sophie decided to try catching Nicky for an update.

'No idea, I'm afraid,' Nicky shrugged. 'In fact, she's been ominously silent about everything. Martin, me and the dress are flying to Bratenac on Friday morning. Could you possibly book us a taxi? Me and the dress, that is. Martin's hiring a car so he can ferry his ghastly family around.'

'Lucky Martin,' said Sophie.

'Don't worry. Mine can be fairly poisonous too.'

'Oh, goody,' Sophie grinned. 'I'll look forward to it.'

'The weather forecast looks good,' Nicky announced happily.

Sophie looked out of the window at the blazing sun and bone-dry landscape. 'Actually, we're having a bit of a heatwave at the moment. The French call it *une canicule*. The winegrowers love it. It ripens the grapes.'

'Let's hope it's over by the weekend when I come. I wilt in the heat!'

The time seemed to be flying past now. It suddenly struck Sophie that no one had mentioned the grandmother who was supposed to be driving here with the château-shaped wedding cake.

'Come on now, Suzi.' Jackie had stayed on with her friend after the latest Ladies' Club luncheon had finished, and was trying to work out whether a cognac or a large glass of water would be of more help in the circumstances. 'You'll get through this. We're all here for you, remember?' She decided on the cognac, and signalled to Guillaume to bring two.

'I know it's a shitty situation, but face it,' Jackie soothed. 'Is it David you're missing? Or just having a man about the place?'

Suzi raised a face on which emotion and mascara had worked together to produce deep runnels of rejection. Echoing those great tragic heroines Anna Karenina and Emma Bovary, she finally spoke: 'What the fuck does it matter? He's still gone.'

'Yes,' replied Jackie, 'but if it's just a man you're missing, there are ways of finding one.'

'At my age?'

'I'm sure Steve could help. He knows everyone.'

The thought of Steve, whose sensibility ranged from football to beer with an occasional foray into sudoku, finding her a suitable life partner made Suzi want to cry again.

And besides, all this speculation didn't solve the other part of the challenge Jackie had set herself. She might have helped detach Suzi from David, but how the hell was she going to get David and Stephanie back together?

Jackie would have been most alarmed had she known that David was, at that precise moment, sitting in his hotel room trying to decide whether to cut his losses in France and simply go home. It was only his acceptance of the invitation to Nicky's wedding that was keeping him here.

When he'd seen Steph standing in front of him in the hotel garden with a look of genuine regret on her face, a barrage of emotions had flooded into his mind. Relief that he hadn't screwed up his life after all; love and tenderness towards the woman with whom he'd spent so much of his life; even a spurt of hope that they could go back and make their venture here work again. And what had it all been about? An ant infestation! Exactly the same as before. She wanted him only because he was useful to her, and even then she wouldn't thank him or give him any credit for how much she relied on his quiet dependability.

Of course, he blamed himself for his involvement with Suzi, but at the same time he perfectly understood why it had come about. As it turned out, he and Suzi had neither of them understood what the other wanted or needed, but the situation had a logic to it that Steph could quite easily understand – and maybe even forgive – if she wanted to. If she ever considered anything beyond her own wants and needs.

So that was that.

He found it in himself to wish he hadn't accepted Nicky's wedding invitation. But he had, and somehow he was going to find the strength to get through what should be a happy day. If not for him.

*

375

Sophie came back to her desk to find her mother staring at the guest list. Jo jumped when Sophie approached and when she turned, Sophie saw that there were tears in her eyes.

'Oh, Mum.' Sophie enclosed her in a protective embrace, angry again at how badly her mother had been hurt. 'I'm so, so sorry they're on the guest list. I did think about trying to put them off and tell Martin it was a misunderstanding, but I couldn't think of a convincing way to do it.'

For a few seconds Jo allowed herself the luxury of letting Sophie's precious love envelop her before the usual maternal guilt reared its head and made her feel she was the one who ought to be in charge. 'It will be pretty ghastly for us both, having them here.'

'I know.' Sophie hugged her even tighter. 'We'll get through it together. Maybe I can get Jean-Christophe to poison their Mediterranean lamb!' she giggled. 'Or at least give them the runs. That'd put the kybosh on any romantic minibreak!'

This time they laughed together. 'I do love you, Sophie,' Jo told her gratefully, and made herself go back to the salutary task of sorting out the French version of Portaloos.

The heatwave meant that they needed to be extremely well disinfected and fragranced. A pong of Portaloo could easily ruin the romantic atmosphere they were going to so much trouble to create.

She rounded the corner to have another look at the appointed site and bumped into Liam, who was staring moodily out over the valley. It was so hot that the river was almost invisible in the heat haze. At this rate Nicky would be fainting into Martin's arms instead of reciting her well-crafted wedding vows.

'How long do you reckon this heat will last?' she asked Liam.

'The weather here can be quite dramatic,' he shrugged.

'Pleasantly warm and calm most of the time but you can get violent clashes between the dry cold winds from the north and warm humid ones from the south.'

'What happens then?'

'Short, dramatic storms. Always worth being ready. But I reckon this heatwave'll pass soon.'

Jo smiled, realizing that her white t-shirt was sopping wet and moulded against her body. Liam was consciously not looking, but she knew he was aware of it all the same.

'What happened to that glorious fresh weather of a few weeks ago?'

'Well,' he grinned, 'if you will have your wedding in the hottest month of the year . . .'

She looked at her watch. 'I'd better go and sort out these Portaloos.'

'I have to say this about you Brits,' Liam commented, only a slight softening of the mouth conveying the humour he saw in the situation, 'you certainly know when to be romantic.'

Sophie decided that of the three of them, it was she who was most excited about the approach of Nicky's wedding, maybe because she would be in charge of how the day unfolded. She had spent a long time yesterday evening lying on her bed watching recent Instagram and YouTube videos of weddings and scanning through their rivals' websites. Fortunately, the world still seemed to love a wedding, and brides adored having them in France.

Her favourite was one where the entire château seemed to have been draped in white blossom. God only knew what that had cost. It made her think of Ronnie and the mysterious flowers. Being Sophie, she couldn't even tell herself it wasn't her problem.

Tomorrow she was going to start on making up the rooms. She sat for a moment gazing out at the valley, a little cooler now but still incredibly hot, and wondering when on earth it would be her turn to exchange ridiculously romantic vows and wear an outrageously expensive dress.

Not for a very long time, as far as she could tell.

To the relief of all, the weather broke in the night. All three of them were woken by the sound of thunder crashing so loudly overhead, it was more like an explosion in some war-torn Middle Eastern city than the gentle Savarin valley. They spontaneously gathered on the landing of the main staircase to watch the sheets of green, yellow and white flashing across the sky like some giant *son et lumière*.

'I love our choice of nightwear!' Sophie giggled. 'Me in my crumpled camisole that barely covers my lady parts, Mum all cosy in her jimjams and Meredith in her Janet Reger silk night-dress with the shoestring straps! What does that say about our personalities?'

'It's Liliana Casanova, actually,' grinned Meredith. 'And I refuse to be summed up by my lingerie!' She looked outside at the lightning-lit landscape. 'At least it won't be so hot for the wedding, thank God. Anyone for a cup of tea?'

Sophie started giggling and couldn't stop.

'What on earth's the matter with you?' Meredith enquired.

'It's the idea of Meredith Harding, châtelaine of St Savarin, in her Liliana Casanova nightdress longing for a nice cuppa tea!'

'As a matter of fact,' Meredith replied grandly, putting an arm around both Jo and Sophie, 'I'm considering a choccy biccy too, if anyone wants to join me?'

*

The perfect weather returned. The rooms were ready, and everyone needed for the event was double-checked and on standby, when the exciting day finally dawned and the wedding party was due to arrive.

There was still no sign of Ronnie, but the flowers made their appearance in the morning at about eleven.

'My God,' Jo whispered to Sophie, 'have you seen them? There's about twenty boxes of the things! Where do you think we should store them?'

'All taken care of.' Sophie ticked her list. 'I've asked the florist to put them in the large jars in the pantry I picked up cheap, in case it's too hot in the outhouse. She turned up her nose at such menial work, but I want to make sure she cuts the stems . . . or whatever florists do.'

'My mum swore by putting a drop of bleach in the water,' suggested Jo.

'Nonsense,' Meredith interrupted. 'Mine always used vodka.'

'Old wives' tales!' Sophie shook her head. 'What's wrong with Waitrose flower food?'

Sophie disappeared in the direction of the pantry. The display of flowers was truly mind-blowing. But not as mind-blowing as the amount they must have cost. For a ghastly moment she thought the woman was going to ask her to settle the bill, but it seemed Nicky's dad had already coughed up.

She didn't have long to dwell on this point, because she could hear a taxi pulling up outside the front entrance. The bride had arrived for their very first wedding.

Twenty-Seven

'Welcome to St Savarin!'

Sophie ran forward to help Nicky carry her dress, feeling almost as excited as if it were her own wedding. 'We're so thrilled to see you!'

Nicky stood for a moment at the top of the grand stone staircase that led into the château, taking in the romance of the place, with its four pepperpot towers and russet tile roof, surrounded by its own vineyards with a beautiful paved terrace overlooking the river.

The two young women hugged each other while Jo and Meredith watched them, smiling.

'Come in, come in,' Meredith greeted her. 'Here, let me take your bag; Jo, why don't you take the dress? I've laid out champagne in the bridal suite to welcome you.'

'Do you mind if I hold on to the dress?' Nicky asked, laughing at herself as she said it. 'It's just so precious. My dream dress! I could never admit how much it cost.'

Not as much as the flowers, Sophie thought, but kept it to herself. 'You're the first to arrive,' she smiled. 'And of course, the most important. Your mother's due in an hour. And your sister and the bridesmaids will be here soon too.' Sophie consulted her list. 'Oh, and your dad and stepmother not long after that.'

'Have you heard from Gran at all?' Nicky asked anxiously. 'No one could stop her driving here with the cake in her little Renault 5. What's the point of having a French car, she said, if you don't take it to France? She's supposed to be here about two thirty.'

'I expect she'll be here soon,' reassured Sophie, leading the way up the main staircase and along what seemed an endless corridor. 'The bridal suite's in the West Tower. I'm afraid it's quite a long way.'

At last she opened the door to the tower, which was, in her view, a gorgeous combination of antique and modern, focused around a huge bed piled with velvet cushions. In one corner of the room was a Chinese screen painted with golden flowers, behind which stood a polished iron bath.

'You can move the screen out of the way, if you prefer the bath in full view,' explained Sophie.

'No chance.' Nicky produced a catlike smile. 'I think it's sexier like that, a little bit of mystery. Plus you can hide the tummy fat you were supposed to lose in a pre-wedding diet but didn't!' She looked round the room. 'It really is perfect,' she breathed. 'Just what I fantasized about.'

Sophie, efficient as ever, handed her a sheet of paper. 'Just a list of who's arriving when, and what's happening tonight. I won't give you tomorrow's – that runs to six pages and anyway it's our job to just make everything wonderful! Now where's that champagne?'

She handed Nicky a glass.

'I got up really early to make the flight,' explained Nicky. 'I think I might just lie down for half an hour.'

'Would you like me to wake you with a tea or coffee?' offered Sophie. 'One thing your phone still can't do.'

'That would be amazing. Or sooner if Gran arrives with the cake.'

'I promise. And would you like me to hang up your dress? I promise I won't look.'

One thing Sophie had learned from her study of weddings on Instagram, Pinterest and other châteaux' websites was the vital nature of The Dress. No other element, possibly even the bridegroom, came anywhere near it in terms of importance.

Reverently she unzipped the special bag that had travelled with its own airline seat. Averting her gaze, she put the dress on the special ivory silk hanger she had bought solely for this purpose and hung it on the outside of the huge mirrored armoire, with its inlays of painted nymphs and shepherds, where Nicky could gaze at it as she sipped her champagne.

Meredith looked at her watch and surveyed the drive that led from the château to the main road. 'When the hell is Ronnie coming?' she enquired irritably, as if Ronnie were one of her employees who dared to be late for a meeting. Not something that happened often, Jo suspected.

'I've tried to ring her about three times, but it just goes to voicemail.' Sophie shrugged. 'I even tried Steph in case she'd gone there, but Steph says to relax, this is pure Ronnie. Creating unnecessary tension is her speciality. Everything else is fine, though,' she added reassuringly. 'Bill and Maureen, dad and stepmum, have just arrived and are installed in the West Tower. Jean-Christophe is busy taking deliveries. The bridesmaids and Nicky's sister Lara are giggling after their third Prosecco – I couldn't stop them, since they brought their own.'

'Oh well, bridesmaids will be bridesmaids,' Meredith shrugged. 'They're going to have a nasty hangover, though.'

'I've tactfully left paracetamol and rehydration salts on the tray with the tea and coffee.'

'Sophie,' Jo marvelled. 'You're amazing, the way you think of everything!'

'Oh, and the gran rang,' Sophie continued. 'She's made it to Bratenac, thank the Lord, and has just stopped to pick something up.' Sophie consulted her list. 'OK, once we locate the tension-creating Ronnie, we are on schedule.'

'Mademoiselle Sophie!' an anguished voice interrupted. 'I cannot have all these flowers in my pantry! The supplies are all arriving and I need to put them there!' It was Jean-Christophe.

'Of course, Jean-Christophe. Come on, ladies, time to put a shoulder to the wheel. We need to put the vases of flowers in the dungeon. Nice and cool down there. And maybe the White Lady will appear and help with the flower arranging.'

Meredith looked shocked at the idea that she might have to do some physical labour, even of such a ladylike kind. But as Sophie was managing the occasion so effectively, she decided to comply without demur.

'Is there light down there?'

'God, yes. It's like Versailles,' Sophie grinned. 'Anyone who fancied a bit of medieval torture would certainly be able to see what they were doing.'

They had just finished putting the flowers in the dungeon when Sophie heard a hubbub of raised voices above them. It sounded as if Jean-Christophe had been pulled away from the kitchen again and didn't appreciate it.

They arrived in the entrance lobby to discover a very irritated Ronnie, wearing a quiet little Roksanda Ilincic number in bright turquoise with wide diagonal pink stripes. She clearly felt that as mother of the bride there should have been a string quartet, or at the very least a piper, to celebrate her arrival.

'I took the Eurostar to Paris!' she fulminated. 'Two hours late because some idiot decided to jump under the train. Honestly, they might think of the people it was going to inconvenience.'

'I suppose if you're going to kill yourself, you tend to forget the social niceties,' Sophie almost said, but decided to make a diplomatic fuss of her instead. 'Ronnie! It's so great you're here! Your flowers are amazing. We've put them all somewhere cool where you can arrange them in peace.' She didn't add that just at the moment, 'somewhere cool' was the dungeon. 'By the way, what are the enormous square boxes that came with them? We didn't have time to open those.'

'Onyx vases. Essential for the Old Master look I'm trying to achieve.'

Sophie took a deep breath and tried not to imagine what a huge onyx vase would cost.

'Is everyone here?'

'Everyone except your mother,' Sophie replied briskly, not wanting to mention the arrival of her ex, Bill, and his wife Maureen. 'But she is in Bratenac. Funny, though, she's been rather a long time. I do hope everything's all right. Perhaps you'd better call her?'

As she spoke, they heard the sound of a car skidding to a halt on the gravel. 'That'll be her now. She's always been a fast driver.'

They trooped out of the front door and down the right side of the grand stone staircase, which Nicky would walk down tomorrow as a bride, to find a hysterical old lady in the courtyard beneath. Despite the heightened emotion, she looked very smart, with newly coiffed hair as if she'd just walked out of a hairdresser.

Which was exactly what had happened, as they soon discovered.

'Veronica! You won't believe it! I drove past this salon with a terrific offer and I couldn't resist popping in. I left the cake in its cool box in the boot, absolutely fine, and I must have not put the lid back on – and look what's happened to it!'

They all peered into the box to see what now resembled a ruined castle that had been attacked by an enemy bent on razing it to ground. What made it even more poignant was that it was *this* castle.

'Oh dear,' murmured Meredith, not entirely tactfully. 'What a host of enemies couldn't do to the château in four hundred years, a shampoo and set in Bratenac has achieved in a couple of hours!'

'I'll get Jean-Christophe,' reassured Sophie. 'I'm sure he can rescue it. Mum, why don't you show Ronnie her room? It's the lovely green suite in the North Wing. The one Steve's just finished.' To stave off any incipient complaints, she added: 'It's one of my favourites.'

'I hate green,' responded Ronnie. 'And it better not smell of turps and new paint. I'm very prone to headaches.' She started to follow Jo, then stopped. 'Where are bloody Bill and Maureen sleeping?' she demanded.

'In the West Tower. A long way from you.'

'It couldn't be too far. Have I got a bathroom?'

'Of course you have. All our rooms have bathrooms.'

'Theirs had better not be bigger than mine. And where's Nicky? I expected her to at least come and greet me?'

'She's having a little snooze. She had a very early start,' replied Sophie. 'I promised to wake her when you all arrived, so I'll do that now and I'm sure she won't be a minute.' She turned to the grandmother, who seemed to have calmed down now that the cake was to be taken off her hands. 'And how about you, Nora? Can I show you to your room as well?'

They set off, with Nora quietly following in her theatrical daughter's wake.

'Everything set for the wine tasting?' Meredith asked Jo.

'As far as I know,' replied Jo, embarrassed that everyone always applied questions involving Liam to her. 'I'd better go and see about the restoration of the château, chocolate version, then I'll check.'

Jean-Christophe took one look and shook his head. '*Je suis désolé, madame,* but I have never been a pastry cook. I'm afraid we will have to ask my father.'

Jo thought for a moment about consulting the patisserie in town, but she didn't know them well. Besides, time was getting on.

'Could you possibly give him a call?' she asked Jean-Christophe.

'Assuredly I can, although on a Friday night he may be very busy.'

Busy or not, an hour later Philippe turned up and carried the ruined cake, still in its box, carefully into the kitchen.

'*Putain!*' he murmured under his breath as he gently removed it from the soggy cardboard, 'to leave a chocolate cake in the *coffre* of a car in this heat! And such a wonderful cake too.' He caught his son's eye and they both laughed. 'I will have to find a way of restoring its former glory – for the honour of the St Savarins!'

As it happened, at that very moment the duchess of St Savarin had sneaked into the orangery and was interrogating Liam as to what wines would be consumed at the wedding.

She was quite impressed at the choice. 'But, most important, what have they chosen for the toast?'

'The Savarin *crémant*, madame.'

'*Pas champagne?*' She sounded as if a sacrilege were being committed. '*Quel grippe-sous alors!*'

'It is not to save money. The suggestion was mine,' Liam insisted quietly but forcefully. 'For the sake of our vineyard. Besides, it is delicious.'

Margot looked round at the dining table behind her, laid for tonight's dinner. 'Quite a small affair, I see. How many are invited to the wedding?'

'*Madame la duchesse*,' Liam bowed, but with a twinkle in his eye. He would actually quite like to lose his temper at the old trout, but that would help no one. 'We are good friends, you and I, and for the sake of that friendship, let us not talk of the wedding. By now the duke will be missing you.' He reached under the table for the bottles cooling in plastic containers full of ice. 'Please, take a bottle of crémant and enjoy it together.'

Margot looked back at him levelly. He could see she longed to say: 'Young man, I *own* the château.' But of course, this was no longer true. 'What a kind gesture,' she replied eventually. 'But it would be even kinder if you gave me two.'

Liam handed over a second bottle and laughed as he watched her depart. Fortunately for the world, Margot was one of a kind.

For her part, rather than be grateful for the free wine, Margot walked slowly back home pondering whether she could think of any ways to discreetly sabotage the wedding.

'I wonder if anyone's been able to rescue the cake?' Nicky's grandmother asked anxiously as she joined the others for the pre-dinner wine tasting in the orangery.

'Do you want me to find out, Gran?' Nicky was still smiling after her tour with Sophie taking in the wedding pavilion where they would exchange their vows, the terrace where the round tables would be laid, the spot for the string quartet. The dancing was planned to take place under the stars, next to the salon so that they could relocate if the weather changed.

'I'll go.' Sophie jumped up.

'Why don't I?' Meredith suggested to Sophie. 'You're running yourself ragged! Sit down with a nice glass of wine for a moment.'

'Not till I find out when Ronnie intends to do those damn flowers!' Sophie whispered back. 'There's a whole dungeon full of them.'

Bill and Maureen came down to join them. In marked contrast to his ex-wife, Bill seemed to be an amiable, tolerant man who didn't like attracting attention to himself. Maureen was one of those cosy, motherly women who got their clothes in M&S and had long ago decided that comfort was more important than chic.

Fortunately, Jo reappeared at the same time and led them straight over to meet Liam. 'This is Bill, father of the bride and general VIP.' She had already explained to him that Bill was picking up the tab for everything. 'And this is Maureen, Bill's wife.'

'Call me Mo,' Maureen said with a smile. 'Being in a castle like this, I feel I've been miscast. I should be the Wicked Stepmother, with at least a poisoned apple hidden in my pocket.'

'Good thing you haven't got any pockets, then,' Bill teased her cheerfully. They seemed a happy pair, Jo decided.

'Let me show you the wines, Bill,' Liam invited. 'They're all grown here at the château.'

When Meredith arrived in the kitchen accompanied by an insistent Nora, Jean-Christophe unveiled the cake like a magician producing a rabbit from a hat.

And indeed the transformation was almost magical. The cake had been entirely rebuilt, its four towers now standing proud and erect, the roofs made of new ice cream cones and all the crenellations picked out in piped chocolate icing.

Nora nearly cried. 'Oh my God, it's even better than before. I could never have done all that detail. I haven't got the right icing bag.'

'Just don't trying cutting up the towers,' Jean-Christophe cautioned, laughing. 'They had to be rebuilt with cocoa tins!'

'I really can't thank you enough, young man. You've certainly saved the day.'

'As a matter of fact –' Jean-Christophe avoided catching Meredith's eye – 'it wasn't me. It was my father. He would have stayed, but he had to get back to his restaurant.'

Meredith struggled with the desire to say, 'He gets everywhere, doesn't he, your dad?' and the knowledge that to do so would be extremely ungracious, not to mention unfair. 'Please thank him from us,' she said at last.

'I think he enjoys being able to help you.' This time he looked her directly in the eye and added: 'If you'll let him.'

Meredith put her hand on Nora's arm to lead her back to the others, suddenly conscious of an overwhelming sense that it might be a pleasant relief to have someone to help you sort things out occasionally.

She was so shocked at this deviation from everything she'd ever believed that she pushed the idea firmly to the back of her mind and ignored it.

Everyone was now assembled for the wine tasting, except Ronnie.

'She's probably fallen asleep in the bath with a glass of champagne,' suggested Nicky.

'Only if she brought her own.' Sophie sighed. 'I'd better go and have a look.'

But there was no need. Moments later, Ronnie swept into the room wearing a floral silk maxi dress in day-glo shades of bright strawberry pink, green and turquoise, which she had teemed with strawberry pink sandals.

'Oh my God,' murmured Nicky. 'I wonder what she's planning for tomorrow.'

'Not exactly clothes for flower arranging,' Sophie sighed.

'Hello, Mum.' Nicky embraced her. 'What a colourful dress!'

'Half price on the internet. It's Fendi. I won't tell you how much.'

Bill and Maureen exchanged a look.

'Hello, Bill,' Ronnie finally greeted him, at the same time totally ignoring Maureen. 'This is your big moment, giving away your little girl. As long as you don't upstage the bride, of course.'

'Not likely to be *me* who manages that,' Bill commented wryly. 'But, yes, it is a big moment. Pity Martin isn't here. I didn't know bridegrooms were banned from the pre-wedding dinner. Is it bad luck or something?'

'No, it's his ghastly family,' Nicky laughed. 'For the sake of peace tomorrow, he felt he ought to spend tonight with them. He told me to remember we'd have the rest of our lives together.'

Bill put his arm round his daughter affectionately. 'He seems like a good man. You know, I'm really happy for you, darling. And proud.'

Watching the heartfelt gesture between father and daughter, Sophie felt a sudden sense of loss. She sought out her mother. 'Are you OK, Mum?' she asked, slipping her arm round Jo. 'About Dad coming tomorrow, I mean.'

'I'll survive. After all, I've got you.' She squeezed her daughter's hand. 'Where's Steph, by the way? Auntie of the bride and the reason we're having the wedding here at all. Surely she's coming?'

'After the wine tasting. She's got her guests to feed and wonderful Jean-Christophe's busy here, so she's doing the cooking.'

'OK.' Liam started to tap a wineglass with a spoon for silence. 'As everyone seems to be here, why don't we start the tasting?'

Lucille Latignac stretched out a purple-painted toe over the edge of the bath, sipped her chilled Sauvignon and smiled her catlike smile. It had been such a clever idea of hers to offer to help out at the wedding, and clearly destiny had taken a hand in making one of Jean-Christophe's staff so ill that, at the last minute, he'd finally got in touch.

She had a very good feeling about tomorrow.

She had emailed Philippe, using her most formal and businesslike tone, and asked if she could stay given how late the clearing up would go on. He had accepted in an equally formal tone. But she wasn't fooled. Once she was there she could slip into his bed and, really, what man could refuse her?

She studied herself in the mirror. Huge aquamarine eyes looked back at her from beneath the fringe of stylishly cut black hair. No matter how broke she'd been, she'd never economized on hairdressers.

But she wouldn't be broke any longer. She'd be back with Philippe, and this time she wouldn't be a waitress. In fact, she wouldn't have to work at all.

She climbed out of the bath and towelled herself, feeling the sudden kick of desire as she pulled on her black thong.

In the background she could hear Bob Marley singing 'Don't Worry', which had been their favourite song when they were launching their first restaurant. 'I think you're right, Bob. Everything *is* gonna be alright!'

The only cloud on her optimistic horizon was the old man. He'd never liked her. But if she was clever enough about it, she was pretty sure she could find somewhere to send him and convince Philippe it was the right thing to do.

The food at the pre-wedding dinner was delicious. Nicky had asked for something simple, and it was simple in that it used few ingredients; but somehow Jean-Christophe had created flavours of amazing freshness and depth out of those few elements. They were all delighted and impressed.

'I can't wait to see what he comes up with tomorrow,' Maureen commented to her husband. 'It's certainly not going to be the usual overdone chicken leg, anyway.'

Bill got to his feet. 'I know tomorrow's the day for speeches, but while we still have you to ourselves, I just wanted to say how proud I am of my lovely daughter. To Nicola!'

'To Nicola!' echoed all the other guests.

'Do you want some help with the flowers, Mum?' Ronnie's younger daughter Lara asked tactfully. 'Everyone's a bit worried you're going to run out of time.'

'How ridiculous.' Ronnie slurred slightly. 'There's plenty of time. I know exactly what I'm doing.'

'There's also the wedding pavilion to deck, the table centrepieces and, of course, the bride's bouquet,' Sophie reminded, trying not to show her irritation.

'I've only agreed to do the main flower arrangements and the bouquet,' Ronnie replied huffily.

Sophie tried to repress an extremely rude word. 'Right,

girls –' she addressed Lara and the bridesmaids – 'it's up early for flower picking in the garden before you get your hair and make-up. I'll bring you all a cup of tea.' Several of them giggled as they went up to bed.

'Oh,' Ronnie remarked, looking very pleased with herself. 'I forgot to give you these. I had them printed specially.'

They all unwrapped their small packages, which turned out to be short pink wraps in imitation silk. Along with the obvious ones saying *Bride* and *Bridesmaid*, there was another with the letters *MoB* for Mother of the Bride and *GoB* for Nicky's grandmother.

'I suggest an earlyish night.' Nicky looked round hopefully.

'You always were a bit of a goody-goody,' replied Ronnie.

'Come on, Mum,' intervened Lara. 'Drink up your wine, or you'll end up with a hangover on Nicky's wedding day. And don't forget you're doing the flowers!'

'Everyone keeps going on about the sodding flowers! I wish I hadn't said I'd do them!'

Nicky had to stop herself replying that they all wished so, too.

Ronnie, realizing she was the only one left at the table, looked round in surprise, her eyes alighting on an almost full bottle which she scooped up and put under her arm. 'Waste not, want not, as Gran would say. Where is Gran, by the way?'

'She went to bed an hour ago, as did almost everyone else,' pointed out Nicky. 'Come on, Mum. It's after one. The staff are waiting to clear.'

'Oh dear,' said Ronnie, in a tone that implied this was not one of her usual considerations. 'We wouldn't want to keep the staff waiting, now would we?'

Jean-Christophe was almost the last off duty, but not quite.

He was about to head for his van when he noticed Sophie, half hiding in the corridor, looking pale and tired and clearly waiting for Ronnie to finally go up to bed. Even now at after one, she was clutching one of her lists and trying not to fall asleep on her feet.

'Sophie!' he called softly, taking the list out of her hand and putting it down on the table. 'When the celebrations are over – if you haven't fired me by then – I would be honoured to cook you a proper vegetarian dinner.'

Sophie's tiredness dropped away, replaced by a twinkling flirtatiousness. 'Jean-Christophe,' she replied with absolutely no attempt at maidenly modesty. 'I thought you'd never ask! I was wondering if I ought to dance naked along the riverbank while you were fishing!'

'Don't let me discourage you,' he grinned, pulling her firmly into his arms and kissing her.

Sophie responded with enthusiasm, deciding this wasn't the moment to reveal her recent fantasy about enjoying a really good steak.

Twenty-Eight

Sophie woke early and rushed over to pull the curtains. Her first thought was to thank heaven that it was a gorgeous day for their first wedding. Her second was to remember that Jean-Christophe had finally kissed her.

Even at this hour the sky was a deep blue, dotted with a few small, high clouds. There was a strange-shaped one on the far horizon she wasn't so happy about, but it would probably blow over soon. Down below she could see Meredith out with Nelly, frisking happily along the riverbank.

What would it be like to be Nicky, waking up this morning knowing you were going to vow to love someone forever? Sophie thought of her father and Amanda, and the hurt and distant look that still clouded her mother's eyes when she thought of him. Love didn't seem a very reliable prop to lean your life on.

She took a deep breath and blanked out the thought. Weddings were an act of faith and for a lot of people marriage was the most nurturing, healing and fulfilling thing in their lives.

You just had to choose the right person to fall in love with.

Jean-Christophe's darkly handsome face invaded her thoughts. Apart from his obvious good looks, there was something grounded and thoughtful about him that made you feel he was a man to be trusted.

She dressed quickly and went down to the kitchen to make tea for Ronnie, Lara and the bridesmaids. She then assembled secateurs and fixing wire so they could decorate the wedding pavilion, since Ronnie had announced that this was definitely not in her brief.

Looking into the small dining room, she was relieved to see that Jean-Christophe's staff had already laid out croissants, *pains au chocolat*, fresh fruit and orange juice for the guests. Moving on, she went down to the dungeons and switched on all the lights. The job was near-impossible without Ronnie, but how the hell would she ever get her up? Then she had the brainwave of ringing Steph, who promised to be there as soon as she could.

Fifteen minutes later, Lara and the bridesmaids descended the big staircase and trooped out onto the terrace in their short silk wraps, to the delight of the unreconstructedly French delivery drivers who were unloading the elegant gilt chairs for the wedding feast.

'OK,' Lara enquired. 'What do you want us to do?'

'The very best thing would be to get your mother up,' replied Sophie. 'Steph's on her way too. Where's the bride? Having a nice cup of tea in bed?'

'Gone for a walk down by the river.'

They looked out to see Nicky on the riverbank, bending down to pet Nelly.

'OK,' replied Lara. 'I'll take on Mum. If you could provide me with a cup of the strongest possible black coffee?'

*

Down by the river, Meredith watched as Nicky stripped off her wrap proclaiming that she was the BRIDE, revealing a bikini underneath. 'It suddenly seemed romantic to swim on the morning of my wedding,' she explained. 'After all, I get hair and make-up later, so I can get as wet as I like.'

'I quite understand,' Meredith replied. 'I used to swim here when I was a child. One of the reasons I bought the château.'

'Why don't you come in, then?'

'I haven't got a bathing suit on.'

'No one's watching apart from your dog, and I doubt she'd mind.'

Meredith laughed and quickly removed her top and slacks, revealing a smart lacy bra and pants. Ignoring the muddy edges, she moved confidently through the reeds and plunged into the deep water. Nelly decided it was a great game and followed.

'Why didn't you ever get married?' Nicky suddenly asked. 'I mean, you're very attractive with pots of money.'

'I think maybe that was the problem,' Meredith grinned. 'I think I scared men off. Either that, or I couldn't find anyone as nice as my father.' She studied the pretty, slightly anxious face next to hers in the water. 'You're not getting cold feet or anything?'

'No, no. Martin's a sweetie. But is it possible to promise you'll love someone forever? I mean – look at my mum and dad. And now Auntie Steph and Uncle David, and he's such a nice man. A bit like Martin, actually.'

'Marriage is a bit of an act of faith,' Meredith agreed. 'But I know some people who find it the best thing in their lives, and that makes me genuinely jealous.' As they climbed out of the water, it occurred to her she'd never admitted that thought to herself before.

She'd just got as far as the edge, where the water was ankle-deep, when Nelly raced past her, doggy-paddling madly.

Standing a few yards away on the riverbank stood Philippe, fishing rod in hand and a wickedly appreciative smile lighting up his olive-black eyes.

'Mum! Mum! Wake up, Mum!' Lara shook her mother gently.

Ronnie groaned and turned over.

'I've brought you a coffee and everyone's waiting for you!'

Fortunately, Steph had arrived as well, and her approach was rather less sympathetic. 'For God's sake, Ronnie, drink this coffee and get your arse downstairs,' she ordered, 'or I'm taking over the flower arranging.'

Ronnie sat up so quickly that the sheet fell off, revealing her ample breasts. Lara looked away, horrified.

'What's the matter with your generation?' Ronnie demanded, narrowly escaping revealing her pubic hair for good measure. 'I blame all this political correctness.'

'Just drink the coffee and spare us the philosophizing. Remind me what flowers you're actually doing?'

'Three fabulously fantastic Old Master arrangements, and the bridal bouquet.'

'That's it? No table centrepieces and just as important, no buttonholes? Let alone decorating the wedding pavilion?'

Ronnie looked sullen. 'I'm sure that's all I was asked for.'

'OK,' Steph shrugged, trying to keep her temper on this special day. 'We'd better raid the garden for the buttonholes and the centrepieces first. Let's go!'

'You are so bossy,' accused Ronnie petulantly. 'No wonder your husband left you!'

'Mum!' threw in Lara. 'Stop behaving like a bitch and get out of bed. After all,' she added provocatively, 'you don't want people to call you a *lazy* bitch, do you?'

*

Under Sophie's efficient direction the giggling bridesmaids decorated the wedding pavilion and took over making six buttonholes, while Nicky picked simple garden flowers for the centrepieces.

'Oh shit!' Sophie suddenly exclaimed. 'Where the hell are we going to find vases to put them in?' She toyed for a moment with running to the kitchen to look just so that she could see Jean-Christophe, but he would be hideously busy.

'Jam jars!' beamed Nicky. 'I've always liked the idea of unpretentious flowers in jam jars. I bet Auntie Steph's got loads at the B&B.'

Nicky had guessed right. Steph, it turned out, had a whole *armoire* filled with Bonne Maman jars, not to mention jars from Dijon mustard since she particularly liked their shape.

Half an hour later a huge cardboard box of jam jars had arrived and they were happily filling them with pink garden roses, lacy gypsophila and some early Michaelmas daisies.

Suddenly a furious voice cut through their girlish giggles. 'What the hell do you think you're doing?'

Nicky swivelled round to face her mother. 'Arranging the flowers you forgot to order,' she replied with quiet dignity.

'But you can't have that tat anywhere near my arrangements!' Ronnie flashed. 'I got the inspiration from the Paris fashion shows! They're the height of chic.'

Reminding herself that it was her wedding day and she refused to lose her temper and spoil it, Nicky exercised supreme self-control. 'I'm sure your arrangements will be fabulous,' she announced calmly. 'Put one in the orangery for the reception and the other in the salon. They'll look wonderful there.'

'There are three,' Ronnie insisted, with a face like a spoiled child.

'The third can go in the entrance hall. Everyone will see them as they come in. Oh, and Mum –' to Sophie's delight, Nicky suddenly seemed to be the one in charge – 'I'm doing my own wedding bouquet. OK?'

Thanking their lucky stars that Margot had planted a whole bed of white flowers in homage to Vita Sackville-West's famous garden at Sissinghurst, Nicky strode out to the garden to make her selection while her mother seethed alone in the dungeon.

Nicky stood in the middle of the flower bed and consulted her watch. By now, the hair and make-up artists would be busy upstairs with the bridesmaids and Lara. She looked round the flower bed, trying to decide between the dramatic heads of white hydrangea, the pretty white ranunculus, star jasmine, cosmos and white roses, when a clump of plain and elegant calla lilies caught her eye. They would be perfect!

She was just picking a generous bunch when she heard an unfamiliar female voice speaking in an intense, almost desperate tone from just the other side of the wall. Nicky glanced round and realized the flower bed she was standing in must be right up against the car park.

'You're making such a mistake, marrying Nicky,' insisted the voice. 'We were really happy together till I stupidly spent the night with Max. I knew it was a mistake the very next morning. Everyone thinks we should get back together, even your mother.'

It was Emma, Martin's ex-girlfriend! What the hell was she even doing here? Surely Martin wouldn't have been crass enough to invite her? He was usually quite sensitive.

She waited for Martin's response. She knew the way he thought so well. He wouldn't scream or shout, just feel faintly uncomfortable at being the focus of Emma's attention.

At least, she bloody well hoped so.

'You'd better go, Emma,' Martin said at last. 'Simon's over there jumping up and down looking for you.'

So that was it. Simon was one of the ushers, and Emma must be his plus one. She'd probably bullied him into inviting her at the last minute so she wasn't on the list, stupid cow.

'Don't forget,' Emma's tone dropped to intimate and seductive. 'It's not too late. If you want to bolt, I'll come with you. My car's in the car park.'

After that it was silent.

Nicky gathered up her armful of calla lilies and headed back inside, trying not to think about what she'd just heard. She wasn't going to worry. She knew Martin would find a way of getting rid of Emma.

Jo surveyed herself guiltily in her mirror. She ought to be still downstairs helping out, but the temptation to slip up here and re-do her make-up, in the hope of looking her best, was too strong to resist. Any woman in her position, she decided, who'd suffered the pain and humiliation of being replaced by a younger model, would want to look fabulous.

The trouble was, she wasn't sure she did. Her self-confidence had been so shattered that even getting up in the morning had been a struggle at first.

'Look how far you've come,' she reminded herself out loud, straightening her back and taking a deep breath. She needed Sophie here to make her say she was gorgeous again.

'Jo Walker, you're gorgeous!' she attempted, but it just made her laugh. Oh well, laughing was OK, laughing was good.

Besides, she wasn't a guest at the wedding; she was on duty, trying to make it the best possible day for Nicky, and prove that the château really was the perfect place for countless other brides to come and celebrate in gloriously romantic surroundings.

She patted down the smart green silk dress, straightened a stray grey-blonde curl and smiled at herself. 'You may have lost a husband,' she informed the mirror, 'but you have wonderful friends. And they're not going to dump you for anyone!'

'There! Aren't they bloody amazing!'

Ronnie stood back to admire her three enormous arrangements of peonies, blowsy-headed roses, huge ranunculus in tones of sugar almond, palest lilac bearded iris, old-fashioned cottage lilies, exotic parrot tulips and tall spikes of blue and white delphiniums, finished off with generous branches of green ivy that hung down in a decorative fringe.

Drafting in a couple of unwilling kitchen staff, she placed them where Nicky had recommended, then changed her mind and moved one to the table where she knew the bride and groom would be sitting to ensure it would be viewed by the maximum number of guests.

Meredith, who was pinning table plans to a blackboard, stopped to look, opened her mouth to point out the drawbacks to this positioning, then shut it again, knowing the reaction she would get.

Ronnie looked at her watch and screeched.

'I must get upstairs and change!'

'Aren't you going to help Nicky with her dress?' Meredith couldn't resist asking. 'Mother of the bride and all that? After all,' she added, deadpan, 'you've even got it written on your wrap.'

'I suppose I ought to,' Ronnie replied. 'But I'll just go and change first.'

'And I thought *I* was the selfish type,' shrugged Meredith. 'I'm in a different league.'

She was interrupted in her musings by the arrival of Sophie holding a giant cardboard box. 'This has just arrived for Nicky. Do you think I should take it up?'

'Absolutely. How else will we know what's in it?' She Blu-tacked another set of table plans to a display board and took it out to the entrance hall, where all the guests would be arriving. Finding out where you were sitting was always a number one social preoccupation, in her experience.

In fact, Nicky was grateful she had her sister dancing attendance instead of her mother.

Lara was gazing admiringly at Nicky's newly made-up face. 'You look absolutely ravishing, O sister mine. Like you, only better, if you know what I mean.'

Nicky couldn't help laughing, even though that horrible Emma's words were still reverberating painfully round her brain and threatening to spoil this longed-for moment. Perhaps she should have gone and got rid of her herself. But she wanted it to be Martin who sent her packing.

'Thank you,' she said to the make-up artist. 'I couldn't have had a better compliment than that. I don't wear a lot of make-up normally and I was terrified of ending up looking like someone else!'

'Shall I get the dress?' Lara asked, handing them both a glass of champagne. 'Or would you rather I tried to dig up Mum?'

'Knowing Mum, she'll be far too busy making herself look fabulous to bother with me.'

Nicky opened her arms, and Lara hugged her as tight as bridal hair and make-up would allow. 'Thank God we've got each other,' they chorused in a familiar refrain.

'And soon you'll have a husband to love you and watch your back, you lucky thing!'

Nicky held her sister even tighter. 'I will, won't I?'

'OK, bride-to-be. I think it's the moment for the dress.'

As if on cue the door opened and they both turned, expecting Ronnie.

'Auntie Steph!' they beamed. 'How lovely to see you.'

'Well, I wasn't missing this for the world. Where's on earth's your mother?'

'Our mother,' announced Lara with more than a shade of bitterness, 'is too busy getting ready herself to honour us with her presence.'

'Is she now? We'll soon see about that.' Sometimes her sister's selfishness took Steph's breath away.

'No, please, Auntie Steph, we're fine,' Nicky insisted. 'Especially now we've got you. You know Mum – she'll probably only say something critical anyway. She won't mean to, but somehow it'll come out. Have a glass of this delicious fizz and tell me I look more gorgeous than Princess Diana when I put on the dress.'

Lara and Nicky disappeared behind the painted screen and when they came out, Steph didn't have to make any comparisons with Princess Di; Nicky looked quite beautiful enough in her own right. The ivory-toned dress, made of some magical material that managed to float and cling at the same time, with a little train and a matching shoulder shrug, was simply beautiful.

'Darling Nicky.' Steph felt a lump in her throat that made it hard to speak. 'You look perfect!'

It was at that moment that Sophie arrived with the giant cardboard box.

'Oh, brilliant!' giggled Nicky. 'Could you get it out and plug it in, Soph?'

'Close your eyes, everyone.'

Moments later, the room was illuminated by a giant sign made of light bulbs blazing out the words MR & MRS.

'Isn't it a hoot?' Nicky grinned at the others.

None of them noticed the door opening again. 'What on earth is that vulgar contraption?' demanded an incandescent Ronnie. She was still wearing the pink MOB wrap, now with the interesting addition of a feather fascinator. 'You can't put that horrible thing anywhere near my flowers!'

'Shut the fuck up, Ronnie,' commanded Steph in steelier tones than her nieces had ever heard from her, 'and come in and admire your beautiful daughter!'

Meredith, as usual, had managed to look both chic and businesslike and even – a new thing for her – ever so slightly sexy. The table plans were now sorted, and she consulted Sophie's lists to see what job next fell to her. It turned out to be Keeping an Eye on the Kitchen.

One glance told her that Jean-Christophe was very much in charge. Everything seemed to be running smoothly. In fact, unusually for him, he was actually singing as he chopped and sliced. Meredith found herself smiling as she wondered why.

'Can I help you?' enquired a voice that, while on the surface of it perfectly polite, seemed to imply that she was an unwelcome trespasser.

Meredith was staggered to find that it was Lucille, wearing a tight black t-shirt and fashionably narrow black slacks. What the hell was *she* doing here?

Lucille clearly read her mind. 'A staff member called in sick, so I'm helping my son out for the day. He wanted someone with experience.'

'You certainly have that,' Meredith replied ambiguously. 'If there are no problems I can help with, I'll leave you to it.'

'I wish you would,' replied Lucille, her beautiful aquamarine eyes beaming out hostility. Under her breath, she added: 'Permanently.'

Meredith simply raised a dismissive eyebrow and turned round to find herself barging straight into Philippe, who was almost running in the opposite direction.

The sudden surprise made her, Meredith Harding, queen of cool, drop Sophie's six-page list all over the floor. 'Don't worry,' she protested, as he bent down to help her pick the pages up. 'You're obviously in a hurry.'

Before she had time to wonder if he'd come to see Lucille, he answered the question for her. 'Have either of you, by any chance, seen my father?' he asked anxiously. Meredith noticed there were dark smudges under his eyes, giving him an even more piratical look than usual.

It was on Lucille's lips to say that really his father ought to be in a home, but she stopped herself in time, remembering how fiercely Philippe was resisting this.

'No, I'm so sorry,' Meredith replied. 'I'll tell the others to keep an eye out.'

'He went to the restaurant and was told I was here helping with the cake.' Philippe turned to Lucille. 'Could you let Jean-Christophe know he might turn up, and to call me if he does?'

'Of course.' Lucille produced her usual catlike smile. 'I will tell him at once.'

'You're going to have a busy day,' said Philippe as soon as Lucille had disappeared.

'We are. But this is what it's going to be like when we get going, so it's good practice.'

'Good luck.' He reached out a hand and held her free one

for a brief second. 'And remember, if you ever need me, I'm always at the end of the phone.'

Nicky looked out of the window while her sister and the bridesmaids fluttered about, making sure their hair looked good and they had their little bags of confetti.

Down below, she could see Martin sharing a drink with the ushers. Emma was still standing nearby, smiling flirtatiously.

Deep inside, a tectonic plate shifted. She had a choice: let this go, or put a stop to it.

Meredith, having made sure the bride's father was ready for his role in taking Nicky to the wedding pavilion, now went to check on the bride.

She found Nicky still staring out of the window. 'Are you OK?' she asked quietly, so the others couldn't hear. 'You seem a bit preoccupied. Do bridal nerves really exist?'

Nicky came to a decision. 'Meredith, could you do something for me? Can you go down there and tell Martin – discreetly, of course – that I'm not coming down unless he tells that woman next to him, the one in lurid turquoise, to leave? She's his old girlfriend, and she's trying to persuade him to do a runner.'

'How the hell did she get on the guest list without you vetoing her?'

'As one of the usher's plus ones.'

'Sly bitch.'

Sudden visions of their very first wedding never taking place invaded Meredith's mind. Why had they gone for a bloody wedding château? Why not a yoga retreat or a posh B&B like Steph's? Then she remembered all the grinding labour Steph and David had to put in.

She took a long look at Nicky. She liked the girl. She showed

407

humour and dignity dealing with her ghastly mother. But should she try and talk her out of this risky course of action, for all their sakes? Probably; and yet, hadn't Meredith herself always been one to dare to take risks?

'Are you sure? What if he says no?'

'Then there's no point my coming down anyway.'

Meredith gave her a quick hug. 'You're absolutely right. You're a girl after my own heart. I'd better go before the guests start to arrive.'

Nicky made herself walk away from the window. The next five minutes were the longest she could ever remember.

Twenty-Nine

Finally Nicky could resist the temptation no longer. She walked over to the window to stare down at the terrace below. Meredith had disappeared and Martin was looking straight up at her window, the sweetest smile on his face.

There was no sign of Emma anywhere on the horizon.

Nicky blew him a kiss, suddenly remembering that it was supposed to be bad luck for the bridegroom to see the bride.

Forget that. It was a lot better luck for the bridegroom to make it clear who he really loved. And that was her.

Seconds later, Meredith reappeared. She was smiling. 'The bitch has gone,' she announced. 'You're also one usher down, but I expect you can cope with that. Martin was brilliant. He just went straight up and told her to go.' She stood aside as the door began to open. 'And here's your father to take you down.'

'Hello, darling,' Bill greeted her. 'You look absolutely ravishing! Are you ready to do the deed?'

'Let me just get my vows.' Nicky picked up a sheet of paper from the dressing table while Lara fussed over her veil and the bridesmaids twittered happily in the background. Finally

Lara handed her the simple bouquet of a dozen calla lilies, encased in their shiny green leaves.

'It's perfect.' Lara embraced her, fighting back tears. 'And so much better than anything Mum would have done.'

'Where *is* Mum?' They smiled at each other, acknowledging how much more peaceful it had been without her.

Almost instantly, the door opened and Ronnie appeared. The cause of her delay was more than obvious in the flawless perfection of her hair and make-up and the perfectly matching dress and shoes in a dazzling lime green. From her uber-confident smile and the dismissive shrug of her shoulder towards her kind ex-husband, it was clear Ronnie had decided she looked the biz.

'Sorry I took so long, darling,' she announced. 'But almost as many people will be looking at me as you!'

A sudden wave of pity for her appalling mother took Nicky by surprise. Someone really ought to tell her her appearance was only one step away from a drag queen's.

'So how do I look, Mum?'

'Absolutely lovely, darling. All brides look beautiful.' Being Ronnie, she couldn't resist the qualification. 'Apart from the bouquet. I'd have done a lot better with that.'

Nicky caught her sister's eye. They both knew their mother couldn't praise without finding a fault, but Nicky decided that by some miracle of survival, she didn't give a damn. 'Right, Dad, let's go for it!' She tucked her hand into his arm. 'And thank you so much for footing the bill for everything.'

'What greater thrill can a father have than seeing his daughter get married to a decent man? And he is a decent man, isn't he?'

Without a second's hesitation, Nicky smiled back at her father. 'Yes, Dad, he's a lot more than decent. He's lovely.'

They walked slowly down the beautiful grand staircase with Lara carefully holding on to her sister's train, out through the orangery and into the walled garden at the side of the house where Margot had carefully tended her roses, and onto the open patch of green. The wedding pavilion, decked with flowers by Lara and the bridesmaids, was at the far end, with the guests ranged in rows either side of an aisle space.

Martin, flanked by his best man, stood in front of the pavilion waiting and watching her progress as she waved and smiled at her friends and relatives.

Finally she was there.

'Nicola and Martin,' the celebrant announced, 'we are all gathered in this lovely place to hear you pledge yourselves to each other, that you may have a long and happy life together.' She turned first to Nicky. 'Nicola, will you share with us what you hope for from this marriage?'

Nicky looked at her list. She had spent hours if not days compiling it, admittedly with a little help from other people's vows she'd read online. How much respect she would have for him as an individual, the joy she found in his laughter, the strength he gave her when she most needed it, and even, rather daringly, the pleasure she found in his touch.

But standing there, looking directly into his eyes, she just remembered the corny but simple message on the card she had sent to Sophie, and that was what she repeated now.

'Martin, I want to be with you all my life because you know exactly what I'm like – and you still love me.'

In the front row, something made Steph turn her head. She caught sight of David, who sat watching her a couple of rows behind.

His face softened slowly into a smile, so dear and familiar that she had to fight back tears. She'd had not the slightest inkling he was coming to the wedding, although now it seemed obvious that he would.

Almost involuntarily, she smiled back. A wave of all the regret and love that she had tried so hard to suppress suddenly flooded through her, so that she had to hold on to her chair in case she fainted in front of everyone. She saw the concern in his face and how, seeing her distress, he had almost started towards her, and she mouthed the word 'Later' to him.

At precisely the same instant, they smiled.

Now it was time for Martin's moment. Without consulting a piece of paper, he loudly and clearly began his vow.

'Nicky, you are my best friend. I love you with all my heart and stand here before our friends and family for the happiest day of my life. I want nothing more than to share my future with you – my triumphs and disasters.' The look of laughter they shared at this moment was witnessed by all. 'I can't promise you that dark clouds will never hover over our lives. I can't promise you that tomorrow will be perfect or life will always be easy.' He reached out and took her hand. 'I can promise my loyalty, my respect and my unconditional love for a lifetime. Nicola, I love you.'

'Well, that beats to have and to hold,' whispered her sister Lara to the bridesmaid next to her. 'I hadn't realized Martin was such a romantic.'

The happy couple proceeded back towards the château, greeting and being kissed by so many friends that it was going to be a slow process.

'Ladies and gentlemen, guests of the bride and groom,' Jo announced, smiling broadly. 'Please make your way back to the terrace for the reception.'

'Oh goody,' announced someone at the back. 'Now we can get plastered while they spend hours taking photos!'

Jo waited till they'd all gone in case anyone needed assistance, her eye fixed on that strangely shaped cloud still lowering above them in the sky. Perhaps it was something to do with how hot it had been lately.

Liam was behind the bar with two assistants, making sure all the glasses were kept filled and the guests happy. Jean-Christophe and his team were passing round delicious canapés to stop people getting too drunk. Weddings were lengthy events, and they had to be crafted cleverly.

The photos were almost finished when suddenly, without any warning, balls of frozen water began to thunder down from the sky, banging loudly on the car roofs in the parking area, in one of the freak hailstorms that were a curious feature of the region even in high summer. Guests started shrieking, feather fascinators drooped and men of the old school took their jackets off and draped them protectively round their partners' shoulders.

Jean-Christophe, knowing exactly what to do as a native of the area, herded all the guests into the grand salon and shouted at his assistants to cover up the tables on the terrace.

Jo tried to find Liam, but he had already disappeared down towards the vineyard.

The last of the guests to run for the salon were Mark and Amanda. He stopped dead, hailstones beating a tattoo on his shoulders, staring at her as if she were a ghost. 'Joanna! What on earth are you doing here?'

Jo realized she really didn't care what Mark or his silly wife thought of her. All she wanted was to follow Liam, and see if there was anything she could do to protect his crop.

'I'll tell you later. I've got to find someone first.'

Ignoring Mark's outraged expression, she ran down the steps at the edge of the terrace and headed for the vineyard without even bothering to look for a mac or an umbrella. It would hardly protect against hail this size anyway.

Liam was standing not far from the riverbank and surveying the neat rows loaded with almost-ripe fruit, his face etched with something close to desperation. 'You can lose a whole year's crop in ten minutes when you get a hailstorm like this,' he stated, his voice devoid of any emotion. 'It depends how long this one is going to last.'

They were suddenly aware of a lone figure with long white hair and a beard standing right in the middle of the vines, waving what appeared to be a crutch towards the sky and shouting up at the heavens. He looked for all the world like Prospero conjuring up the weather with his staff.

The guests thought so too. A crowd stood watching him from the long windows of the salon as if he had been laid on for their entertainment.

'Jean-Christophe,' Meredith whispered urgently. 'Call your father. Your grandfather is in the middle of the vineyard, shouting at the sky. He must be soaking wet. I'll take him down a coat till Philippe gets here.'

As she passed the drinks table she grabbed a bottle of cognac destined for the cocktails and headed off across the terrace, ignoring the hail, which soaked her hair and made her dress almost transparent.

By the time she reached Antoine, the hailstones had stopped as dramatically as they had started and the skies were once more a deep, almost Mediterranean blue.

The guests, who had returned to the terrace, clapped loudly as Antoine, clearly loving every minute, took a deep bow.

'Here,' insisted Meredith, 'put on this coat and take a drink. It'll warm you up.'

Before he deigned to raise it to his lips, the old man examined the label.

'Don't worry,' she laughed, 'it's the best in the house.'

He took a large swig. 'They are very stupid, your guests,' he pronounced in disgust. 'They thought it was I who stopped the hail falling.'

'I don't think they actually thought that,' Meredith smiled. 'But they thought you gave a magnificent performance. And personally, I'd like to thank you. You have rescued the wedding.'

'*Avec plaisir, Madamoiselle Meredith.*' Antoine rewarded her with a slow, knowing smile and took another swig of the cognac.

Near to the riverbank, Liam examined his grapes tenderly.

'I think this time we've been lucky,' he smiled. He suddenly stared at Jo. 'You left the wedding party to see what had happened to my crop, when you should probably be firing me for deserting my post.'

'I knew how much it mattered to you,' she replied simply, and turned back towards the wedding.

He reached out a hand to stop her. 'You know, the only reason I held back was that I realized you'd be my boss, in a manner of speaking. But now I know what a lovely woman you are, that seems ridiculous. I just wanted to say that if you were up for it, I think we should start again.' He grinned and spread out his hands. 'That was hardly the most romantic speech, but you'll know by now, I'm a straightforward guy.'

Suddenly Jo had the most powerful feeling that this was a man she could trust. Some of her old self-confidence surged back as she looked him directly in the eye. 'Straightforward guys sound pretty good to me. Now, I suppose we'd better get back to the party. The guests will be wanting a refill.'

They had almost reached the steps when they bumped into Margot lurking in the bushes. '*Bonjour*, Joanna. I am so sorry for you. The hail has ruined the wedding, no?' She could barely conceal her glee at such a terrible catastrophe.

Jo just laughed. 'From what I can tell, everyone rather enjoyed it. In fact, they thought it had been laid on specially.'

Margot shook her head. 'As long as I live, I will never understand the English.' She turned for home in disgust.

'Poor old Margot,' Jo laughed gaily. 'She really doesn't want us to make a go of it at the château.'

Climbing up the steps, they just missed Philippe coming down at the other end of the terrace.

'He's here at last!' declared Antoine jovially when Philippe arrived, looking wet and dishevelled. 'You've missed all the fun, *mon fils*. I have made the heavens open and the hail come down in the middle of this young couple's wedding. Maybe we could tell them it is a good omen in France to have hail at your wedding, *hein*?'

'Come on, you old menace,' Philippe replied. 'You've led me a merry dance today and I've had just about enough, OK?'

'*D'accord*,' Antoine consented merrily. 'But let me give you a little advice.' He indicated his snowy locks. 'I have not earned these white hairs for nothing. It's time you had another woman in your life, and if I were you, I'd have this one.' He indicated Meredith. 'She knows her cognac, for a start. And she is *genereuse d'esprit*, not like that other one. That is my advice. Take it or leave it.'

Philippe caught Meredith's eye. She was struggling to keep a straight face until she saw that Philippe wasn't laughing. His eyes were fixed on hers with an expression that was almost uncomfortable in its intensity. And there was no mistaking the message in them.

Sophie, temporarily left to manage the wedding, carried on with her effortless efficiency and six pages of notes. From the window of the salon where she had gone to indulge her small vice of a roll-up cigarette, she caught sight of Meredith with Philippe and, with her usual perspicacity, instantly guessed what was going on.

She went to seek out Jean-Christophe in the kitchen. He instantly stopped serving up and came towards her, oblivious to the reactions of the waiting staff, a melting smile illuminating his olive-dark eyes.

Sophie put out a hand to halt his clear intention to kiss her again. 'Jean-Christophe,' she apologized with an answering smile in her eyes, 'I'm so sorry to disturb you – but I suspect your dad has finally told Meredith how he feels about her. Could you get the carer to come and look after your grandfather, so that Philippe can stay? I don't think we should let this moment go!'

It was at this moment that Lucille returned to the kitchen, carrying a dozen plates piled right up her arm in that almost magical trick a good server can pull off. She stopped dead, taking in every word.

Glancing through the open terrace door, she saw Philippe and Meredith approaching together, a look of loving conspiracy passing between them.

The plates clattered to the floor with an almighty crash. Lucille turned to Jean-Christophe. 'I am very sorry, Jean-Christophe, but I find I must return to Bordeaux for an emergency.'

'Lucille . . .' attempted Philippe as he entered the kitchen.

'No – no sympathy.'

Jean-Christophe, ignoring the debris on the floor, led her away and called for a taxi.

'I will wait at the front of the château,' Lucille announced with dignity.

'Oh dear!' Meredith found herself actually feeling a little

sorry for the woman, despite her calculating personality, as she and Philippe picked up pieces of broken china and assorted cutlery from the floor.

'Don't waste your sympathy on that one,' Antoine announced with satisfaction. 'She is like . . . What is that insect that eats its mate after sex?'

'A praying mantis?' asked Meredith.

'*Voilà!*' nodded Antoine. 'My son would be eaten alive if he let her come back. What are *you* doing here?' He had spotted Amélie, his carer, arriving by the back door; someone had obviously already summoned her.

'Come to get you, you old magician,' Amélie replied. 'Quite enough excitement for one day. I'll drive you home and you can do some more of your tricks for me. And I've brought you a nice lunch of *ris de veau*,' she tempted him with the local speciality of casseroled sweetbreads.

'I don't need more brains!' he responded, laughing. 'I've got enough already!'

'Put some in the brain bank for another day, then,' she suggested, taking his arm.

They both waved goodbye as they left.

'Are you sure he's not too much for you?' Philippe asked Meredith. 'He would have to live with us, I'm afraid.' And then, realizing he had jumped far too many hoops, he blushed.

Meredith kissed him again. 'I really like him. It's like having my own father back, only what he might have been like all these years later.'

Guilt overtook Meredith and Jo at about the same time and they both went to find Sophie, who, wonderful girl, was calm as a moonlit sea.

'It's all going according to plan,' she reassured. 'Although you missed a sensational bust-up. Nicky's dad moved the ridiculous floral arrangement off their table and when Ronnie blew her top, he calmly told her that as he was paying for the wedding he could do what he bloody well wanted. And then he tipped the whole thing over the balustrade! I think it's the only time I've ever seen Ronnie lost for words.'

'I like that man more and more,' Meredith remarked.

'Me too,' seconded Jo. 'Now, what can we do to help?'

'All under control at the moment. Let's go and watch the speeches.'

Bill's father of the bride speech was predictably sweet and heartfelt. 'To my darling daughter, Nicola.' He finally raised a glass. 'She was an adorable girl and she's a wonderful woman. Martin, you're an exceptionally lucky man!'

Thankfully, Martin looked as if he already knew that. His own speech managed to be both funny and romantic.

'Maybe he's the best kind of bet,' Jo whispered to Meredith. 'On the outside he looks almost ordinary, but inside there's a beating heart full of romance.'

The usual tension rose as the best man's speech approached. Would it be hilariously funny or embarrassingly bad? Martin had managed to find a best man who had known him since he was three and was endearingly entertaining. He even produced video clips of Martin's most embarrassing moments.

Even Grandma's cake was a huge hit. Possibly because she insisted on wheeling it round on a trolley to show it off to all the guests first.

'Whatever you do, don't touch the towers,' she hissed at the bride and groom as they reached for the knife. 'They're made out of cocoa tins!'

Once the cake had been ceremonially cut, Jean-Christophe wheeled it away to be divided up in the kitchen.

'Now for the first dance!' Sophie elbowed Jo, prompting her to let Meredith know. It was time to get everyone up to the other end of the enormous terrace to wait for the bride and groom.

Overtaking the best man's speech, the build-up to the first dance was fast becoming the new source of tension at the hip modern wedding.

'I blame *Strictly*,' Jo whispered. 'Thank God we didn't have it in my day.' She glanced across at Mark, who already looked rather drunk. Lucky Amanda. 'At one wedding I went to, the bride and groom danced to "You've Lost that Lovin' Feeling"! Everyone thought it was a bit soon for that.'

'Couldn't have been as bad as the one I went to where the bride chose James Blunt's "You're Beautiful",' Meredith murmured. 'And the awful thing was, she really wasn't.'

'I thought all brides were beautiful!' They turned to find Liam standing behind them, smiling at Jo.

Nicky and Martin had very sensibly chosen 'It Must Be Love' for their first dance: a sweet song that was quirky enough not to be corny, yet required no dazzling arabesques or embarrassing lifts like something out of *Dirty Dancing*.

The applause when they sat down again was deafening.

'Right, everybody!' Sophie announced as soon as it had died down. 'Come and watch the fireworks over the river!'

'You wouldn't believe how many hurdles we had to jump because of the fire risks,' Liam confided to Philippe. 'Special licence from the town hall, only certain fireworks allowed and a fee for the local fire brigade to be standing by. So let's hope it's worth it!'

He needn't have worried. The display was so spectacular that even Nicky's father, smiling broadly next to his cheerful and unassuming wife, managed to forget that it was costing

420

him a thousand pounds a minute and cheered along with everyone else.

When it was over, Bill clapped loudly to get everyone's attention.

'Before you get back to the dancing, I'd like to thank our amazing hostesses. Here's to Meredith, Joanna, and not forgetting the wonderful Sophie!'

Sophie suddenly noticed Jean-Christophe standing at the back of the crowd, nodding enthusiastically.

'Thank you for creating a beautiful wedding for my daughter,' Bill continued, 'in a truly romantic location which I hope will be the first of many, many more!' Suddenly realizing what he'd said, he added: 'Though obviously not for my daughter!'

As the last firework fizzled into darkness, a full moon appeared from behind the clouds and illuminated the entire château.

Gazing skywards, Meredith found that Philippe had materialized from the darkness and was standing next to her.

'Your father would have been very proud of you,' he whispered in her ear, 'for making his dream come true.'

Just below them, he spotted somebody approaching from between the vines. He stared down into the darkness.

'Christ almighty, it's Margot!' he exclaimed in a low voice.

Laughter threatened to shake Meredith and she had to take a deep breath. 'Margot!' she shouted. 'Come and have a glass of wine.'

Meredith looked up at the château. It had stood on this spot for six hundred years, enhanced by the light of the moon and the perfect natural beauty of the landscape. Everyone around her was relaxed and happy, and it truly was as romantic a location as anyone could possibly want for a wedding.

She felt Philippe's arm around her, strong and reassuring. And Meredith decided that, although she'd never felt the lack of a partner, there were definite advantages to finding the right one.

With his usual sensitivity, Philippe guessed what she was feeling and turned her round to face him. 'So, Mademoiselle Meredith Harding, the time has come for me to ask you, could you put up with a man in your life?'

'Only if he was the right man.'

'And am I the right man?'

Without waiting for an answer, he took her in his arms.

Suddenly, from the direction of the château, Nelly burst through the vineyard, gambolled up the steps and began to howl noisily at the moon.

'I might be gaining Grand-père,' Meredith remarked to Philippe, 'but you'll be inheriting eighteen kilos of British bulldog with a perennial slobber and a snoring problem.'

'Nelly,' Philippe enquired of the engaging heap of sinew and muscle that had decided to settle on his feet, 'I hope you're not going to take that lying down?'

From the terrace above, David and Steph stood watching them, each holding a glass of Liam's prize crémant de Savarin. 'It seems to be a night of declarations,' said David wryly, 'so why not another? I've missed you, Steph.'

'I've missed you too,' Steph admitted as he reached for her hand.

David raised his glass towards the moon. 'To the triumph of love!'

From the darkness below, Nelly stopped howling and barked contentedly, as if this was the ending she'd always intended.

If you enjoyed *A Very French Wedding*, then you'll love these other titles by Maeve Haran . . .

The Greek Holiday

There's nothing like friendship and sunshine to get you through . . .

Penny, Dora, Nell and Moira had always meant to keep in touch, but life got in the way.

So when Penny gets an unexpected legacy, she decides not to tell her overbearing husband but to spend it instead on a reunion on the sun-drenched Greek island they visited at eighteen. But many years later, what was a tiny village full of donkeys and cafes is now a major tourist attraction. And the friends have to face the fact that their own personal difficulties can't always be cured by a holiday in the sun.

On the way back to Athens, they stop at a tiny island, not yet on the tourist map. In Kyri, they find an opportunity to contribute to a community needing their help and, at the same time, to recapture lost romance and have some healing fun.

But will they relearn the most valuable lesson of all: the true importance of their friendship?

More laughter and love in ...

In a Country Garden

**Are your best friends the last people
you should end up living with?**

Lifelong friends Claudia, Ella, Laura and Sal celebrated sixty as
the new forty, determined not to let age change things.
But now they are looking at the future and wondering how
to make growing old more fun.

Why not live together – helping and supporting each other
when any of them need it – and still keep enjoying life?
Joined by Claudia's reluctant husband, Sal's energetic new
fiancé, and the intriguing Mrs Lal, they ignore the protests
of their children and pool their resources into a manor house in
the country. Only Laura holds out, determined she still
has some living to do, especially now she has met the
dashing Gavin through an online dating app.

Life and love certainly haven't finished with them in what
the locals dub a new-age old-age commune. But are your best
friends the last people you should end up living with?

Find more sunshine and friendship in . . .

An
Italian
Holiday

Sometimes you have to go through
the clouds to find the sun

Springtime in glorious Southern Italy can go to your head.
Especially if you're escaping not just miserable weather but
an overbearing husband, the embarrassingly public loss
of your company, an interfering mother who still tries to run
your life or the pain of a husband's affair with a girl young
enough to be his daughter.

As the sun ripens the lemons in the groves that tumble down
the hillsides and the Mediterranean dazzles beneath them,
bossy Angela, extrovert Sylvie, unconfident Claire and
mousy Monica leave their trapped lives behind, and begin
to blossom in quite unexpected ways.

Packed with memorable characters, *An Italian Holiday*
is a witty and entertaining reminder of why going a little mad
in the sunshine can sometimes be exactly what you need.